Buried for Now

BOB HOWARD

BOB HOWARD

Cover art by Lorena Martin of Premade Ebook Covers

DEDICATION

This book is dedicated to my wife, Dawn. She continues to be the rock that is the foundation for my life.

CONTENTS

About the Author

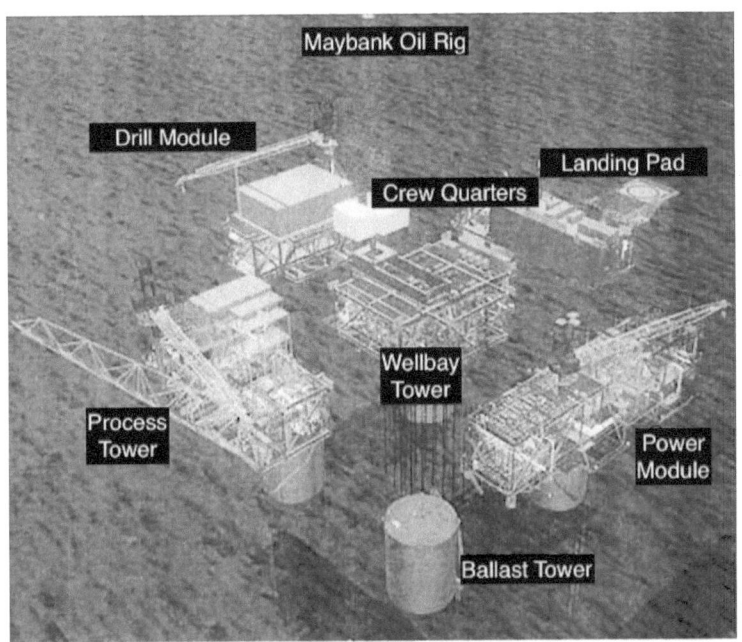

ACKNOWLEDGMENTS

I think every contemporary author has at least once hoped someone famous would contact them and express an interest in their work, and while I don't dwell on it, I have at times wished for that email or social media message. Over the last three years I've heard from so many people who have wanted to say something to me about the impact I've had on their lives. Honestly, I didn't expect that. Did I hope to get good feedback? Was I happy when my books reached the top ten on the bestseller list? Of course, but what I didn't expect was the emails from people who gain some measure of hope, joy, or comfort from escaping into my fiction. I've heard many times from readers who were in the hospital, and my books helped them pass the time. I heard from a nice lady who was hoping I would write another book in the series because her father enjoyed my books so much. He was a Korean War veteran who had lived a rich and fulfilling life, yet there was room in his life for my books. That made a real difference to me.

The email that made the biggest difference to me last year was from Tim Moriarty. He signed up at my website, and I took a few minutes to send him an email thanking him for reading my books. He answered with an email that meant the world to me. He said his youngest son, Teddy, also enjoys my books. He told me that they race to see who can finish first, and then they spend some time talking about the book. He said his son is sixteen, and then he thanked me for getting his son to read. I believe his parenting plays a bigger part in his son reading, but I was humbled that he had given me some credit. My thanks to both Tim and Teddy for allowing my books to be part of their time together, and I hope to hear they enjoyed Buried for Now.

I always like to give credit to the people who help me get the book done once it's written. My wife Dawn reads for content, enjoyment, storyline consistency, and understanding of descriptions. Her suggestions are invaluable. My son Drew has shown he has a good eye for finding those elusive little typos, and his grammar skills are impeccable. I know he was stunned when he found a double negative. I know I was. My daughter Julie continues to play a big part in motivating me to write. It's nice to know she can take the credit for getting me started in the first place. Six books later, I haven't forgotten. Gary Graham, an old friend from almost forty years ago, found me last year. He has been proofreading for me this time, and I remembered why we were such good friends when we were younger. His memory for details and trivia makes me wonder where and when he had the time to learn what he knows.

Lorena Martin of Premade Ebook Covers continues to be my first choice for the cover. If you would like to contact her, you can get her information from my website. Best practice dictates that contact information not be placed here, but don't worry. We're both easy to find, plus I can shamelessly invite you to my personal website.

I hope you enjoy the book!

BOB HOWARD

1 MAYBANK

Beginning of the Decline

Daniel Maybank stood at the highest platform on the oil rig. From there he could turn in a complete circle and see the horizon in every direction. Ever since the first news reports started broadcasting about an infection that made people turn into cannibals, he had alternated between the television screens, the internet, the helicopter landing pad, and hundreds of last minute system checks. The Gulf was calm and as flat as glass in every direction, and there was nothing but blue sky above.

He searched the horizon and didn't see a single dot protruding above the straight line separating the water from the sky. If things were as bad as he was hearing, there should be someone, anyone trying to escape the carnage. Enough time had gone by for people to begin showing up, and from what he was seeing on the news broadcasts, the marinas had no shortage of people pushing their boats away from their slips.

"Where are they?" he mouthed the words without making a sound. He had noticed he was having entire conversations like that even when he made one of his rare trips to the mainland. He knew it was because the trips had become exactly that. They were less and less frequent until he couldn't stand to be around crowds. He thought it was something that old people preferred whether they lived on the mainland or on an oil rig, but he was glad he had a choice to be so far out in the Gulf.

Maybank had rolled out of bed just before sunrise without an alarm clock and immediately went to his favorite place to enjoy his morning coffee.

That was another characteristic of old men as far as he knew. They didn't need to sleep the day away, and he was glad for it. His favorite place was an observation deck that faced directly to the east. He had an unblemished view of the sun as it appeared on the horizon. At first it was a faint, purple glow. Then it was brighter shades of orange and yellow just before it exploded into view. He never got tired of seeing its arrival, just as he was always there to see its departure to the west. As far as he was concerned, sunrise and sunset were the only times of day that mattered. Everything in between was just daylight or darkness.

After sunrise of this day everything had changed. He was getting his second cup of coffee and thinking about what to have for breakfast when he turned on the television. He did it so absentmindedly that he didn't even notice there was no volume. He stirred a teaspoon of sugar into the coffee and walked back out to the observation deck.

Half in and half out of his chaise lounge he remembered the TV. He sat his coffee cup on the small table next to the chair and turned in the direction of the TV. If there was something interesting on the screen he would waste the energy to walk to the shelf by the coffee pot where he had put the remote down. He laughed at his own laziness when he considered not walking to a remote instead of walking all the way to the TV the way people used to.

Maybank froze in mid motion. He could see himself reflected in a nearby mirror, and he was amused by the ridiculous pose he was striking. His silver hair was in disarray, and he had a passing memory of a wild eyed scientist in a movie about time travel.

"What did that kid call him, Professor? Yes, that was it."

Maybank had been much younger when that movie was in theaters, but he had watched it here on his oil rig.

Across the main living quarters was a seventy-five inch flatscreen. One of the perks of getting free technology upgrades whenever he wanted. A sound system that would be the envy of any teenager was connected to the TV, but most of the time it was silent. Maybank preferred the sounds of the wind and waves over the strident sounds of human voices, especially on news channels. He could hear the faint rushing sounds of the Gulf of Mexico behind him, but he could imagine the sounds that went along with the images on the large TV screen. He could almost hear the screaming without turning up the volume.

He shook himself out of the trance that felt longer than it probably was and found himself lunging for the remote. The volume popped on as soon as his finger hit the button, and the screaming matched his imagination.

The scene that filled the entire TV was chaos. It was a national twenty-four hour news channel, so he didn't expect to see a local broadcast. He considered a local broadcast anything that came from Florida, Georgia, Alabama, Mississippi, or Louisiana. Texas wasn't local. The chaos he was watching could have been anywhere, but he was fairly sure it was New York.

Smoke was casting a gray and black shroud over cars, buildings, and people. The people were darting in and out of the smoke.

"That's not entirely true," he mouthed. "Some of them aren't darting. They're just standing around watching, and when people run into them, they grab the running people and bite them wherever they can."

Maybank shook his head from side to side. He told himself to shut up and just watch.

Two women were standing next to each other. There was something unnatural about the way they were standing. One of them was leaning to the right and was almost leaning on the other woman. When the smoke cleared away from them, Maybank saw that the woman was missing her right foot from the ankle down. They were oblivious to the smoke that swirled away from them and then back into their faces. It didn't seem to bother them at all.

"Why should it?" mouthed Maybank. "What's a little smoke when you're missing a foot?"

He grimaced at his inability to stop talking to himself, but at the same time he considered the possibility that he might start doing it more often in light of the broadcast he was watching.

A car burst through the smoke and hit the leaning woman head on. The force launched her into the smoke so fast that the yelp that escaped Maybank's lips was well after she disappeared. The other woman didn't seem to notice that her friend was hit by a car, but she did notice the man that jumped from the front passenger seat. He fell to the pavement as he tripped over something, and she fell on his back with her teeth bared.

Maybank didn't understand why she fell, but he was smart enough to understand that she really was biting the

4

side of the man's head. She lifted her head away from his, ripping off the man's right ear and a long strip of skin from his hairline to his lips. The man's pain was undeniable, and his scream rose above the other chaotic sounds in the street. The red blood stood out in stark contrast to the gray and black smoke.

The driver of the car was a woman, and Maybank could see she was turning the wheel and backing away from the place where her companion had jumped from the car. She was paying so little attention to her friend that she didn't notice someone else had climbed in through the open passenger door. The car backed up, stopped, and then backed away into the smoke. Maybank's eyes were glued to the spot where it had disappeared, so he was still watching when the car slowly rolled into view for a second time. The driver side door was open, and no one was behind the wheel.

He was still watching the car when it occurred to him there was a voice coming through the speakers. It had been there all along, but he had to mentally tune into what was being said. A reporter in the studio was describing the scene, but the smoke was apparently too boring because he asked someone if they had a better view.

The producer was happy to oblige, and the scene switched to another city. This time the historic landmarks of Washington DC made the scene more recognizable, but there was nothing familiar about a group of people on their knees biting a jerking body that was stretched out on the sidewalk.

The cameraman who was filming the attack was yelling something at a reporter who kept asking him if he was getting the shot. The camera jerked almost as much as the victim on the sidewalk as the cameraman shoved it into the hands of the reporter.

Maybank heard him clearly when he yelled, "You want that shot? Go get it."

The camera was heavy, so the end result was a good shot of the sky. Then there was a view of the retreating cameraman's back. The reporter kept talking into her microphone as she turned the heavy camera back toward the original subjects of her report, and when she finally got it pointed in their direction, she was surprised to find they were no longer shredding the man on the sidewalk. They were standing in front of her.

Her screams were cut short as the entire group, attackers and victim, fell onto the camera. The picture was a side view of a woman's foot as it was jerked loosely from side to side. For a brief moment there was a profile of a face, teeth bared and biting into the soft flesh above the back of the ankle.

The studio cut away from Washington, and with a shaking voice the anchor said they were going live to their London correspondent.

"Patrick, this is Diane in Atlanta. Can you describe the scene outside Parliament?"

"It's incredible chaos in the streets of London, Diane. People have been told to go home and shut their doors. Authorities are saying not to open their doors until public announcements say it's safe to do so."

"Are they saying what's causing this, Patrick? The US government is saying it didn't start here."

"Diane, everyone is denying responsibility, but the European networks are calling it The Decline of Man."

"What does that mean, Patrick?"

"They can't stop it, Diane."

Maybank didn't remember sitting down, and he didn't remember when the picture on the TV had gone blank. He had a vague recollection of live broadcasts from major cities around the world. Paris, Rome, Moscow, and many more reports came and went. There were so many shots of people being attacked and dismembered that he felt like he had watched a horror movie.

It seemed to take more effort than usual to get up from his chair, but he eventually pushed himself to a standing position. He found that he hadn't bothered to get dressed, and all he had put in his stomach was coffee. It wasn't exactly a humorous smile that shaped his mouth when it dawned on him that he had seen plenty of people becoming well fed today. The smile changed to an expression of twisted agony and he felt the knot in his stomach and the burning bile as he vomited on the carpet right in front of him. Maybank's knees buckled, and he fell on top of the mess he had just made.

He didn't know if he had blacked out or just blocked everything out, and maybe there wasn't much difference between the two. He pushed himself up for a second time, and that was when it came to him that this was the day they had planned for. This was the day when the shelters would save a few lives. This would also be the day when people would try to escape to the safety of his oil rig. They wouldn't know about his shelter, but they would be coming any time now just to be safe on one of the man made steel islands.

From what he had seen on TV, oil rigs were going to be a lot safer than cities, and the irony wasn't lost on him. Plenty of the people who would think of the oil rigs were the very people who tried to prevent offshore drilling. Regardless of their politics, they would be trying to reach safety now, and so would his designated guests.

Maybank raced into the bedroom and found his pants. It wouldn't do for him to greet dignitaries in his underwear despite the fact that he would greet them naked if he hadn't promised Titus Rush that he would behave. He didn't know who they were, but the promise given to him was that they were worth keeping alive.

Once he was presentable, he began going through the checklist he had prepared for this day. There were parts of the oil rig that were always in a state of readiness, but some had to go through a series of extra safeguards.

The living quarters were exposed in their present state, but a few simple switches moved to the proper position changed it from a resort home into a fortress.

When the survivors club had asked where he planned to put his shelter, he wasn't surprised by their reaction. Part of the reason they had formed the club in the first place was to bring likeminded people together to test each other's ability to survive an apocalypse. That meant critiques, critiques, and more critiques. Their job was to find every reason why their shelter ideas wouldn't work, and the owner of each shelter had the unenviable task of altering designs based on those critiques. His idea to put a shelter on an oil rig seemed to draw the heaviest amount of criticism.

The hardest apocalypse to survive was a direct hit from a nuclear device. Some of the members of the club considered a nuclear war to be in the top five disasters, so their shelters were hardened until they were likely to accomplish their mission. Mud Island, Fort Sumter, Green Cavern, and the President's shelter in Columbus, Ohio were the first to come to his mind. He was told that Ambassadors Island was also impervious to a direct hit, but he didn't have the same faith in the soft strata under a lake that he had in the bedrock around the others. He had visited each shelter, and even though Ambassadors Island had the same metal shell as Mud Island, he felt like an ocean was a better layer of protection than a lake.

Nonetheless, Maybank hoped each of the shelters were online. There hadn't been a nuclear attack, and it remained to be seen exactly what kind of apocalypse was in progress. Judging by the reports on TV, he was leaning toward the probability of a pandemic, and that meant he had to seal off the shelter and close all areas that were exposed to the air.

There was one master switch that was intended to begin the lockdown procedures for any disaster. With a simple flip of his hand, walls dropped into place, electrical systems received signals that internally told his system this was not a drill, and the entire oil rig complex went to internal life support. Until he knew whether or not the pandemic was airborne, he would take every precaution he needed to.

Maybank understood better than some of the survivalists. It was a simple point that Titus had preached to them. One of his favorite expressions was that every oyster would eventually be pried open. Their job was to make it take as long as possible. Maybank didn't think nuclear devices would be aimed at oil rigs because even the madmen with their fingers on the buttons would need oil after a nuclear war.

The pandemic scenario wasn't that simple because viruses tended to go where they wanted to go, especially if they were airborne. His ears popped, telling him there was positive internal air pressure inside the shelter, and the air quality system was already testing the air for pathogens. To some extent the positive pressure would force airborne pathogens to stay outside. He would know within the hour if there was an airborne virus out there. In the meantime, he had his checklist.

Maybank had designed his shelter with multiple control rooms, each one capable of operating all systems. This one in his living quarters allowed him to keep one eye on the news broadcasts while he checked off the items on the list. He saw that the network was still showing cities in Europe, but the always present ticker tape banner was going by at high speed on the bottom of the screen. It began with The Decline of Man and was displaying the names of cities reporting the outbreaks of violence that included cannibalism. He wondered why they didn't just say, "Everywhere."

That reminded him. Some of the cities on the list had shelters in them. It was probably the oldest technology he had in his shelter, if he didn't include the electric can opener, but a panel with green lights was disturbing him. They were all still dark. It was way too early to worry about his friends, though, and it could be a simple malfunction.

Malfunctions were also an inevitable curse according to Titus. He had warned them that malfunctions would be the likely cause for their shelters being penetrated, along with human error, but that didn't have to be true. Malfunctions didn't have to be major to be life threatening, and major malfunctions didn't mean all was lost. That was what crossed Maybank's mind as he considered why his panel of lights was still dark. A computer monitor at another work station gave him his answer. The satellite feeds were down except for some communications. He had TV, he could talk to people when the time was right, but the satellite feed to the shelter transponder signals wasn't operating.

That was a malfunction he could live with. He would eventually make contact with the other shelters, and when he did he could find out which of them were online. He had a momentary thought that maybe Titus had made it to Mud Island in time. Then he remembered that his good friend had died. He had forgotten because he hadn't been at the funeral. Maybank and all the others had honored his request and stayed at their shelters instead of going to the service. Titus thought it would be the ultimate irony if the world ended while they were away from their shelters for the funeral of a club member.

When the checklist was done, Maybank made his first trip topside. If a biohazard was detected, he would receive warnings long before it arrived at the oil rig. A string of buoys with air samplers and other monitors attached to them formed an invisible line of defense for the oil rig, and the satellite that relayed that data was functioning well. If the pandemic was an airborne pathogen, he would have at least an hour to get inside even if a brisk wind was pushing it his way.

There was a light breeze blowing, but it felt good. As a matter of fact it felt so good that he found it hard to believe what he had seen on the news. The solitude of his shelter was one of his reasons for putting it in the deep water of the Gulf, and he was at least going to survive the initial phase of this particular apocalypse, or so it seemed. He let his mind wander as he climbed and thought about how he had come to his decision to put his shelter on an oil rig.

Maybank loved thinking about that day long ago when they were all so much younger. He had been laughed at when he announced his choice for a government funded shelter, but he seriously doubted the others knew much about oil rigs. He knew that he wanted a semisubmersible rig because everyone thought an oil rig is just one big contraption that sat on top of a well and drilled down through the center. Even Titus didn't know there were different types of oil rigs.

After the meeting when he had been nearly laughed out of the room, Titus had approached him and asked for permission to visit the shelter while it was under construction. As the president of their club, and Titus hated being called president, Maybank knew Titus could visit his shelter any time he wanted without asking. So he invited Titus to travel back with him to the Gulf.

It was Maybank's turn to laugh when their helicopter descended toward the landing pad. When Titus turned to him with total understanding on his face, Maybank swelled with pride. It clearly wasn't what Titus had expected.

The structure was massive, and as Titus would learn on his tour, it was like an iceberg. Even though the visible portion was an impressive sight, almost two-thirds of the rig was under water.

There were four cylindrical towers that stood straight up from the water almost as if they went all the way to the floor of the Gulf. They were so big that almost everyone made the mistaken assumption about its size when they saw the rig for the first time. Each of the towers was a corner post for the rig, and each served a separate purpose.

One of the huge towers had nothing built on top of it. Maybank explained that it was full of water and simply kept the rig balanced. The Process Module was built on top of the tower to the west, and the giant crane above it was used to offload supplies from the ships that would dock at the rig. The tower forming the next corner could have been straight out of an architect's nightmare. It was the tower that supported the Living Quarters Module, the Drilling Module, and the Wellbay Module. The whole thing was a monstrosity of metal buildings and pipes that reminded Titus of a house built on a cliff. Their helicopter had landed above it all, and Titus felt like there was no reason for it not to tip over. The last tower was the Power Module, and although it was functional and providing power to the oil rig, the power for the shelter came from below the surface of the water.

The highest spot on the rig was actually the helicopter landing pad. Maybank reached the top of the ladder and his thoughts came back to the present.

At the moment he had a deck chair and a cooler of bottled water sitting on the center of the crosshairs painted on the landing pad. If he saw guests arriving by helicopter he would know they were coming long before they could land. If they had the correct codes, he would grab his deck chair and cooler and move to an observation hut at the top of the ladder. If they didn't have the proper landing codes, he had ways to deal with them.

The hut was lower than the landing pad and had some nasty surprises built in. From that vantage point he could detonate explosives to destroy invaders. That wouldn't be his first choice since helicopters and boats were his connection to the mainland.

His first choice was to do exactly what Titus had said to do. He would drop down through a hatch next to the observation hut above the Quarters Module, which was designed to look like any other living quarters of a semisubmersible oil rig, and then make the long descent through the Wellbay Module. Below the four towers at each corner was the massive submerged hull of the oil rig, but instead of being the flooded ballast compartments that held the rig stationary above the oil well, it was his impenetrable shelter.

The main entrance to the shelter was in the Wellbay Module, and the door would have been familiar to the members of the survivors club. The emergency exits were located in the Process Module, the Power Module, and the tower section with nothing built above it. Although the towers supporting the other modules were all part of the hull, this particular section warranted its own name as the

Main Hull because it literally provided the weight needed to keep the entire structure from tipping over. If it was penetrated and lost its ballast, there was an anchor system that would deploy in seconds and take over, but that was just one more redundant system every shelter had. Titus had called it Plan B.

Maybank walked to the chair and turned it to face north. He got comfortable and brought his binoculars to his eyes.

******

The clear blue sky meant plenty of sunshine, and Maybank pulled the battered baseball cap from his back pocket. That reminded him of something else he had in his other pocket, and he retrieved a piece of paper that had been folded so many times it was ready to separate along the lines. He gently spread it across his lap.

"Let's see who won the pool."

He had read the paper so many times that he already knew what it said, but it was like winning the World Series. Even though you knew your favorite team had won, you read the sports page just to see it all happen again.

It was a list of disasters and extinction level events that could happen. It was also the reason for the shelters. It began with nuclear war and was followed by pandemic. The list was used as a guide for building the shelters. If it was on the list, contingencies had to be designed to keep the shelter safe. The disasters were on the left, and they were followed by the odds of each one happening.

A meteor hitting the Earth came in at about a million to one, and as a joke someone had written below it the odds of winning a Powerball jackpot. That had come years later because there weren't big lotteries like that when the paper was passed around the room for the first time.

The military already had their list, but the survivors club was asked to create their own. The expectation was that the collection of unorthodox thinkers would come up with something the military hadn't considered. When they turned their list over to the military, it was a lot longer than theirs. For some reason, the military minds didn't even have an invasion by an alien race on the list, but the survivors club had given it a high probability.

Another cataclysm that the survivors agreed on didn't even have an official name, so they just called it The End. It was the only apocalypse on the list they couldn't plan for because they didn't know what would cause it. Needless to say, it caused real concern for the sponsors of the shelters, not because it couldn't be prevented, but because it didn't make sense to them.

Titus explained it to the officers who sat together in a tight group at a meeting.

"Imagine this," he began. "You go to bed tonight, and you aren't here tomorrow."

"You mean I'm dead?" asked a General.

"No, you just disappeared, and so did everyone else in the world. Organic life ended. Any one of a hundred different things happened during the night that removed the ability for life to exist on Earth. It could be something on this list, but it's more likely something none of us thought of. Maybe gravity stopped working, or the atmosphere got sucked into outer space, or simply became unbreathable. What we're saying is the laws of physics aren't all known yet. Some are theories, and a new one could pop up while you're comfortable in your bed. That new law may say it's impossible for life to exist."

The General wasn't entirely sure what to say in response to the explanation, but he hadn't gotten to his rank by being stupid.

"Gentlemen, you're either toying with me, which comes naturally to you, or you're stating the obvious. We can sit here until the end of the world and add new disasters to this list, and we'll never think of all of them. So, anything we do think of is fair game and possible. That's why someone wrote zombie apocalypse on here."

Someone behind the General clapped a big hand down on his shoulder and said, "General, you're officially one of us."

Maybank remembered the expression on the General's face, and if he read it correctly, the General was proud to join the club.

The first dot on the horizon brought Maybank back to the present, and he returned the worn piece of paper to his pocket without checking to see who had won the pool. It was growing fast, and it was only seconds before he could see separation between it and the surface. His first post-apocalyptic contact was an aircraft. It grew fast enough for him to be sure it wasn't a helicopter, so he doubted it would be a rescue vehicle for important people escaping to his shelter.

A second dot appeared behind the first just as he was beginning to focus the binoculars enough to make out the outline of a fighter jet. He guessed he had no more than thirty seconds to reach safety.

He abandoned everything and ran to the escape shaft. The door would shut automatically when his weight passed over a panel a few feet below, and within ten seconds he was sliding through the hatch into the Wellbay Module. It theoretically served as access to the well, but in reality it was the fastest way to enter the shelter.

He checked his watch and saw he had made it with ten seconds to spare, and if the two jets were going to bomb the rig, they would do plenty of aesthetic damage, but the shelter would still be there. Even if they blew off the tower that served as ballast, the rig might fall over before the anchors could deploy, but it wouldn't take the shelter with it. The shelter would separate from the oil rig as easily as Titus Rush's houseboat from Mud Island. It would just appear to be worse.

Secure in his shelter, Maybank went to the monitor that showed the approaching fighters. They were close enough for him to see they were loaded with munitions, so they had a target in mind. He didn't have long to wonder if his oil rig was their target as they screamed by at incredible speed.

On a monitor facing south he watched them fade away but not before they began launching their weapons. Whatever it was they were hitting, it was well beyond the horizon. He didn't know if he would ever learn what it had been, but a few minutes later they flew by without their payloads.

There was a thin black line reaching from the horizon upward that resembled a scratch against the glassy blue sky. Maybank opened a log book and noted the times and dates of the events. The length of time that the target burned would give him some idea of what it was they had bombed. Judging by the color of the smoke, he guessed it was a ship. It bloomed like a flower and the black line became thicker.

Maybank considered his dive to the shelter as the first successful test of the escape system. He had practiced the drill many times, but this was the first time his life could have depended on how well he did. His estimate of thirty seconds could have been wrong, so he was pleased that he had given himself an extra ten seconds by making it to safety in only twenty.

Only one thing went wrong, and it had to be fixed immediately. There should have been an audible alarm as soon as his radar detected the aircraft. He had made it below in twenty seconds, but if he had been climbing the ladder instead of sitting on the landing pad, he would have arrived at the top as the fighters screamed past.

The equipment room for the radar system was inside the shelter, and it didn't take long for him to find the problem. It was as dark as the green lights on the shelter panel. A few simple test inputs proved that the system wasn't receiving a signal.

"Great. Malfunction number two."

Titus had offered one piece of advice to the entire survivors club, and Maybank could repeat it in his sleep.

"Once it starts, the best place you can be is inside your shelter. Go there, shut yourself in, and stay there. The only thing you'll be giving up is sunshine."

He had everything inside the shelter that he had up above, and he knew Titus was right, but it felt like he had time before the rest of the world caught up with him. Besides, he really liked watching the sunrises and sunsets, and in the end, he wanted to spend just a little more time up there.

It didn't take long for him to make the climb back to the living quarters. He took a few minutes to gather together a few personal effects that he could have left behind but really wanted. He closed up the quarters just like a shopkeeper at the end of the day, but his security devices were better than most banks. Steel walls slid into place and the twenty foot ladder that went from the lower level up to his home retracted into a hidden recess that closed a door over the opening.

Sooner or later someone would reach the oil rig. When they did, they would have to figure out how to get from the water up to the modules. There were no visible steel rungs or handrails on any of the towers, not unless he wanted them to be visible, and he certainly didn't plan to do so.

Despite the difficulty, someone would figure it out. That was expected. When they did, they would find lots of steel everywhere except one place. There was food, fuel, and most importantly, drinking water in only one place that could be reached by other survivors, and that was the crew quarters above the Wellbay Tower. If everything worked according to plans, the crew quarters would distract survivors from searching for the shelter.

Maybank spent the rest of the day on the landing platform but saw nothing cross the horizon again. He didn't doubt that there would be anything different on TV, but that could wait. He wanted to savor the open sky and the smell of the water surrounding him. When the sun dropped below the horizon to the west he decided it was time to go back to the shelter and test the rest of his security system.

Closing the door to the shelter had a feeling of finality to it. He wasn't really surprised that no one had arrived on the first day, but he was sure someone was already on the water and headed for the oil rigs. He was concerned about the dignitaries who were assigned to his shelter, though. The topic had been broached many times over the years, and one thing they all had been assured. People would make it to their shelters within the first twenty-four hours. After that, it was likely they weren't coming.

The final security test was the camera system that was laced throughout the miles of pipes on the rig. They weren't like the lights on a Christmas tree that would all go out if one decided to quit, but Maybank had told Titus when he did his last upgrade that it would look like Christmas if every camera had a light on it. In fact, there were so many cameras that there were literally no hiding places on the rig.

An added bonus of the last camera upgrade was the motion sensors. If something moved anywhere on the rig, he would get a text message that told him where the motion had happened. It was a nuisance at first because birds actually managed to reach the rig from time to time, but the advantage outweighed the nuisance. It became a real-time test of the motion sensors that was better than a scheduled test by two people.

There was one more security measure in place that Maybank couldn't imagine ever using, but when he flipped the switch that activated the system, it occurred to him that until this morning he never imagined seeing cannibalism on network news. Throughout the maze of steps, ladders, platforms, and pipes there was an ever-present hum. When the switch was off, power was supplied to thousands of different systems. When the switch was on, there were very few safe places to walk as the oil rig became a big electric chair.

2 MOLLY AND SAM

Six Years After the Decline

It was Molly's idea to start a journal, but she thought I should write it. She felt like one day everyone would want to read the words of Ed Jackson, the man who saved so many people because he had a shelter.

When she suggested it to me, she said I should be the one to do it because I knew how everyone had survived. It had been my shelter that had kept everyone alive, and I knew how all of them had lived long enough to find me. She said she also wanted to read about herself rather than to tell her story. Telling it would be too painful. I never suspected at the time that I would be writing about how we lost her. The very idea of life without Molly was too foreign to consider.

I had told her that everyone was a survivor because they made it past those first days, and those days were the worst. I had never really spoken with her about the things I had seen at the beginning because she had always been a little girl to me. Now, almost five years since the trip to Columbus, Ohio, she had grown into a teenager who was less like a little girl every day. She had also become restless and bored with her life in the company of the soldiers at Fort Sumter. I imagine I had grown a bit, too.

I was seeing the same behavior from Sam. Both of them used to be about as polite as kids could be, but more than once in the last year I had seen them giving an attitude to someone older than them. Whether it was a soldier on guard duty or a member of the original Mud Island Family, Sam and Molly didn't give them the respect they used to show adults. The sad reality was there weren't other kids their age living in the shelter, and they felt left out. Whitney was closer to the ages of the soldiers and her friendships with adults had pulled her away from the younger girl. Sam was a little older than Molly, but he was still younger than the youngest of the soldiers. They were protected, given menial jobs to perform around the fort, and they felt like they were being looked down on. Maybe they were.

I guess it shouldn't have come as a surprise when they vanished at the beginning of summer. One day they were sitting on the wall that surrounded Fort Sumter just talking and watching the sun go down on the other side of Charleston. The next day Tom was searching every level of the shelter. Of course the rest of us were helping, but none of us held the same amount of hope as Tom. The note she had left for him was short and simple. She and Sam wanted to find a place of their own. Tom was devastated, and Kathy was at a loss for how to console him.

As we searched the shelter, the helicopters were loaded with provisions for an extended search and rescue mission. On the off chance that they managed to avoid being spotted quickly, the Chief wanted the helicopters to be able to cover a large area without having to return to Fort Sumter for anything except fuel.

Once all rooms in the shelter had been checked, everyone used the elevators to ascend to the top floor. We didn't waste any time getting to the ladders and the surface where the waiting choppers were bringing their operating temperatures to optimal levels. The crews were ready for us as we climbed aboard.

Only two of the Navy VH92A's were warming up alongside the executive model Sikorsky S76D. Captain Miller had made it a standing order that one would always remain behind on standby because Fort Sumter was not as well defended when they were gone. If our friends across the harbor at Patriots Point saw all of them leave, it might make them feel bold enough to attack the fort.

That was our other problem. Someone had converted the Yorktown, a World War II aircraft carrier, into a fortress of their own, and they had rejected all friendly attempts to establish contact. Over the last five years we had watched as they expanded from the carrier all the way to the middle of the massive Arthur C. Ravenel bridge that spanned Charleston harbor.

The bridge had been like every other bridge in the country after the first days of the apocalypse. It was a graveyard with cars and trucks as the grave markers. People escaping from downtown Charleston toward Mt. Pleasant had probably wondered why so many people were on the other side of the bridge trying to escape in the opposite direction, and the same was likely to be true for people over on the other side. No matter which way they were going, they were driving toward death, and just like other bridges, traffic came to a stop. People abandoned their cars and left the worldly goods they had snatched up to take with them. They ran for their lives back the way they had come, being chased by the infected and running straight into the arms of the dead that waited for them.

For weeks after that first day, the dead had wandered among the twisted wreckage on the bridge. They would occasionally find someone who had managed to remain hidden, but eventually there were no more desperate screams. There were no more pleas for mercy.

At some point in time, the only infected dead on the bridge were those that were trapped in that endless, tangled maze of vehicles. They were exposed to the elements, and over the years they had either decayed or had become food for other predators. The rats and birds had picked the bones clean. The soldiers on watch at Fort Sumter reported seeing swarms of rats running along the railings of the bridge, and we knew anything moving on that bridge would be gone before long.

A long period of quiet fell over the bridge graveyard. For over a year there were no changes we could see from Fort Sumter. Then we noticed a few of the cars were in different places. The changes were so subtle that we didn't spot them at first, but some of the vehicles were more obvious than others, and when they were moved, we started watching more closely.

Under the cover of darkness, someone was rearranging the graveyard. Sounds carried across the water at night as metal was bent and twisted free from the wreckage. Smaller vehicles near the top of the highest span were pushed down toward Charleston, and from what we could tell, a lane had been opened from Mt. Pleasant all the way to the top of the bridge. Trucks towed containers to the crest of the highest span, and somehow they managed to stack them on top of each other. First they were stacked across the width of the bridge, then they were stacked along the sides in an attempt to keep prying eyes from seeing what was happening behind them.

Satellites were no longer providing imagery for us, so Captain Miller sent up helicopters to take a look from safe distances. Pictures taken during those flights told us all we needed to know. Someone had organized the survivors into a safe zone that included the bridge, the entire maritime museum at Patriots Point, and a corridor of roads that ran all the way to the docks on the Wando River. The fact that they were organized might have been good news if not for their unwillingness to meet their neighbors at Fort Sumter. They ignored radio hails, and would shoot across the bow when approached by water. All we could do was watch the bridge take on the appearance of a rusty red and yellow, rectangular fortress as container after container was raised into position.

We had been spending a lot of time speculating about how to establish a good relationship with the bridge people, but so far there was no solid plan. As we lifted off from Fort Sumter in the helicopters, all eyes were pointed in that direction, and we silently hoped that we were right in our guess that Molly and Sam wouldn't have gone that way.

Our best guess was that they had crossed the marshes toward Fort Johnson and then gone inland across James Island. The marshes were still treacherous, but if they were cautious enough, Sam and Molly could have navigated the quicksand-like spots and reached dry land. The thick woods where they could have left the marshes would provide excellent cover during the first hours of their disappearance.

We didn't believe there was much chance they had gone along the coast of Morris Island in an attempt to cross over to Folly Beach. They knew as well as we did that Folly Beach had remained heavily populated by the infected. Limited access to Folly Beach made it difficult for anyone to leave the coast, and that included the infected. Molly and Sam also knew that they would be easily spotted from the air, and it would take them longer to reach cover because they would have to travel in the open.

The same was true of them leaving by water. If they went up the Ashley River, they would have needed to row against the current of the river, and they would have taken hours to reach the first place they could abandon the boat. There was also the likelihood of being seen by the infected dead that tended to wander into the boat landings.

So, that left Fort Johnson. The three helicopters fanned out on a course that would take all of us in that general direction, but the two on the left and right of us would also be able to at least scan the less likely escape routes. With Tom in the copilot's seat, we went straight down the middle of the best path.

Although it was difficult to see anything useful in the mud flats that sat temporarily above the tide, Tom spotted footprints that could only have been made by two people. One person was walking behind the other, which was how they would have done it. They would also have tied a rope around their waists, and if one got stuck in the mud, the other would have freed them. The tandem footprints made their path easier to see from above.

The Chief steered the sleek Sikorsky along that path, and Tom aimed his binoculars ahead in the same direction. There was a heart stopping moment when he leaned forward out of reflex and shouted that he could see something moving in a place where the water was pooled around the marsh grass.

We all thought it was Molly and Sam as soon as we located the spot where Tom frantically pointed, but as we drew closer we knew that it wouldn't be good news if it was one of them. The green, shiny body of an alligator was twisting and turning as it dragged its prey toward the water. Its powerful jaws were closed around the upper torso and shoulder of someone with black hair. Hair the color of Molly's.

The Chief poured on the speed, knowing that we had to get there before the alligator went under the surface. We had to at least know whether or not it was Molly. The only thing worse than seeing her die would be wondering if it had been her.

The prey was wearing a red flannel shirt and jeans, and as we sped past the horrible scene, the Chief put the helicopter in a steep bank to give everyone on the right side a longer look. The face that was turned toward us by the twisting alligator was a mass of torn flesh, but it had obviously been a man. He had been heavier than Sam when alive, but the sheer number of old injuries was what identified him as an infected dead.

The rivers along the coast had become a breeding ground for the alligators. They had found food to become plentiful in the early days of the apocalypse, but the number of bodies falling into the water had decreased with time. Now the alligators attacked quickly because there were so many of them that they were competing for food. They were also competing against the hordes of blue crabs that would steal the victims of the alligators from the underwater lairs where their bodies were hidden.

As the Chief completed his steep bank and brought us back on our original course, we saw the alligator and its prey slipping below the surface. If the infected dead could be described as having one last expression on its face, it would have been indifference.

The footprints disappeared when they reached a narrow tidal creek where the water had begun to get deeper, but then they resumed on the softer sand closer to the trees. From this point on it would become even more difficult to find the kids because there was plenty of cover.

The Chief brought the chopper into position hovering just above the trees and panned the nose from left to right. In front of them was only a small island of trees covering a few acres of land. Beyond that was more marshland and mud flats, but a small gravel road had been built along the edge of the marshes, and it went almost all the way to Fort Johnson. If they had made it to that road far enough ahead of the search party, there would be very little chance of spotting them from the air.

I leaned forward from the crew cabin and got the Chief's attention. I didn't have to shout because the executive Sikorsky was built for comfort and was much quieter than military helicopters.

"We need to land and search this wooded area. We'll never spot them from the air."

The Chief shook his head in my direction and then said something over his radio. He gestured in the direction of the helicopter that was flying on our left side. I followed his hand and saw it was already getting lower as it descended toward the gravel road.

The Chief's voice came over the internal speakers.

"If they made it past these woods, then they are already at Fort Johnson or somewhere beyond. We would lose valuable time searching for them. We're going to go ahead to a spot they couldn't have reached yet and then work our way back. The crew that landed will search those trees and then begin searching along their trail if they don't find them."

The Chief told everyone to wait a moment as he received a radio call. He gave some instructions to the crew on the ground and then came back to us.

"New footprints were found in the mud near the gravel road. They're deep and going in the right direction, and they're in tandem. They must've been running, and the prints may be fresh."

We could feel the tilt of the Sikorsky as the Chief increased his forward speed. Fort Johnson flashed by beneath us, and we were all surprised to see how many of the infected still wandered out from the trees surrounding the buildings. The Chief didn't bring our helicopter in for a landing as we expected. Instead, he raced inland and began to descend toward an unpaved bare patch that was cut in a perfect square surrounded by trees. Judging by the rows of boats along one side, it appeared to be a boat parking lot.

A sign at the entrance of the lot sat next to a building, and it confirmed my thinking.

It said, "South Carolina Department of Natural Resources, Boat Titling and Registration."

"We'll work our way back from here," said the Chief. "Chopper three is flying ahead to set up chokepoints where they would have to pass if they get by us. These woods are thick, but there are so many infected stumbling around that I can't imagine they could be making good time."

The side door opened and we piled out onto the packed sand of the parking lot. Besides the Chief and Tom who sat up front, the passenger cabin could comfortably seat over a half dozen people. I handed my rifle out to Cassandra and climbed out with my wife, Jean. She had been a mother to Molly since our first day with the little girl, and I could tell by the grim expression on her face that she was focused on finding her, but she was afraid. Jean was so petite that we called her "Pixie" sometimes, but she could be formidable in a weapons fight. If it came down to rescuing Molly, Jean was good to have along on the trip.

Cassandra Gibbs was a former Army soldier who had been working as a security officer on a Mercy Mission ship. She was fearless and had stayed alive on a harrowing journey at sea while everyone else on her ship had died. She was a quick thinker who would take on an army of the infected if she had to.

Her companion was a former member of the crew of Executive One. Terrance Simmons, Sim as he liked to be called, had been the navigator on the plane that had gotten the President out of Washington. He had chosen to come south with the Mud Island survivors when the rest of his crew had chosen to go north where the cold lasted most of the year. They reasoned that the infected wouldn't survive there, and they could live peacefully. Sim and Cassandra had taken to each other over a glass of iced tea, and it was no surprise to any of us that they were still together.

Colleen and Hampton were exchanging whispers privately. Two of the kindest people I had ever known and perfect for each other, they were probably talking about where the young boy and girl were hiding. They had survived in a suburban neighborhood near Charlotte and had some experience with house to house combat. Behind Colleen's little Irish nose, freckles, and red hair was a keen mind and a sharp wit. Together with Hampton's knowledge of the coastal regions, they were a skillful pair. Hampton had only left the coast when his home town had been overrun by the infection that caused people to die and then begin eating their neighbors.

Bus, our doctor for the group, was talking with Kathy, Tom's girlfriend and one of the survivors from a cruise ship who had landed virtually at the front door of my shelter on Mud Island. Kathy, along with Jean and the Chief had spotted me off shore when I had gone out in a boat to do some target practice. We had been family ever since.

Bus had known Molly her whole life and had been a close friend of Tom and his wife Allison. When Allison had died while trying to escape from the infected city of Charleston, Kathy had become close to Tom, and Bus was quick to accept her. He knew she was good for Molly and for Tom.

All in all, our group was Molly's best chance for survival in the infected world, but we had to find her and Sam fast.

"I feel a bit conspicuous in this parking lot," said Hampton. "What's the plan, Chief?"

They could all imagine what must be trying to reach them from the thick walls of trees surrounding the parking lot. The foliage was so dense on all sides that they could only see a few feet into the trees. They had all begun to swivel at the hips, weapons ready and watching for the first of the infected to emerge.

"If they're following a map," said the Chief, "they would have crossed the last tidal creek close to the boardwalk that goes from the water to Fort Johnson. That would bring them onto land by the College of Charleston Marine Laboratory. That's about a half mile from here. The question would be whether or not they would stay on the road or head for the trees."

"I don't think they would have much choice," said Tom. "As a matter of fact, I'm betting on the third option."

"Where would that be?" asked Kathy.

"The buildings. These woods are thick. That means running into the infected without seeing them way in advance. The roads are just as bad because they can see you out in the open. By now they may be in big trouble."

The Chief pointed toward the southeast.

"This way through the woods to the road, or we can use that driveway and stay on the road the whole way."

As a group we weren't too keen on the idea of going into those woods. We were used to the woods on Mud Island and even on the other side of the moat that surrounded the island, but this was different. The trees were close together, and the brush under them was dense. Not much light could be filtering down to the floor of these woods.

With the helicopter secured, we broke into a trot and silently formed a line behind the Chief as he led the way to the parking lot entrance. A quick left and a second left almost immediately put us out onto Fort Johnson Road.

I felt like we were somewhere else in the world, not just a couple of miles from the suburbs. We were looking down the middle of a virtual tunnel made of trees that interlocked their branches above the road. It was a great place for tourists, but the dark shapes we could see in the road ahead weren't about to welcome us to Fort Johnson in a friendly way.

"We can't shoot our way through that," said Hampton.

Tom answered a bit more sharply than he had intended. "You have a better idea?"

Before Tom could answer, the Chief stepped between them and said, "We approach slowly staying quiet and as low to the ground as we can. As we encounter the infected, we take them out with knives and machetes. We only shoot if we have to fall back or if they get behind us. Understood?"

Everyone nodded agreement, and we moved forward again. The Chief eased closer to the right side of the road as we shouldered our rifles and drew our machetes. We were practically brushing against the trees, and it gave me the feeling that we were going to be swarmed from the dark places under the leaves at any moment.

We came to the first of the infected only twenty or thirty yards down the road. The moaning that escaped from the shattered face of the man that had become an infected creature quickly drew the attention of more of the dark shadows that had been milling around in the middle of the road. They turned in our direction as if they had been called by the first walking corpse, and they joined in with him in a chorus of moans.

"We have to work fast," said Kathy. "We need to shut them up before they draw more into the area."

Arms reached out from the infected as they gathered, and arms reached out from us as we moved in with our blades in front of us.

We had learned, mostly through trial and error, how to take out the threat of being bitten as fast as possible. It started with approaching the target with the blade extended. It was surprisingly easy to push the machete tip upward under the chin of an infected, slicing neatly into the brain. A quick pull backward would free the blade, and we could approach the next one.

We used to slash at the infected because it seemed that was the best way to use a machete, but it was too easy to get a blade stuck in a skull or a neck. While we were trying to pull the blades free, the infected were trying to bite the arms that were so tempting as they flailed in front of their faces.

As we took down the first of the infected to reach us, we tried to keep moving along the right side of the road. If Molly and Sam were going to be in a building, it would be on that side.

We worked well together and didn't let ourselves get bunched up. Before long we had a rhythm going, and five blades were going in as five blades were coming out. The road was so littered with bodies of the infected that we were leaving a barrier behind us. When the infected finally began coming out of the woods behind us, they tripped and fell over the bodies. They weren't making much progress getting to us because they would no sooner get up from a fall when they would trip over another corpse.

Light began to filter through the trees and we found ourselves at what we thought was our goal, but it was the driveway to a smaller building. The sign at the entrance said it was the Charleston location for NOAA, the National Oceanic and Atmospheric Administration.

"The National Weather Service," said the Chief. "The kids wouldn't have made it this far if they stopped to take a break, or if they took the time to check out the Marine Laboratory."

"How far to the College of Charleston buildings?" asked Kathy.

"Maybe a half mile," I said. "I visited the place a long time ago. They were doing some amazing things growing fresh water shrimp."

"Thanks for the strategic update," said Tom. "Anything you can remember about the place that might be useful?"

I didn't take offense at Tom's sarcastic tone. If it had been my child out there with no one but a teenaged boy protecting her, I might have sounded worse.

"There was security on the building," I said.

I hoped that would make Tom feel like his daughter could have found a safe place to hole up if they had been chased into hiding by the infected. I was surprised that it had brought everyone to a stop.

"What kind of security?" asked Cassandra. "Hard to get in or hard to get out?"

"I guess both," I answered, still uncertain about the reaction.

Then it came to me. This secluded strip of land that jutted out toward the harbor was the perfect place to take a last stand, and FEMA had most likely brought resources here. Resources meant lots of people, and that was why there were so many infected on the road and in the woods. I could only imagine what it was like inside the buildings. The people who had died inside them were still in there, but they weren't people anymore.

"They probably couldn't even get inside," I said.

My voice sounded weak even to me.

We had another thick group of the infected to push through before we reached the next entrance, but then we had a clear stretch where we made up for lost time. Colleen had a close call when an infected literally fell from a thick tree limb that stretched over the road. It knocked her over, but since she was toward the front of the group there were plenty of us who were able to impale its head before it could bite her.

Colleen let loose a colorful stream of profanity that I was sure contained new words, but she ended with the question of how an infected had gotten up into the trees.

Hampton did his best to calm her down and suggested that maybe the man died in the tree and had been stuck in the branches since. Everyone must have been on edge because she snapped back at him that she really wasn't expecting an explanation, but since he was in the mood to give one, he should consider the possibility that it had fallen from a plane.

I had to admit, it would have been funny if it hadn't scared all of us so badly. I thought I saw a very slight twitch at the corner of the Chief's mouth as he tried to suppress a grin.

Colleen shook herself loose from Hampton and went up to the front of the group alongside Tom. Kathy conceded her spot up front and dropped back next to Hampton.

"Don't take it personally," she whispered. "She's only mad because I think she wet herself a little."

Hampton choked and pretended to be fighting back a sneeze as he moved to the back of the group.

"There's our turn up ahead," said the Chief. "Keep moving unless I say to stop."

The entrance to the College of Charleston Marine Laboratory had been blocked by sandbags and barbed wire. It looked suspiciously like the place I had seen on TV in the first days of the infection. I had no doubt that we would find the infection had gotten inside the barriers.

We picked our way over the barbed wire fences being careful not to snag our clothing on the razor sharp blades, and it was exactly as we expected inside. Security doors were smashed, and furniture had been piled on the stairs. Even if this wasn't the same building I had seen on TV, the scenario that had played out as people retreated to safety must have been played out in hundreds and thousands of places. The survivors in this building would have made it to a higher floor, but then they would have discovered their lack of water and food. Maybe someone in their group had been bitten, and keeping them alive was not going to be good for the group.

The lobby of the building was mostly debris and pieces of glass. Wrecked computers and overturned shelves were evidence of a battle fought almost seven years ago. Moist walls covered with mold made the place smell like old, wet paper, but one smell permeated the air. People had bled and died here, and the infected had roamed the halls long after people stopped seeking refuge in this building.

"I don't think they would have found this place too interesting," said Kathy. "After Fort Sumter, the smell here would have been too offensive, and the humidity is unbearable."

The group was in agreement that Molly and Sam would have done nothing more than give the building a quick look. They had both survived some close calls in bad conditions, but Kathy was right. If they wanted to find a place of their own, they would have something romantic in mind. Maybe a hut on a peaceful lagoon. A moldy deathtrap wouldn't be their idea of roughing it with a smile on their faces.

We shouldn't have been surprised by the reception committee that had gathered outside the building. Before they could even get clear of the front door, the parking lots and driveways had filled with the infected.

"I don't think the kids came this way," said Tom. "At least I hope they didn't."

3 RECRUITED

Before the Decline

Maybank was in his last week of high school when he met Titus Rush. A friend had given him a magazine about the end of the world, and about how everyone should get ready. There were pictures of shelters under construction and lists of companies that would build them for anyone who could afford them.

The magazine had some really great tips about what you could or could not eat, what plants to avoid, and how you could burn a crayon like a candle for hours. He liked the pictures of the best places to build shelters, but what really caught his eyes were the pictures of the weapons recommended by the survivalists.

There were big things happening in the world, and he didn't have to be convinced that everything was going to get blown up sooner or later. Vietnam was in his future. That was another thing he was sure of. Body counts were posted on the news every day, and the only way out of it was college, something he couldn't afford, not on his pay. He could get a few scholarships, but not enough to make up the difference. It was a rotten way to plan for college, but he figured if he could survive a year in Vietnam, maybe he could get the GI Bill benefits to pay his way through school. He considered other branches of the service, but a recruiter had visited his school and told him he would have to enlist for a few more years, and he could still wind up in Vietnam.

One of the magazines on the shelf at the grocery store where he worked had an article about a survivalist group that was having a meeting in Columbia, South Carolina. What he didn't know was that the public meeting was a cover for a secret meeting the group was having with the Army at Fort Jackson. At least he didn't know about it when he read the article.

The public meeting was being held at a county library, and the article said the topic of discussion was survival of the coming apocalypse. His dad said it was all just a bunch of bull and anti-war propaganda. He said they just wanted his money. Danny figured it wouldn't hurt to go listen because he didn't have any money. Besides, it sounded like fun.

It was fun, but not for the reasons he expected. He sat in the back row because everyone else was older than him, and there were a lot of hippies. It wasn't that he had anything against hippies. It was his paranoia about getting busted. Looking around the room at all the long hair and bell-bottoms, he was sure everyone had something illegal on them.

Despite the paranoia, he started enjoying himself as soon as people started taking their turns talking. There were several people scattered around the room on their folding chairs who claimed to have been abducted by aliens. They all told similar stories about bright lights, electronics going haywire, and being subjects in experiments. They were all poked and prodded. Listening to them was a riot.

"Okay, who do we have up next?"

There was a man running the meeting who was looking at a sheet of paper attached to a clipboard.

"Danny Maybank, you're next on the list. Why do you want to join American Survivalists?"

The man was swiveling his head around making his shoulder length hair and beard give him a mountain man appearance. His eyes searched the faces waiting for someone to admit their name had been called.

Maybank was caught off guard. He had heard them calling out names before people started speaking, but he missed the part about this being a membership drive. He sank a little lower in his chair, but the guy sitting next to him cleared his throat really loud and then pointed at him.

"Well, son. What've you got to say?"

Since he was discovered, he hesitantly stood up and said, "Hi, I'm Danny Maybank."

He didn't know why that was funny, but a lot of the people in the room laughed.

"This isn't an AA meeting," whispered the guy who had pointed at him. "You sound like your next line will be that you're an addict."

"Oh, sorry everyone. Hey, listen, I just thought this meeting would be interesting. That's why I came to it. You can go on to the next person."

He sat down and thought that would be the last of it, but the guy next to him handed him a card and said, "Give me a call."

When the guy up front called on the next person on the list, Danny saw a big guy in front stand up. He thought he only glanced that way for a second, but when he turned back to ask the man why he should call him, he was gone.

After the meeting Maybank went into the library and checked out a stack of books about home remedies, survival, and weapons. Part of him said this stuff might keep him alive in Vietnam.

He was leaving when he saw the leader of the group in the parking lot talking with the guy who had been sitting next to him. He couldn't resist interrupting them.

"Hi."

That was all he got out of his mouth before the big guy said the rest.

"I'm Danny Maybank, and I'm an addict."

Their laughs were so natural that he didn't feel like he was being laughed at, or he might have just walked away.

"Vince Clayborn," said the big man. He held his hand out to Danny to shake. Danny felt like the hand had a baseball glove on it because it was so big and calloused.

The second man, considerably shorter and extremely relaxed, held out his hand.

"Titus Rush. Nice to meet you, Danny."

"Call me Maybank," he managed to say in a voice that sounded different from a kid who was just about to graduate from high school. As he spoke he realized it was the effect this man had on him. There was something calming about him that made Maybank like him and trust him immediately. Even though he had outed him in the meeting.

"Why did you ask me to call you, Mr. Rush?"

"You can call me Titus, and Vince here has never liked being called Mr. Clayborn. What did you think of the meeting?"

"Well, it was interesting. There were some entertaining stories."

"To say the least," said Titus. "If you were the guy in charge…"

"President," said Vince.

"Man, you know I hate being called that."

"Yes, why do you think I call you that?"

"Wait a minute, you're the President of the club? Why were you on the back row?"

"To watch people better. If you were the person in charge of a group like that, would you allow those space travelers to join?"

"I imagine you have a hard enough time being taken seriously without adding nuts to your club."

"Exactly," said Vince. "Our funding source already wants us all to get haircuts and dress better."

"Funding source?"

"Kid, got any plans for the rest of your life?"

Maybank was caught off guard for the second time in the last hour.

"Yeah, but not what you would call good plans. Why?"

"You might call us a rather select group. We need just a couple more members, and almost everyone in the room was there to judge the newbies who want to join. Our funding source gave us until tomorrow if we want to go forward, and you were almost a unanimous choice."

Maybank felt a little dizzy, and he wondered what he had gotten himself into.

"Don't decide right this moment, kid. Go home and think about it, and if you decide you're interested give me a call by 9:00 AM tomorrow. We'll send someone by to pick you up."

"I have a car."

"You won't be able to take it where we're going," said Vince. "You can ride with us."

The men left Maybank standing in the parking lot of the library, and if not for the fact that he didn't want to die in combat, he would have torn up the card with the phone number on it.

******

By the end of the next day, Maybank knew his life had reached a turning point. He made the call, and he was picked up by a guy in a Volkswagen Beetle. For some reason he had expected a Jeep, but at least his parents weren't suspicious. He didn't know why he expected a Jeep, but when they drove up to the front gate of Fort Jackson and asked to climb into an Army Jeep, he had a feeling like he was where he was supposed to be. Then again, in a few weeks he expected to be at the same Army base for basic training.

The meeting room was in a hot, metal building, and everyone was sweating already. Columbia wasn't the hottest city in the country, but the humidity could kill you. He was surprised to see a General at the podium, and he was eyeballing the long hair in the room like he wanted to personally do the honors with a barber's clippers.

Maybank tried for the back row again, but Titus motioned for him to take the seat next to him up front.

Without wasting time or words on introductions or greetings, the General asked, "Are we ready to move forward?"

Titus answered without getting up, "We have the number of people you need. We'll have a list of members for you in a few minutes."

"Good. Each of your people will be assigned a team of Army engineers and someone who will handle the money. They will meet at the end of next week and travel to their sites to discuss construction. I have ordered them to give you whatever you ask for, but I want to remind you that this is a top secret operation. If even one of you gets the urge to tell someone about it, we'll scrap the whole thing. Questions?"

"A few of my people have received draft notices. Can we get those taken care of?"

The General had addressed the entire group with a scowl on his face, but when he faced Titus to answer his question, he visibly softened. Maybank could see that the General had a measure of respect for Titus.

"Please indicate next to their names who needs attention, and we'll code those with a college exemption."

Maybank still didn't know what was going on, but he was either going to college, or someone was making it look like he was. Either way, he wasn't going to die trying to earn his tuition money.

Just as quickly as it had started, the meeting ended. The list was given to the General who passed it to his Orderly, and a whirlwind of processing and paperwork started.

They were escorted through the building, normally used to process new recruits, and one by one their pictures were taken for ID cards. Maybank noticed there were Army barbers standing by next to a row of barber chairs and long mirrors, but their anticipation changed to disappointment when the group was rushed away into the next room.

They didn't escape the Medics who were standing in pairs ready to give them a series of vaccinations.

"Why do we have to get shots?" Maybank whispered to Titus.

"The Army doesn't want us to give important people any diseases."

Maybank wasn't entirely sure that Titus had given him a straight answer, but he got in line behind him. He was getting out of the draft, and a few shots were a small price to pay.

By the time the processing was done, they were each introduced to their individual "project teams". Every member of the survivalist club was given five people to work with, and Maybank was taken away to a private room to talk with them. He wasn't sure of the chain of command. His dad called it "the pecking order". He felt like he was still a kid, but his team kept calling him Mr. Maybank. He finally asked them to just call him Maybank, and they seemed fine with that. He didn't realize it at the time, but he put them all at ease because military people tended to refer to each other by their last names.

One of them explained that he would be handling all of the expenses. He would keep track of everything they spent and get approval for whatever he needed. Maybank didn't ask because he didn't want to seem dumb, but he didn't know what the guy was talking about.

The answers began to take shape when the military man started talking. Maybank just sat and listened while the rigid officer told him things as if he had asked questions.

"The location of the shelter will be your choice and yours alone. If you want it somewhere, that's where we'll put it."

Maybank nodded.

"There is no budget, but keep in mind that big ticket items should be requested as early as possible to allow us time to arrange the funds"

Another nod.

"Mr. Rush has already made it clear that technology in the shelters must be upgradeable. When the shelter is finished it will have the latest technology, and it will be upgraded once a year unless there is something that can be incorporated sooner."

He risked a question.

"What's the latest technology?"

He thought he had screwed up because the officer stared at him like he didn't know how to answer.

"Is there a problem?" asked Maybank.

"No, uh."

The officer let that last partial answer kind of drag out. He thought he was being tested.

"Well, uh Maybank, we don't have all of the specifications for your technology yet. What do you want in your shelter? You'll certainly have radar and TV reception. I imagine shortwave radio will be in every shelter. If they ever improve on that, we'll certainly install it."

That was when Maybank really started to understand. He was supposed to be telling them what he wanted and where to build it, in which case he didn't have a clue because he hadn't thought about it.

"Can you gentlemen excuse me for a minute? I'll be right back."

Maybank left the room and went looking for Titus. He finally found him with his group about thirty minutes later. He had a large map rolled out on a table, and Maybank could easily tell who was in charge in his meeting.

Titus saw him coming and intercepted him at the door.

"Why didn't you tell me what was going on before leaving me alone with them?"

"Well, if you didn't shoot yourself in the foot, I had complete faith that you would figure it out fast enough."

"Why me?" he asked.

"Why you? You mean why did I pick you to join the club? Because you were the only applicant who wasn't nuts. You were genuinely curious about survival and came into the meeting with no expectations that we were going to save you when the apocalypse hits."

"Seriously? So, now that I'm a member of the club I get my own shelter, and these guys are going to build it for me?"

Titus leaned in closer and asked, "Can you keep a secret?"

"Yes."

"Good. Don't tell anyone. Now get back to your group and design a shelter that can withstand any apocalypse."

Titus walked away as if this was all normal to him.

"Wait a minute, Mr. Rush. What kind of apocalypse?"

Once he was back with his project team and had a chance to think about the answer he got from Titus, Maybank realized what Titus meant.

He had simply shrugged his shoulders at Maybank and said, "I don't know. You tell me. Something killed off the dinosaurs."

******

From that night on, Danny Maybank had watched the news from a different perspective. The Air Force was bombing Vietnam, and almost daily it seemed like someone was coming out with a new movie about the end of the world. His favorite was a movie about an astronaut stranded on another planet where humans were an inferior species to apes, and the apes could even talk. In the end the planet turned out to be Earth in the future, and some kind of apocalypse caused apes to evolve until they passed humans.

Maybank didn't really care about how the astronaut got to the future. He just cared about the apocalypse that caused monkeys to pass humans on the intelligence ladder. He laid awake at night staring at the ceiling and tried to picture different scenarios, and his mind kept going back to the list the survivor group had done.

Eventually, he decided that Titus wasn't really asking him to answer his question that day out at the Army base. He wanted him to be ready for anything, and he came to the conclusion that you couldn't be ready for everything on the list.

When that happened, he started wondering why he felt like the list had a flaw, and that was what was really keeping him awake at night. Then it came to him. It couldn't just be a list of possible apocalypses. It had to be a list of likely worldwide catastrophes, and what Titus and the rest of the group didn't realize was that it could have a totally unbelievable outcome. So, the survivors shouldn't be working from a list of apocalypses, they should be working from a list of outcomes.

Maybank gave up on sleep. He turned on a lamp and got out a note pad. He wrote everything on the list over again but left space in between each apocalypse. Then he went back and wrote under each one the likely outcomes of the events. He wrote the long term and short term outcomes because the shelters were supposed to last forever. It surprised him how much he was writing and how easy it was to come up with ideas, but hours later he sat back and looked at his work. There was one shocking similarity. No matter what apocalypse he chose, whether it was man-made or an act of God, he had the word "mutation" next to everything.

Maybank laid his head on his pillow with one thought on his mind. The next day he would have to contact Titus Rush and tell him that they needed to design shelters that would protect them from mutation. He woke up eight hours later with his light still on, and he knew for certain where he wanted to build his shelter.

******

If Columbia felt hot and muggy, New Orleans was bound to feel worse, but Maybank couldn't really tell the difference. The city felt old, and he didn't know much about it other than what he had learned in high school. When he arrived in the French Quarter, he realized just how little of the history he had retained. There were lots of tourists, and his project team told him to dress like one. He wasn't sure what that meant, so he picked up a souvenir t-shirt at the airport that had a big picture of Bourbon Street on the back.

His team told him to check in to his hotel and then they would all meet at a local restaurant. The idea was to be inconspicuous, so they would do some of the tourist activities and then drive out to the Coast Guard Base. An Army helicopter would be ready for them to take their first ride out over the Gulf of Mexico.

It wasn't hard to recognize his group. When he walked into the restaurant, the hostess told him his party was already seated, and then she commented about how popular his shirt was. He didn't have a clue what she meant until he saw that four of them had bought the same shirt. He wasn't sure if it was funny or a little scary that they were thinking alike.

Over a meal of crab and crawfish they talked over the choice Maybank had made. Logistically, his shelter wasn't the hardest one to construct. As a matter of fact, there was an abandoned oil rig that could be easily modified to meet their needs. The well had been capped, which was what they wanted because they didn't want to complicate things by hiding under a working rig that was actually shipping oil to a refinery.

It was also going to be a much more private project than some of the others. The engineer on the team talked about the nightmare of building a shelter under downtown Columbus, Ohio, and he was glad they wouldn't be blasting granite from a mountain. He explained that they would build the outside hull of the shelter above the water along with some of the compartments, then they would submerge it and push it into place under the oil rig. All things considered, he seemed excited about it.

The money man was also happy. His projected costs were far lower than several of the shelters. He said they were a fraction of the cost of the Fort Sumter shelter, and the only one that cost less was the location chosen by Titus. If not for the moat around the island, they wouldn't even be close in cost, but the money man was still very satisfied that the oil rig would be easy to fund.

The Army officer wasn't happy. He didn't fit in with the relaxed atmosphere of the restaurant even with his Bourbon Street t-shirt. He was frowning and sitting stiffly in his chair even though he was an expert when it came to getting the meat out of a crab leg or sucking on the head of a crawfish. Maybank wasn't too thrilled with the crawfish.

What bothered the officer was his belief that the shelter would be an easy target for his number one theory of an apocalypse. To him it would undoubtedly be a war that led to nuclear escalation and then annihilation. He didn't think they would need any other theories on the list. When Maybank asked if he didn't think a pandemic was possible, the officer said a pandemic would cause a war.

They debated the issue through the entire meal, each making some good points about what would cause the end of the world, but the engineer gave them both a surprise.

"I think my shelter could withstand a direct hit from a nuclear weapon," he said, "even in the water."

Maybank didn't believe there would be a nuclear war, but this was good news to him.

"I thought everyone was worried about my choice of location because of a nuclear strike."

"They are, but this new metal we're working with is remarkable. As soon as everyone started getting excited about how easy it would be to blow you up, I started working on how to keep it from happening."

"You have a way to prevent a nuclear war?" asked the officer.

"No, but I never intended to build this thing with flat walls. A big explosion passing through water and hitting a curved wall would give you one helluva ride, but after you're done getting your brains rattled, it would still be in one piece."

Neither of them were afraid to argue their beliefs, so the rest of them ate their meals and listened to them fight. The third man in the group was the man who would report directly to the President, and he was wondering if he could get his counterpart on the Columbus project team to trade with him.

Early the next morning they lifted off from the Coast Guard station and flew out to the oil rig. Maybank had to admit, after leaving the Mississippi Delta, the water was much more blue than the South Carolina coast. Everything was new to him, so the ride was over quickly as time seemed to fly by. The landing platform was in need of repair, and everyone was uncomfortable at the sight of so much rust, but the engineer clapped his hands together excitedly.

"This is going to be great."

4 NIGHTMARE ESCAPE

Six Years After the Decline

Crossing the marshes at night had been every nightmare they had imagined and then some. Molly and Sam had spent days discussing what they would take with them, how they would leave, and most importantly, how they would survive.

Despite the fact that they were behaving more like two star crossed lovers than survivors of an apocalypse, they were light years ahead of the kids they had known in school. They were aware of the dangers outside the safety of the shelters, and they were in their own minds prepared to face those dangers.

They moved fast when they left. They knew the slightest noise or even hesitation would put an end to their plans, and a thousand things could go wrong in the first few hours. They also knew the Chief, or any one of the survivors for that matter, would deduce which way they had gone. It was reasonable to expect that they would be caught, and that expectation was what made them think ahead.

There was no way to hide their tracks and still make good time, so their only hope was that a search party would think they decided to stop at Fort Johnson, either to rest or just take a look around. For that reason, they decided Fort Johnson would be where they would begin moving as fast as they could. Once they made it past the heavily wooded areas they would be in the neighborhoods. From there they would find places to hide during the day and travel at night. They still had to cross several stretches of marshlands that were connected by bridges and highly visible roads. If they knew the Chief, he would have someone at those locations before the day had gone by.

The marshes were muddy and more than once they were bogged down when one of them would be sucked in all the way to the knees. When that happened, the other would stay where they were. To move meant the possibility of finding another soft spot, and if they were both stuck in the mud, they could die. Their experience with the marshes taught them that the one on dry ground could pull the other one free, but it had to be done before the alligators or the blue crabs heard their efforts to pull themselves out.

Then they had to move even faster in order to be gone before something else arrived. The infected didn't know to be careful or quiet. If one of them heard the teenagers out on the marshes, they would start their incessant moaning as they stumbled across the mud. Sound carried too well at night, and although they couldn't always tell where it was coming from, they could hear everything. There were popping noises, cracking of dry brush and branches, and splashes. All of those noises had been part of the marshes for many centuries, but the moaning was relatively new. Regardless, it was more than enough reason to be afraid.

When they saw an alligator moving along the bank of one of the last inlets before reaching dry land, they were sure they would have to turn back. They weren't sure if the alligator was stalking them or if it had another form of prey in mind. All they knew was that they couldn't cross that inlet without drawing its attention.

They had just crossed over an island that was covered with trees and had been surprised by the number of infected they had seen, but the tiny island was as loud as a rock concert with all of the popping, cracking, and moaning, and the infected hadn't seen them. Now the noise was behind them, and the alligator seemed to almost pause to listen.

Molly and Sam lowered themselves to the ground slowly and watched as the dark shape pulled itself out of the inlet and stood as still as a statue. The alligator was facing almost in their direction, but it was waiting for something. It turned toward a splash that came from some place back in the direction from where they had come, and dashed toward it with more agility and speed than they expected.

They didn't realize they had been holding their breath until they faced each other. Both of them exhaled in ragged fear, and if not for the alligator being between them and home, they might have turned back.

Making more noise than they wanted to, they both crossed the last inlet onto dry land. Unlike the marshes and mudflats, the inlets often had firm ground beneath the water, and they were relieved when their feet pushed against it.

The next mile was a crucial part of their plan. When they had studied the area on a map, Molly told Sam that her father and the Chief would expect them to hole up at Fort Johnson. That's why they had to go further while they could. They would also expect them to stay somewhere close to the road, so Molly pointed out the way the shoreline ran along the edge of the last inlet. She was afraid they might run into another alligator, but if they could follow the shoreline far enough they could make it past the first of several chokepoints before dawn.

Now that they found themselves standing on that narrow strip of shoreline, they realized that their options were already chosen for them. They could see one narrow section of road that passed by the College of Charleston buildings, and it was heavily populated by the infected. They wouldn't be able to use the road even if they wanted to.

Molly pulled Sam down next to her. She cupped her hands around his ear and whispered in something hardly louder than a breath.

"Where could they all be coming from? They've had years to die off."

Sam shrugged silently in the dark. She sensed his movement more than she saw it.

He cupped his hands over her ear and breathed the words, "It doesn't matter. They're here."

Molly sat back on her heels, and Sam had an idea what she was thinking. They had discussed the beginning of the infection for hours. They had speculated about how it began and if it was a man-made mistake or if it was a natural occurrence. They both believed it was a virus, no matter where it began, but the bottom line had always been the same. It didn't matter. There was nothing they could do about it except try to survive.

Molly had argued with Sam, though. She told him that it did matter because understanding how it had started would always be the first step in stopping it. Now she sat quietly in the dark and thought the same thing about where they were all coming from. If the human population had been wiped out, there had to be a reason why there are so many infected here at Fort Johnson.

Sam felt her tug on his sleeve and knew it was time to leave that spot. Neither of them knew it yet, but they were both thinking the same thing. By leaving Fort Sumter, they were placing friends and family in danger by making them come to Fort Johnson. There were far more infected dead in the area than they had expected, and it was too late to go back.

Molly hesitated, and Sam froze where he was. They had watched the infected through the trees for too long, and they were surrounded. It didn't look like the infected had noticed them yet, but they couldn't move as a large group of them stumbled into a small clearing right behind them.

"Don't move."

Sam's words were hardly loud enough for him to hear himself, but Molly was too afraid to move. She didn't need Sam telling her not to.

In the darkness the young couple could have been anything to the infected dead as they aimlessly wandered by. They were so still they were nothing more than lumps of clothing. One of them actually staggered through the narrow gap between Sam and Molly. One leg dragged behind the other, and Molly held her breath when the infected snagged the trailing foot in some vines. If the rotting remains tripped and fell on her, there would be no way to stay hidden.

It seemed to take forever, but when the last of the infected walked noisily into the bushes, Sam and Molly turned away from the already crowded road by the college and hurried in a straight line the opposite way. When they got to the trees, Molly dropped to her knees and shook violently.

Sam didn't know what to do, so he just knelt next to her and began turning his head to the left and right. He didn't know if they would ever feel safe again.

"Want to go back?"

His voice was weak, and he knew it was more of a statement than a question, but he didn't want to be the one to give up. He was surprised when she nodded yes. Out of reflex his head snapped around in the direction of Fort Sumter. It was his turn to start shaking.

Molly sensed his change and strained her eyes against the darkness that still blanketed the marshes. There was a slight drop from dry land down to the mud they had crossed, and the crest of that drop was as crowded as the road by the college. The infected were walking along the crest in single file. Molly and Sam watched as one lost its balance and tumbled out of sight. If they tried to go back the way they had come, they would have to get past that narrow rise and then probably outrun the infected.

Sam helped Molly up into a crouch, and they eased forward into the cover of the trees.

"We can go this way until we see an opening," said Sam. "Then we can go back down to the marsh."

Molly was still nodding in the darkness, but she wasn't saying no to his plan. To Sam it was all about getting back to Fort Sumter.

They moved in a straight line parallel to the mudflats and marshes and kept their eyes on the gray patches between the trees to their left. The sun was still a long way from making its appearance in the east, but the light over the marshes didn't seem to be as pitch black as the light between the trees.

Several times they had to stop and wait while the infected thrashed by in the brush. They were making so much noise that Molly and Sam wouldn't give away their position unless they collided with one. They finally saw their chance and angled their way out of the trees.

The fall to the mudflats was only about ten feet, but it was one of those bone jarring landings. Sometimes the mud was soft, and sometimes it was hard. This mud felt like concrete, and Molly was trying to shake the white dots out of her field of vision. At least she thought they were white dots. They were swimming everywhere, and she couldn't focus her eyes.

The dots bloomed brighter and seemed to explode in front of her as something hit her forehead. Before it went totally dark, she only had time to tell Sam that it hurt. Sam didn't hear her say anything because he was unconscious before she was. The fall had stunned him the same way as Molly, but it felt like he fell again as soon as he lifted his head.

******

"What did you do that for?"

The gruff voice was male and had a rattle to it that identified the man as a heavy smoker. His question was followed by a half cough as he tried to clear his throat.

"What did you expect? I thought they were ripe meat that wandered over the edge. Isn't that what you thought?"

The second voice was softer. The woman had a heavy southern accent.

When Molly and Sam dropped in from above, the woman had swung her heavy flashlight out of reflex at their heads. They had been easy targets because they didn't stay on their feet when they landed.

"That one said something," said gravel-throat.

"I know, stupid. I heard her. Help me get them in the boat. We need to get out of here in case they were being followed by ripe meat or something."

Both of them looked at the ledge above them as if the woman had just reminded them of how it felt to have two bodies drop in out of nowhere from above. They grabbed Sam by the feet and arms and lifted him from the hard mud into the flat bottom boat next to them.

"This one doesn't have much meat on his bones," said the man.

"Shut up, stupid. If ripe meat up there hears you and decides to drop in, I'll just let you take care of them by yourself."

She didn't have to say it loudly to get him to listen. She knew his attention span was short, but it was long enough for him to not want to dodge falling bodies and maybe get bitten. He also knew that the penalty for getting the unwanted attention of ripe meat was that she would leave him behind if he was bitten. He would become ripe meat, too. After that he would most likely become alligator and crab food.

He clamped his mouth shut so hard that it was an almost invisible line in the middle of his tangled facial hair.

Molly was tall for her age. Her mother hadn't been short, but her father had been a baseball player with the body of an athlete. The man didn't say it out loud, but he struggled enough lifting her to show that he thought Molly was heavy.

They gave the ledge above a final glance as they climbed into the boat and then pushed away from the shoreline. The creek was very narrow, so anything that fell from above could still land on top of them, but it meandered away after only a few yards. They felt better when they were farther out from shore.

"What are we going to tell Stokes when we get back?" asked Randal.

"What do you mean by that. There's nothing to tell. These two came over the edge out of nowhere, and I thought they were ripe meat."

She was getting tired of Randal. Of all the people she went out with at night, he was her least favorite. The problem was that no one else wanted to go out with him, either. That meant everyone got stuck with him sooner or later.

As they drifted slowly through the snake-like twists and turns of the tidal creek, Sarah Beth wondered how she had sunk so low. Her life as an upperclass Charlestonian seemed to be something she had read about rather than her own memories. It seemed like one day she had just finished prep school, and the next day she was hiding in a tidal creek swatting at mosquitos.

******

Beginning of the Decline

The invitation to go boating with friends was such an expected event that she didn't even bother to acknowledge the invitation. Of course she would be there. If you didn't invite her along, you could get dropped from the social circles that mattered, so everyone invited her. She showed up, but she had hesitated when she saw the size of the boat they would be using. It was hardly big enough for someone as popular as her.

By the end of the day, the small size of the boat had most likely been responsible for her survival. A bigger boat would have been out in the harbor with the other big boats where they were repeatedly overrun by armed and desperate people trying to save themselves and their families.

They were drifting near the Fort Johnson boat landing when they heard gunshots from across the harbor. They were far enough away from the Yorktown at Patriots Point to wonder what the sounds were, but when they didn't stop, they started passing around a pair of binoculars to see if they could tell what was happening.

Sarah Beth saw people falling from the Yorktown, but it didn't register with her way of thinking. It was the same reaction that people had when they saw the planes hit the Twin Towers in New York. It just wasn't real to the civilized mind. She had turned to her friends in the boat for an explanation but only saw the same expressions mirrored back at her. Six young men and women who had lived pampered lives that included table manners and social etiquette stood on a small boat and watched hundreds of people die.

Paul, the son of a prominent Charleston lawyer, was the first to speak, but it was only to say someone was going to pay. He was still thinking in terms that would apply to the normal world. What was happening across the harbor and around the world was far from normal.

Warren said, "Shouldn't we do something? We can't just sit here. We have to go over there and see if we can save somebody."

They reacted as a group, and his words spurred them into action. The small engine was started, and since they had been drifting without an anchor in the water, it was only seconds before they were moving fast in the direction of the commotion without even looking back toward Fort Johnson.

Just as quickly Paul cut the engine, and they were bobbing further out in the harbor where they had a better view of the entire scene. They were all holding onto the side rails and seat backs to watch, and the gunshots were louder.

On the Battery there were sirens and cars crashing violently into each other. There was automatic rifle gunfire down by the State Ports Authority, and smoke was rising from the city. Being born and raised in Charleston meant each of them knew precisely where the fires were. Then they saw the fate of the larger boats that were being swarmed by people in the water. The original occupants were shot or just thrown overboard.

Paul started the engine again, and he turned slowly back the way they had come. They were filled with resignation, not because they understood what was happening, but because they understood they would die if they kept going.

Paul aimed for the dock at Fort Johnson. He shouted to the others that they could get help there and maybe even a ride home. Those plans lasted about as long as their rescue attempt had.

At Fort Johnson hundreds of people were jumping into the water. Some were fleeing and some were attacking people at random. It still didn't register as they watched a heavy man and a skinny woman dragging a gray haired woman to the ground. They were biting her as she collapsed under the attack.

Hands were already reaching from the water and gripping the side rails of their small boat, and it began rocking furiously from side to side. Paul had the presence of mind to power up the engine and cut the wheel hard to the left. The right side of the boat rose high out of the water as the speed increased, and the hands began letting go.

He heard Sarah Beth screaming, but he didn't have time to find out why. Paul was focused on a small inlet that had appeared when the tide had come in, and he knew it would disappear when the tide went out. All of them had been to Fort Johnson, so they knew the inlet was a tidal creek that led to the homes of people wealthy enough to find the sort of privacy and isolation only money could buy. Some were clients of his father's law firm, and they would help.

The small boat raced dangerously close to the shallow banks of the submerged inlet, but Paul didn't have time to worry about hitting them. He knew if he missed the entrance to the tidal creek while it was deep enough to enter, he would hit the mud, and they would most likely be killed by being thrown from the boat.

He cut the power a little as they passed between the steep banks on the right and the mud flats on the left. There was a straight section for about thirty yards, but then the creek would start zigzagging to the left and right every few feet. They would be moving at hardly more than a crawl, but they would be moving away from the mayhem behind them.

It was when he began his first really slow turn that he had a chance to check on Sarah Beth and his other passengers. Sarah Beth had stopped screaming, but she was making some kind of wailing noise that he wished she would stop. He was surprised to see that she was the only passenger in the boat with him.

"Where's Warren?"

His girlfriend, Patricia, was gone, but he asked about Warren first. Somewhere in his disorganized thoughts he had a vague feeling that he had gotten that wrong, but Warren had gotten permission to come along today only on the promise that Paul would bring him home in one piece.

Linda, Brad, and Robin were also missing, and Paul's mind wasn't filling in the blanks. He had plans to become a lawyer, and he would probably have been a good one, but surviving the beginning of a pandemic apocalypse wasn't something he was prepared to process. He had kept himself and Sarah Beth alive, but he had failed to consider the other four people in the boat. They had gone over the side when he had unexpectedly increased power and cut the wheel hard to the left. They were somewhere behind him and over a hundred yards away. Even if he wanted to go back for them, the creek was too narrow to allow him to turn around. Sarah Beth was huddled in the stern and wailing.

He wanted to go to Sarah Beth, and more than anything he wanted her to stop that noise, but his motor was already kicking up silt from the bottom that was only inches from the spinning propellor. Paul knew he had to keep his forward momentum. If the boat came to a stop and settled deeper, they would be stuck where they were. He no sooner had the thought when that was exactly what happened. The motor connected with a slight rise in the bottom of the creek, and they came to a stop. When he increased the power, a plume of mud shot out behind them.

Sarah Beth quit wailing at the same moment that they stopped moving, and it seemed too quiet out on the wide tidal basin. On one side he could see the back of Fort Johnson. In the far distance to their left was Morris Island and Fort Sumter. They were less than fifty yards from a private dock, but that was as the crow flies. For them to reach it by boat, they would have to wait for the next high tide and then hope to get the propellor free. Then they would follow about two hundred yards of meandering tidal creeks. Personally, Paul was for crossing the fifty yards of marshland to the dock, but he didn't know what Sarah Beth would be willing to do.

Sarah Beth was regarding Paul as if he was an axe murderer when he approached her.

"Stay away from me."

She drew herself deeper into her corner of the stern.

"I didn't know," said Paul.

He knew his voice was making it a poor defense, but he really hadn't known. All he could think about at the time was getting away from the hundreds of hands that were going to pull them all into the water.

"We have to try for that dock," he added.

Paul gestured toward land.

Sarah Beth either didn't hear him, or she ignored what he said, so he held out his hand to help her up. The violence that erupted from her came as a total surprise. She slapped his hand so hard it felt like a hundred bee stings, and she lunged at him with her other hand.

Paul wasn't a jock in school, but Sarah Beth was no match for his size and strength. When Paul overcame his initial surprise, he blocked her swings and then threw his weight on top of her.

"Stop," he yelled.

He was about to add something about the people hearing them when he realized there were people. Hundreds of them.

The dock he was hoping to reach, the shoreline beyond the dock, the mudflats, Fort Johnson, the water...everywhere there were people running, swimming, and pushing the motors of their boats to their limits. Most of all, there was the screaming. Whether it was screaming for help, screaming in pain, or screaming in anger, the air was filled with voices raised to a fever pitch.

Sarah Beth and Paul had stopped fighting and just sat in the bottom of the boat watching the people as if it was a movie. A cruise ship was drifting away from the port over by Charleston, and smaller boats were dashing ahead of it for open water. There were more gunshots, some close by.

On the dock less than fifty yards away, an elderly couple had retreated as far as they could before reaching the end of the wooden sidewalk that extended out into the marsh. The man had a huge hunting rifle in his hands and appeared to be fumbling with bullets. Paul had seen one rifle like it and was fairly sure it was an elephant gun. The man lifted the stock to his shoulder and sighted through the scope.

Paul turned his attention to the other end of the dock where over a dozen people were all trying to walk on the dock at the same time. Even though there was a railing on both sides, they managed to jostle and push against each other so hard that one of them tumbled over into the marsh grass below. The others didn't seem to notice or even care.

"This can't be happening," said Sarah Beth.

Paul didn't see the point in disagreeing with her. He just watched as the old man took careful aim at the people on the other end of the dock.

When the rifle jerked in his hands, Paul's head snapped back to the left, and he saw the head of the man leading the pack explode. The powerful bullet of a .460 Weatherby Magnum went through the man's head and then through the neck of the man behind him. Paul would normally have been shocked beyond belief to see someone's head explode, but he was too confused by the reaction of the second man.

The bullet had removed most of the flesh and bone in the neck that held the man's head in place. The head laid over at an angle and was resting on his left shoulder where Paul could still see his face. At fifty yards, he couldn't make out the details, but the sun was glistening on the red blood that had erupted from arteries, and one muscle that was being drawn tight by the weight of the head. Paul's mouth had already dropped open when the man kept moving forward, so it didn't drop open when the man's head rolled backward off of his shoulder until it hung onto his back.

The gang of people indifferently moved forward toward the elderly couple. The old woman was behind the man with the rifle trying not to fall into the water. Many of the docks had small boats moored below them, but some had nothing beyond that point. They had fished for flounder and tossed cast nets for shrimp from the end of the dock, but they had apparently never seen the need for a boat.

The rifle bucked for a second time, and another man went down. This time the others behind him began to mindlessly trip and fall over the body, and the man with the head pointing in the wrong direction fell with them. The fall made the head snap free from the last of the muscle connecting it to the body. Sarah Beth moaned when the head rolled over the side of the dock. Paul felt like the eyes were staring straight at them as it disappeared in the marsh grass.

The rifle fired at a steady pace as the old man got his nerves under control. He had undoubtedly been hesitant to shoot a living man at first, but once he had fired the first two shots, he was resigned to finish what they had started. He had to stop to reload after each shot, but he wasn't fumbling anymore. One by one the pursuers fell onto the pile until there were no more advancing toward them.

Paul lifted his hand and waved.

"Hey, can you help us?" he shouted.

He felt the blood rush from his face when the rifle turned in their direction, and out of reflex he ducked into the bottom of the boat, pulling Sarah Beth with him.

There were shots fired, but no holes appeared around them. The big bullets of the .460 Weatherby Magnum would have ripped a hole through both sides of the boat if they had been lucky enough not to be hit, and it was possible that the bullet would still make a second hole in the boat.

Paul lifted his head and saw that the shooting was by Fort Sumter. The big white hull of the cruise ship was broadside to the mudflats, and he could see that someone at Fort Sumter was firing at them.

When he turned his attention back to the old man with the elephant gun, he saw that the elderly pair was cautiously approaching the pile of bodies in an effort to free themselves from the narrow wooden dock. The old man poked and prodded at the bodies until he was satisfied that they could cross over them. A few tentative steps into the pile a head lifted up at him, and the teeth began snapping at his legs. The rifle fired at point blank range, and the couple went back to making their escape.

Paul didn't want to get shot, but he still intended on making it to the dock. He was just going to let the man with the cannon for a rifle go his own way first.

Sarah Beth had begun to let their situation sink in. She didn't understand why any of it was happening, but she was aware of what she was seeing. She was still in disbelief about losing four friends so quickly, but something made her understand it had not been because Paul had wanted them to die. She wasn't really believing he had been reckless when he had powered up the boat so fast that they had fallen overboard. She had felt that way at first, but once the shock had worn off, she remembered seeing her friends extending their arms toward the people in the water. Now her gut was telling her that would have been a bad idea.

She lifted the cushion on the starboard seat to see what was in their cooler and pulled out a bottle of water.

"How much is in there?" asked Paul.

"It's full."

She didn't ask him if he wanted some, so he got it himself. He stayed low as he did so, not really concerned about the old man anymore, but not wanting someone to see them exposed in the tidal creek.

"At least we won't die of thirst," he said.

He sat with his back against the front seats and watched the cruise ship clear the jetties beyond Fort Sumter. He only absently wondered if those people were any better off than he was with Sarah Beth. Eventually, the sun dropped below the horizon as they drank their water in silence.

5 DIGNITARIES

Beginning of the Decline

It wasn't hard for Maybank to know it was a helicopter coming his way. It was catching the morning light reflecting off of it at just the right angle, and even though it was little more than a black dot on the horizon, he had seen the way helicopters appeared to hug the water until they were closer. Then they popped free of their background and took on a familiar shape.

This one was having problems. It was straying off course and then overcorrecting. The trail of black smoke was only visible from a distance when it strayed far enough off course. Maybank hoped the pilot decided to ditch the helicopter in the water rather than to land while burning. It would be better to pull the passengers out of the water than out of a fire.

He had a momentary pang of guilt when the helicopter strayed off course and didn't attempt to correct. It was still a few miles away, so he was sure the pilot wasn't ditching the craft, but there was no doubt that it was going into the water. He would probably never know why it crashed because it wasn't even close to being a controlled landing.

It was a strange feeling watching the crash without sound because the pilot had lost all control by the time the helicopter hit the water, and it was violent. It was almost upside down, so the blades hit first, and the craft disintegrated.

Maybank didn't expect survivors, but watching the helicopter had taken his eyes away from the horizon long enough for him to miss the arrival of a pair of pleasure boats. He saw them when they changed course for the place where the helicopter had gone down, and he was surprised when they began throwing life preservers into the water. Someone must have survived the crash.

For a moment Maybank wasn't sure what to do. The helicopter was most likely bringing people that he was supposed to protect, but the boats weren't part of the plan. He opened his laptop and looked for the manual the Army had given him. It took a few minutes, but he found a direct reference to the situation. He read it twice to be sure, but then he packed up his gear and headed for the Wellbay.

The contingency manual said the surviving dignitaries could only arrive under the protection of their personal escort and were considered to be compromised if they arrived in any other manner. In other words, don't let them in.

The shelter was already sealed from the outside world. All Maybank needed to do was get inside and shut the door. Once that was done, he turned on the monitors to watch the two pleasure craft approach the oil rig. He had come to the rig by helicopter more often than by boat, but he remembered how he had felt when he arrived by boat the first time. The sight was breathtaking.

Maybank could see it on the faces of the people in the boats. They were awestruck by the size of the rig. Seeing it from above, it appeared big. Seeing it from the water made you feel small. It probably felt to them like they were floating next to an ugly cruise ship, and that meant they would live.

The boats circled together. They were moving to the west in search of a way to climb onto the rig. Maybank knew they were trying to find metal rungs, a ladder, a hatch, or anything that was used to board the oil rig. They paused for a long time at the cargo receiving area. The huge crane above them could lift their boats completely out of the water, and Maybank could almost read their lips as they shrugged their shoulders at each other. They had to be asking if anyone knew how to board the oil rig.

Unlike operational oil rigs, everything about this one was different. To the average person it was just another oil rig, but to the experienced eye of someone who had worked on rigs, there were some very odd differences. The people on the two pleasure craft didn't have an experienced eye.

Maybank did his best to count heads on the boats, and his best guess was that there were eight people on each. He could see wounded people being tended to that were wearing military uniforms, and one guy was wearing a suit. They were likely to be the guests he had been waiting for. He was surprised anyone made it out of that crash, but he couldn't take his eyes off of one injured man who was still wearing his flight helmet. There was something about the way he kept trying to sit up that reminded Maybank of the news broadcasts.

The boats gave up at the supply tower and moved toward the Hull. They picked up speed because it was already obvious to them that there was nothing on that tower. The boat in the lead made a sharp turn and drove toward the Process tower, but the second boat kept going straight. Maybank zoomed his camera in on that boat and saw that the injured man who was trying to get up had succeeded. He had already begun his attacks on his unsuspecting rescuers. The white deck of the boat was covered in dark blood, and bodies littered the lower end of the boat. Some of those bodies were trying to stand up while the boat rocked on the swells from the leading boat.

They began falling overboard as they tried to walk to the living bodies on the lead boat. It had turned toward them to investigate why the other boat had gone off course. Within a few minutes, almost everyone had gone into the water, and Maybank could only see two people in the boat. Whether they were really alive or not, he couldn't tell, but the boat was traveling away from the oil rig at low speed. It was moving away toward the open water of the Gulf, and the first boat was slowly following.

Maybank could only watch, and a part of him felt a tremendous amount of shame for not helping. He was also tired. He was alive, and he would survive, but for the first time he wondered why he should. He had grown old waiting for this day, and now that it was here, he would have a front row seat to the end of the world, but he wasn't sure why him and not others.

The two boats kept moving further away, and he watched until they disappeared over the horizon, never aware that he had been watching. He snapped out of the daze when he heard one of the proximity alert sensors broadcasting that something was going to collide with the Wellbay tower.

He brought up the image from that sensor and saw that he had guests after all. There were at least three people in a raft and maybe two more under a tarp that was intended to protect occupants from the sun. It resembled a floating pup tent, but it had WSS printed in big letters on the side of it. Maybank had heard of Worth Security Service. They were a private company that did a lot of contract work for the military. A man in a paramilitary uniform was keeping the raft steady against the tower, but one of the hazards to inflatable rafts was the chance of being punctured.

Years ago it was decided that there would be no attempt to remove the barnacles from the towers. There were several reasons why barnacles were a good idea to have around, and the main reason was that they would make it dangerous for anyone to approach the oil rig in a raft. Even SCUBA divers wouldn't find it easy to avoid being sliced by the sharp growths.

It seemed almost ironic that one of the best thought out defenses was likely to be what prevented the people from reaching the shelter. When the towers were erected using the strange new metal that the military said was indestructible, the barnacles didn't grow. Even they couldn't penetrate the metal enough to maintain a purchase, and that made the towers stand out too much. If they were to blend in, they needed to be painted, they needed to rust, and they needed to allow barnacles to grow below the waterline.

The military grew a measure of respect for Maybank when he suggested a layer of sheet metal wrapped around the towers. Compared to the elaborate construction of the underwater shelter, it was a minor detail and a minor expense. Of course it meant the hidden ladder rungs had to be modified, as well. They were each covered with a thin sheet of steel and had to fit into the wall of the tower so seamlessly that no one would guess their function.

One of the designers who was drawing the plans for the shelter commented that the little "trapdoors" that covered the rungs were obviously handholds when seen from a distance. Maybank asked him what they would look like if there were hundreds of them drawn on the sides of the towers. They painted hundreds of them on each tower, and when they were done, no one thought they were obviously handholds. As a matter of fact, when inspected from close up, people tended to push on them and then disregard them completely because they didn't appear to do anything.

Maybank reached for a switch and sent power to the handholds. The paramilitary man who was holding the raft in position fell backward into the raft as a row of handholds popped out of the side of the tower. The row ascended upward and disappeared at the top of the tower, but the man had recovered quickly as he understood someone had just put out the welcome mat.

He was already climbing when Maybank turned back toward the monitor. The man went up by himself while another took over the job of keeping the raft steady. When he reached the top, he smoothly unslung his M-4 from his back and was rotating left and right. It didn't take him long to realize that there was no way he could know if the area was clear. The top of the Wellbay tower was a nightmare of walkways, ladders, stairs, pipes, and doors. It seemed like every pipe had a wheel valve attached to it, and there were gauges everywhere. If someone had asked him later, he would have sworn the ladders had wheels and gauges, too.

Maybank watched him return his rifle to his back and stand up straight. He didn't doubt that the man understood he would be dead already if someone was going to shoot him.

The man continued to rotate where he was standing as his eyes scanned the maze of metal searching for something familiar. He spotted what he was trying to find only a few feet away. It made perfect sense to have a rescue locker close to the edge of the tower. The red cross on the white background was a welcome sight.

He retrieved a rope and a harness from the locker and hurried back to the ladder. Maybank continued to watch and wished he could do more to help the man. There was a metal stretcher with a winch not far from the Wellbay tower, but the man had searched for rescue equipment rather than a communications station. If he had communicated with Maybank, he wouldn't be trying to lift the full weight of an injured man by a rope.

After what seemed like an hour, two injured people, a man and a woman, were being tended to by three uniformed men at the top of the tower. Both were having open wounds treated, and there was a considerable amount of blood coming through the bandages before they were even done.

One of the security detail finally found an interior communications phone. Maybank had insisted on the old fashioned telephone equipment with the pigtail cord because they would give visitors the impression that everything was low tech on the rig. He didn't want anyone to guess what was really behind all of that metal.

The phone rang in Maybank's control room. When he answered, the man immediately launched into a tirade unlike anything he had ever heard. Maybank couldn't get a word in between the profanity and the yelling, so he quit trying and hung up the phone.

He saw the man on his monitor holding the phone out in front of him like it was personally responsible for hanging up on him. He showed it to one of the other guys, then he turned and started slamming it against a metal rail.

"That's going to help," said Maybank.

Maybank wasn't sure if he would answer when the man called back, but he was sure that he would hang up again if he started yelling.

When it rang and he answered, the man said, "If you hang up again, I'm going to…".

That was as far as he got before Maybank hung up, but he didn't hang up because of the man's behavior. Maybank wasn't even listening to him. He was watching the monitor and what was happening behind the man.

The platform at the top of the Wellbay tower ladder wasn't large, but it was surrounded by railings to keep clumsy people from falling into the water. A fall that far would more often than not be fatal. The injured man and woman had been left in a reclining position against the railing while the uniformed men gathered around the phone. After Maybank had hung up for a second time, the other two men were trying to get the phone away from the first guy. They apparently had some feelings to share with Maybank.

What drew Maybank's attention away from the angry men was the injured couple. One moment they were blood soaked and near death, and the next moment they were like a pair of newborn colts trying to get their legs under them. It didn't escape Maybank's attention that they weren't using the railing to pull themselves up the way normal people did. It took them awhile, but they were eventually upright. Upright and moving on shaky legs toward the three uniformed men.

If he had realized what was happening, he wouldn't have hung up the second time. He would have warned the men. Maybank punched in the number to the phone the man was holding. Nothing happened because they were still fighting for the phone. He heard the busy signal and tried again. Just as he finished entering the number, one of the men turned toward the injured people. He didn't even have time to react before they fell forward into the private security guards. Maybank felt like he was watching a news broadcast from the night before.

There was hardly room to move in the corner of the platform, and two of them were bitten before they could even start to defend themselves. Blood made the steel deck slippery, and all five of them fell together in a pile.

Maybank had read once that being bitten was very invasive to the victims. There was an element of disbelief that the victims had to deal with before they could react defensively. It was a disbelief that it was really happening. The article he had been reading at the time was about animal bites, and the author actually said the bite victims had to go through the disbelief, but they also had to go through a brief moment where they felt sorry for the animal. Once they reached the moment of sorrow for the animal, they could better defend themselves against further bites.

He remembered that he had more than a little doubt about whether or not the author of the article had ever been bitten because he didn't think he would feel sorry for the shark that had just removed his leg. Now that he was seeing people actually being bitten and how they reacted, he was inclined to believe the first part, though. From what he could tell by the expressions on their faces, the uniformed security guards couldn't believe they had been bitten. One was so busy staring at the wound on his wrist that he could have forgotten they were still trying to bite him. Maybank didn't see sorrow on the man's face, but he saw plenty of shock.

The third man had managed to keep from being bitten when they all became tangled together, and he rolled away from the pile to get to his feet. He pulled a pistol from its holster and fired four quick shots into the couple. His training had been to shoot center mass, so that was what he did. Two rounds hit the man in the heart, and two rounds hit the woman with the same accuracy.

They fell backward from the impact, and the two uniformed men who had been bitten used the opportunity to put some distance between themselves and their attackers. One of them was bleeding furiously from a deep wound to the upper part of his arm by the armpit. The other was wrapping a rag around his left hand where he used to have a thumb.

Maybank didn't think the guy with the arm injury would survive more than another fifteen seconds. As part of his preparations for this day, he had done a considerable amount of training in first aid, and he figured there wasn't much you could do for a big hole in the brachial artery. He watched as the man staggered and then was unable to stay on his feet. A few seconds later he was dead.

The uninjured man lunged across the platform and grabbed the phone that was swinging from its cord. Maybank didn't know if he should bother to answer because he already knew there was no way he was going to open the shelter for the man. The question was settled for him, and all he could do was grab his phone and say as fast as he could, "Look behind you."

For a second time the man was trying to push away the injured couple. He knew they should be dead because there were fresh bullet holes where their shredded hearts had been. He knew he couldn't have missed. Somehow he managed to get each of them in his grip at the same time, and he pushed as hard as he could. They fell on top of his dead comrade and almost comically kept trying to get up by knocking the other down.

The man with the wrapped hand kept his back to the railing and circled around to his friend by the phone. His friend reached out and helped to pull him the last few feet. Even on the monitor Maybank could see them face to face, experiencing the disbelief.

Both of them got their pistols ready as the couple finally became untangled from the deck of the platform, but this time their disbelief had grown because they were watching their dead comrade stand up, too. He was facing away from them as if he was seeing the oil rig for the first time and found it interesting, but then he saw his living friends, and they were far more interesting to him. He turned and joined the other two bleeding corpses as they moved closer to the men huddled by the phone.

The man with the injured hand had lowered his weapon, but the other man raised his and fired three shots, each one to the foreheads of the advancing corpses. He stood with his eyes lowered to the bodies for several minutes then seemed to remember where he was.

He snatched the phone for a third time and dialed the number. When Maybank answered the phone the man didn't yell, but he still tried to issue orders as if he was in charge. Maybank didn't know why he said it, and he wasn't trying to be funny, but before he hung up the phone he said, "Wrong number." He didn't know what else to do, but he felt awful.

******

The phone rang for so long that Maybank finally disconnected it. He had things to do, and he wanted to put the entire scene behind him. He knew how it would play out up on the oil rig, and no scenario had a happy ending. If the man somehow managed to be the last one standing, he wasn't likely to be someone Maybank could ever completely trust. That ship had sailed.

He decided to close off that particular control room until he could get over the events of the day. He was tired already, but he could imagine how it was going to be if the first day had gotten this bad. He didn't have an appetite yet, but he would have to eat if he was going to stay healthy. He closed the door to the control room and began following a maze of tunnels that connected the various modules of the shelter. Just like the oil rig above, this underwater shelter was divided into watertight sections. Each section could serve as a shelter independent of the other sections if the structure sustained any heavy damage. He sealed each door after passing through until he reached the next control room.

Maybank spun up several computers and began a systems check. He wanted to tune into the news channels, but that would have to wait. He brought up a view of the Wellbay module and saw the two private security guards going up the ladder toward the crew's living quarters. He knew they would feel better once they saw the food, beds, and shower facilities, but it was only going to last as long as the one man stayed alive. After that, if the uninjured guy survived, it would only be until the supplies ran out, and then he would get desperate.

He tried not to think about it, but his mind kept going back to the question, "What if? What if the guy really was a nice guy? What if he understood why I had hung up? What if I save him? Wouldn't he be grateful then?"

When he put himself in the shoes of the man outside, he came to the conclusion that the first thing he would do was shoot whoever was inside the shelter. To the security man, Maybank was just some guy with a shelter who was supposed to save him and his clients. He probably didn't know anything about the shelters, who built them, and who ultimately owned them. In the end, Maybank did his best to put the man out of his mind.

The oil rig shelter wasn't like the hotels at Fort Sumter and Columbus. The military hadn't given up on their concerns about its vulnerability to attacks by foreign navies. More than once he had heard the argument that a nuclear tipped torpedo was all anyone would need, but Maybank stuck to his belief that madmen respected oil above gold. As a result, his shelter wasn't designated for anyone in the presidential chain of succession. He didn't know who he was getting, but they weren't going to need protection from Secret Service Agents.

Titus Rush was given the choice not to play host to anyone, and Maybank didn't choose an oil rig because it would shorten his guest list, but he was glad that he wouldn't have some pompous politicians expecting him to fetch for them. The fact that they were arriving with a paramilitary escort concerned him some, and he decided to waste a little time trying to find out who they were. After all, time seemed to be something that wasn't in short supply.

The second control room was down one level from the first but on the opposite side of the shelter. Each level was air tight and self-contained, which meant part of the shelter could be damaged without effecting the operations of the rest of the shelter. One of the best features was the way the levels were connected. Each level had a separate access to every other level. There were five levels, so that meant a lot of space was given to stairs and ladders, but they did double duty. Supply cabinets lined the stairwells, and even the steps were storage cabinets.

After dropping down one level, Maybank crossed his armory and medical level. If either was needed, he wanted them closer to the main shelter access. Beyond the medical bay he entered his second control room and went straight to his security cameras. Everything needed to power up, but in a matter of seconds he had a camera view of the Wellbay tower and the three bodies that were still in full view.

There was little doubt to him who the important people were even through the blood. They were movie celebrities who had undoubtedly been campaign donors, but there was one thing all of the shelter owners anticipated, and that was uninvited guests who had learned about the shelters from influential friends. There had even been rumors of a blackmarket that sold space in the shelters. Maybank wondered if these two had been buyers, especially since they arrived with belligerent private security.

He had seen the couple in plenty of movies, and he wondered if he would have let them in if they had arrived differently. He put the thought aside because it was all conjecture, and there was no point wasting time on something that wasn't going to happen. If more celebrities showed up, he would decide then.

A few minutes of scanning the security cameras to locate the two security guards was all he needed. They were in the living quarters above the Wellbay tower. Maybank thought of the quarters as his shelter houseboat. The idea Titus had was adopted by every shelter owner because it made sense. Even the President's shelter had an elaborate fake shelter between it and the Ohio State University campus. The guards didn't know where Maybank was, but they wouldn't suspect he was in an elaborate shelter under the water as long as there were decent accommodations in the oil rig.

|

What saddened him was that one of them had been bitten, and his friend was trying to keep him alive.

"Yep. If I was him, I would hate me, too."

Now that Maybank was more or less confined to his shelter, he was doing what Titus said would keep him alive. Climbing around the catwalks outside wasn't part of the survivors club philosophy, which was go to your shelter, shut yourself in, and stay there.

He opened an app on a tablet and made an entry in the journal that resembled a captain's log with one notable exception. The first entry began with, "Captain's log, star date 000001." He described the events of the day and then moved to the next function on the app. He could do a systems check from the bridge, as he often called the control rooms, but there was no better assurance than seeing the systems with your own eyes.

It would take years to inspect every detail of the shelter, but he also wanted to see the surroundings of the major systems. If moisture was building up in a computer cabinet, he might smell it before the diagnostics detected it. At least he thought he might.

So, he began his inspection tour that would take most of the day. He scheduled his route so he would pass through the galley at supper time. His appetite hadn't returned yet after the episode on the Wellbay tower, but he knew he needed to get into the habit of eating on a schedule. He had gotten bad about that while living in his topside quarters, often skipping meals in favor of a cold beer and a bag of chips. His excuse then was that he felt like he lived on a tropical island, but that excuse wasn't going to work anymore. All of the tropical islands were getting lots of visitors right about now, and some of those visitors would be bite victims.

He checked off the armory and the medical bays because he had already passed through them. He would give them each a closer inspection when he returned the next day. The schedule on his calendar app showed he would have target practice just after supper. He hadn't neglected that training the way he had meals and had become fairly proficient with rifles and handguns, so he had something to look forward to.

A watertight door beyond the control room led to a decontamination chamber. He checked the seals on the doors that went from decontamination into decompression and then the doors to the infirmary. He knew that the path he had taken would lead him in a circle under each of the towers, and once he finished a circle, he would drop down a level to inspect the next compartment.

Almost an hour later he was on the next level down when he heard voices. Chills ran up the back of his neck, and he froze where he was until he realized he was hearing audio from the TV broadcasts. Whoever had gone through this particular area the last time hadn't bothered to turn off the satellite reception on a TV or seal the watertight door that went into the control room on this level. One more good reason for the visual inspection. It had probably been one of the enlisted personnel who had gotten the job of storing the treasure trove of supplies in the shelter.

That was another reason for this inspection. He needed to see if anything important was missing. More than once the project had uncovered issues with theft of some of the really cool toys they were stocking in the shelters, and Maybank didn't really blame some of the young kids who were given the jobs. It was preferable to combat duty, but every time they upgraded the technology, they had to break in new people who couldn't always keep a secret or their hands to themselves.

Maybank recalled one breach at a shelter on the west coast that put the entire project in jeopardy. The shelter was in a hostile environment near the Canadian border. Just like Titus Rush, the shelter owner preferred a small island for his location, but he felt like the cold weather would deter any interest by survivors after an apocalypse.

Someone important who was to be saved by the shelter had told his girlfriend about how they would be safe if there was an apocalypse. When he ended the relationship, a news crew camped outside the hidden entrance to the shelter for two weeks. They never found the entrance, but it was clear that the shelter builders had to find incentives to make people keep the locations secret. For the important people who were to be saved, the penalty for disclosure was loss of that privilege, but just to be safe, they weren't told the locations in advance. Those who already knew were told the construction had been abandoned at the first location and moved to an undisclosed site.

It was harder to find incentives for the military personnel. The only things they could come up with were higher pay, combat duty transfers, and federal prison. In the end they found that higher pay was usually sufficient as long as they were also told the alternatives.

After stepping through the door and sealing it behind him, Maybank made a mental note that the inspection had not been a waste of time. He congratulated himself for following the rules.

The audio was coming from a computer that also displayed other camera views besides TV broadcasts. One was an outside view of the crew's quarters. Maybank sat down and guessed that at the moment, the uninjured man was probably trying to assure his friend that he would be fine. Maybank didn't know how much they knew about what was happening on the mainland, but the man would either lie to his friend, or he didn't know yet that the bites were fatal. His best chance of survival would be to kill his friend, but there was always the possibility that he was just unable to do what had to be done.

Thinking of the men made Maybank remember why he had let them board the oil rig in the first place. He didn't know any of them had been bitten. It also reminded him that he had forgotten to close the door behind them, so to speak. He found the right panel and hit the button that retracted the handholds back into their hidden doors on the side of the tower.

He turned off the monitor to conserve power and crossed the control room to the next sealed door. The galley was on the other side, and his appetite had returned. He was also thinking that maybe he would spend two hours in the armory target range instead of one.

6 TIDAL CREEK

Beginning of the Decline

Sarah Beth wanted to stay in the boat for a while longer, but Paul wanted to reach the dock. She couldn't explain why she felt like it was worse than Paul realized, but whatever was happening, it wasn't over. Paul kept going on about the authorities, the government, safe zones, the Red Cross, FEMA, and everyone else who would rescue them.

The old couple had disappeared hours ago, but they heard the boom of the rifle a few times. She hadn't blamed them for going back. It was better than sitting at the end of the long dock. Maybe they were somewhere safe by now, but the boat was at least safe for the time being. She wanted to stay in the boat until one of Paul's life saving agencies showed up.

She felt the boat move as Paul managed to gather a little forward momentum in the tidal creek. The current wasn't swift, but he was satisfied that they were drifting in the right direction. He was using a pole to reach into the marsh grass and push against the roots, and he had to be careful not to get the pole stuck in the mud. Pulling it free would have had the same effect as pulling them back in the other direction.

Paul let out a whoop of satisfaction when they made the last turn and had a straight line to the narrow dock, but then he moaned with dismay when he saw there was no ladder or even a rope he could climb to reach the platform above them. It was at least ten feet above the water, but he thought maybe he could jump up and grab the edge of a board.

He guided them into position then carefully got up on the seats. Once he had his balance, he jumped and grabbed. He had it for a moment, but he came down with a crash and a painful handful of splinters.

Several more attempts met with the same results, and Paul finally announced that they would have to reach the shore by wading through the water.

"I'm not getting in that water," said Sarah Beth.

"What's eating you?" he said. "We've swum in tidal creeks before."

"That's my point. Nothing is going to eat me. We haven't gotten in tidal creeks after bodies have fallen in the water. I saw that head go off the dock into the water, and there were several people who fell in."

"They're long gone by now," he argued.

"You don't know that. I'm not getting in the water."

"Suit yourself. I'm going."

"You're just going to leave me here?"

"No, you can go with me."

Sarah Beth got up and walked to the bow. She sat down and crossed her arms as if to say the discussion was over.

Paul sat down and then swung his legs over the edge. He gave a push with his hands and launched himself over the side into the water. It wasn't deep, so he bounced on the bottom with his tiptoes until he was facing toward shore then gave himself a push in that direction.

The cool water felt good after spending the day in the boat, and the stress of the things they had seen made the day seem that much hotter.

"You should go with me," he shouted over his shoulder at Sarah Beth.

"You can come back for me after you get a ladder or something. As a matter of fact, I'll stay here until you come back with help."

Paul had just passed out of sight in the taller patches of marsh grass, and Sarah Beth heard some splashing, but she couldn't see if it was him. Swells gently rolled across the surface of the water, and Sarah Beth leaned around one of the big poles that supported the dock.

"Paul?"

She could hear the water lapping against the banks, but otherwise it was quiet.

There were still some boats burning in the harbor, but it was like the aftermath of a war. She had stopped trying to tell where the random gunshots were coming from, but they were obviously not a danger to them. The big elephant gun wasn't booming anymore. She watched as the smoke from the boat fires seemed to swirl and drift until it merged with the big fires in the city.

Sarah Beth took in the view as a spectator at a car wreck would. She felt detached and immune from what she was seeing, and when she got wherever she was going, she would tell everyone what she saw and then go on with her life. Everyone would say how awful it sounded and offer her sympathy as if it had happened to them.

Something had made her forget that Paul didn't answer her when she called out to him. She used the piling of the dock to keep the boat steady and tried to see through the grass. There was another splash, but then it was quiet again.

"Paul?"

Sarah Beth heard the fear in her own voice, but she had no sooner called out the second time when the thrashing started. She heard Paul repeatedly yelling, "No, no, no….."

He was half swimming and half crab walking on the marsh grass as he burst into the creek, but the whole time he kept yelling that one word. Sarah Beth got the impression that he was not so much yelling at someone as he was shouting a denial in answer to a question. Like he saw something that couldn't have been there.

Paul didn't even seem to see Sarah Beth. She saw his face above the water, and it was so pale he was bone white. His lips were even white, and his eyes were bulging so big she thought they would explode. It struck her that Paul resembled a guppy that was gulping as it tried to breathe out of water.

He grabbed the back of the boat and tried to pull himself over the stern, but Sarah Beth saw he was hurt. Watered down blood washed along the inside wall of the boat and puddled by the motor.

"Oh, no. Paul, let me help you."

Sarah Beth somehow managed to get to the back of the boat despite the fact that Paul was making it rock as he tried to climb aboard. She grabbed his arms and pulled, but her grip was slippery because her hands were quickly covered in blood.

Paul screamed in pain, and she let go. As she did, she saw the big ragged tear in his arm and the white bone exposed from the wrist to the elbow.

She didn't know what to do at first, but she knew she had to get him into the boat and get that wound bandaged. She grabbed him again, but this time she reached past his head and down to the middle of his back. She grabbed handfuls of his shirt and pulled, and this time he came up high enough and flopped over the railing into the boat.

There were plenty of towels in the boat that she could use as bandages, but Paul had never believed in wasting space with a first aid kit. She could wrap the wound, but she couldn't clean it.

Paul began shrieking, and in between the screams of pain she caught words that could have been, "It can't be." She didn't get the chance to figure out what he was trying to tell her before he passed out cold. Sarah Beth laid him back onto the seat cushions and went to work trying to stop the bleeding.

As the sun went down, Paul was breathing in raspy shudders. He had lost so much blood that Sarah Beth wondered how he could even be alive. She retreated to the bow and squeezed herself against it with her legs drawn up under her. For some reason she was afraid to be near Paul.

The darkness closed in on them despite the many small fires that still dotted the harbor. A few of them were larger, but they flared brightly and then sank below the surface. The cruise ship was long gone, and there had been a lot of shooting at Fort Sumter, but it all seemed so far away.

Paul opened his eyes, and even in the darkness she felt like he wasn't really seeing her. It was like someone else was looking at her. He lifted the bloody arm and regarded it with a detached expression and said, "What happened?"

That surprised Sarah Beth beyond belief. She didn't know what she expected to hear, but she didn't think it would be a coherent question. She didn't know if she should go to him or stay where she was.

"You went into the water so you could get to shore. I don't know what happened after that. You came back hurt."

She didn't consider whether or not he could see her when she gestured toward Paul's shredded arm.

"Something got you, but I didn't see what it was."

Paul was silent for a few moments like he was trying to remember something, but when it came back to him, there was that one word again.

"No, no, no...."

He pushed himself up on the seat and was trying to get to his feet. He made it to a standing position long enough to grab the piling under the dock and gave it a hard shove. He fell over in the boat, but they drifted away from where they had been sitting just far enough for them to see what was walking around above them on the dock. It was crowded.

There was a huge splash as a body landed in the water. Sarah Beth screamed, and there was a general increase in the amount of pushing and shoving followed by railing boards pulling free from their nails. The metal nails shrieked as they came out of the wood, and the moaning grew into a chorus as the bodies rained down faster.

Hands pulled at the boat, and the rocking back and forth increased. Somehow Paul got the pole into the water and pushed against the ugly, mangled bodies. Sarah Beth didn't know what had happened to these people, but it looked like they had been too close to an explosion. All of them had injuries that made Paul's arm look like a scratch.

Paul wrestled with something that was holding onto his pole, and when he eventually pulled free, he fell back onto his seat. In the pale light, Sarah Beth saw there was something still attached to the pole as Paul dropped it in the bottom of the boat. It was moving, and at first she thought it was a gigantic blue crab. It was biting into the pole and making a sound like a groan.

"What is that thing?"

Even as she screamed the question she knew the answer. Just like Paul, she just wanted to deny what she was seeing. The hair was matted down against the skin, and the ragged flesh where the head used to connect to shoulders was flapping against the boat making a wet sound that reminded Sarah Beth of a fish on a hook.

"Get it out of the boat," she screamed.

The snapping teeth had clamped onto the pole, and Paul was trying to lift it upward using just his bad arm. He had one end of the pole under his armpit, and the other end was six feet away with the big, dark mass hanging from it. It seemed to start bouncing in the air as Paul tried to rotate it away from the boat, and when it fell off, Paul fell backward.

Paul screamed as the pain in his arm was replaced by the white hot pain on the back of his neck. He had fallen far enough for something to reach from the water and grab him, and when he sat upright he was reaching with his good hand to the new wound.

Sarah Beth felt helpless as Paul curled into a fetal position in the bottom of the boat. Both of them wailed in deep, wracking sobs for hours as hands rocked the boat. Her sobs were out of helpless fear. His were from pain.

Just before dawn, Sarah Beth realized Paul wasn't sobbing anymore. She lifted her head and saw that he was trying to move. His face was turned away from her, but she doubted she would have been able to see it even if he had been facing her. It was a combination of low light and all that blood in his hair. She absently thought he must have been laying on his face because his hair was plastered forward.

She opened her mouth to ask him if he was okay, but something made her bite back the words. At first she thought it was the way he twitched and jerked as if he was stiff. Then she saw what it was. He was leaning with all of his weight on the shredded arm, and there was no sign of pain. He had also stopped bleeding, even though the wound was wide open.

Sarah Beth eased her feet under her so she could stand up. The boat rocked a little, but Paul didn't appear to notice. He was lifting his head upward toward the sky, and for an insane moment she thought he was sniffing the air.

Paul pushed even harder on the arm that should have been too damaged to move. The exposed bones appeared to bend out of the arm from the pressure. Just as one of them snapped in half, he got his feet under him and stood to his full height. She felt something escape from her throat when she saw the bone break. She had her hand over her mouth, but he heard her anyway.

On legs that seemed like they weren't used to walking, he rotated to his left as if taking in the sunrise in the east, but he continued to turn. There were gunshots somewhere by Fort Sumter, and that held his attention for a moment. Then he turned to face her.

There was just enough light for her to tell she wasn't looking at Paul anymore. Whatever he was, he wasn't Paul. On unsteady feet he tried to step toward her, but the boat rocked too much. Sara Beth scrambled forward on the bow as far as she could go, and the shaking of the boat made the creature sway and then fall. She didn't know what he was, but right now her only defense against him was that he couldn't stay upright when the boat shook, and that wasn't going to stop him from eventually reaching her.

As if he knew she would rock the boat again, he started to crawl toward the bow. He would have to stand to climb up to where she was, but that wouldn't stop him forever.

She started to cry again, but this time she was begging him to leave her alone. He couldn't hear her because he was dead. Sarah Beth knew that, but she begged anyway. He pulled himself to his feet and leaned forward with his arms outstretched. All she could do was move her legs back and forth to stay out of his reach.

She felt his fingers catch one shoe, and out of reflex she jerked it back and kicked. The heel caught Paul in the middle of the nose and sent him sprawling backward. Without hesitation he climbed to his feet again. This time Sarah Beth didn't wait. She threw her weight left and right, and the creature fell again. She had hoped he would fall overboard, but no such luck. She only slowed down his advance, and he was crawling again. Even though he fell over on his side, he kept coming. Somehow she managed to get her fingers wrapped around one of the poles she had seen people use to reach for ropes. She swung it at Paul, but it was much heavier than it looked, and it wasn't keeping him away.

There was a whistling noise, or something like a whistle. Sarah Beth heard it long before she realized it was there because it started as a low rushing of wind and increased gradually until it filled the air. She had the vague feeling that there was a helicopter somewhere.

The sound seemed to pass by over her head, moved away, and then was coming back again. She saw it the first time when it passed behind Paul toward his left, but it didn't make sense. It was square, but it was flying.

Sarah Beth almost forgot about Paul as the gray object got closer and closer. She could tell it was going to connect with Paul's head if it stayed on the path it was following. There was a straight line that ran through the air from the gray square all the way back to the dock, and for the first time Sara Beth understood.

The man on the dock was short but very husky. Not many men could swing a cinderblock around in a circle on a rope even one time. This guy was not only swinging it in circles, but he was paying out more rope with each turn, and the block was closing in on Paul's head. The man had a big smile on his face that erupted into a shout when the cinderblock found its target.

There was a sound like a ripe watermelon hitting the pavement after falling from a four story building, and Paul's head disintegrated. The cinderblock was moving so fast that it almost stayed in the air, but the impact had caused the line to go slack, and it tumbled into the water.

A second man stood up next to the husky guy and put his hands on his hips. He stood like a supervisor or someone in charge. He had apparently been sitting on the dock to stay below the rope as it passed over his head. Once Paul had been removed from the picture, he was free to stand up.

The man launched into some kind of explanation without introducing himself.

"I asked Randal if he could hit that piece of ripe meat with that cinderblock from here, and he said he could. I was actually asking him if he could throw it that far. I didn't know anybody could swing one like that on a rope. I gotta tell you lady. Even I'm impressed."

He clapped the husky guy, presumably Randal, on the back. Randal look pleased with himself. He was busy pulling in the rope with the heavy cinderblock on the end, but he took the time to give Sarah Beth a little wave.

"I had to do it nice and slow, Ma'am. I didn't want to overshoot and get you by mistake."

Her throat was as dry as gravel, but she managed to croak out a weak thank you and something about being glad Randal didn't overshoot, too.

Randal tossed the rope at one of the cleats near the stern and pulled the boat closer to the dock. He leaned as far as he could over the edge and extended a beefy hand to Sarah Beth. When she held her own out to him, she was surprised by how easily he lifted her up to the dock. She was also surprised when she saw the other end of the dock was crowded with injured people.

"What was that you called them?"

She gestured back toward Paul and then at the crowd that was slowing its own progress by bumping and shoving each other.

"Ripe meat?" asked the taller man.

"Yeah. Why do you call them that?"

The man couldn't tell if she was serious or not. Then he understood and considered the possibility that she did not understand the full gravity of their predicament yet.

"Lady, have you been in that boat for a long time?"

She had to think about it for a minute, but she shook her head to clear her mind and said, "A day or two. I don't know for sure."

He held out his hand in a gesture that seemed oddly out of place considering where they were, and that she had just watched an old friend get his head crushed. Now this man was standing in front of her wanting to shake hands.

"My name is Stokes, and this here is Randal. We saw that you were about to become lunch for that ripe meat, so we figured we would lend a hand."

"That ripe meat, as you called him, was an old friend of mine. Do you live near here?" asked Sarah Beth. She tried to keep her voice more calm than she felt inside.

"As a matter of fact, we just moved into that big place at the end of the dock."

When he said it, Randal laughed like he thought something Stokes said was funny.

"You're welcome to come home with us," said Stokes.

He kept his hand out in front of her, waiting for her to accept his gesture.

"Sarah Beth," she said. "I'm Sarah Beth."

She shook his hand but only because something told her it would be dangerous to reject it.

"Well, hello Sarah Beth."

Stokes made a sweeping gesture with his hand like he expected Sarah Beth to start walking down the dock, but she stayed where she was.

"Tell me what's happening. Do you know?"

She directed her question to Stokes, but she glanced at Randal to see if he was going to answer.

"How long did you say you've been in that boat, Miss Sarah?"

Stokes used the formal way of addressing her that was common to the south, especially Charleston.

The thought of being in the boat rattled her a bit, and she couldn't completely wipe out the tremor in her voice.

"I think since yesterday, but it could have been two days. What's been happening?"

It was the first time she saw something in their eyes that she had in common with them. They were nervous and maybe a little more than scared. Randal and Stokes both seemed like they had been reminded of something, and their heads swiveled on their shoulders to take in their surroundings.

"We need to get back inside," said Stokes. "We'll explain everything in there. We also have more work to get done on the ditch up at the road to the house. If we get that done fast, we can flood the area and seal it off."

"Seal it off from what?"

Neither of them answered this time, and Stokes dropped his facade of southern charm. He didn't wait for her to take the lead as he walked down the dock. Randal fell in behind him like a big puppy dog. He was winding the rope around his arm in loops and carrying his cinderblock.

"Wait, I'm sorry. I didn't mean to be rude. It's just been bad out there. I mean, I don't really even know what day it is, and I don't know what's going on."

"No time to be all blubbery, girl. Just follow us. You'll find out what's happening in due time, then maybe you can explain it to us."

She took that to mean Stokes and Randal didn't know much more than she did, but at least she was alive because of them. They could take care of themselves, and that was a lot more than she could say about Paul. She fell in behind them and noticed they were both watching their surroundings closely as they walked toward the house at the end of the dock.

There had been around six or eight "ripe meat" gathering at the end of the dock, but several had already fallen off into the marsh. Instead of trying to get back up onto the dock, they tried to walk through the water to reach the trio of living people. When they reached the deeper water, they disappeared.

Now, there were only four of them staggering along the wooden planks of the dock. One more fell through an opening in the railing, and Randal threw the cinderblock at the remaining three. He was remarkably accurate, and one by one they were eliminated.

The dock met solid ground about twenty feet from the back porch of a brown house that would have fit nicely on any piece of beachfront property. The back yard had an eight foot privacy fence around it that gave her a feeling of safety, but Stokes and Randal were even more vigilant now that they were off of the dock. She started to say something, but Stokes' left hand shot upward at the elbow, and they both stopped walking as if someone had yelled for them to freeze.

Sarah Beth instinctively did the same, and she watched as Stokes very slowly began stepping to his right, and Russel did the same while carefully stepping in the same places as Stokes.

She knew it was totally random, but she thought they were acting like they were crossing a minefield. Then she saw that Stokes was carefully avoiding small twigs and branches, and Randal was able to stay quiet as long as he followed Stokes. She decided she would stay where she was until they told her to come forward.

Stokes pointed at one section of fence, and Randal nodded. They walked like a pair of cats across the yard until Stokes could press his face against the wooden fence. He held up one finger, and Randal nodded in understanding. Randal walked quietly for a stocky man, and he eased over to a lawn chair. Sarah Beth was amazed that he carried the chair over to the fence and climbed onto it without making sound. He hefted the cinderblock and reached over the fence with it.

Randal swung the cinderblock like it was a boxing glove on his fist, and they heard the sound of it hitting its target. Just as quickly, he ducked back down below the top of the fence and moved back in her direction.

As Stokes passed by, he said under his breath, "There's ripe meat all over the place in these woods. Once we get the road finished, they won't be wandering up on us like that."

"What exactly are you doing to the road?"

"This place is an island except for the road. We're digging it out so that it fills in with water. Anything that gets across we can deal with."

Sarah Beth followed them to the house wondering how they planned to dig out the road. She didn't know they had driven to this end of James Island on a backhoe from a cemetery. The scoop on the front could be used to break apart asphalt then dig a nice, wide trench across the road. They had already gotten a good start and had at least partially flooded the area, but the racket they had made driving it to the house had been an open invitation to every piece of ripe meat for miles around.

There were other people in the house. That surprised Sarah Beth. She didn't know why, but she had expected the house to be empty. The others were going about jobs that were assigned to them by Stokes. For some reason he was the chosen leader even though none of them had seen how truly evil he could be. When they had arrived, one by one or in small groups, everyone took for granted that he was the one who made all of the decisions. He wasn't going to disagree with them.

Sarah Beth had enough education to know that a leadership vacuum could be filled quickly if there was a shortage of leaders, but she hadn't ever seen people defer to one person more quickly. Maybe they sensed something the way she did. She just knew she would try not to cross Stokes.

"You look lost."

The voice that spoke to her was a young, dark haired guy who looked like he was a college student. She was used to boys finding a reason to talk with her at parties, but she had never felt lost the way she was at the moment, so his line was more accurate than the pick up lines she was used to hearing. She really did feel lost.

He held out his hand, and unlike her mental alarms that made her hold back from shaking hands with Stokes, she readily accepted the gesture.

"My name's Gervais. What's yours?"

"Sarah Beth."

"Ah, Charlestonian?"

She tilted her head to one side and said, "You're from the Midlands, maybe a USC student."

"Gamecock all the way," he smiled.

To an outsider, it would have seemed that they were squaring off for a fight, but where they were from was actually an ice breaker in South Carolina social circles. She was from the Lowcountry, and he was from the Midlands. That wasn't a great combination, but it wasn't as bad as someone from the Lowcountry socializing with someone from the Upstate. For a small state, South Carolina had well defined borders within its borders.

Gervais continued, "It looks like where we're from doesn't matter so much right now. The fact that we're alive might be the most important thing."

He wasn't unpleasant, and Sarah Beth didn't detect danger the way she had with Stokes and Randal, so she was grateful to have him stepping up.

"Does anybody know what's happening?"

He shook his head. "Most of us were here for the day to sit in on some labs at the College of Charleston. I hardly know any of these folks. All I know is that people started biting other people. Crazy people were running around killing each other, and campus security couldn't handle it. Next thing I knew there were security officers attacking students, too. Police showed up, and they didn't last ten minutes before they were either dead or attacking everyone. Afterward, there was no one left to attack."

"How did you get here then? Why didn't you become one of them?"

"Same reason you didn't become one I guess. You didn't get bit by anyone."

Sarah Beth thought about Paul. He had left the boat feeling fine, but he came back dying. She finally understood he got bit when he went to get help.

"Stokes and Randal found me in a boat and brought me back here. Are we safe here?"

"So far," said Gervais. "They dug out enough of the road to make it hard for those things, whatever they are, to get to the house."

"They call them ripe meat," said Sarah Beth. "I still think of them as people, so I don't really like what they call them."

"I would get used to it if I were you. If we're lucky we won't be stuck here for long, but I have a bad feeling we're going to be here a very long time."

7 CAPTURED

Six Years After the Decline

All of that seemed like it had been someone else's life. Sarah Beth thought about that first night every time she came back and reached up toward the wooden ladder they had added to the dock. The tide was in, so they had drifted quickly past the spot where she and Paul had spent the night. She was having trouble remembering how many years had gone by. She thought it was six, but it could be seven or even eight.

"We're going to need help getting them up to the dock," said Randal.

"Do ya think?"

Sarah Beth had given up any attempt to disguise her feelings toward Randal. As for Randal, he figured if she fell overboard, he would throw her an anchor before he would throw her a life preserver.

Despite being constantly insulted, Randal dutifully ran ahead down the length of the dock to get some help. He returned a few minutes later with two stocky men trailing behind. A few others tagged along just to see what was going on.

One of the stocky men dropped down into the boat and easily lifted Molly over his shoulder. When the second guy saw the pretty face and thick black hair of the teenager, he offered to take her from the first guy.

"Keep your hands to yourself, dirtbag. You can get the other one."

Bert Smalls was about as popular as Randal. That's why Stokes had pointed at him and Al Wilkes to go help Randal and Sarah Beth with whatever was so important that Randal had burst into the house stuttering.

Bert's eyes went down into the boat hoping to find a second attractive teenager. It was another teenager, but it was a skinny boy. He grumbled the whole time, but he knew better than to keep Stokes waiting, so he made quick work of retrieving the limp body from the boat. He caught up with Al at the end of the dock, and they followed Sarah Beth and Randal to the big house that was mostly hidden by trees.

Noise was kept at a minimum as everyone walked inside, and even though there was very little light in the big living room, each of them wiped their feet on the mat by the door and then removed their shoes. They were left neatly along the wall in pairs. Stokes liked to keep his house clean.

Sarah Beth saw that the shades were all drawn tightly shut on the windows, and only two candles burned in the room. It had to be a precaution due to the unusually high amount of ripe meat walking around on the mainland.

"What have we got?" asked Stokes.

His voice was soft and low, but everyone in the room knew it was because sound carried too well at night, and he didn't want anyone to discover their home.

Sarah Beth stepped forward to explain. She didn't want Randal to give his version of the events because he would screw it up. She didn't know how, but she knew he would.

"It was a routine night patrol, Sir. Me and Randal….".

Stokes raised his hand with the palm outward, and she knew to stop speaking. Then she realized what she had said. Stokes had a rule about good grammar. If you knew how to speak properly, he wanted you to do so. If you didn't already have the skill, he just tolerated you.

"Randal and I were on our way back from the campus when these two dropped in on us from above. I thought they were ripe meat, so I swung at their heads as soon as they landed. Turned out to be alive."

"That's it?"

Stokes was leaning forward from a large leather sofa. His long hair was pulled back in a ponytail, and there was an array of weapons spread out on the coffee table in front of him. His right hand was lingering over a knife with a beautifully carved handle. Sarah Beth knew that much of what he did was for show, but everyone was on edge about the sudden increase of ripe meat in the area. The home was separated from the mainland by creeks and a moat they had dug by the main entrance to the property, but ripe meat could still get across if they didn't get stuck in the mud.

She didn't know what he expected, but she did know he didn't want speculation. He wanted facts.

Stokes focused his eyes on Randal for just a moment, and Randal took it as a sign that Stokes wanted his version. As he started to speak, the hand came up again.

Sarah Beth went on before Randal could make a mistake and wind up wandering in the woods with his entrails in a loop around his neck. Although when she thought about it, that didn't seem like such a bad idea.

"Sir, they fell over ten feet, and they were likely to have been stunned already when I hit them, so they haven't been questioned."

Stokes smiled. Even in the dim light his yellow teeth made Sarah Beth feel ill. His greasy hair framed his face and made him resemble someone who had just been pulled from a grave. He would actually enjoy it more if he had all of the information first hand, and he could get it straight from the two teenagers as soon as they woke up. He would do it privately and then decide how much to tell his followers. His hope was that they knew something about Fort Sumter or the people on the aircraft carrier.

"Where exactly did you find them?"

"Where the creek passes close to shore between the college buildings and the government buildings. It's the highest bank along the marsh."

"So you didn't see where they were coming from?"

Stokes liked Sarah Beth because she did what she was told and had no ambitions of her own. Most of his followers felt like they should be in charge, and he had to make an example of them from time to time. Sometimes he wished Randal would try something so he could have an excuse to get rid of him. Randal made everyone feel just a bit safer, as if he was a layer of insulation between them and Stokes' temper.

"No, Sir. We didn't even hear them coming, so they must've been running when they jumped."

Stokes gave orders to have the teenagers locked up. Then he disappeared to his private rooms. His trusted officers were allowed to stay in the house, but everyone else had to stay outside. Sarah Beth preferred to be outside because she felt like she was one step closer to escaping if she had to. She always felt like she was going to either have to escape from Stokes and his cutthroats, or the ripe meat would find a way onto their little island paradise in large enough numbers to overrun them.

She walked outside onto the broad front porch and peered into the darkness. It was oppressively hot and humid, and the mosquitos seemed to be getting bigger. For about the thousandth time she wondered when the infection would mutate and be able to spread by mosquito bites.

"That would really stink," she said half out loud.

"What would?"

She didn't jump or let on that the question from the darkness had spooked her, but it had. When she had spoken, she knew deep down that none of the ripe meat would be close enough to hear her, but she had forgotten about Gervais.

Sometimes Sarah Beth thought at least half the people in South Carolina could trace their roots back to someone rich or famous in the history books. Gervais certainly could. He proudly told people to call him by his last name because his ancestor had been a South Carolina state senator as well as a delegate to the Continental Congress. She had grown up in a family like that, so she understood his desire to hang onto his family roots. A lot of good it did for any of them now.

"I was just thinking out loud about the infection and how much worse it would be if it could be carried by mosquitos. One itchy little bite, and bam. You're ripe meat."

"You're in a dark mood tonight."

He didn't have to be able to see her well to know that she was glaring at him. It was a bad play on words even for him.

"Hey, I'm sorry. What's eating at you tonight?"

That one was unintentional, but even she had to stifle a laugh. Somewhere in the distance a piece of ripe meat moaned.

"The teenagers we found this evening. Good looking kids. Well cared for. Probably been eating well and had people to look after them. Why they were at Fort Johnson is beyond me. They should be home with their families, but now Stokes has them."

"Why do you care so much?"

Gervais wasn't trying to be mean or insensitive, but after years of death from the infection and at the hands of people like Stokes, it was hard to worry about someone he didn't even know.

"Don't you ever wonder what happened to your family? I do all the time. I've given up on the idea of finding them even though they could be right over there, but no one's alive that I knew back then."

Sarah Beth gestured in the general direction of Charleston. They couldn't see it from their location on James Island, but they both knew where it was. If you lived in Charleston long enough, you always knew which way to turn to face the peninsula.

"Well, they aren't your problem now. You aren't thinking of doing something stupid, are you?"

When she thought about it for a minute, Sarah Beth knew the honest answer to the question. She had learned on the first day of the infection that she didn't have the luxury to care about other people anymore. If she wanted to stay alive, she could only care about herself. Whoever those kids were, they were on their own.

"No, I'm not going to do anything stupid. There's nothing I could do even if I wanted to. Do you think Stokes is going to let them go?"

"Are you kidding?"

Gervais asked her the question so quickly that Sarah Beth realized she should have thought about that before bringing them back to camp. There was still Randal, though. If she had let them go, Randal would have fallen all over himself getting the report to Stokes, and if she hadn't knocked them out, Randal would probably have killed one of them just taking them into captivity. Either way, Stokes wanted information about Fort Sumter and the Yorktown, and he was going to get it.

Gervais didn't really expect her to answer. They both knew Stokes wouldn't let them go even if they didn't have any information he could use.

There was activity behind them, as Randal and a few others came outside.

"What's happening?" asked Gervais.

"We're movin' out," said Randal.

"In the middle of the night?"

Sarah Beth couldn't have sounded more surprised when she stepped in front of Randal and asked the question.

"That skinny kid woke up, and the first thing out of his mouth was what the Army would do to us if we didn't let them go. And there's some guy he called the Chief who's some kind of super hero to the kid. The boss said we're out of here tonight."

Sarah Beth brushed past Randal with Gervais on her heels.

"Don't do it," he said as he grabbed her by the back of her arm.

She pulled herself loose but stopped trying to go inside. She knew the secluded house wasn't going to be a permanent solution to their survival, and the time would come sooner or later when they had to move on. She just wasn't so sure about Stokes' plan to go south to the Gulf of Mexico.

Sarah Beth had always believed they should find a barrier island that didn't have any ripe meat wandering around on it. They could build a fort and then carry supplies out to it. Stokes liked her idea, but he wanted to take the idea a bit further. He wanted to go to the Gulf of Mexico and take over an oil rig. He wasn't sure how they were going to do it, but he felt like it would be pretty easy. He kept saying they would figure that out when they got there.

The part that bothered Sarah Beth the most was that Stokes never took prisoners. Now that the boy had figuratively spilled his guts, Stokes was likely to spill them literally.

Before she had a chance to think about it, and before Gervais could stop her, she wheeled around and went inside. Stokes was on his couch with a map spread out on the coffee table. He was going over the best route to New Orleans with several of his officers.

"Stokes, why not let the kids go? We could leave them somewhere. There's no need to kill them."

Stokes tilted his head to one side, which he tended to do when he was actually thinking about something, but sometimes he did it for show. It made people think he was considering what they were suggesting. Sarah Beth didn't know which tilt she was getting.

"Okay, Sarah Beth. I won't kill them. I'll find a place to leave them just for you."

Gervais had come up behind Sarah Beth, and he arrived in time to hear everything. If he had watched Stokes the way Sarah Beth had, he would have missed the grins from the other men. Whatever Stokes planned, he was sure it didn't include letting the prisoners go.

The best thing Gervais could do was get Sarah Beth out of there before Stokes decided she should share the fate of the two teenagers, whatever it was. He took her by the back of the arm for a second time and gently pulled her from the room. Stokes must have said something funny after they left because his officers all laughed.

******

Molly had regained consciousness after Sam. She had a splitting headache, and she wanted him to shut up. He was yelling at someone about how they would pay for taking them prisoner. She heard a door slam shut, and they were alone.

Sam could tell in the darkness that she was trying to sit up and went to help her even though their hands were tied behind their backs. Through the fog in her mind, Molly knew that was a bad sign.

"Molly, are you okay? You've been out for a long time."

Besides her head hurting so bad that the sound of his voice was like a needle in her eye, she was furious with him about the things he had been yelling at whoever that was who had left the room.

"When did you become such an idiot?" she yelled.

Molly thought she would pass out from the pain she caused herself when she yelled at Sam.

Sam recoiled from her, expecting Molly to be glad to see him standing up to their captors.

"What did I do?"

"I can't believe you actually yelled at that guy that our friends would take care of him. That's just the kind of information they would want. Numbers, firepower, location. What else did you tell them?"

"Nothing."

Sam broke eye contact with Molly when he answered, and she turned her back on him.

"I may have said Fort Sumter."

Sam's voice was low, but it was loud enough for Molly to know Sam may have said more than just Fort Sumter.

Molly stepped over to a boarded up window and looked for gaps. Even if she found one, it was still dark outside. The only light in their room was coming from a gap under the door, and it was only enough to make the area by the door a little bit gray. She couldn't really tell yet if their room was small or large. The corners were so dark that there could be someone in there with them.

Sam was whimpering something about getting hit on the head and being worried about Molly. Molly was wondering where her knight in shining armor had gone.

"Does anything look familiar to you?" she asked.

"I've only seen this one room. I don't think I've ever been here before."

Sam had been on the outside for a long time after the apocalypse began. He and his friends had foraged for food through a lot of the houses in downtown Charleston. If they had somehow been carried over to the mainland, they may be in a house he had searched.

"Besides," he continued, "a lot of those places burned down, and the Chief says that the buildings are really crumbling."

"This room looks kind of modern," she said. "I think we're still on James Island somewhere.

They heard footsteps coming from somewhere else in the house. It sounded like people were moving from one place to another like they were in a hurry.

The door burst open so suddenly that they almost fell over trying to move away from it. One guy pushed Molly onto a bed that had only become visible in the light that came from the hallway. The other two grabbed Sam by the arms and lifted him easily between them. Without a word from them, they left just as quickly as they had arrived.

Sam had resumed his yelling as if Molly had never mentioned it. Before the door shut behind them, he said enough that he might as well have given them a written diagram of the shelter.

Molly began frantically searching the room, trying to remember the locations of furniture and doors she had seen during the brief period of light. From the bed she had seen two other doors. It was a fair guess that one was a bathroom, and one was a closet. Maybe she could find something in one of them that she could use to cut the ropes around her wrists.

She found the first one and put her back to the doorknob. Her wrists were bound so tightly that she couldn't grab the smooth piece of metal at first, but she eventually got her hand around it. It turned, but the door didn't open. She tried turning it in the other direction, and this time she felt the door move inward as soon as there was a metal click by the knob.

The room beyond the door could have been either a closet or a bathroom. With no light coming from anywhere, she couldn't tell. Molly shut her eyes and tried to breathe evenly. She pictured a bathroom and imagined she had been there before. In her mind she looked around for anything familiar, something she would find in any bathroom.

She saw the vanity in front of a mirror and realized the first thing she would have done if her hands had been free was turn on the light switch that would be to the left of the door. She turned her back that way and leaned hard against the wall, sliding along until her back scraped against the switch. There was no way she was going to get her hands high enough to push the switch upward, so she tried using the flat of her back between her shoulders.

A couple of minutes of effort went unrewarded, and suddenly Molly knew she had let the situation get the best of her. Otherwise, she would have turned the lights on much sooner.

Molly turned around and faced the wall. She started searching again, and it didn't take long to find the switch with her mouth. She bit down on the piece of plastic and pushed upward.

The lights came on and blinded her, but she smiled at herself in a big vanity mirror to the right because she had been mildly successful. The smile disappeared from her face because the second reflection in the mirror was big and ugly. He towered over her, and his amused smile revealed yellow, nicotine stained teeth.

Before she could start her scream, his hands came up behind her head with speed she wouldn't have believed possible from someone his size. A black burlap bag whipped downward over her head, and once again she was in darkness.

If she could have seen him raise his fist, she would have fainted before it arrived at its target. His punch was to the right side of her head, and her legs crumbled under her. He caught her and easily lifted her in the air and draped her limp body over his shoulder.

******

Sam was taken back to the living room where he was unceremoniously dumped on the floor in front of Stokes. He never stopped complaining and threatening the men who had carried him from the dark room, and Stokes wasn't sure how much of what he was hearing was true. Still, he preferred to question the boy because he had a feeling he was going to be short on time. He didn't know if the girl would give up information as easily as the boy, but could save time by just encouraging the boy to threaten him.

Stokes leaned toward the boy and said, "When your friends get here, I'm going to kill them all."

Maybe it was because Sam was scared, but he took the bait.

"Oh, yeah? Do you have over a hundred men?" he spouted. "Do you have helicopters?"

Stokes had seen the helicopters coming and going from Fort Sumter since about a year or so after they had discovered the secluded house not far from Fort Johnson. It was perfectly situated in the middle of an overgrown island that was surrounded by tidal creeks and mud. A narrow gravel road led to the front gate that could keep out a fair number of the ripe meat, but it had become their second line of defense when he had his men dig out a big section of the road. It had flooded from both sides as soon as the dirt was removed and had effectively stopped the ripe meat from using the road to reach them.

The helicopters had passed overhead plenty of times. They would have seen the roof of the house, but it was doubtful that they could see his small gang. They had made it a habit to turn off the lights whenever possible, and the small generator that gave them power for brief periods of time wasn't used every day.

Tonight was one of those rare occasions when they needed the lights. They were packing their gear to leave, and they needed to go in a hurry. If the people at Fort Sumter were as dangerous to them as Stokes thought they were, they had to be gone before they arrived. He had no doubt that they would be sending out search parties at sunrise.

"Shut up, kid."

Stokes didn't have to say it loud. The menace in his voice was enough to stop Sam from saying another word.

"I don't need to know everything about you. I just need to know one thing. How long will the people at Fort Sumter search for you?"

Sam was confused by the simplicity of the question.

"How long?" asked Sam.

"Did I stutter? Will they search for you until they find you, or will they give up in a day or two?"

Sam still didn't understand the point of the question, but there was no doubt in his mind that the Mud Island family would tear the place apart to find them. He didn't know that Stokes planned to leave and assumed all along that Stokes planned to hold them for ransom.

He defiantly said, "They'll never give up searching for us, and when they find us, you're going to be sorry."

Stokes motioned with his hand to someone behind Sam, and he tried to see what was happening. His face turned right into a fist that knocked a tooth out. He didn't feel it because it also knocked him out.

A bag was pulled over his head, and he was carried off to join Molly.

******

Stokes was ruthless, but he wasn't stupid. He knew he had to keep the search party busy for as long as possible. He had to keep them in the area until he had his people far enough away, and that meant he had to give them something to look for. He couldn't just kill the teenagers. If they found the bodies, they would want revenge.

He hadn't been happy when Sarah Beth and Randal came back with the kids in the first place. He had asked Sarah Beth why they knocked them out and bagged them, and he could understand the part about being surprised when they dropped in from above. Sarah Beth thought they were ripe meat, and she had a split second reaction.

He had a hard time understanding the rest of it. Sarah Beth said Randal wanted to bring them back, and she wanted to leave them. Unless Randal had suddenly become the brains in their gang, Stokes couldn't wrap his mind around why Sarah Beth had listened to him. She could have left them to become ripe meat, and the people in Fort Sumter would have assumed the teenagers had been bitten. Then again, he could do the same thing. He could take them out to the woods and shove them into a crowd of ripe meat.

Stokes felt like he was missing something, but then it came to him. If the people from Fort Sumter had a reason to believe their kids were alive and somewhere nearby, then they had a reason to stay in the area and keep searching for them. The last thing he needed was for them to think the kids were either killed by them or kidnapped. All he needed was a way to make sure they came to the conclusion that they were still on a search and rescue mission long enough for him to put some distance between himself and Charleston.

When the idea came to him, he wondered what had taken him so long. He needed to leave someone behind, and Sarah Beth was the perfect candidate. She didn't want go to the Gulf, so she would jump at the chance to carry out the plan. He couldn't understand why she was still so attached to Charleston. It was a dead city of overgrown and wet buildings. The smell alone was enough to keep people from going there.

Her job would be to put on an act for the people from Fort Sumter. The kids didn't know she was the one who knocked them out, so she could pretend to be on their side and lead them to believe he and his men had gone north instead of south.

Stokes was fairly sure Sarah Beth would do it for him, or maybe there was a way to make her help him without knowing she was. After all, he was the one who had saved her back when the infection had started, so she owed him. If not for him, that ripe meat floating in the boat with her would have made a meal out of her a long time ago, and since that day he had protected and fed her. Actually, Randal had more to do with her rescue than Stokes, but the man in charge should always get the credit, according to his way of thinking.

Stokes had been out on a work release program from the county jail on the first day of the infection. They had assigned him to work for a cemetery digging graves and doing general maintenance. Most of it was landscaping, and he preferred to be outside, so it wasn't that bad.

They had just finished the graveside service for someone, and people were filing out of the cemetery. He was waiting nearby for the word to be given to lower the casket and fill in the hole. He was bored and wished they would hurry up. When he thought about it, that was probably the last time he had ever been really bored.

The last of the mourners stumbled away from the grave, and he waved to the two halfwits that were going to help him. No one put him in charge, but they were the kind of people who had to be told what to do, so they had been quick to listen when he stepped up. He started folding up the chairs while they lowered the casket. It had looked like it might rain, so they had a pavilion to take down, too.

"Hey, Boss."

Just hearing either of the halfwits speak grated on his nerves.

"What?"

His yell was loud enough for him to be heard by the last family members as they were getting into their cars. It earned him a few looks that he was sure the cemetery director would hear about.

"Now you got me in trouble, stupid. What do you want?" he snarled.

"Ah hear somethin' in there."

His thick southern drawl fit perfectly with the confused look on his face as he pointed at the coffin.

Stokes had understood clearly what the halfwit was telling him, and he stole a glance at the parking lot before he answered.

"Keep your voice down, idiot. As a matter of fact, don't speak until those people are gone."

The other helper still had his hand on the crank that operated the chrome winch that lowered the casket, but he had stopped turning it. Some automatic feeling told him he wasn't supposed to be lowering a coffin into the ground if there was someone moving around inside it.

"What are you waiting for? Start lowering that thing before those people decide to come see what's wrong."

He made a circular motion with his hand in the guy's direction, and the winch started turning again. There was a steady clicking sound as the gears engaged and disengaged repeatedly.

Curiosity got the best of one of the family members, and he took a few steps in their direction. He had his head cocked to one side and was watching Stokes as if he had just asked a question and was waiting for an answer.

Stokes didn't know why, but he felt like he had done something wrong and was about to be caught. At first the feeling was just guilt because that's what he was used to.

When you spend your whole life getting into and out of trouble, blame and guilt become everyday emotions. Not that he felt bad about what he did. He just felt like he was always found guilty in court.

He suddenly realized if a mistake had been made, he wasn't the one who had made it. As a matter of fact, he would be the hero if someone was closed up inside that coffin and he rescued them.

"Hold up."

The family member paused within hearing range as if the command was aimed at him. Stokes could see he was probably one of the sons. He couldn't have been over twenty-five.

The guy turning the chrome handle stopped and waited for Stokes to give another order. Stokes reversed the hand motion he had done earlier.

"Bring 'er up."

That made the young family member start walking again, but this time he was walking with a purpose.

"What do you think you're doing?" he asked.

Stokes didn't have to answer as there was a loud thumping sound from inside the coffin.

The two helpers both backed away from it at the same time while Stokes and the young man just stood as still as statues and stared at it. The coffin had only been partially raised, so it was just level with the pile of dirt on the other side of the grave.

It was safe to say they were trying to decide who was supposed to lift the lid. Stokes shook his head to the unspoken question, but the young man had mastered the expression that conveyed authority, and Stokes knew he was going to be the one who was going to open the coffin.

The next few minutes were somewhat fuzzy in Stokes' memory. He remembered stepping down from the seats to the edge of the hole where the coffin seemed to be hovering in place. He remembered reaching for the hole in the side of the coffin with the key that would turn the locking mechanism. The rest of it he wasn't totally sure of. Despite everything that had happened since that day, he had never been able to completely wrap his mind around seeing the pale old man trying to sit up as he raised the lid.

There was the screaming, the blood, the people tearing holes in the bodies of other people using their teeth. It seemed like it would never end, yet somehow it did. The two nitwits had followed Stokes as if he had a plan, but all he did was run.

Somehow he found himself at the secluded house a few miles away. The people who had lived there were dead, and all he had to do was take over. Over the next few days he let survivors join his ranks as if he was the ruler of a kingdom. One of his official acts as the lord and master of the home in the marshes was to rescue the young lady in the boat. She was swinging a pole at a young man who was trying to climb into her end of the boat. His shirt was covered with blood, and he was making a groaning sound.

******

Sarah Beth remembered that first day like it was yesterday, but her best guess was that it was close to six or seven years ago. Gervais was still with her, and of course Stokes and Randal were just stupid enough to live forever, but the rest of the faces were gone. A few of his trusted officers were all that were left.

Supply runs, never-ending close calls with ripe meat, and friends being bitten and keeping it secret from the others were all things that took their toll. It had been a long time since they had seen another real, living person, and she regretted taking them as prisoners for Stokes. She realized too late that she should have used them as a means to finally escape from this house that had become a prison.

Now that Stokes knew they were from Fort Sumter, there was no telling what he would do with them. He had set his mind on escaping to the Gulf of Mexico, and if she had been smarter, she would be in Fort Sumter right now and not about to be dragged off by those morons.

Sarah Beth was sitting with her back against a wall outside, just thinking about what she could do to change things. She saw the dark shape coming her way and readied herself for the attack, thinking some ripe meat had made it through the woods.

The years had taught her that nothing could sneak up on you if you had your back against a wall, and you always got to prepare for what was coming. This one stopped and lit a cigarette, and she relaxed. Only Randal was that stupid.

He walked straight up to her, and she was just about to comment about how dumb he had to be to light a cigarette at night, but the words didn't make it past her lips before he punched her.

The blow caught her between the eyes, and she was unconscious in the next second. Randal pulled a cloth bag over her head and tied her hands and feet. He picked her up and carried her off to dump her limp body with the others.

8 DESPERATION

Six Years After the Decline

Our search party wasn't having any luck. There were signs that others had been in the buildings looking for food or other useful items, but it had been a long time since the infection began.

Evidence of scavengers was subtle at first, but we had all become experienced living in this new world. In the chemistry labs we saw the fuel canisters that were used for portable Bunson burners were gone. Of course the labs had their own gas lines for the equipment, but these labs were part of the field training for Marine Biologists, and it was expected that they would want to run some experiments while camping along the coast on the barrier islands.

Field packs were gone, as were the dissecting kits. The blades in those kits would be invaluable to survivors who didn't have a shelter like ours. Cast nets, fishing gear, SCUBA gear, spear guns, and tents were probably the first to go, but those things were also likely to be the cause of the high infected dead population in the area.

On the first day, survivors would have scattered into the woods, but hundreds of survivors in the same area was also a guarantee that hundreds of the infected would be in the woods following the sounds of the injured, the frightened, and the desperate.

Some of the injured would have been bite victims. As a matter of fact, the majority of the injuries were likely to be bites. I tried to imagine what it must have been like to see classmates, boyfriends, and girlfriends bleeding from bite wounds and not knowing that those wounds would be fatal.

There couldn't have been much information available even on a campus with so many open lines of communication and a college safety office with armed security officers. They knew the same thing everyone else did, and the information about the bites being infectious had to have come after the population of the campus had become scattered. Those who remained within the fenced perimeter of the campus weren't prepared for the onslaught that would come within the next two days and would go on until they were all counted among the victims.

After the fences were breached, the campus had become a walking cemetery, a graveyard for the infected dead that couldn't find their way back out of the enclosures.

The woods on the other side may have been populated by survivors even longer than the secure buildings of the campus, but one by one the small pockets of the living were consumed by their friends who died in their arms, unaware that the danger was within their own camps. By the time the mistake was learned, it had already been made too often, and survivors who returned to scavenge for supplies suffered tremendous losses for a few precious items.

Judging by the lack of footprints and campsites out on Morris Island and in the marshes, the students had either chosen to stay on the mainland or had been forced inland away from the beaches. Either way, the population of infected dead grew steadily in the area.

As we moved from room to room we cleared the infected we encountered using blades. The plan was to move quickly and quietly to the upper floors in case the kids had become trapped up there. We had drawn too much attention getting into the building, so we hoped to work our way out the other end.

Cassandra was in the lead at the moment, and despite her tough exterior, she was finding it difficult to be the witness to the loss of so many people. She wasn't seeing the infected as the monsters they had become, but as the future they used to represent. She said it best when she stopped and asked how we were ever going to replace so many bright, young minds. Creativity would be gone for a century.

"Stairwell is clear," she said from above, and we hurried up to the landing outside the door to the second floor.

We cleared the second floor as quickly as the first, and we saw no fresh evidence that the floor had been visited by survivors. A quick meeting at the last room resulted in the decision to move on to the next building since we were all in agreement that it was unlikely that Molly and Sam had been in the first one. We had two more buildings to search, and the Chief wanted to take a look at the docks where the Marine Laboratory kept its boats.

As we had hoped, a sizable crowd of infected had gathered at the other end of the building, and it was far enough away for us to move unseen into the second one in line. It had its fair share of infected in the classrooms and offices, but not nearly as bad as what we had already seen. The students had probably known there were more labs in the first building and more lecture halls in the second. There wasn't much survival value in the computers and desks in the lecture halls.

The last building was more like a warehouse inside, but the contents were useless to survivors. Large aquariums and breeding ponds filled the building, and the second floor was lined with faculty offices.

That left the campus docks. We had ignored the docks for years because we could see them well from the air and from the deck of the Cormorant when we would cruise by. They had fallen into ruin on the first day when burning boats had tried to dock at the campus. Explosions from fuel supplies had destroyed the other boats, and the slips had all become clogged with debris.

We had an unlimited supply of boats at our disposal because we could fly to the marinas along the coast, or we could use the Cormorant to carry small invasion forces to the boat centers. We had talked about bringing more boats to Fort Sumter, but so far we hadn't determined a strategic reason to do so.

Tom and Hampton led the group out the back door of the last building and were cutting a hole in the chainlink fence before the rest of us caught up. They held back the wire for everyone to go through, and we made our way to the docks in a hurry.

It was as bad close up as it was from a distance. The remains of clothing and bones in the boats told the whole story. Fire had melted the entrance to the main dock, and it was obvious that no one had escaped from the campus by boat. To make matters worse, people had tried to escape to Fort Johnson as others tried to leave it behind.

There was a row of buildings on each of the two docks. Kathy found a door on the dock on the left that was unlocked and led to a single room. There were visible sight lines in all directions, so we wouldn't be trapped if the infected discovered where we had gone. It was an excellent place for us to have a group discussion about our next moves, and we were in desperate need of a plan.

Once we were all inside, we took up positions at the windows to keep watch while we focused on what to do next. Hampton led off the discussion by stating the obvious. It didn't appear that the kids had come to the college campus, possibly because they knew how easily they would have become bogged down. That would have given a search party the chance to gain ground on them.

We still didn't believe the kids could have gotten off of James Island before we set up a blockade, so Tom set up a radio and checked in with the helicopter that had flown ahead. The crew answered immediately and confirmed that the infected population was high across the island, so travel would have been slow. If they had gotten out of the area, it wasn't by any of the main roads.

The Chief turned over a large table that had been flipped over and used as a barricade over a broken window. He spread out his map of James Island and began marking key points.

"Where are we?" I asked.

The Chief drew a circle around the dock.

"We're here, and this is where we landed the Sikorsky. We used this road to reach the building we cleared. This is where the search crew in chopper three is waiting, and here's where we left number two."

He located the place where the kids were likely to have come ashore and then stood back from the map.

"What am I missing?" he asked the group.

Cassandra had the most combat experience other than the Chief. She leaned in and put a finger on the map where the marshes met with the trees.

"If this was a combat mission instead of search and rescue, I would be worried about this flank. It's totally uncovered. Can we get chopper two to give us a flyover as soon as they're done checking that little island?"

"They should be done by now," said the Chief. "Somebody get them on the radio and tell them where we need a quick look."

Jean had taken over at the radio while Tom joined the Chief at the map, so she hailed chopper two. It only took a few seconds for her to get confirmation from them that they were airborne and proceeding to the coordinates Cassandra had given her.

The report came back almost immediately.

"Chopper two says this area is flooded with the infected, and they want to know if we need to be extracted," said Jean.

The Chief thought about it for a moment before he shook his head.

"Too many of us to extract without drawing them all into the area. The parking lot outside is the only place to land, so we can either have Captain Miller send the Cormorant to get us, or we can go out of here on foot."

Tom was objecting before the Chief could even finish.

"That would take too long. It would also be like starting over."

Kathy was running her finger along the beach to the east of Fort Johnson, and then she followed a curve along a tidal creek. She didn't stop until she had traced a line from the college campus all the way to a heavily forested area that also had inlets that surrounded it.

"Do you see this big shadow inside the trees?" she asked all of us. "It has to be a house, and these inlets don't look like they dry up at low tide. If we stay along the marshes, we would be able to retreat if it gets too bad. The choppers could pick us up on the mudflats. Once we reach the house, it looks like we can double back to our chopper without running into that big horde."

"You think the house stays surrounded by water all the time?" asked Colleen.

I added, "A smaller version of our moat at Mud Island."

"There's a driveway coming out of the trees way over here to the west," said the Chief. "It has to be the only way to get to the house without crossing the water, but it's too far away. We'd lose too much time."

"Then we have to cross the water," said Tom. "We've already lost a lot of time by searching this area."

Everyone knew Tom was worried about Molly. She was all he had left from his life before the infection killed most of the world population, but there was also an accusation in between the lines. He felt like it was someone's fault that they searched an area where Molly and Sam didn't go.

The unspoken blame hung in the air between Tom and the Chief, and I couldn't remember ever seeing the Chief's eyes with that level of smoldering anger.

"You need to get something off your chest?" he said.

Tom was about to say something when Kathy took a chance and put one hand on his arm.

"Tom, it was my idea to search the campus first. If we had passed up the chance to check it, and they were trapped here, we would never have forgiven ourselves. Besides, that's the Chief you're talking to. You know how much he cares about Molly and Sam."

It wasn't easy for Tom to let it go, but we could all see he was embarrassed for making it sound like the Chief was somehow at fault for their delays. As for the Chief, a vein had popped out on the side of his forehead, and I could literally see it disappear. I told myself to remember that vein.

Tom opened his mouth to say something to the Chief, but the Chief stopped him.

"Let it go, Tom. We don't need to waste more time rehashing the obvious. They weren't here, but at least we have the satisfaction of knowing they didn't get trapped in the campus buildings. They wouldn't have survived a single night."

"I just wanted to apologize."

"Apology accepted. Now, let's move out and work our way around to that spot that looks like it might be a house. If they made it to there, then we're likely to find out they're safe."

Getting to the trees that lined the edge of the marshes and mudflats was harder than it looked on the map. Almost immediately we ran into a swarm of the infected that had followed us to the docks, and we were forced to use our handguns to break through.

The good news was that we would be doing an end run. The infected would be drawn to the place where the gunshots made noise, and we would be crossing behind the infected as they converged on the docks. Plus, our combined firepower was undeniably effective.

As soon as we cleared a big gap in the advancing crowd, we began running back toward the Ashley River. We reached the place where the trees met with the water and ran across the wet sand to get to the other side of the trees. As far as we could tell our plan was working because the infected we could see in the trees were still heading in the wrong direction.

The tide was out, so we were able to jump across the tidal creeks and run along the sand at the base of a steep bank. The footing was firm close to the bank, but it made all of us nervous to be directly below the tree line. It wasn't hard to imagine what it would be like if the infected fell from the woods above us.

"Hold up."

Jean didn't really have to yell it, and she was just as worried about the infected dropping in from above as everyone else, but she had to get us to stop. She had tripped over something that made her look down. She gave an evil eye to the driftwood that she had stumbled over, but there was something next to it that was familiar. She picked it up from the sand and held it out where the others could see it.

Everyone recognized the sterling silver chain that Molly had worn as a reminder of her mother. Allison had given it to her when they had been reunited at Mud Island. It had a little trinket hanging from it that was nothing more than a souvenir from the state park at Guntersville, Alabama, but it had meant the world to Molly.

We all looked up at the bank a few feet above our heads and wondered if Molly had passed by above, or if she had run along the same bank that we were using. At least we felt closer to Molly for the first time since we arrived at Fort Johnson.

Sim had been quiet since they left the helicopter. Even after five years, he was still trying to get used to this group of crazy survivors. His perception of us was that we weren't afraid of anything. Ever since we had shown up at the President's shelter in Columbus, Ohio, he had marveled at our determination. This time it was one of our own we were searching for, and our level of determination was well beyond what he had seen before. He felt safe with us, but at the same time he felt like we could be dangerous.

"We should slow down our approach," he said.

Tom became visibly rigid from head to toe, and Sim was sure he would be shot if he said another word. The Chief stepped between them, but his eyes were fixed on Sim. Kathy got close to Tom's face to make him get good eye contact.

"We're close," said the Chief, "and you want us to slow down?"

Sim had been the navigator of Executive One, so he wasn't stupid. He knew that most of us were ready to charge the rest of the way to the house that was hidden by the trees up ahead. He also knew that the next thing out of his mouth had to be something that made instant and perfect sense to all of us.

"What's your plan, Chief? Are we going to assault the place like a SWAT team?"

The Chief had a plan for everything, but the plan for finding Molly was to search quickly so she wouldn't get too far ahead of us. That plan hadn't worked out so well because we had lost a lot of time in the college buildings.

"Maybe I shouldn't say we should slow down," Sim added. "Maybe I could have said it better, but if the kids are close by, we don't need to sound a bugle charge. That could make them run, and this isn't a good place for them to run."

Tom surprised everyone. All of us thought the Chief would be the one to agree with Sim first, but Tom beat him to it.

"Thanks, Sim. It took a lot of nerve for you to stop me, and you're right. If they blindly run from us, they're going to run right into the infected."

Everyone breathed easier. The Chief grabbed a stick and drew a map in the sand that included the house and their approximate position. As soon as he did it they saw Sim had been right. If they had continued on their present path, they would have found themselves stopped short by the tidal creek. They could see a dock in the distance that was likely to be the same dock that was attached to the house where they were going. The only way to get there was by boat or to go up into the trees above them.

"But they needed a boat," said Jean. "We know Molly was here because of the necklace, so they didn't go through the trees. That means they must've gotten a boat from somewhere."

"Maybe they weren't alone," said Colleen.

That should have been reassuring, but it wasn't. Everyone looked like they were immediately on guard. There was something ominous about the necklace being at the bottom of the steep bank, and it wasn't likely that it just fell off her neck. Our intuition told us that something had happened here that made it fall off. Something violent.

"Okay, we don't have a boat," said the Chief, "and even if we did, I wouldn't want to be out in a tidal creek approaching the dock. I don't like being that exposed, and we all know how these tidal creeks can be. One moment you're alone, and the next moment something has a grip on your ankles. We have to double back."

"What about the water that surrounds the house?" asked Hampton. "Can we cross it?"

"It doesn't look deep on maps and the photos we have," said Kathy. "If it turns out to be too deep to cross, we can always keep going until we reach the road that goes straight to the house."

There was a rumble in the distance that signaled the arrival of a storm. It was going to be typical for this area with the usual lightning and heavy raindrops.

"The sound of the storm will give us a little cover," said the Chief, "but remember it will do the same for the infected. No talking and stay in formation. We don't need to get bunched up against a horde, so we'll move single file until we reach the house. The bank will be to our left the entire time. If we get swarmed, everyone go over the bank. No one stays behind, and we'll take our chances with the creeks."

We didn't have to double back as far as we had expected because there was a place where we could use tree roots to climb the steep bank. Cassandra, Tom, and Hampton went up first and set up a perimeter for the rest of us to join them. When we were all ready, the column started for the house. The rain got as heavy as we expected, and soon the only sound in the trees was the downpour. Talking wouldn't have done us any good because we would have been forced to shout.

The house was only about two hundred yards away, and we only had to slow down twice when we saw a dozen or so of the infected trying to walk through the dense brush. While we lifted our feet to go over logs, branches, and vines, they tended to trip and fall every few feet. Even if they had spotted us, we would have been able to out distance them without jumping over the bank again.

We eventually came to a spot where the tidal creek wrapped around a small, muddy island. The walls of the house blended into the trees and blocked out the light. We could make out its shape long before we could see details, but we could see why it would have been a safe refuge if resources were used wisely. The house sat on a base of broad tree trunks that acted as stilts. Stilts were common along the rows of beach houses, but they were almost always man-made. These trunks were either trees that had been cut to the present length or had been pushed into the marsh like pilings. The seemingly random pattern of the trees suggested both methods had been used for maximum support.

The end result was a house that would survive a flood during a really high tide or hurricane, and was also impossible for the infected to reach. The tidal creek was deep around the house, but it obviously flooded under the house at high tide. Any infected that managed to get under the house probably became food for the thousands of blue crabs that would swarm onto the banks at low tide.

We followed the bank of the tidal creek, circling the house and watching for a place to cross. It became obvious that we weren't going to find a place and would come to the road sooner or later. We were surprised when we finally reached the road and came to a crude drawbridge. It was in the down position.

Kathy said, "That's not good. If the bridge had been up, it would mean someone was still home. Being down might mean someone has already left."

"And doesn't plan to come back," added Jean.

Cassandra took the lead again. She had a keen eye for traps because of her time fighting in Afghanistan. She had told us once that there were so many IED's over there that there had to be less infected dead. Hordes would be tripping over every improvised explosive device in the country. We all took it more or less as a joke, but there was a certain amount of ironic sense to it.

After Cassandra pronounced the bridge safe, we all crossed and then took a few minutes to raise the bridge.

There wasn't any sense in allowing unwanted company onto the little island while we were visiting.

We picked up our pace a little, reasoning that keeping to the center of the single lane gravel road was likely to be safe. The rain had stopped, so the only sound was our boots crunching into the gravel as we ran.

The big house came into view, more exposed from our side than from the others. A steep set of wooden steps came right down to the road. The bottom had been fortified by a steel gate that had probably been in place before the infection had begun. Someone valued their privacy when they built this home.

There had been no signs of the infected since we crossed the bridge, and we had a nagging feeling that the bridge hadn't been open very long. That quite possibly meant someone had left only a short time ago. We had to know if anyone was at the house, though.

The Chief signaled for everyone to spread out and wait while he took the radio from Jean's backpack. He called chopper two and told them to locate the road that led to the house and follow it in the other direction.

While we waited for chopper two to report back, the Chief spread out his map again.

"The good news is that we have almost made it back to the Sikorsky. It's not far from here to the north."

"The bad news?" I asked.

"The woods are too thick. We would be better off using the road to get back. We'll check out the house as soon as we get a report."

Chopper two didn't take long. The gravel road looked like it had been traveled by a piece of heavy equipment, but there was nothing moving on it now. The Chief asked them if it was visible anywhere along Fort Johnson Road, and chopper two replied that there was a backhoe parked just inside a cemetery gate. It looked to be about the size of the tire tracks on the gravel road.

"Okay, folks. Let's check out this place and then head for that cemetery."

As everyone started for the steel gate, the Chief radioed chopper two and instructed them to land and see if the engine was still warm on the backhoe. The answer came back before they were halfway up the steps, and it only added to their sense of urgency. It was still warm.

"Change of plans," yelled the Chief. His lack of concern for stealth didn't go unnoticed by anyone.

"Two teams. Sim, Jean, Hampton, and Colleen are with me. The rest of you search the house fast and then wait for me to pick you up where the road is in the open so I have a clear landing zone."

"You don't expect to find anything here, do you?"

Tom wasn't showing fear when he asked the question. It was more like dread.

"I think they were here, but we missed them. If they are here, it would be best if you were the one to find them. Move fast, and they won't be too far ahead of us. If nothing else, they might have left us a clue."

The two groups split quickly, one sprinting up the stairs and one sprinting down.

******

There was a wide porch on the house that wrapped around all four sides. As was the case where most small groups managed to survive, the place had probably kept the original occupants alive for only a short period of time.

139

Until people caught on and stopped trying to save their loved ones after they had been bitten, most survivors died from within their sanctuaries. When survivors began culling the bitten from their groups and doing formal inspections, places like this became safer and took in new occupants. The question now was whether or not the occupants were still here, and did Molly and Sam stay here with them.

The remaining members of the group reached the top of the stairs and chose to go in through the front door rather than to look for another place to enter from the wraparound porch. Speed had become more important than caution.

The first floor layout was designed to show off the size of the house, so we could see the living room, kitchen, and dining room all at once.

The only doors turned out to be a small bathroom and a pantry. The pantry still had food on the shelves, so we knew that someone had left in a hurry. It also gave us some idea about whether or not the kids were alone. It was looking more and more like they had hooked up with another group.

I took the stairs to the second floor two at a time. Cassandra was right behind me, and Tom was on her heels. There was a balcony overlooking the living room and a hallway beyond the balcony. I crossed the opening and only took a glance down the hallway. Before I could even get in position on the other side, Cassandra had her handgun aimed around the corner toward a series of doors.

"Go," she said to Tom.

Tom almost jumped over Cassandra getting to the first door. His foot flew up and connected with the door, and it shattered. Two infected dead were just inside the door, and Tom collided with them both. They went flying across the room and landed in a pile on the bed. Tom managed to keep from falling with them and placed well timed shots into their heads.

Cassandra said, "I didn't expect infected, did you?"

I looked past her into the room. "Maybe we should open the next two a little more carefully."

This time we did it by the book. With two of us in place to the sides of the doors, Tom kicked in the next door. Cassandra and I each shot one infected dead.

"What are the odds of two in each room, and what do you want to bet there are two in the last room?" I asked.

We weren't surprised when Tom kicked in the third door and two infected tried to come out. Each of the rooms were furnished, so we quickly searched for clues. One of the closets had a lot of mud on the floor. That could mean anything, but the mud was fairly fresh. There was at least the possibility that someone had been held prisoner inside the closet.

No other clues were found in the bedrooms, but there was a crude drawing on the mirror in the bathroom located in the master bedroom. It was a drawing of several large trees with thick trunks. In between the trees there were stick figures of people with wings, and above the trees in big, bold letters was the word "PLEASANT". Spaced between the trees there were four crosses.

Bus had been feeling like he was just along for the ride because everybody was moving so fast. He was still in good shape, but he was the oldest member of our group, and the pace was wearing him down. His real value to our group was the fact that he was an outstanding doctor. If someone needed emergency treatment, we all wanted a good doctor, whether he was athletic or not.

"What do you think that means?" I asked.

"Angels," said Tom. "Those must be angels. Do you think it has something to do with that tourist attraction with the big oak tree? Isn't it called Angel Oak?"

"Yeah, but the word above the trees means something," I said.

Bus was rubbing the stubble on his chin when he asked, "What's the name of that cemetery where chopper two said they saw the backhoe?"

Even before we got confirmation back from chopper two, we knew they would say the cemetery was named Pleasant Oaks, and our biggest fear was not knowing why the clue had been left for us. The question on all of our minds was what would we find at a cemetery except graves, and did four crosses mean something. If it had been two crosses, we would have felt more dread, if that was possible.

We ran outside onto the wide porch of the house and started trying to get the Chief on the radio, but there was no response. Tom was frantically yelling into the radio for the Chief to get the helicopter back to the house as fast as he could. Then he raised chopper two and told the pilot to land at the cemetery and have the men begin looking for graves that had fresh dirt piled on top as if they had been recently filled.

The Sikorsky wasn't coming in over the treetops yet, and as much as we hoped the Chief would arrive soon, we couldn't help but try to get to the cemetery in time, so we ran down the road. In time for what, we didn't know, but the unspoken fear was that we would find new graves at the cemetery. Graves that belonged to Molly and Sam.

9 A NEW LIFE

Year One of the Decline

The first year was what Maybank called his year to worry. For some reason he felt like that was when something would go wrong, and he was sure he would survive if he made it a full year. He was having plenty of doubts by the end of the third day.

Boats had him on edge. Every time he saw another on the horizon, he worried that it was coming to his oil rig. Every time they continued in his direction, he was convinced they were going to attack. By the time the tenth boat sped past without slowing down, he was a nervous wreck, and that was only the third day after the world fell apart.

The news broadcasts continued, and he was grateful for those satellites that kept sending their signals back to an ever diminishing audience, but what he saw was not what the survivors club had expected. Even though it was on their list of catastrophes, none of them thought it was a real possibility. As a matter of fact, they only added it last because they felt like everything before it on the list was possible. They tried to explain to the military why they believed an alien invasion was possible, and a zombie apocalypse was not. The problem was that their sponsors had totally bought into their shelter project, and if it was on the list, they believed it could happen.

There was no shortage of experts who gave explanations for what was happening, but none of them satisfied Maybank. He could believe it was an infection, and he could believe it made people sick enough to eat people, but he couldn't understand how an infection could reanimate dead people.

His interior communications phone rang, and despite his ragged nerves, he didn't even flinch. That was when he realized he was too tired to react because he hadn't slept since it all started. He felt far too old to be losing sleep. Answering the phone just seemed like the right thing to do.

"Hello?"

He absently wondered if he had really spoken or if he had just thought the word.

"I'm surprised you answered, old man. Are you going to let me in?"

"No, but you're welcome to stay in the crew's quarters as long as you want. I'll even resupply you."

The phone disconnected, and Maybank wondered for a second time if there was something wrong with his mind. He saw the answer to the question in the monitor that showed the crew's quarters from the outside.

The door into the crew's quarters was very similar to a mobile home. The only difference was that it was elevated high above the Wellbay module, and when someone would walk out through the front door onto a small platform, they had a spectacular view of the Gulf of Mexico. When the rig was under construction, the quarters provided housing for the Army engineers, and it wasn't unusual to see them standing on that platform at the railings before they started work each day.

Today it was the view of the platform that was spectacular because so much blood had been sprayed on the door. In the morning sunshine it appeared to be even more red than it was, and the two men wrestling on the top of the steps rolled under the bottom rail, bounced against several levels of pipes, and dropped out of sight into the ocean below.

Maybank had something on the tip of his tongue that he was about to tell the man before the phone had disconnected. He was going to tell him that he could only stay if he disposed of the man who had been bitten. The man was dangerous and would attack him sooner or later.

He tried to remember what he was going to say but decided that it didn't matter anymore, so he pushed himself up from the bank of monitors and staggered away in the general direction of the stairs. He hated the idea that his quarters were on another level, but at least it was down and not up.

******

The big yacht showed up next. It was easy to spot when it crossed the horizon because of its size. Maybank had gotten a few hours of much needed sleep and was watching on a monitor, so he was scrolling through websites with boats on them and feeling more alert. In his mind that meant he was able to remember what he was doing from one moment to the next. He was more interested in how many people would be on a boat than he was the boat itself. The beast that was cruising toward his oil rig had three decks and was one hundred and thirty feet long.

Unlike the others he had seen, this one didn't pass by on its way to somewhere in South America. News reports from Venezuela were as bleak as anywhere else, so it didn't make sense to go there. Maybank concluded that there were plenty of small islands and secluded places that were fortified in South America, and the people with money were at least smart enough to get out of the Gulf Coast cities.

This one came straight at his oil rig and left little doubt that it planned to dock. It began to slow as it approached, and it circled to the Process tower. Whoever was navigating the yacht knew the layout, and even more surprisingly, who was on the oil rig.

"Maybank oil rig, this is Lady Blue out of New Orleans requesting to board, over."

The message came through on one of his standard ship to shore radios rather than his computer network. At least he wouldn't have to look at them on a video camera, and better yet, they wouldn't see him. He looked like something the cat dragged in. He made a mental note to work on that.

"Lady Blue, please state your purpose to board, over."

"Ah, Mr. Maybank, it's so good of you to answer."

The man had a South American accent and sounded very charming.

"We were afraid you would close your doors to us. If you don't mind, it has been a difficult few days. We can talk after we board, over."

Maybank didn't particularly care for assertive people, and this guy sounded like he had written the book on assertive behavior.

"Lady Blue, I didn't catch your response regarding your purpose to board, over."

The man on the other end of the transmission must not have been used to saying the magic word, and it really had been a harrowing few days because his fuse was really short.

"Listen, we need shelter, and I understand you have supplies. There wasn't exactly much time to order food and water for a trip. We were lucky we already had fuel. Are you going to let us board or not, over?"

"Lady Blue, supplies are limited. How much food and water do you need, over?"

The truth was that there were enough supplies for at least one hundred people to last over forty years, but those supplies were in the shelter. Topside, in the oil rig levels there were caches of supplies that were meant for other survivors, and if he knew the needs of this yacht, he could give them access to the correct cache. The crew quarters above the Wellbay were to be resupplied from those caches.

"I didn't ask you how much you can spare. Do you have any idea who you are speaking to?"

All pretense of courtesy was dropped. Before Maybank could say anything else that would further irritate the man, he elaborated on his last transmission.

"This is Hector Dominguez, and as of today I am declaring the territorial waters of Venezuela are extended to include these coordinates. This oil rig and its contents are now the property of the sovereign nation of Venezuela, and you will turn it over to me immediately, over."

"Lady Blue, permission to come aboard is denied."

"Less than four full days into an apocalypse, and someone is already trying to take away my shelter," he said out loud. "And the winner is, Hector."

He did the sound of a fake crowd cheering and waved his arms over his head. Then he did an imitation of Hector blowing kisses to his adoring crowd.

"Did you say denied?"

There was a sound that reminded him of hail at first. When he turned up the speaker he could tell it was automatic weapons, but he wondered what in the world they could be shooting at. The monitors showed several men shooting upward, and the funny part was when they hit one of the additions that was reinforced with the special metal used to make the towers and the shelter. Bullets bounced off of it and began flying in all directions, including theirs.

They were too busy diving for cover to realize the bullets hitting their boat were ricochets. From different decks Maybank could see heads cautiously peering around corners as the gunmen searched for the imaginary shooters on the oil rig. They uncertainly waited for new orders from their boss. When Hector finally decided to see if an olive branch would work, he was less charming, but he was more sincere. Still, people like him had a hard time losing face in front of their minions.

"Mr. Maybank, perhaps we have gotten off on the wrong foot. I was less than polite because we have injured people on board."

Before Hector had a chance to end his transmission, Maybank cut him off.

"What are their injuries, and how many are there, over?"

The pause was longer than he expected, and Maybank began to suspect they were weighing other options. By now they must have realized there was no way for them to climb on board unless they were carrying a powerful launcher used to shoot lines across between ships at sea.

He got his answer when he checked a camera angle that showed the stern of the lowest deck. They were setting up a launcher and preparing to send a line up to the spider web of catwalks and railings above them. He shook his head and keyed the radio.

"Lady Blue, you don't need to do that if you cooperate."

The launcher sent the line over the rails, and they fed out the line as quickly as they could. The idea was to shoot a light but durable line over the target and then retrieve the end of it. They would then tie a heavy rope to it and reel in the lighter line until they had the rope replacing it. Then they could climb up.

"Well, if you'd rather do it the hard way," he said without using the radio.

As big as the yacht was, it easily passed through the opening between the huge towers, but it was drafting too deep to pass over the top of the submerged shelter. When it was designed, he decided it would be better to have it close to the surface so he wouldn't have to bother with decompression. The shell protecting the shelter was more durable than the hull of the ship, but the scraping noise still bothered Maybank.

The cabin crew of the Lady Blue reversed their engines and pulled away from the rig, undoubtedly yelling at the sonar and radar operator to watch his depth finder. This left them short of their goal, which was the other end of the line they had launched over the railings.

Despite misgivings about being shot from above by the imaginary people on the oil rig, they launched their life raft to retrieve the line. Maybank saw there was a guy in the bow of the raft who was swiveling around with an AK-47 trying to spot a target.

The raft only had to go about fifty yards, and it didn't draft deep enough to reach the shelter, but just as they were stretching with a pole hook for the line, the raft lurched to a stop. Everyone fell over on top of each other. It resembled a tag team wrestling match with everyone in the ring at the same time.

Hector Dominguez was watching his men as they progressed toward their target, and all he could tell was that something had gone wrong. A camera high above was telling Maybank what was happening in better detail, but even he didn't understand at first. The raft shook from side to side on top of the water and seemed to rotate under its own power. Then the bow dipped and popped back up into the air. The men in the raft were jumping away from the middle of the raft as if something had gotten in with them, but just as quickly they got down from the sides of the raft.

With all the shaking and jumping around, it wasn't long before the man with the AK-47 went over the side. He went in backward the way SCUBA divers do when they leave a boat, but his dive wasn't planned.

He screamed as he hit the water, and a slick of red blood surrounded the raft. The change in color added a contrast against which Hector could see the arms and legs that were already in the water, and he knew they didn't belong to his men.

Maybank could see the outline of the shelter through the blue water, but just before the man with the rifle fell in, Maybank saw something walk toward him in slow motion with outstretched arms. Another figure was on the other side of the raft, and it was reaching as high as it could.

The man who had been steering the raft began beating furiously at a pair of hands that had gripped the material of his loose fitting shirt. It was probably the first time he ever wished denim wasn't too strong to tear. The other two men didn't know if they should be helping him or going for the line that dangled only a few feet away.

Hector was yelling instructions from the yacht, but his voice was drowned out by the AK-47 that had started firing wildly in all directions from under the raft. Bullets shredded the raft and ran in a straight line up the back of the man in the denim shirt. The impact threw him overboard, and the change in the weight caused the other side of the raft to tilt the other way just as one of the men managed to catch the line in a firm grip. He swung out away from the raft and pulled his feet as high above the water as he could.

The remaining man in the shredded raft fell inward, and just as his friend hanging on the line thought the guy had been lucky, there was a second burst of bullets that found the spot where he had fallen.

Hector continued to yell, the man on the end of the line was crying, and there was splashing under the raft. Gradually the only sound was the crying, and it faded away as the man skillfully climbed the durable line. It was either a skill or survival instinct. Either way, he gradually made it to the top and pulled himself over the bottom railing of a catwalk where he collapsed in a sobbing heap.

Hector was yelling instructions again. Maybank could hear him, but it was in Spanish, and he didn't understand. The man on the catwalk thought he was yelling at him, so he peered over the edge. Over eighty feet below him, he saw the man in the raft trying to stand up, but there was no solid footing, and he fell backward over the side. The raft kept shaking back and forth until it finally lost enough air to be pulled under. Bubbles popped to the surface, and between bursts of bubbles, hands extended upward as if they were floating and reaching.

Up above, the lone survivor had recovered enough to remember why he had gone up the rope in the first place. He was signaling wildly to feed him the line so he could pull the heavier rope over the catwalk. Thirty minutes later, he had enough rope to secure it in place, and two more crewmen made the climb with additional ropes. Now anyone who made the climb had a safety line attached to them in case they fell.

Maybank watched with morbid fascination as the shadows continued to move around on top of the shelter, but now there were five of them. From time to time the shadows would stop where they were and a pair of hands would appear above the water. One of the shadows had moved very close to the edge of the shelter, and when it reached for the surface, it took one step closer to the edge and quickly slipped away into deeper water. He could see that the men up on the catwalk had also been watching, and they knew from that day forward not to ever trust water they couldn't see through.

He could have told them about the chain ladders stored in lockers around the oil rig, but if he was going to do that, he might as well have extended the rungs from the side of the tower. Hector didn't seem like the kind of person who played well with others, so Maybank decided they were on their own outside. They could stay as long as they wanted.

He knew that Hector was also not going to be satisfied with the supplies in the crew's quarters. He would have his men beat on the steel doors of Maybank's former apartment with everything they could find, and if they did manage to get inside, there wasn't much for them to live on. They could watch TV for a bit, but Maybank wouldn't want them getting too comfortable, so he would turn off the power to that section.

Maybank remembered there was one thing he needed to do before the Internet went completely dark. He switched from the internal monitors to his search engine and looked up his neighbors on the yacht.

He was right about Hector. There were several indictments but no convictions. Most of them were felony assault charges, but his main source of income was drug trafficking. Maybank mentally reminded himself to continue trusting his gut when the time came that he couldn't look someone up.

One of the men outside had found the chain ladders and lowered two over the side. Armed men were climbing each of them, and Maybank was trying to make a decision. Judging by the number of weapons he could see, Hector had his priorities set on survival at the cost of others. There were going to be plenty of decent people who would approach the oil rig, and Hector was going to treat it like his own private kingdom. He would undoubtedly take their supplies and then kill them.

The decision wasn't reached lightly, but it was only the fourth day, and that army was going to be living off of his outside supplies until they were gone. So, there was only one choice Maybank could make. He counted the number of people already spreading out on the catwalks and the ones who were on the chain metal ladders. Two dozen in five minutes.

Maybank's left hand popped the cover up over a switch, and he didn't hesitate. The switch clicked and isolated a large section of the catwalks from the rest of the maze. No sense in doing damage where he didn't need to.

He couldn't hear the hum that grew in the metal outside, and he knew it was being drowned out by the screams as two dozen armed men were hit with enough voltage to drop an elephant. Everyone was trying to let go of whatever they were holding, but the shock from high voltage was causing their muscles to contract and grip the metal harder. They began falling from the ladders and catwalks into the water. If they were alive when they went in, they were unconscious as they drowned.

Several landed above the shelter, and Maybank saw the shadows under the water converging on the bodies as they sank. Those men were lucky to be unconscious as the water around them turned red.

Hector was on the upper deck of the yacht doing his own screaming. Maybank could see exactly what kind of person he was as he barked orders at his crew. It appeared that he was telling them to help one of his men who had fallen from a ladder back onto the yacht. In reality, he wanted the body off of his deck and was shouting instructions to toss the man overboard.

"Nice guy and boss of the year," said Maybank.

When they were all dead, Maybank switched off the power. Most had fallen into the water or back onto the boat, but several were still sprawled out on the catwalks. He didn't see them at first, but three of them had already started to twitch, and after that they were trying to get up.

Maybank had seen enough on the news broadcasts to know that there was no way to predict how long someone would stay dead, but these guys were coming back fast.

"This is as good a time as any to test a theory," he said to himself.

He threw the power switch on for a second time. There were sparks from the bodies that were still prone on the catwalks, but the dead people who were stumbling around didn't seem to care about the voltage in the metal. Smoke was coming from inside the shoes of one man, and Maybank saw the flicker of flame as it ignited the pants.

The man made no effort to put out the fire, and it didn't seem like he even knew his pants were about to turn him into a walking torch. The flames were licking at his left knee, and the fire on his right leg was catching up quickly.

It wasn't out of a desire to escape the flames. It was simply the availability of an opening in the railing. The man took three steps, and the third one was thin air directly above the yacht. He rotated once before hitting head first right where Hector had been standing. Hector was mad enough to kick the man twice before he realized the smoking, ruined body wasn't recoiling from the kicks. It was trying to grab his foot, and as it grabbed, it also snapped its teeth at him.

Hector stopped kicking and stepped back farther than he meant to. He was staring down at the thing with so much shock and disgust that he backed over the safety rail.

His crew still on the yacht rushed to his rescue as he came within inches of going over the rail again one deck lower. They grabbed him by his clothes and put him back on his feet.

There was a loud popping sound as the other bodies ignited. Several were in the process of standing up, but all of them burned right where they were. Maybank's theory had been that he could kill the zombies with electricity, and he was satisfied with the results until he saw the charred remains were still moving. He didn't know if it was still alive or not, but neither the electricity or the fire had stopped it from moving.

The ammunition blew up next. The armed men were all carrying plenty of ammunition, and as they burned the rounds in their pockets loudly erupted in every possible direction. Hundreds of bullets went into the bodies of the burning men, and just as many rounds flew downward and riddled the luxury craft below. Several of the men who had stopped Hector from going overboard were shredded where they stood.

Hector didn't know which way to go, but he finally figured out the oil rig was a bad idea. He shouted obscenities and shook his fist at the oil rig as if he knew exactly where Maybank was standing. There's no way he could have known that Maybank was below him. Between obscenities he shouted orders to his helm crew, and the boat quickly pulled away.

Someone came out onto the deck of the boat as the distance increased, but Maybank could see that the person was a woman. She swayed from side to side and fell over when the boat rolled to the left for too long. Several people rushed to help her, and to Maybank it resembled a fight on the ice at a hockey game.

The last Maybank saw of the people out on the deck, the woman was on Hector's back as he tried to crawl away from her. There were others pulling at her arms, but her face was buried into the back of Hector's neck.

Maybank turned his attention to the ammunition cook-off out on the catwalks. The rounds blowing up were a guarantee that the fires would keep burning long enough to incinerate the bodies, but he was curious about whether or not they were dead.

He didn't think there was anything that could get him to go out there and check, but he was seriously concerned when he saw one of them crawl under a rail and drop to the next catwalk. It resembled an over cooked roast with stumps for arms and legs, but the head swiveled to the left and right as teeth snapped blindly at the air.

A breeze kicked up and whistled through the metal jigsaw puzzle of pipes and catwalks, and the smoke swirled with clouds of ash and burning embers, but when it cleared Maybank could see that there were at least ten bodies that were still moving. None were recognizable as people, but they were moving.

Maybank decided there wasn't anything that had to be done about the bodies. The first good rain would wash away the piles of black ash, and there wasn't anything that could have been hit by a bullet that needed to be repaired.

From a distance the oil platform would just appear to be weather worn and dirty. The brief battle with Hector, who was most likely a drug lord judging by his armed guards, had done Maybank a small favor by keeping the rig from seeming to be too shiny and new. Hector didn't have a clue what he was dealing with when he decided to take over this oil rig. Of the one hundred and seventy-five rigs operating in the Gulf of Mexico, he had simply picked on the wrong one.

10 PLEASANT OAKS

Six Years After the Decline

The Chief's group heard the gunshots in the distance, and they knew Tom's group had at least encountered the infected. He couldn't imagine they would be shooting living people since there wasn't any return fire.

One thing the Mud Island survivors had learned a long time ago was that gunshots only worked against the living when it came to giving away their position. When they heard a shot in the woods, they couldn't always tell which direction it had come from, but for some strange reason the infected always seemed to know. If you wanted to draw a horde of infected away from somewhere, shoot off a round wherever you wanted them to go.

In this case, the Chief knew the group would draw the infected into the creek that surrounded the house in the woods, but there was bad news, too. The number of infected they were likely to encounter on their way back to the Sikorsky was likely to increase.

It had only taken them ten minutes to reach the intersection with Fort Johnson Road, but they ran into the first large group of infected as soon as they made the turn back toward the Department of Natural Resources boat parking area where they had landed.

Dozens of infected were already in the road, and more were trying to free themselves from the brush and trees lining the left side of the road. The first gunshots had started them moving into the trees along the right side, and some were already snagged on branches there.

"Too many for us to take on unless we move now," yelled the Chief. "Single file straight through the middle while they're spread out."

The Chief led the way using his machete, but he pulled his Glock from his holster and had it ready with his left hand if the horde closed in on them too quickly. Some of the infected he simply pushed hard enough to make them fall into the others of their kind, and a wide hole appeared for the group to follow him through.

When there were only stragglers in front of him, he turned around and made sure everyone got through okay. Jean was covering them at the back, and the Chief could see the path was closing on her. He stepped back into the fight and cleared a hole for her while Hampton and Sim took his place up front.

From that point on it was a footrace with the infected. They could outrun any of them, but it was constant weaving and dodging until the entrance of the parking lot came up on their left. They only bothered to waste precious time on the infected that were too close to avoid, and many of those were only slowed down. A quick backhand with a machete to the side of the knee was a very effective way to remove their ability to stand upright.

The Sikorsky was surrounded by the infected, no doubt because of the ticking sounds the engine made as it cooled. They had been gone long enough for it to be completely cool, but their landing had been noisy enough to empty the surrounding woods into the parking lot. The gunshots were drawing some away, but they would have to fight their way to the doors of the chopper.

Hesitation would only allow the infected time to close in on them from every direction, so the Chief moved ahead.

"Hampton and Sim, up here with me on my flanks, blades only. Jean and Colleen, guns to the sides and behind us. I don't want any stray bullets hitting our only ride out of here."

They formed up on the Chief and began cutting a swath through the parking lot. Much faster than they could believe possible they found themselves at the doors of the Sikorsky. All five of them began firing their pistols at close range and then further back into the crowd giving them plenty of time to open the doors and climb inside.

As the rotors began to pick up speed, the wind from the blades began knocking over the infected. The clearance was high enough to keep the rotors from hitting them, but they were hoping to see what Kathy had described to them after the Chief had used the Sikorsky like a weed-whacker at the Air Force Base.

The Chief could guess why they had their faces pressed so close to the windows.

"Sorry, folks, but the Army mechanics told me not to do that anymore. They said that the specs for the blades are good enough to withstand direct contact with a crowd without getting bent, but they wouldn't test the specs more than I already had."

They were disappointed, but smart enough to know they had survived by trusting the talents of everyone at Fort Sumter, and they were lucky to have mechanics to keep the choppers in the air.

The Chief lifted the Sikorsky from the ground while watching the crowd on the left side. He gently rocked the chopper to the left and pushed the infected away from that side, then he did the same on the right.

He answered the unspoken question from his group and said, "It wouldn't help us to find one or two of them hanging from the chopper when we lift off."

Sim and Jean let him know that he was all clear on both sides, and he eased forward while he banked away to the left. He quickly lined up with Fort Johnson Road and increased his forward speed, but almost immediately began to slow down. When everyone looked down to see why, they were surprised to see our group running at full speed down the middle of the road.

There were infected following us, but the road ahead was mostly clear. The Chief passed us and landed the helicopter neatly on the center line of the road.

Kathy had always been the Chief's right hand man in a fight, even though she was Tom's girl. She spoke for all of us and gave the Chief a quick summary of what we had found at the house. He was lifting the Sikorsky into the air as soon as she told him about the clue, the cemetery and the backhoe.

The urgency we had felt when we realized the significance of the clue was like a physical presence inside the helicopter. Even though it could cross James Island from Fort Johnson to Pleasant Oaks Cemetery in a matter of seconds, we were all filled with dread, and I had to admit there was a strong sense of pessimism. We didn't expect to find them alive. We were only hoping we would.

The cemetery came into view, and the Chief came in for a fast landing. It was a cemetery that didn't have headstones above ground. Bronze nameplates were arranged in neat rows, and the statue of one angel stood in the center. Chopper two was already on the ground, and the NCO in charge had radioed for chopper one to leave its position at a bridge on Harborview Road where it had been waiting in case the kids had tried to leave James Island by land. Nothing could have gotten by them at that spot.

Chopper one landed almost simultaneously with our helicopter, and the soldiers quickly spread out in a large circle to take up positions at a brick wall that surrounded the cemetery. It was high enough to stop the infected from coming over it, but the iron gates in two places were old and not likely to hold against a large horde.

The NCO from chopper two was waiting for Tom at one gravesite, and a soldier was already driving the backhoe toward him. We piled out of the Sikorsky and ran to join them.

Jean and Kathy were already crying. The thought that Molly could be buried under the fresh pile of dirt was more than they could bear.

The NCO yelled for us to be careful as we ran to him, and he pointed at something on the grave. When we were closer we saw he was pointing at something white that was sticking out of the ground. It looked like a PVC pipe about an inch in diameter.

"I think it's an air pipe," said the NCO. "If someone is buried down there, they may be alive if someone gave them a way to breathe."

The driver of the backhoe approached from the other end of the grave and carefully dropped the rear digging bucket into the soft dirt. He backed away and dragged a great scoop of dirt with him. He was good at what he was doing because the pipe remained where it was.

Tom hopped onto the pile of dirt and wrapped his hands tightly around the pipe. The next scoop could easily pull away the air supply. He nodded to the soldier, and the backhoe advanced on the grave again.

The big metal scoop came down dangerously close to Tom and pulled back for a second time. This time the jagged teeth of the bucket made a scraping sound as it slid across the outside of a coffin. The shiny surface of polished mahogany appeared as more dirt slid away.

We all began using our hands to scoop and throw the dirt as fast as we could while Tom held the air pipe in place. Tom started yelling across the open end of the pipe in hope that Molly could hear him.

"Molly, it's daddy. Hold on, baby. We're coming for you. You'll be out of there in just a minute."

We worked frantically, and gradually the entire casket appeared. It was just as the last of the dirt fell away from around the pipe that we saw something that made our hearts stop beating and our blood turn cold. The pipe ended at the casket. It didn't go through a hole in the wood and provide air to the inside.

We only paused for a few seconds, but it was long enough to hear a sound from inside the casket. Tom jumped out of the way, and we began prying at the lid over the upper half of the coffin. The lid flew open, and the Chief grabbed Tom from behind as he started to reach for the struggling teenager inside the coffin.

In his haste to rescue Molly, Tom had not even considered that it would be Sam, and when he saw Sam squirming around in the narrow confinement of the smothering coffin, it didn't even register in Tom's mind that Sam was not trying to get out. He was trying to bite Tom.

The crying that had briefly stopped while we dug away the dirt began again, but it wasn't just the women. Even the Chief had to turn away, and we could see his big shoulders shaking with grief as he fought back a tremendous sob.

There wasn't one of us that was strong enough to recover quickly from the sight of the young boy we had watched grow up under our protective watch. He had survived so long on his own, and this was a horrible way for him to die. We were all momentarily frozen in time, and no one moved with the realization that there was another grave somewhere.

It was the soldier on the backhoe who recognized the catatonic shock that had paralyzed us all. He revved the engine making it roar even louder, and when our heads turned his way, his shout rose above the sound of the engine.

"Where's the girl?"

We all turned to each other as if someone knew the answer to the question, and our heads began snapping left and right as our eyes searched the cemetery for another freshly filled grave.

From his vantage point in the seat of the backhoe, the driver could see better than we could, and he pointed excitedly toward the southern corner of the cemetery. He shifted the backhoe into gear and started driving it at high speed in the direction he had pointed.

We were right behind him as he lined up with the second grave and dropped the teeth of the scoop into place. This time he moved more quickly, and even though the air line had been a decoy on the first grave, Tom hadn't given up hope. He gripped the pipe as hard as he could, hoping beyond hope that it meant Molly was still breathing.

Before long we were shoveling with our hands for a second time, and the casket was quickly uncovered. This time when the bottom of the PVC pipe appeared, it went through a neat round hole that had been drilled through the wood.

We pried at the lid and flipped it open, and the sunlight outside shone down on the face of a pretty blond girl who started screaming and sobbing at the same time.

Our shock at finding someone we didn't know was only partially paralyzing because she wasn't trying to bite anyone, and she had started screaming for help. The infected didn't do that. We all reacted together and opened the rest of the coffin to allow her to be lifted to safety.

Doctor Bus moved in to take over while Kathy and Jean comforted the girl. The catatonic state that had held us all frozen in our tracks earlier didn't hit us this time as was obvious from the fact that each of us was standing in a circle around the grave and scanning the cemetery.

This time it was Hampton that burst into a sprint like a runner coming off of the starting blocks. We didn't need to see what he had seen. It was enough for us to follow him, and that's what we did. Behind us the backhoe was turning away from the second grave, and within seconds it was rumbling as it drove alongside us.

******

It was like a dream to Molly. A dream that she kept trying to wake up from but couldn't. It was dark, and she wasn't sure if her eyes were open, so she kept blinking them just to feel them move.

Sometimes she thought she could smell a change in the air, and sometimes there was a tiny pinprick of light above her, but it kept disappearing, replaced by darkness and a rank smell.

She was having a hard time breathing, and it didn't help when the smell got so bad that she threw up in the darkness.

165

That was when she hit her head hard against a ceiling that was only a couple of inches from her. She had grabbed at her stomach when she retched and tried to sit up as she doubled over to one side. Her vomit was sour, and the smell made her gag repeatedly.

Wherever she was, she knew it wasn't the closet anymore, and now there were two lumps on her head. One was on her forehead. That was the new one. The other was bigger, and it was on the back of her head. It hurt when she touched it, and her hand came away with something sticky on it. It had a smell like copper pennies.

Molly saw the pinprick of light for just a moment, and she got dizzy when she tried to focus her eyes on the spot where it had appeared. She didn't know if she was looking at the light, or if she was looking at the spot where the light shined off of her chest. She gave up after a moment and almost gratefully drifted off into unconsciousness. As she drifted away, not knowing that she was very close to running out of air, she thought she heard someone yelling something at her.

******

We weren't inclined to become experts at opening graves, but practice does make perfect, and the third grave opened even faster than the last one.

Kathy and Jean couldn't stand to be left behind as we dug Molly out of the ground, so they had enlisted the assistance of a couple of soldiers to help them and Bus carry the girl with them to the third grave. Since she was also a victim of the maniac who would bury kids this way, they wanted her nearby to answer questions as soon as Molly was found.

Uncovering the grave and finding the air pipe going into the casket for a second time lifted our spirits with hope, and once again the lid was pulled open.

We pulled ourselves back from the snapping jaws and clutching fingers of a young man we didn't know. He looked like he was in his early twenties.

Each of us felt the energy in us dry up. Adrenaline can give you plenty of strength when you need it, but afterward the price of that extra strength was the total opposite. Strength leaves you, and hope leaves you. All we could do was sit back and look at the young man, not really feeling anything.

The young girl from the last grave began to scream, and none of us was spared from the instant terror we all experienced. Those screams in these days and times always meant someone was dying or very close to it.

We all braced ourselves for the attack we were sure was coming, but all around us was nothing but the quiet cemetery. There was no infected horde charging down on us. No one was being bitten. Instead, the pretty girl with the dirt streaked face was on the ground and crawling toward the open grave.

"Gervais," she sobbed. "No, not Gervais."

We were tired. The entire day had taken its toll on us, so we were slow to understand that this young man had been the girl's friend. She was as heartbroken as we were when we found Sam, and as glad as we were to have rescued her, at the moment we would have gladly traded her for Molly. That's how mentally and physically exhausted we felt.

Bus moved in front of the crying girl and gently turned her away from the grave. We all felt guilty as the NCO stepped down into the grave and used a knife to end the existence of the infected who had been known to the girl as

Gervais. It was only then that we realized that in our rush to find Molly, we had left the NCO to do the same merciful act for Sam.

We turned one by one in the direction of the open grave where we had found Sam. It was silent around the mound of dirt.

Somehow we began to move. We stood one by one and surveyed the cemetery, but as hard as we strained our eyes, we couldn't spot a fourth grave. We began to turn to each other to verify that we had failed Molly.

The NCO radioed the soldiers along the walls, instructing the platoon sergeants to have their men join the search. One of the men took it upon himself to climb the brick wall that surrounded the cemetery. It was risky, but it gave him a much better view of the cemetery from above.

Below the soldier the infected began moaning louder and crowding against the wall. He could feel the vibrations in the wall, but he was sure it would hold. Around the perimeter of the cemetery more soldiers followed his example, and it wasn't long before an excited shout carried across the open ground.

We all looked in the direction of the shout with hope, but just as we had been confused when the first grave had been opened, we found ourselves questioning the sanity of the soldier who had shouted. He was pointing, just as we had expected he would be, but he wasn't pointing at a spot inside the cemetery. He was pointing outside.

The NCO with us radioed the squad leader by the man and asked him to verify that his man had spotted a grave. We waited, and saw the squad leader climb the wall to where his man was standing. He looked down at the open mouths and the arms waving in the air and carefully got his balance before turning his attention to the spot where the soldier pointed.

He raised binoculars to his eyes and focused them on a mound of freshly turned soil. If he had to guess, he would guess it was a grave, but this time there were infected dead walking over the soft dirt. One tripped and fell over what appeared to be a piece of white PVC protruding from the ground.

He raised his radio to his mouth and told the NCO it was affirmative.

This time we moved as an assault force. Three helicopters and almost fifty shooters escorting a backhoe. We had no illusions about attacking thousands of the infected and winning the war, but we didn't doubt we could hold them off long enough to rescue Molly if she was in that grave.

The grave was at least a hundred yards from the brick wall in the middle of a wide open field. Why there were so many infected was anyone's guess. The only thing that mattered was that they were here. Someone had managed to dig a grave and bury Molly out in the middle of the horde, and they could settle up with those people later.

The three helicopters lifted off together and drifted slowly toward the back gate of the cemetery. The backhoe drove toward the gate and waited as instructed for the gates to be opened.

When the helicopters cleared the wall, they hovered together and then slowly sat down in a triangular formation. The Sikorsky was in the center of the road, and the Navy helicopters were to the left and right but slightly behind. The rotor wash was tremendous, and the infected dead were blown around like tissue paper.

The soldiers on the wall opened the gates inward, and the backhoe raced forward. The cab was high enough to give some protection to the soldier driving it, but if he became swamped by the horde, it was possible he could be overturned. Since their arrival at the cemetery the horde had grown so fast that the wall around the cemetery was beginning to buckle.

The backhoe moved into position in the middle of the helicopter triangle, and the entire procession moved forward. Gunners on the Navy helicopters had a clear view of the backhoe and could shoot any infected that managed to stay on their feet. Their instructions were to shoot only the infected that were on the road and had a possibility of grabbing the backhoe, and then any infected that were able to follow behind the backhoe. They wanted it to reach the grave and go right to work.

When the road turned away from the gravesite, the Chief steered the Sikorsky off of the road. Its original path was parallel to the suspected grave, and they moved slowly only to draw as many of the infected dead away from the spot as they could. It was agonizingly slow to Tom, but he knew that getting Molly out of the grave safely wasn't going to be easy.

Twenty yards from the grave, the helicopters deployed their shooters, and they began targeting everything in their path. The Sikorsky continued past the grave and stopped a few yards beyond it. The backhoe came up from behind and started digging as Tom and the rest of his friends arrived to help. Two large scoops of dirt came out, and the metal bucket hit the casket.

Tom held the PVC pipe in place while everyone else dug away the dirt around it. We were all relieved when we saw that the pipe entered the casket through a hole. It hadn't helped Gervais to survive, but we had to hang onto our hopes.

Tom was pulling at the lid even before all of the dirt was removed. We all wanted him to be careful, but if his baby was inside, he was going to be anything but careful.

Molly was limp, and she was either unconscious or dead. Bus pushed his way into the hole with his stethoscope. As much as Tom wanted to just pull her out of the casket, Bus needed to know how bad it was going to be. We gave them both the room they needed, and Bus listened intently for a heartbeat.

He finally looked up and gave a half smile and a nod to all of us. He pulled Tom over to get close to his ear and said something we couldn't hear, but we could guess what he said because Tom gave him a big smile and then a hug.

One of the Army medics climbed into the hole with an oxygen bottle and a mask. Molly was most likely unconscious because she had come close to suffocating, so the mask was strapped in place. A stretcher was placed next to the coffin, and after a brace was put on her neck she was finally lifted free of her prison.

A quick inspection of her head and body revealed a nasty bruise on the back of her head that had bled for a while. There were other small bruises and rope burns, and judging by the slow response of her pupils, she had a severe concussion. Someone had hit her harder than they probably needed to in order to knock her out. The important discovery was that there were no bites.

Shooting around the grave kept us all aware of where we were, and we began our evacuation. Molly was carried to one of the Navy helicopters because they were designed to carry wounded service men and women. Tom and Kathy rode along with her. The unknown girl had been kept under guard even though she didn't appear to be a threat. She had been examined and was also free of bites. We decided to have her ride back to Fort Sumter with us in the Sikorsky because the bodies of Sam and Gervais were being transported in the second navy helicopter. It was a sad day for all of us, but we would stay civilized and bring back our dead for proper funerals.

The three helicopters lifted off together and banked away toward the east. The trip to Fort Sumter would only be a matter of a few minutes, but we all knew that the sooner we could get Molly into our hospital ward, the sooner she could get some x-rays and proper medical treatment.

******

Stokes and his remaining gang of misfits were too far away to see what was happening at the cemetery, but for over an hour he sat with a pair of binoculars and watched the helicopters dipping in and out of the area. Two were clearly military choppers, but he wasn't familiar with the design. The insignia said they were US Navy.

He was leaning on the window sill of a room on the top floor of a house on the corner of Harbor View Road and Shamrock Lane. It was a logical choice for them to hide in the house. Besides facing in the right direction, it was taller than the neighboring homes and gave him a good view of the surrounding area. When they searched the house, there was the added bonus of the discovery of an extensive wine collection. The last owner of the house must have been an expert when it came to choosing only the best wines.

They were also far enough from their old house to keep them from being caught. That, of course, depended upon how well Randal and those other idiots could stay hidden. If they could stay hidden long enough, and if the people from Fort Sumter stopped searching, he planned to keep his people in the area for a few days before making the long trip south.

He felt like he had enough of the Atlantic coast. It was hot just like the Gulf of Mexico, but it was a different kind of heat. It was so humid here that sometimes he found it hard to breathe. He longed for the dryer heat on the Gulf and thought about eating some real Cajun food. He never thought blue crab tasted nearly as good as crawfish.

The fastest route from Charleston to New Orleans was less than eight hundred miles and took about eleven hours back in the days before the infection. As a matter of fact, that was by driving to Atlanta first and using interstate highways for the entire trip. It wasn't even a straight line, so he figured it was between six and seven hundred miles as the crow flies. If they could find transportation to use for at least a week, he thought they could make the trip in a week or two. Of course it also depended upon how bad the ripe meat problem was on the roads they would choose.

Something was happening at the cemetery because all three helicopters had lifted off and then just as quickly landed facing in the same direction. A few minutes later the helicopters took off and immediately went to high speed in the direction of Fort Sumter. He wondered who they had found alive. He knew it wasn't that smart-mouthed boy who tried to threaten everyone every chance he got. He had carried on about someone called the Chief like the guy was some kind of super hero. Stokes laughed to himself and thought he would like to meet the Chief and show him a thing or two about being a super hero.

******

Fort Sumter was on high alert even before we landed. As we waited for the first helicopter to touch down, and for the crew to rush Molly inside, we received a radio call warning us to stay to the south over Morris Island. A follow up call gave us the reason why.

Only moments before we departed from the cemetery, a sentry on duty on the walls of the Fort spotted light reflecting from the marshes between Patriots Point and Sullivans Island. When he trained his binoculars on the spot, he could see a small, flat bottom boat. If not for the light reflecting off of something in the boat, the sentry would never have seen them because they blended in so well with the terrain.

There were two people in the boat wearing hunters camouflage, and all of their equipment was painted olive green. Whatever had given them away was obviously something they had corrected because they once again blended in with the surrounding marshes. The real surprise was the weapon that was laying across the shoulder of the man in the bow. It was an RPG of some kind. From the Fort it was impossible to identify the model, but it was well within range of a small aircraft that was approaching from the west.

It was identified as a Cessna, and it was too far away to hear the engine, but if they had a working radio, they needed to be warned of the danger they were about to encounter. The radio operator in the control room was frantically calling on all frequencies to tell the pilot about the RPG, but there was no answer. As the helicopters arrived at Fort Sumter, they joined in with emergency calls.

Everyone watched and held their breath as the small blue and white plane drew closer to the Ravenel Bridge and the container city that stretched to the middle of the Cooper

River. Its ugly rust red colors were a stark contrast against the blue sky behind it.

We couldn't have been more surprised when the Cessna suddenly did a controlled descent into the area behind the Yorktown. The golf course at Patriots Point had some flat fairways that could easily accommodate the small plane. Not only were the occupants of the Yorktown antisocial, they had planes.

11 THINKING VIRUS

Year Six of the Decline

The radiation from the failed Oconee Nuclear Power Plant didn't kill the infected, but it caused their bodies to become even weaker than they already were. The normal course of decay made the soft, fleshy parts of their bodies rot and fall away. The bones, cartilage, tendons, and ligaments were often seen walking around with only a few muscles or organs between patches of skin, but the radiation eventually caused even those parts to fall away.

In the early days when the radiation was high and its killing particles drifted with every breeze, the infected that were contaminated rapidly decayed practically where they stood. The normal bacteria that caused flesh to break down into putrid smelling liquids and gases were killed by the radiation, but the virus that had caused the worldwide pandemic was resilient and did the job for the weaker bacteria.

Without new victims for the virus to attack, without people searching desperately for more provisions and exposing themselves, the virus turned inward to survive. Instead of dying off along with its hosts, the virus fed on the infected as it waited for the day when the radiation decreased to safer levels.

The "thinking virus" had the genetic instinct to know it was time to move again. It was time for the infected that were capable to rise up and once again search for the living. Of course there weren't as many of the living in the previously sprawling city of Charlotte. Those who had survived and remained in the city when the radiation came were exposed, became sick, and died a very ugly death. After the radiation ate away at their living bodies until it killed them, their weaker corpses pushed themselves upright and began to walk. The virus knew it had to leave this place to begin once more to spread, but for that to happen, it had to walk far enough away from what was destroying its hosts.

All over the three hundred square miles covered by Charlotte, all along the sixty one mile circumference of the city, the infected faced outward from the radiation contaminated area and walked.

Thousands upon thousands of the infected walked first into the suburbs, surprising and overwhelming the small enclaves of people who had sealed themselves inside the borders of private, walled communities. For over five years they had prepared, and as time went by they built bigger and better defenses.

They thought they had survived the pandemic. They thought their walls would hold, but their new barriers of steel and spikes were pushed aside by the incredible numbers of the infected. Not since the first days of the pandemic had they seen such vast numbers of the dead, and with every community that fell the numbers increased even more. The infected that had died from radiation poisoning were joined by the newly bitten victims. It was day one again for the area surrounding Charlotte.

Thousands of the infected didn't make it far because they were too decayed. They encountered barriers that they couldn't go around or over, but they were the ones pushed from behind into the spikes until the pointed defenses broke from their weight. They were the ones that were pushed from behind into the brick, wooden, and metal walls until the structures groaned under the pressure and fell inward. They were unknowing and uncaring sacrifices for the virus that willed them to spread.

They also fell prey to the natural predators that feasted on carrion rather than to hunt. Emboldened by the lack of interest shown by the infected dead, animals that normally waited for prey to stop moving began to attack them even as they walked. Survivors that saw the sky darken as the vast hordes approached thought they were only seeing the dust clouds stirred into the air by the thousands upon thousands of dragging feet. They were shocked when they saw the air was full of vultures, crows, and ravens that would land on the infected, tear off great strips of flesh, then fly away.

All along the expanding front line of the infected, the horde would dwindle as it ran into resistance, only to break through once again and move onward with its newer, stronger replacements. What was left behind were bewildered pockets of people without enough food or water to survive another day, or enough ammunition to fight back. It was as if the infected dead were cleaning up and finishing what they had started.

Once the horde reached the outskirts of the cities and suburbs, they were free to spread out through the fields, woods, and highways. The interstates were natural funnels that offered no resistance to their advance, but to the people who were scratching out an existence along the interstates, the sound of thousands upon thousands of the infected was inconceivable.

By the end of the third year after the infection began, people in the farmlands had begun to feel safer because they were isolated. Survivors had learned to stay away from the cities, and the biggest fear had become the roving gangs that survived by taking what they wanted from anyone they encountered. That problem was answered by the farmers themselves.

As they came out of hiding from their personal shelters and found surviving friends and neighbors, they prepared for the future in a way they never had before. Strangers were turned away unless they arrived as families and were able to demonstrate their worth. Most of all, they had to prove their health.

Bitten travelers were executed, and some enclaves went so far as to execute the families of the bitten rather than to allow enemies to leave. Armed camps communicated with each other about movements of rogue gangs and the infected, and temporary truces were formed when one or both had to be dealt with.

Life adjusted to deal with the new reality, but those who had survived between Charlotte and Charleston didn't know they represented less than one thousand souls in the southeast compared to millions of the infected dead. If they had known, they probably wouldn't have done anything differently because there wasn't anything else they could have done. It was also man's nature to survive, or at least try to survive.

After five years of uneasy existence, the sound of the infected walking on four lanes of interstate highway could be heard for miles in all directions, and when the infected heard a loud sound, they went toward it. So it was on I-26 that the largest of hordes began to form. Even the massive horde that flowed down I-95 was drawn east by the combined roar from the feet and moan from the mouths of the I-26 horde.

The only benefit that came from so many infected being in one place was that they slowed each other down. The procession that gathered on the interstate was slow and clumsy. It moved only as fast as the infected in front could move, and sometimes that wasn't fast enough for the infected that were the least decayed or damaged. Pile ups in front caused logjams of bodies as the slow infected were pushed to the ground.

The survivors who were in the path of the infected exodus didn't think they needed to run because the entire mass moved so slowly. Scouts would move to interstate overpasses and watch in horror as they tried in vain to guess the number of infected moving their way. Their mistakes were repeated over and over again as they underestimated the magnitude of the new tragedy that confronted the remainder of mankind. They saw the infected as marching down the interstate and failed to anticipate that the fastest of the infected would be walking along the fringes.

Each scouting party planned to return to their enclaves with news of the advancing horde, and if any had made the short trip home, at least some would have understood that they did need to run. As the main body marched, its tentacles of faster walking infected surged ahead and surrounded the scouts on the overpasses. Much too late they tried to run, but they found hundreds of infected already on both sides. Within minutes the scouts were added to the growing numbers of the death march.

When scouts didn't return, the walled settlements of survivors were slow to react. Instead of gathering their children and whatever belongings they could carry, they sent out more scouts, and as the mistakes were repeated, the horde had drawn even closer.

The scenario that played itself out on I-26 between Columbia and Charleston was the mirror image of every interstate highway around Charlotte. The mountains turned the tide of infected away, but wherever there was a gap or a highway acting as a funnel, they followed it. It was the second wave of the pandemic. It was slow in coming, but it was coming.

******

It had been a long time to be underground, but the survivors in the shelter at Ambassadors Island weren't complaining. If you asked any of them how long it had been, few of them would have known if it had been five, six, or even seven years. All they cared about was that they had been given a safe place to live for a very long time. That was a lot more than thousands of other people could say.

Supplies had lasted so well that they never even considered rationing, and the community had flourished as if it was in a safe place on the surface. Water had continued to test safe due to the well designed filtration system installed by the Army Corps of Engineers, and power never so much as blinked off and on. When a lightbulb needed to be replaced, they made a production out of changing it just for fun.

The idea to build a shelter with a mall in the center was genius. It wasn't just a mall with entertainment and social events. It was a mall with stores that resembled the chain stores everyone had enjoyed before the end of civilization. People worked in the stores and shopped in them. It kept them busy and gave them a sense of purpose as they clung to a sense of normalcy. After work they could go to the restaurants to enjoy the company of friends.

Crime was practically nonexistent. The closest thing they had to a problem was tempers, and most of the citizens knew how to control theirs. There had been one domestic violence case that resolved itself quickly when the couple involved learned their punishment for a second offense would be banishment to the surface.

There was some concern that abused spouses or children would be afraid to speak up, but that was easily fixed by continuing to do the bite inspections. It wasn't hard to understand that the biggest fear would be that the infection would somehow get inside, and a bite would go undetected. Over five years of being checked for bites had made the community feel like one very large family, and a bite inspection could uncover bruises as easily as bites.

A natural death had created a crisis when a man died and turned while his family was sleeping. His family managed to restrain him without anyone becoming infected, and even though they were grieving, they put the community first and requested to be inspected for bites.

There had been births during the years since the doors had been sealed shut, and children went to school almost willingly. The older kids were taught trades, and a health clinic was able to deliver the babies and treat most problems. When chicken pox was diagnosed on two children, there was an attempt to quarantine families to prevent the spread, but in the end, everyone just suffered through it together.

When Iris Mason looked in the mirror, she was well aware of the new wrinkles at the corners of her eyes. She also knew they were called crow's feet, but she preferred to call them laugh lines. They were there just as they should be, but she wondered if Joshua Barnes would notice them. It was something she would only ask herself in private, and if she ever saw him again, she knew he was too much of a gentleman to say anything about getting older. As for him, she doubted he would look a day older despite the differences between life on the surface and life underground. She could only imagine what the Chief had gotten himself into since she saw him the last time.

Iris pulled back her long, silver hair and admired her healthy figure. She had led the way by example and made the gym part of her daily routine. If she did see the Chief again, he would comment about how good she looked. She allowed herself the liberty of pretending he had just given her the compliment, and she felt like it was good to wish even after everything that had happened. She knew one thing for sure, and it wasn't part of her fantasy. She would make sure the next time they met that he would know beyond any doubt how she felt about him. It was something she had kept to herself for far too long.

The last time they had seen each other there was no sense complicating the situation. They both had feelings, but she had to stay with her people, and he had to go back to his. While she could help almost a hundred people keep their sanity underground, he would have felt confined. It was best that he was out there doing whatever he could to fight the infected.

Communications had been their weak link. There were radio reports from random places for a while, but gradually the radio signals dwindled to nothing. She had heard a report about helicopters, and as sparse as the report was, Iris knew in her gut that Chief Joshua Barnes must have been involved.

Reports were given to Iris this morning that the radiation monitors were sending back negligible readings. The heavy rains over the last two years had been particularly helpful at washing the earth clean. If they were careful, they could avoid any of the hot spots that still dotted the area. They were already developing a topographical map of the previously contaminated area. Everyone in the shelter assumed it was because they would need to know where they could search for supplies when the time came, but Iris had other motives.

She realized that was probably why the Chief was on her mind. When the day came that they could go to the surface again, she knew that she would leave Ambassadors Island in the hands of the others and go find the Chief. She knew that it would be a difficult journey, but she was resourceful and ready to do more than just survive. Besides, there were a few old friends in the shelter who had approached her about doing the same thing, so she wouldn't be alone. At first she had tried to reason with them and convince them their place was in Ambassadors Island, but deep down inside she was grateful.

What Iris didn't know or couldn't possibly suspect, was that the apocalypse was beginning again. She didn't know what to expect on the surface. It had been a topic of discussion at almost every meal or social gathering for the first year, but as time went by it became a boring conversation as the same ideas were hashed and rehashed. When it was discussed, it was almost always ended by the comment that they would find out when it was safe to have a look.

As the infected swarmed toward the interstates and walked away from the lake that held Ambassadors Island, they left nothing behind. Iris Mason and her friends would emerge from the shelter and think the battle was over. They would think the infected were all dead. There just wasn't a reason for them to believe that there was a tidal wave of infected so vast that it would consume everyone who had survived the first time.

There was a knock at the door that broke Iris away from the pleasant thoughts she had allowed herself to enjoy. She had even momentarily allowed herself to subscribe to that popular theory that they would find the infected had ended their reign of terror. That the virus was gone. She couldn't begin to know that it was gone, but just not the way she thought.

When Iris opened the door, she was surprised to find it was one of the young apprentices that was being trained in communications.

"We've had some contacts, Ms. Mason. More than we've had in a long time. The watch captain felt it was best to send a private message."

"Thank you."

She eyed the boy and saw how excited he was. He was a mere child when they had closed the doors to the shelter, and she momentarily wondered if it would be better if they were never opened again. The boy might live a life different from the one originally intended for him, but at least he would live it.

"Please run ahead of me and tell the watch captain I'm following."

She could have been escorted by him, but then she would have been forced into conversation. For some reason she didn't feel like talking. She had a suspicion that it was simply a wish to have a few moments to relive some of the enjoyment she had been indulging herself moments before.

As it turned out, Iris could have spared herself several interruptions. With an escort she could have begged off more quickly every time she was stopped on the way to the communications center.

When she finally arrived, she was greeted by several people who were on duty at the different electronic monitors that still functioned. There were also several cameras that continued to provide excellent views of the surface, and they were watched every minute of every day.

The watch captain was a young woman who had grown into the position quickly. One of the first apprentices, Andi had admired Iris as a role model. Iris thought if Andi was a little older she would be a good candidate to replace Iris when she relinquished her position as mayor, but she knew that it wouldn't be fair for her to pick her replacement if she was going to leave. It would be far better for her to allow the citizens to have an election.

"What do we have, Andi?"

"Good morning, Ma'am. Several radio contacts we didn't have before. All of them are shortwave. No AM or FM, so they're not likely to be radio stations."

"Anything worth hearing?"

"They're strange. They're reporting widespread attacks by the infected and heavy losses, yet the monitors on the surface don't show anything moving at all."

"Do you have locations from the reports?"

"No, Ma'am. We haven't received any confirmations from any of the sources that they are receiving our broadcasts. It's one of the first questions we've been asking."

Iris checked the view on the nearest monitor and saw several birds. That was a good sign because it meant the radiation levels were getting better every day, but other than the birds there was no movement. She panned around and zoomed in on the roads. There used to be bodies, and after the bodies were gone, there were the random sightings of the infected that still wandered slowly in the direction of sounds.

"What is the sense of urgency in the broadcasts, Andi? Could they be fake? Didn't we get some suspicious reports once before?"

"That's just it. If these are fake, the broadcasters are good actors. They sound like they're in full blown panic mode. Listen for yourself. We're still getting one now."

Andi handed a headset to Iris rather than to put it on speaker. Although the communications room was one of the upper level rooms with a ceiling, it was best not to have a report of this nature echoing down the hallways.

She put on the headset and got chills at the level of frantic fear in the broadcaster's voice. The man was breathless and his voice shook.

"......scouts aren't reporting back. We sent out more when the first scouts didn't come back, and we haven't heard from them. An infected wandered out of the woods, and a perimeter watch said it looked like Charlie Gibson. He was with the first scouting party. I don't know if it was true, and there's no way to know for sure. We're evacuating and will be off the air until we know we're safe."

Iris' hand shot out and keyed the broadcast button. She had to know where this was happening, and the problem with shortwave was that it could be anywhere in the world.

"Unknown broadcaster. What is your location. Please do not terminate broadcast without advising of your location."

Iris tried to convey her own sense of urgency. If the man heard her voice he would feel like he had to answer. After all, he was sending out the message as a warning.

There was a long pause, and Iris was afraid contact had already been broken. She was just about to repeat her message when the voice came back through the headset, but he wasn't answering her question.

"There are infected in the settlement. Hopkins is surrounded on three sides. Security forces have retreated from the fields into the main settlement to eliminate the infected. Some of us are gathering children and minimum rations and heading south, but some want to stay. No time to say more. Ending broadcast. God help us all."

"Wait."

Iris practically shouted into the microphone, but the sound of the radio switching off was too audible to ignore. There was nothing but silence.

"Are there any other broadcasts in progress?" she asked to no one in particular. Her somber tone had caused a stillness in the room after her plea to wait.

One of the men at a station nearby handed over his headset.

"Scanning all frequencies, Ma'am. We have one broadcast that's intermittent but clear. This one said something that made us think he's somewhere near the Virginia border with North Carolina."

When she put on the headset, she heard a much more calm voice, but the man seemed almost to be confused rather than afraid. She lifted one earphone away from her ear and turned to Andi.

"Watch captain, please have your staff begin reviewing all maps to find a town named Hopkins. I have no idea which state, so start with the southeast and work outward."

She lowered the earpiece into place before she heard an answer from the watch captain, but she had no doubt the order would be carried out. The man's voice broke up a bit, so she asked the man assigned to the station to try to tune it in better. Computers made good shortwave receivers because the software could make the adjustments.

"Towers along the ridge updated their count to four hundred sightings. That's an increase of three hundred and fifty in the last twenty-four hours and is equal to the entire count for the last year when we were receiving reports of one per day. The watches estimate forward progress to be unusually slow for most of the infected. The faster dead seem to be new victims while the slower dead are extremely decayed. Speculation among camps is that they were radiation victims that have begun to move outward from the greater Charlotte area."

There it was. She finally had her answer about the location of the broadcast. Towers were common along the western borders with North Carolina back when forest fires were a bigger concern than zombies.

The momentary thought of zombies made Iris think of the Chief. His humorous insistence that they weren't zombies still amused her.

Confusion appeared in the lines of her own forehead, and she turned to take in the faces of the communications room staff.

"Why are we just now getting these broadcasts? I've gotten more information in the last five minutes than I have in the last five years," she said.

"Best guess is all I've got," said Andi.

"Let's hear it."

The idea wasn't that farfetched once she heard it put into words. As a matter of fact, they could have been planning for this day instead of manning every station as they had for years. Still, even though they had listened to static, it had given the radio operators a sense of purpose just as it had to the people working in their stores.

Andi pointed at one particular station and said, "This is the station that controls our communications array, or antenna if you prefer. Our manuals gave us instructions on how to realign them to the satellites that would in turn give us the ability to detect broadcasts rather than to just randomly search for them by turning a dial."

She paused to give Iris the opportunity to ask questions, but Iris had read the manuals, too. Andi thought of her as their mayor and didn't really know the depth of her skills, one of which was ship to ship communications when she had been the chief enlisted officer on a cruise ship.

"Go on, please."

"We were acting under the assumption that we were realigning the array whenever we sent a signal for it to change positions. We had every reason to believe that was true because we received a status signal as feedback each time. What we never considered was whether or not the array was able to receive signals after it was realigned. Was it actually exposed to a clear sky above it, or was it enclosed?"

Iris could tell the question was rhetorical because the obvious answer was that the array had been enclosed, and somehow it had become clear to receive signals.

"Does your best guess include a theory about why the array could suddenly have a clear sky above it?"

"Yes, Ma'am. As you are probably aware, we keep a log of times and dates when we realign the array."

This time Andi didn't pause because she knew Iris had been the driving force behind not only the recorded history of life in the shelter, but the need for a specific routine. It wasn't enough to monitor the stations. The smallest of details could be important, and this practice had proven itself to be true.

"Review of the logs showed an interesting anomaly, and we tested it to see if it was real. Now, keeping in mind that this is just a best guess, we became curious when we noticed that the status feedback signal came back faster than it had in the past. A typical signal came back ten seconds later for every degree of turn on the main array. As of this morning, the signal came back after one second per degree of turn. That was significant, so we rotated the array three hundred and sixty degrees and timed the response. Then we did the same in the opposite direction."

"And your best guess for the speed of the array increasing was what?"

"A body or bodies jamming the machinery, and whatever had decayed enough to allow the array to turn faster also allowed the enclosure above the array to finally open. We've been shooting radio waves into a ceiling for years. Now the ceiling is open."

Iris couldn't help but smile.

"I can't wait to find out if your best guess was accurate. Personally, I like the odds given that the array also turns faster, but I have one question. Was the rate of turn always ten seconds per degree before, or was that the average?"

The communications staff was impressed by the mayor's question. She could tell by their beaming smiles.

"It was the average, Ma'am. Sometimes it was faster, and sometimes it was slower. That would suggest it was having to push bodies around on its tracks."

"Let's act on that assumption for now," said Iris, "and start mapping contacts. We need to have a clear picture of the world before we go up there. Speaking of which, has anyone had any luck finding Hopkins?"

The answer wasn't the good news she wanted to hear.

Andi sat a map on the table nearest to Iris and put her finger on a small town just south of Columbia, South Carolina. It sat in the middle of farm country and was situated along a road that ran roughly parallel to I-26.

******

Before the infection arrived and destroyed civilization, Hopkins, South Carolina was a small town of less than three thousand people. Off the beaten path, the secluded farm community was popular with people who wanted to live where they didn't have to deal with noise, traffic, or other people. At the same time, it was close enough to Columbia, Charleston, and Myrtle Beach when it became too quiet. Hopkins was one of those places that seemed to be ignored by time because it was far enough away from the main highways, but when people started dying, it was in the way just like every other town.

It was a fair assumption that the current residents of Hopkins had all come from somewhere else before the infected had arrived. They only stayed in Hopkins because someone organized the survivors who had nowhere else to go. There were no natural barriers that provided permanent protection from the infected, but the survivors had worked long and hard on their fallback plans.

Lake Weston was popular because there were bigger and better places for fishing and water sports available to the public. After it was wiped clean of life during the first few weeks of the infection, the dead just wandered away. There really wasn't anything to keep them there.

When survivors discovered the campgrounds and rental cabins, they realized they could build barriers along one side and keep the lake at their backs on the other three sides. The lack of infected dead in the area was something that bothered the survivors only because they couldn't explain it, but they weren't going to let it bother them enough to make them leave. If they had known it was only because there weren't any survivors at the beginning, maybe they would have thought twice about staying.

They began working as fast as they could to build their barrier, and there were plenty of trees for the task. When it was finished, the only way for the infected to get inside the new town of Hopkins was by walking out of the lake. Unfortunately, the infected could do that, and it was a stroke of luck that they arrived during daylight hours.

The survivors had just begun working on the second phase of their plan when they got their surprise. They decided to build a long dock out to the center of the lake. At the end of the dock would be a floating fortress, and it could be disconnected from the dock by a drawbridge. The principle wasn't a new idea. Centuries ago the foundations of Venice, Italy had been strengthened by driving trees straight down into shallow water and then building on top of them.

The dock was close to finished when the bloated bodies started crawling up onto the banks. It was a wake up call, and guards were posted all along the waterfront. It was a nervous community, and despite their previous efforts the survivors had to build a fence at the waterline. The water served as a way to slow down the infected, so it was safer than open ground behind them, but the end result was the speed at which they worked to finish their fort on the lake.

The fort became the home of the Hopkins survivors before it was finished, but to their surprise it was enough to be what they hoped it would be. It was a safe haven for them and a trap for the infected.

At sundown on the first night, all of the guards were brought out to the fort, and the drawbridge was raised. The decision was made to let everyone rest for the first time in weeks. If the infected dead found their way into the camp, they would be dealt with.

In the darkness of that first night, they heard the splashes, and by moonlight they gathered to watch as the infected labored up the wet banks, fell through the bars of the log fences, and dragged their heavy bodies to the long dock that led to the fort. It was almost a final insult when they reached the end of the dock and fell into the water where the drawbridge would have been. It was a weary group that settled into an uneasy existence in Hopkins.

12 CHANGES

Six Years After the Decline

The mood at Fort Sumter was a mixture of sadness and anger with more than a touch of worry. Molly was still unconscious, and the soldiers were covering their worry with their anger. They would have liked nothing more than to mobilize and go in force to search for the scum that had killed Sam, but Captain Miller was seriously concerned about the increased numbers of infected that had been encountered.

After Molly was flown back to Fort Sumter and left in the capable hands of Doctor Bus, the helicopters were fueled and sent back to James Island. They were given two mission plans. Their first mission was to attempt to spot any clues that would reveal the hiding place of the people who had killed Sam, and the second mission was to assess the reason for the increased numbers of infected.

This time the Sikorsky stayed behind while the Navy VH-92A's were all refueled and armed for combat. There was no shortage of volunteers when crews were assigned. Captain Miller gave orders for the helicopters to go to the beginning of Harborview Road at Folly Road. From there they would begin an organized search pattern hoping to accomplish both missions.

The main clue they expected to find that would indicate they had located the people who buried Molly and Sam was a concentration of the infected. Where you found living people, you could expect to find the infected trying to get to them. In this case, they were searching for armed killers, so they would most likely leave a trail of bodies. James Island was so infested with new infected dead, that it would be obvious to see a large number of them on the ground. They weren't disappointed as they hovered into a parking lot in front of a grocery store on Folly Road, all three having spotted the bodies that were scattered around one street not far from them. They radioed Fort Sumter and asked for confirmation that they could mount an attack on one particular house because they were sure they saw one infected dead go down as they flew by. The body flew backward away from the door of the house as if it had been hit by a bullet. They hoped their perps were that stupid.

******

Randal expected Stokes to be angry when he got back and saw what had happened. The infected had been banging at the doors on the house on Shamrock Lane ever since Stokes decided to check out a small strip mall they had never searched. He saw a gun store during their earlier escape from Fort Johnson, and he decided it was always worth checking a gun store even if they came up empty handed.

He had left Randal with simple instructions. Stay in the window and watch for the helicopters. If it stayed clear for a few hours, it would be time to move out when he got back.

He was anxious to start their trip south to New Orleans, and they would have been on the road already if not for the helicopters from Fort Sumter.

Despite instructions to lay low, Randal got bored. There were infected everywhere, and he was dry firing a rifle at them, pretending that he was really loading a round in the chamber each time. Randal was just being himself, so eventually he forgot what he was doing and slapped the bolt handle backward, laid a bullet inside, shoved the bolt forward, and a round was in the chamber. He dry fired at an infected in the street right in front of the house and was surprised by the recoil.

The rifle was a big gun that they had found in the house when they had taken up residence at Fort Johnson. He had never fired it, but Stokes had said plenty of times that it was an elephant gun. There were pictures around the house of a man carrying the gun. He looked too old to shoot a gun with that much kick, but Stokes had explained it was all a matter of technique.

The boom of the single shot was deafening, but Randal had never learned the technique of firing the rifle, so the recoil threw him backward. When he brought the rifle upward with the recoil, he tore out the entire window and frame, advertising his position to every infected dead except the one that had his feet flying through the air past his head.

Randal got to his feet and peered around the destroyed window frame to see how bad he had messed up. Judging by the number of infected converging on the steps to the front door, his guess was that he had messed up pretty bad. To make matters worse, he switched to an M4 and started shooting them. He didn't know what else to do.

Stokes was at least a half a mile away inside the gun store, but the distinctive boom of that cannon from the house was unmistakable. He froze and tilted his head with one ear aimed toward Shamrock Lane and listened. The rattling sound of a rifle on semiautomatic wasn't what he wanted to hear.

"Did I leave anyone at the house with Randal?"

His question was directed to a messy looking man named Franco. Franco always seemed to need a shower and a shave and smelled like the infected, but he was smarter than the rest of his misfit followers. He knew the answer to his own question as soon as he asked it. There were four men with him in the gun shop. That meant Randal was alone at the house.

"Did everyone bring their backpacks with them?"

The others all nodded or held up their backpacks.

"Good, because we aren't going back to the house."

"What about Randal?" asked Turk.

Stokes returned Turk's gaze with the most sarcastic expression he could muster up.

"Are you related to Randal or something, Turk? You want to go back and hang out with your cousin until the helicopters get back?"

Turk was busy shaking his head from side to side.

"We're moving now," said Stokes. "We can't get to Folly Road before the helicopters block it off, so let's just find a place to hole up until tomorrow morning."

Stokes was surprised when Turk asked for a second time why they weren't going back for Randal.

"Because Randal is stupid, and Randal is about to have company. If you haven't figured it out yet, that was him doing the shooting we just heard. Now he's shooting the infected, and if those helicopters fly over him again, they're going to see all the bodies. Satisfied?"

Turk nodded that he was satisfied, but Stokes was tempted to send Turk back to the house anyway. The only thing that stopped him was that they were both so dumb lucky that they would probably get away and lead everybody right back to him.

They went out the back door of the strip mall and dodged packs of infected as they looked for another place to hide. Fortunately, the infected were being distracted by the shooting that was still coming from Shamrock Lane and were drifting away in that direction.

******

The assault wasn't the most difficult mission ever attempted by Captain Miller's troops. They would have preferred to be dropping in from Blackhawks, but they were happy to have the Navy choppers. They weren't intended for this type of operation, but the soldiers were craving a little action to get some payback for Molly and Sam.

The wind from the rotors would knock down a large crowd of infected that had gathered at the front of the house on Shamrock Lane. The side and back yards were heavily fenced, so there were no infected trying to get into the house from those places.

One of the helicopters did a high speed flyover from back to front. That was intended to startle anyone who was in the house and momentarily drive them back from the windows. It would also hopefully draw them to the front of the house as they would try to get a look at what had just come over their rooftop. As soon as the chopper passed the roof, it banked to the right to get out of rifle range.

The second helicopter followed the first one closely, but it stopped directly above the house and deposited a dozen soldiers on the roof. They expertly dropped their ropes and followed them down in seconds, so at least for a few moments the people inside would think the rotor wash had been from the first chopper. The second chopper banked away without exposing itself to any windows on the front of the house.

The third helicopter did the same thing over the back yard at exactly the same time. One moment the air was filled with wind and noise, and the next moment the only sound was the moaning from the street out front.

Randal didn't have a clue that two dozen well trained soldiers were in the house with him. The dozen on the roof had dropped into windows while the noise was so loud that the sound of breaking glass blended right in. They overwhelmed Randal so quickly that they found it hard to believe this guy had survived six years. The second group was searching the first floor and they were surprised that there was no resistance.

All in all, it was a fairly disappointing raid with one exception. Randal gave up information with little more than a twist of his arm. He told them where Stokes was and how many people had gone with him. He also told them Stokes was going to New Orleans.

When the information was radioed back to Fort Sumter, the soldiers were disappointed when they were ordered to return with the prisoner, but their spirits were lifted when Captain Miller said some of them would be making a trip to New Orleans. There was no reason to believe that Stokes would still be at the gun store, and he may even know his hideout had been compromised. If anything he had become more dangerous if he had found weapons and ammunition at the gun store.

It took a few minutes to retrieve everyone from the house on Shamrock Lane. The infected had gotten inside by overwhelming the front door with their weight. There was no problem blocking off the second floor, but it was remarkable how many infected there were. The squad leaders reported to Fort Sumter that something was replenishing the population of the infected. If the infected could be compared to each other as new or old, recently turned, and so on, these were new.

The only thing they could think of was the possibility that there were more shelters in the area, and people had stocked them to last five years. After five years, the survivors had to come out into the open, probably in small groups, and they weren't surviving the infection very long. The more quickly they were bitten, the more quickly the next group got infected.

There was also the likely chance that people were leaving their shelters for supplies and then carrying the infection back with them by hiding a bite. People hiding bites was the oldest story of the apocalypse. From small shelters to cities, relatives hoping a family member would survive would choose not to disclose a bite nine times out of ten.

For added information, the soldiers managed to get plenty of photographs to take back with them. The medical staff would welcome the opportunity to look into the question of where the new infected dead were coming from. As a matter of fact, they had requested that a few infected should be brought back to Fort Sumter for study, but the idea was put to rest quickly by Captain Miller because he had seen that idea backfire onboard Navy ships.

Landing safely at Fort Sumter, the crews escorted their blindfolded captive into the shelter. It wasn't very easy because Randal was one of those people who managed to stay fat even though most survivors had lost weight. The main access to the shelter was down steep ladders in a large shaft, and Randal didn't seem like climbing down a long ladder was on his list of strengths. They wound up lowering him in a sling rather than to remove his blindfold, and he complained so much they wished they had gagged him, too.

For someone who was not in the company of people who would be very fond of him, Randal was being too friendly, and the soldiers didn't like it. They would have preferred to put him against a wall and shoot him, or maybe drop him down the entrance shaft. They were finding out that Randal was one of those people who just didn't have a conscience. He had no remorse for burying those kids because it was what he had been told to do by Stokes. When he had been told not to drill an air hole in one of the coffins, he didn't question the order even though he knew the kid inside would be dead long before he could be found and dug up.

One of the storage rooms had steel cages in it where supplies could be stored with extra security, and the designers of the shelter must have considered the possibility that there would be a need for a jail because a toilet and sink were in one of the cages. Randal couldn't imagine where he had been taken, but he felt air conditioning. In his warped mind he wondered if his captives would let him become a soldier. When the blindfold was removed, he looked around with surprised satisfaction and actually asked what time to expect food.

No one answered for a few minutes as the soldiers locked him in and set up a guard rotation. It wasn't so much that they were ignoring him as it was anger. They couldn't believe his audacity.

When Randal asked for a second time, one of the soldiers couldn't resist.

"Haven't you heard, Porky? We're not going to feed you. We're going to eat you. There's enough meat on your bones to feed the whole camp."

How everyone kept a straight face was a good question, but they did it. No one so much as grinned. A few of them gave Randal sideways glances to see his reaction. At first it was a big smile as if he knew they weren't serious. Then it faded to a blank expression, especially when one of the Corporals walked over to the bars and looked Randal over from head to toe in appreciation.

"At least two meals," said the Corporal as he walked away.

The Chief showed up as the soldiers were dispersing back to the squad rooms to file their reports, and judging by the expression on his face, Randal wasn't done having a bad day.

They thought the Chief was going to interrogate the prisoner, but that wasn't exactly what he had in mind. The Chief wanted to leave Randal with a lasting impression of just how mad the Mud Island survivors could get. As soon as he stepped inside the cage, Randal backed toward a corner. He was big, but the Chief dwarfed him in size.

"What time's chow, bro?"

The soldiers doubted that Randal heard the answer. The punch to his jaw couldn't really be called a sucker punch because he had to have seen a fist that size coming at him. Everyone who heard it connect also heard the awful cracking sound in the jaw. Loose teeth and a broken jaw were going to help Randal lose some of that weight.

The Chief walked out of the cell and stopped long enough to tell the soldiers not to let Randal die and to make him clean up his own mess when he regained consciousness.

******

The Chief felt better as he rode the elevator to the floor where the medical ward was located. He wasn't going to get over the loss of Sam easily, but Bus said Molly was going to be fine. He said her vital signs were too good for him to suspect she had been without oxygen long enough to suffer brain damage.

He walked into the ward and heard female voices coming from the end of the room and expected nurses. He was surprised to see it was Molly and the other girl they had brought back from the cemetery. He moved fast for a big man, and Molly knew what was coming as he caught her in a big bear hug that matched his size. She couldn't help laughing even though she was still hurting over the loss of Sam.

When the Chief let her go, the smile lingered on her face long enough for him to see she was glad to be home, but he saw the sadness there, too. The other girl was sitting up in her bed and had been talking with Molly. There was apprehension on her face because she didn't know what kind of reception to expect.

The military people who had carried her to a helicopter and transported her to safety had been professional and kind. She didn't know if she was a guest or prisoner yet, but no one was treating her like a prisoner.

When they had landed at Fort Sumter, she knew exactly who they were because she had seen them coming and going from the fort for years. She had always wondered if they would be the enemy as Stokes had described them, and she was finding out they just might be the good guys.

In the early years after the beginning of the infection, they had seen different groups of people take over Fort

Sumter, and she remembered clearly seeing the group that dragged women from their boats. Bound and gagged and often already with tattered clothing, she was going to be wary of anyone with power. Stokes was a jerk, and he was surrounded by jerks, but for some reason his moral code kept her from becoming that kind of victim. It was odd that he could kill so easily but not cross other lines of civilization.

When Molly had woken up, Sarah Beth called for the doctor she had met, and he rushed in with a big smile on his face. He was seriously kind to her, despite the fact that she already had enough time alone with him to confess that she had been the one who knocked Molly unconscious when they first showed up. Doctor Bus had understood it was more of a reaction because Molly and Sam dropped in out of the blue. It must have scared Sarah Beth. He was glad she didn't just leave them there despite what happened to Sam. They probably would have died when the next infected fell over on top of them.

After all Sarah Beth had been through, this one act of kindness from Bus had made her regret how cynical she had become, and all she could think of was how to repay him. She told Bus immediately that Stokes had made every effort to make her think they were going north, but she was sure it had been an act. She was convinced he was still going south toward the Gulf, and he planned to take over an oil rig.

The connection between Bus and Molly was obvious to Sarah Beth, and she enjoyed seeing their reunion. He gently lectured her about leaving in the first place, but his gratitude at having her back more than outweighed his disappointment about her doing something so dumb.

After the tearful reunion he gave her a quick exam and then introduced her to Sarah Beth. In his usual well developed bedside manner he gave Molly a moment to ask a couple of questions before he told Molly he was going to leave them to talk because Sarah Beth needed to tell her something.

Sarah Beth didn't beat around the bush and went straight to telling Molly she was sorry, and Sam's death was her fault. Molly was terribly hurt that Sam died, but she told Sarah Beth something had come back to her from that night. The last thing she remembered before Sarah Beth hit her was running through the woods and then having the ground disappear under her feet. She saw that she was going to land right next to someone, and she assumed it was an infected. She knew they had scared Sarah Beth, and if someone dropped in from above her at night, she would have hit first and asked for forgiveness later.

Sarah Beth was relieved to find the people from Fort Sumter were everything she had hoped they would be, and she wished she had tried to contact them sooner. Now she was looking at the Chief and wondering if it would stay that way just because he was so big.

Before she had a chance to find out, another man rushed into the room and went straight for Molly. If Bus had acted like Molly's grandfather, then this had to be her father, and Sarah Beth asked herself just how lucky could one girl get. He was tall and muscular but not like the Chief. He looked like an athlete. Molly kept reassuring the man that she was fine and that she was sorry for leaving.

It was probably her way of taking some of the attention off of herself, but Molly said, "Dad, Chief, this is Sarah Beth. She helped take care of me and Sam after we were taken to the house." She left off the way they met because she knew it would be too much at one time.

Tom and the Chief both crossed the short distance to Sarah Beth's bed and gave her a hug. She had held out her hand expecting a handshake and was caught off guard again. She felt herself flush when Molly's father hugged her and wondered if he had a girlfriend.

The Chief stepped back and studied her a little longer than Tom. She saw the questions behind his eyes, and braced herself for the worst.

"Sarah Beth, did you notice there were more infected than usual? We've had a steady decline over the years, and suddenly there were as many as there were at the start. Well, not that many, but there were definitely more than there have been."

Sarah Beth looked off into the distance as if she was seeing something from her memory.

"We patrolled the area around the college campus at least once every other day, and once a week we would go inland as far as the cemetery."

Everyone seemed to fidget or recoil at the mention of the cemetery. No one kept eye contact for a few seconds.

"I'm sorry. That's a bad memory," she said. Before it could get more uncomfortable she went on.

"When we ran low on supplies, we followed Harborview all the way to Folly Road. There's a grocery store at that intersection, and the place became dangerous so fast on the first day, that it's been a good source for us. It's like no one could ever go there and stay alive after the infection spread."

"So, you've been surviving in this area since it started," said Tom. "That's a miracle if you didn't know it, especially since the number of infected seems to be increasing."

That was the second time she heard them called infected, and she had answered out of reflex the first time because the Chief's size was so intimidating.

"You mean ripe meat?"

She saw a reaction when she asked the question. She didn't know if it was good or bad.

"That's what Stokes called them, so it kind of stuck with the rest of us."

She knew the term was less than sensitive, but she could see they weren't overreacting. They were only trying to hang onto their humanity by using a term that recognized the infected used to be people.

"There were a lot of infected at the start, and they used the backhoe to make the creek surrounding the house safer by making it wider. They gave it steeper sides and put spikes at some spots so the infected couldn't climb the banks. Then there were less infected for a long time. We thought it was finally over."

"You've been on the ground around here. Any idea where they're coming from?" asked the Chief.

"Judging by how well you're doing, Chief, I'd guess you guys have seen some action yourselves. Maybe even been to other cities."

"You wouldn't believe it," said Molly.

"Well," added Sarah Beth, "then you know there are more infected out there. I think they've started getting out of places that were sealed tight before."

A female voice from the door said, "No, that's too simple of an explanation. Plus, they would be better preserved, and why would they all be getting out at the same time."

Kathy walked into the room and walked over to Molly's bed first. Molly was all smiles as Kathy gave her a big hug and kiss.

"We'll talk later, young lady."

Sarah Beth couldn't help noticing that Kathy acted like Molly's mother even though her hair was a brilliant blond and Molly's was jet black. Her observation made sense when

Kathy walked over and stood at Tom's side. She comfortably leaned into him with an arm sliding around his waist.

"I'm Kathy, welcome to the Mud Island family."

Kathy gave Sarah Beth a genuine smile, but there was something about her intelligent eyes that gave away her curiosity about Sarah Beth. It was as if Kathy knew there was more to Sarah Beth than what the others could see.

Sarah Beth didn't hesitate.

"I know what you're thinking, Kathy, and you're right. I didn't survive out there for years on my own. I was part of Stokes' bunch, but I never did the things his men did. I don't know why, but as long as I pulled my weight with chores and easy stuff, he treated me okay. It was just at the end that he turned on me."

Kathy couldn't help but soften her expression just a touch. Her instincts as a police officer must have shown, and Sarah Beth was perceptive enough to see it. She stepped over to Sarah Beth's bed and held out her hand.

"Sorry I wasn't more sincere. Seriously, welcome to our family. I'm glad you're okay. Getting buried out there must've been horrifying."

"It was awful," she said as she shook Kathy's hand.

She was touched by the tenderness she felt from her gesture. At the same time there was strength and cool intelligence in her eyes.

"Don't mention it. If I were you, I would be skeptical of me."

Tom and the Chief were both a million miles away and had missed the entire exchange. All they knew was that the ladies were talking and being nice to each other. They had both heard what Kathy said when she came in.

The Chief snapped his fingers.

"I have a theory. Did anyone notice how different the infected were when we were on the road trying to find Molly?"

Tom and Kathy turned to see if the other had an answer.

"I didn't really think about it," said Tom. "I just wanted to find Molly."

"Same here," said Kathy.

The rest of the group chose that moment to walk into the hospital ward. Hampton and Colleen were in the lead followed by Olivia and Chase, Cassandra and Sim, and the room was suddenly filled with activity as everyone got in their hugs and introductions. Captain Miller and a few of his soldiers were among the new arrivals. They felt personally responsible for Molly being able to leave Fort Sumter, and they all wanted a look at the local girl who had survived for years on land.

The room got loud, so the Chief waited for things to settle down before going on.

"Okay, everyone. I'm glad you're all here so I can get your opinions on something. Would everyone agree that the infected appear to be of all kinds? Some are old, some are recent, some are waterlogged, some can walk, some can't, so forth and so on."

"Now that you mention it," said Cassandra, "but isn't that normal?"

"Kind of sad to see our definition of normal sink so low," said Colleen.

"That's why we didn't notice," said the Chief, "there was a perfect mixture, almost like they were brought here."

"And almost like it was easier for them to get around," added Sarah Beth.

"What do you mean?" asked the Chief.

Sarah Beth closed her eyes part way, and her expression was like she was seeing something both far away and in the past at the same time. She was remembering the nights when they had patrolled the roads on James Island and Gervais had asked her if it seemed like some of the cars had been moved.

The memory of Gervais hurt, but she pictured him as he gestured toward a group of cars in particular and then toward the road.

"Those cars had been blocking the road before. Now, they're out of the way, so the dead meat can just walk right down to Fort Johnson," he had said.

"Why would someone move the cars out of the road?" asked Colleen.

"I can think of two reasons," said the Chief.

"The infected can walk to Fort Johnson in larger numbers, and Fort Johnson is practically the back door to Fort Sumter."

13 ROADS

Year Six of the Decline

The trip from Charleston to New Orleans was anything but easy. Even avoiding places that had been heavily populated before the infection was useless, and Stokes was traveling alone by the time he reached the border of South Carolina and Georgia. The way he figured it, he was alive because he was smarter than his companions. If he chose to be a little more honest with himself, he was alive because he was luckier than them.

Stokes told his handful of misfits to expect to run into ripe meat, especially in the places where the land was flat and there were less predators. He lectured them about the difference between the living people they would sometimes encounter and the ripe meat they would very likely see every day. Survivors would be more dangerous because they would be thinking about staying alive. The dead would stumble toward them with no regard for themselves, and they certainly weren't thinking about staying alive.

The biggest concern was getting shot. The first to die of his remaining crew from Fort Johnson was shot by a survivalist who obviously believed in shooting first and asking questions later. It never occurred to Stokes that the guy had picked his target at random, and it could just as easily have been him. He just thought his companion had been stupid for letting himself get shot.

The survivalist had proven to be worth killing to gain access to his supplies. He had every different kind of gadget Stokes could imagine for staying alive. If he had been smarter, he would have hidden until Stokes and his noisy bunch had gone by, but apparently the temptation to shoot someone was greater than his common sense.

After they had circled around behind him, it was just a matter of time before he poked his head up for a look, and Stokes shot him in the back. Stokes didn't even have enough humanity left in him to shoot the survivalist in the head. They left him to turn into ripe meat as punishment for shooting one of his people.

They went through the man's supplies and found all kinds of books about survival. Much of it was just second nature to Stokes, and he thought it was funny that the man needed reference books about what was safe to eat, how to butcher game, or how to dress a wound.

"I guess he just looked it up when he saw zombies strolling toward him."

Stokes laughed at his own joke.

"Someone write that down," he said. "That was too funny."

His men knew better than not to laugh, but it was more likely that they didn't get the joke. It wasn't a stretch to say they had gotten pretty far on dumb luck.

The next in their group to die had forgotten that any body of water in the Lowcountry of South Carolina was possibly inhabited by an alligator or two. Since the beginning of the infection the explosion in the alligator population had been aided by the terrain of the Lowcountry. You didn't have to drive far to cross a tidal creek, a river, a lake, or a swamp. The swamps were the worst places because there was water on both sides of the road for miles.

When the reptile burst from the shallow water where it had laid perfectly still as they approached, Stokes had stepped neatly behind one of his men. The alligator pulled the screaming man off of his feet and dragged him back to the water. Stokes put his hands on the barrels of the raised rifles to his left and right and told the men if they saved the man they had to carry him. The alligator had already made a mess of the man's legs. There was no resistance from them.

That left him with Franco and Turk, and Stokes didn't give either of them much chance of surviving. As a matter of fact, he was a bit surprised they were still with him. The only reason he remembered their names was because he was always calling them stupid.

They dumped the backpack out on the road that belonged to the guy that had become alligator food. As if to prove his earlier thought, he tried to remember the man's name, and all that would come to mind was Gator Bait.

Franco and Turk died together, and none of them would have expected it to be started by ants. In a world where the biggest threat to life was being bitten by ripe meat, it was ant bites that brought them down.

Another feature of South Carolina that is seldom given any thought by tourists is the rich insect population. If the mosquitoes don't drive you crazy, the gnats will. Especially the sand gnats that could pass right through a mosquito net. Then there were the Black Widow and Brown Recluse spiders. The Black Widow could kill you, but most people survived their bites. It wasn't the same with a Brown

Recluse. One bite would leave you with a terrible scar of necrotic flesh, or it could kill you in minutes.

If those weren't bad enough, fire ants were everywhere, and their victims suffered terrible deaths. Most people find out they are allergic to ant bites when they get bitten the first time. Swelling, difficulty breathing, puffy eyes, and pain on the place where one ant left its bite were the symptoms, but when hundreds or thousands bite you at the same time, it feels like your body is on fire. It's also not going to be difficult to breathe. It's going to be an inability to breathe.

Franco felt the itch on his right leg and absentmindedly scratched at it. Then he felt the sting on the back of the hand he had used to scratch his leg.

They had stopped to rest at a small gas station next to one of the many tidal creeks and were considering the attached convenience store as a possible place to spend the night. Stokes was checking it out for himself while Franco and Turk sat with their backs against the gas pumps. Fire ants have a nasty habit of infesting things that sit still too long on dirt or things like gas pumps that don't get used. Things like cars, barbecue grills, and lawn mowers are great places to find spiders and ants in South Carolina.

When the ants bit his hand, they got his attention. He slapped at his pants legs trying to brush the ants off. That only irritated the ones that had climbed his boots to the inside of his pants. The bites increased, and he didn't know why, but he didn't feel right. He was dizzy. His neck was already swelling, and the pressure on his windpipe was increasing. He couldn't swallow, and the bites hurt.

He managed to croak out, "Can't breathe. On fire."

Turk started laughing as soon as Franco had started jumping around and slapping at his pants. He stopped laughing when he saw that Franco's neck would have been more at home on the body of a gorilla than it was on a man. Worse, he felt the first ant bites on his own legs.

Not everyone is allergic to ant bites, but they hurt just the same. Turk could only think of one thing, and that was to get the ants off of him and Franco. He grabbed his friend by the arm of his jacket and yanked him in the direction of the small two lane bridge that crossed the tidal creek. He knew the ants could be washed off if he could get there in time, and the cool water would soothe the stinging bites.

When they reached the low concrete wall that ran along both sides of the bridge, Turk shoved Franco over the side into the water. He didn't hesitate and jumped along with him. They both hit the water and went under. Relief flooded across Turk's body.

He surfaced and spit out a geyser of the brown water, but it felt so good he started whooping because he knew Franco would be better too. Stokes ran out and followed the sound of the commotion at the bridge. He leaned over and saw Turk, laughing and yelling as if he was at a pool party. It was a stark contrast to Franco who was clutching his neck with both hands. Stokes didn't have a clue why Franco's neck was bigger around than one of his legs.

"Franco, what's wrong with you, stupid?"

Turk yelled something he didn't understand, but Stokes waved him off and told him he would deal with him in a minute, and while he was at it to shut up.

Stokes turned back to Franco to repeat his question, but Turk yelled something else. This time he understood what Turk said.

"Ripe meat. There's ripe meat in the water."

Turk was slapping at the water, but this time he was also kicking his feet to push away from something. He was putting distance between himself and a big brown lump that had surfaced a few feet from the bridge, and just like Stokes he was making sure that he was behind Franco.

Stokes was still confused about why they were in the water in the first place, and he was almost more focused on Franco's huge neck than he was the fact that there was ripe meat in the water with them. Stokes didn't understand why Franco was choking himself so hard that his neck was going to explode.

"Franco, I said what's wrong with you. Let go of your neck and get out of there."

Franco's eyes were bulging so far out of his head that he resembled a puffer fish, but there was still a spark of recognition in those big, white orbs because he turned to face the muddy ripe meat that stood up in front of him. The water was only waist deep in places, and the ripe meat was only an arm length away.

Franco had the presence of mind to fall over into the water, but it was much too late. As he did, the ripe meat fell forward and connected its face with Franco's hip before it disappeared under the water. Turk heard it better than Stokes, but they both learned you could hear someone scream under water if they screamed loud enough.

Turk was sitting in the water almost to the bank, and he started walking like a crab with his hands behind him. When Franco surfaced the ripe meat still had its teeth buried in his hip. He came out of the water screaming and immediately went under again. That made Turk crawl faster without thinking about where he was going.

Stokes could have warned him. From his vantage point above the two men he could see that Turk was backing into the marsh grass where more ripe meat eagerly waited for him with outstretched arms. Stokes just didn't care enough about other people, and watching the two idiots die was almost entertaining to him.

When Franco didn't come back up a second time, Turk finally turned to face the direction he had been crawling. The ripe meat in front of him actually scraped dirty fingers across his cheek and drew blood, but it couldn't get a grip on him.

Turk half crawled and half ran up the bank of the creek and sprawled onto the asphalt road. Stokes walked over and tapped him with a boot.

"Are you bit?"

Turk was gasping for air, partially from fright and partially from ant bites. He wasn't feeling the effects as bad as Franco, but he had gotten more than his fair share of bites. He rolled to a sitting position and pulled up his pants leg. It was hard to tell one bite from the other. His leg was red and swollen. The clicking noise by his right ear was the sound of a gun being cocked.

"Wait, Stokes. It's just ant bites."

Turk's pleading voice was wasted on Stokes.

"You know I can't take that chance, Turk."

Stokes pulled the trigger before Turk could plead again. At close range, the bullet threw him over onto his stomach like a rag doll. The leg of his pants was pulled all the way to his knee, and a big swarm of ants was crawling back to the pavement.

Stokes examined the back of the dead man's leg and watched the ants pouring from the rolled up pants leg.

"Well, what do you know. I was wrong. Sorry Turk."

Stokes walked onto the bridge to see how Franco was doing and saw several ripe meat standing in the water. Franco was one of them. They were making slow progress up the bank, and Stokes cursed himself for making noise when he shot Turk.

"Where are the gators when you need them? Might as well find another place to spend the night."

******

Year Six of the Decline

Opening the big door was an event that required a ceremony and much fanfare. Iris wanted her departure to be low key with as little attention as possible. She had made her best effort to convince everyone that the escape hatch at the end of the island was the best bet, but even she knew it wasn't. Going out that way meant she would still have to cross water, and there was no way to know what was waiting on the bottom of Lake Norman.

She managed to convince some of her biggest supporters to stay behind, though. They were needed if the community was going to continue without her. Besides, they had families to think about.

Two of the couples who didn't have children asked to go with her, and she felt like their reasons for wanting to leave were good. They told her they had never really adjusted to being underground for so long, but they were smart enough to know it was what had kept them alive. Death from radiation poisoning wasn't a pretty death.

Another reason they wanted to leave was because they knew something the rest of them didn't know. They promised they wouldn't tell the others if Iris wouldn't take them with her, but they couldn't promise they wouldn't leave on their own one day. Iris felt like it was better to have them with her than to go alone, especially since they had a similar goal.

What they knew was the locations of the other shelters, or at least some of them. It wasn't a secret that could be kept forever because too many of them needed to be involved with the day to day operation of the Ambassadors Island shelter.

Once word got out about other locations, it was more than likely to be a temptation for people to leave with the idea that a loved one might be at a shelter near to where they had lived. At least a dozen occupants of the Ambassadors Island shelter had lived near Charleston, and from what the Chief had told Iris, the Fort Sumter shelter could hold hundreds of people comfortably, maybe even thousands.

Iris was worried about plenty of things, but one thing that stood out as her biggest worry was how many of them were going to die in the next few months if they set out on their own to find their lost families. In a sense, that's what she was doing so she couldn't question the motives of the others.

When she made the formal announcement, she was surprised by how many of them understood why she wanted to leave, but she was more surprised by how many wanted to stay a bit longer or even permanently. They wanted to know what happened to their families, but most knew what they would find.

As many people as possible were crammed onto the platform that spread out in front of the bank vault door that sealed the shelter. The people had left enough room for Iris and the two couples to pass between them, and she had to stop to take one last look at the shelter from the top of the ladder.

It all looked the same as the first time she had seen it, but now it had a familiar, lived in look to it. She could almost reach out and touch the happy times she had shared with the other survivors in those corridors and rooms below. They had been saved by a miracle, but now it was time to go and try to make another one for herself.

There were no more speeches to give. They had all been given the night before at a banquet held in her honor. She had passed the torch, and the new mayor was a widely respected man who would be as kind and gentle with the survivors as she had been.

The door was opened just as the group arrived, and for the first time in years she smelled and tasted the outside air. It was better than she had expected, but it was still bad, almost evil tasting. Even though the sun was bright and a slight breeze was swaying trees in the distance, the quiet of the outside world meant there had been death.

Iris stepped through the open door and squinted against the bright light of the sun. Nothing moved, and there were no remains of humans or animals on the slope that led up to the road above. Her companions followed her out, and they all turned to watch the big door close. The brick covering the door blended back together, and it almost completely disappeared even though they knew it was there.

That was it. Just like that, they were outside and ready to live or die on what was most likely a fool's errand. They shared a nod of agreement and walked up the slope.

It took several hours just to walk far enough around Lake Norman to a highway that would take them south. The complete absence of infected dead, whether moving or rotting along the road, troubled them all. The radiation would have destroyed millions of them, but it almost seemed like they had fled from the area to escape.

Her companions were George and Sherry Worth and Sora and Yuni Tanaka. Sora and Yuni were born in Tokyo but had come to America to work for an automobile parts manufacturer. The cruise had been their way to celebrate their promotions to work in the South Carolina facility. When the infection broke out, they were still working on their language skills, but living in close proximity to everyone in the shelter had enabled them to master the language.

It had been important for Iris to be aware of detailed information about everyone in the shelter, so she knew they were a relatively young couple. Sora was thirty-two, and his wife was twenty-seven. They had tried to start a family, but the stress they had felt being underground had taken its toll on them. They weren't surprised that it just didn't happen.

George and Sherry met inside the shelter. They had been recent additions to the survivor group before being miraculously pulled from the surface into the safety of the underground world. They had formed an instant bond when they met within the first few days inside, but neither was feeling the pull of parenthood. They were close in age to the Tanaka's and had almost as quickly taken the Asian couple under their wings. It was easy to see they all were in need of friends, and they were a natural fit.

Iris liked the way the four of them moved as they walked down the debris covered road. There was a spring in their steps that couldn't be measured inside the shelter. It wasn't that they wanted action, but something had built up inside of them the way it had inside Iris. They all felt the greater purpose they had lacked in the safety of the shelter. They had also kept pace with Iris on the exercise equipment and were four of the most fit people in the shelter. Yuni ran fitness classes as part of her shelter employment, so she could outrun the rest of the group if she had to.

Sora and George had worked on the structural and maintenance teams. There were very few things to fix, but when something heavy needed to be lifted, the two of them were the first in line to help.

All five of them were equipped with M4 carbines and Glock pistols, but they had remembered what the Chief and Kathy had told them about using machetes first if they had a choice. The machetes were all in their hands, and they stayed as far out in the open as possible to be able to see the infected from a longer distance. They were concerned about other survivors, but not deeply worried. The radiation had given people reason enough to stay out of the area.

When they made camp for their first night in the open, they had plenty to talk about. The radiation was gone, but that was all the more reason why there should be at least some infected dead. They had seen a few birds and rats, but there weren't even any decayed infected. Mostly, there had been nothing but silence.

They felt like it was safe enough to build a fire, and they didn't know how many evenings they would have like this one. They took advantage of the break while they could.

"I never thought I could go a whole day on the surface without hearing one moan," said George.

"I'll be sure to wake you up with a good moan for your turn on watch tonight. You'll be wide awake in no time," said Yuni.

"I didn't say I missed it. I meant why aren't we hearing any? Where are they?"

"They don't migrate," said Iris. "Or do they?"

Everyone was wondering the same thing, and they all seemed to be studying their hands while they waited for someone to come up with the answer.

Sherry said, "One night when I was on watch in the control center, I saw one on a monitor that was being held together by the last bits of tissue. The radiation had eaten away almost everything else and it could hardly move, but it was still trying to go somewhere. Months later I could tell the radiation was dropping because I saw an infected in better condition crossing the same spot. I didn't think about it at the time, but the last time I was on watch I saw one that was recently bitten. Poor guy didn't even look dead at first."

"Imagine surviving this long and then getting bitten," said Sora.

The gravity of his comment made him say it in a low, almost mournful voice, and serious moments tended to make him revert to his native language. There was something at the end that only Yuni understood, and she nudged him with her elbow.

"My apologies," he said. "I was just saying we must not let that happen to us, and I believe I may have interrupted Sherry. What happened to the last one you saw?"

Sherry picked up her thought where she had left off.

"He was definitely an infected, but I felt almost like he was going somewhere on purpose. Like he was just passing through."

"Remember that doctor with the theory about it being a virus that could think?" asked Iris.

She had her rifle unslung and cradled in the bend of her elbow, but she sat down near the camp fire and poured a cup of coffee.

"They called it the thinking virus, didn't they?" asked Sherry. "That's what I meant. He was walking as if he knew where he was going. As a matter of fact, I usually call them 'it' when I talked about them. That one was walking like he was still alive."

"Well, they've all gone somewhere," said Iris. "I hope they aren't going to the same place we are."

Early the next morning they were on the move again, and it was Sora who pointed out the obvious to the rest of them. They were so intent on where the infected had gone that they hadn't noticed they were walking on a highway that was virtually cleared of all traffic. The broken down and rusty cars were still there, but they had all been pushed to the side of the road.

Sora jumped up and grabbed the top of the concrete divider in the middle of the interstate. He pulled himself up and balanced himself so he could see both sides.

"You guys should see this."

The divider was at least eight feet high, and although all of them were capable of climbing it, it was a good way to break a leg.

"Save us the trouble," said George. "What's the difference between one side of the road and the other?"

"The other side is one long, solid car wreck," he answered. "Why are all of the cars pushed out of the way over on our side but not on the other side?"

Iris was tall, so she made it seem easy when she jumped up to where Sora had sat down with his feet hanging over on the other side. She stood up as tall as she could and tried to see what it was like up ahead.

"See anything worth mentioning?" asked Sora.

"Yeah, but you're not going to like it. Do you see where the concrete divider ends about a mile from here?"

Sora couldn't see as far as Iris, but when he stood up he could see what she was pointing at. When the concrete divider ended, a wide grass median began, and down the middle was a steel wire cable. The steel wire cable was strong enough to stop a vehicle as it crossed the median, but something had snapped it into big, coiling loops.

"Remember that movie about a Civil War officer who joined up with an Indian tribe?"

Sora didn't wait for Iris to answer.

"They found the trail where a herd of buffalo had crossed the prairie, and the grass was so trampled that you couldn't miss which way the buffalo went. It was about a mile wide. That's what this reminds me of."

Iris could see it for herself. After the place where the wire had been cut, the grass median had been flattened. To the left and the right of the median, all four lanes of blacktop had been cleared of vehicles. On both sides of the interstate, the cars and trucks had been pushed out of the way.

"Did someone actually clear the interstate?" asked Sora.

"Someone or something," said Iris.

"What's happening up there?" said Yuni.

Iris and Sora lowered themselves down to join the others.

"About a mile from here something happened to the interstate. Before I make a guess about it I'd rather see it close up."

Further ahead the shoulders of the interstate were lined with cars. Piled on top of each other, upside down, even standing on end where they were pushed by something with a lot of force. Then they smelled it. The stench was overpowering even though it had to be days or weeks old.

Yuni leaned close to a car being careful not to touch it.

"They're all like this," she said.

Everyone gathered around the car she was examining. It was sitting upright with the driver side door facing her. The side of the car was curiously flat as if it had been inside a metal crusher. As a matter of fact, every car was flat along the side facing the asphalt for almost a hundred yards. They leaned in with Yura, and they could see that the gaps in the metal were packed with human flesh and clothing.

"A horde went through here," said Iris.

George let out a low whistle.

"Would anyone like to venture a guess about the size of the horde?"

"Big wouldn't describe it," said Iris. "They came from the Charlotte area and got squeezed into this section of the interstate because of the concrete walls along the center and the thick woods along the right side. When they came to the place where traffic had backed up, they probably started to go between the cars, but the horde was so big that the ones in front got crushed up against the cars. The pressure from behind was so great that it literally pressed the bodies into the cars like putty."

"No way," said Sherry. "That horde had to be…."

Sherry couldn't finish the sentence. Saying what she was thinking wasn't something she wanted to put into words."

"Yeah, that many," said George.

"Are we talking about thousands?" asked Yuni.

"More," said Iris. "Maybe hundreds of thousands. When they reached the end of the concrete wall down the middle, they spread out until they reached the retaining cable. It made them keep pushing cars out of the way like a bulldozer until the cable snapped."

"Can you imagine what it was like when the cable snapped?" asked George.

Sora answered for him.

"Imagine a steel rubber band getting stretched to its limits. When it broke, all that tension made it whip around like a fireman's hose with no one holding onto it. It probably chopped up thousands of the infected before losing that pent up energy."

Iris picked up the description when Sora stopped.

"Then they pushed the cars out of the way on both sides of the road until there was enough room for the horde to pick up speed. Notice the cars are still flattened for about a hundred more yards, then they're pushed out of the way but not flattened."

"Are we following a horde?" asked Yuni.

Her husband put his arm around her shoulders and gave her the obvious answer.

"It would appear we have no choice. We happen to be going the same way."

Sherry asked, "Why can't we go across country to the coast and then go south?"

Iris said, "The Chief told me about the horde that marched down the coastal highway in South Carolina. He said they crushed each other into trees along the road, but the horde kept getting replacements along the way. They made so much noise that the infected that were scattered throughout the trees, forests, small towns, and wherever they had gathered were drawn to the crowd. If we go toward the coast, we'll run into the infected that are trying to join the parade."

"So we should just keep following them?"

Yuni didn't like the idea of seeing thousands of infected up ahead.

"Better than the other way around," said Sherry.

"Which reminds me."

Iris was facing back in the direction they had come from.

"When the horde went through here they made plenty of noise that drew the infected from miles around, but not all of them would have caught up with the horde. We need to keep an eye on the road behind us from now on. When we stop for the night we have to consider strays that are still trying to catch up."

"And we have to be careful not to catch up to the horde ourselves."

Yuni sounded like she had a pretty good idea what it would look like when they finally saw the horde up ahead, but she also couldn't shake the feeling that they were already surrounded.

14 MISSION PLAN

Year Six of the Decline

The Chief always made a plan before doing anything else, and he believed in making backup plans because sometimes things went wrong. This time was different, though. Somehow the man responsible for Sam's death had gotten off of James Island before he could have the roads blocked. It was partially due to Captain Miller, and for the first time, we were seeing the two friends unable to make eye contact without a hint of anger.

The dining hall had become the informal conference room for strategy sessions, so the tables were all crowded when the Chief started to lay out a plan for going after Stokes.

It had become a heated exchange almost from the start. Kathy and Jean had been with the Chief the longest, and they had told me before that they had never really seen the Chief get angry, but it seemed like he was going to lose control when Captain Miller said they couldn't afford to send the military helicopters after one man. The threat from the people behind the Yorktown had become much bigger when we saw the plane land at Patriots Point, and the munitions we saw them setting up were not to be taken lightly. It was clear to him that the people were fortifying their area and that they considered Fort Sumter to be unwelcome.

The Chief had reacted with a fury that scared everyone except Captain Miller. He dwarfed all of us in size, but when he got mad and stood up, he seemed even bigger than before. He went so far as to call Captain Miller a coward, and the only reason punches weren't thrown was because Bus got between them. Bus may have been old and short, but he was muscular enough to put a stop to it.

I don't think anyone could ever say Captain Jim Miller was really a coward. He had managed to break away from the military with about a hundred soldiers not long after the apocalypse had begun. He wasn't a deserter in his own eyes, nor was he a deserter in the eyes of the men and women who served under him or our group of survivors.

His reasons for breaking away were good enough for us. When his senior officers ordered him to capture the infected and return with them to the ships where the military had set up their headquarters, it was a recipe for disaster. The plan was to experiment with the infected to find a cure, and even though it was understandable, attempts to contain the infection on ships hadn't always gone too well.

When Captain Miller questioned the orders, he was informed that they were also assigned to capture survivors and bring them back for further study under laboratory conditions. Miller never felt that the military should be used against the citizens of his country, so he took as many men and women as he could and escaped to the mainland.

Miller had eventually teamed up with us because we had crossed each other's paths once before, and on that occasion the Chief had sacrificed a large amount of our reserve fuel to rescue Captain Miller and his soldiers.

They were pinned down with no way to escape and likely to be overrun by the infected within the hour. Chief Barnes expertly flew in low over the heads of the infected and sprayed them with fuel. Once it was ignited, it consumed the infected while the soldiers escaped.

If not for the debt of gratitude, and Bus getting in between them, Captain Miller would probably have given the Chief a black eye. If I knew the Chief as well as I thought I did, when he cooled down he was probably going to ask Miller to give him two black eyes because he was the kind of guy who would regret letting his emotions get the best of him.

But that was going to take some time. I didn't think it would take too long, but like I said, I had never seen the Chief this angry.

When Bus separated them, the Chief stormed out of the room. I could see Jim Miller finally relax, but his shoulders slumped further than normal. He was clearly deflated by the cross words they had exchanged. For the most part he had maintained his even disposition. It was one of his character traits that made his troops so loyal to him. He didn't like being called a coward, though, and he had responded with something along the lines of the Chief thinking he was Rambo. The fact was, he cared enough for the Chief that the insults had hurt both of them.

Miller had hit a sore spot with the Chief, and he knew it because we had found Rambo to be one of the movies in the Fort Sumter video library. The Chief had joined in with all of the good natured jokes the soldiers made during the movie. They loved the movie and the actor, but whenever one of the men acted too bold or too tough, the others jumped on the chance to call him or her Rambo. Just as I suspected the

Chief would apologize for calling Miller a coward, I expected Miller to apologize for calling him Rambo.

The room stayed silent for a few seconds after the Chief left. Miller stayed on the same spot, likely to be unsure of what to say to the rest of us.

"Does anybody else think I'm wrong?"

He didn't say it in a voice that made us feel like it was a challenge.

One by one we met his gaze and told him basically the same thing. We understood, and the Chief would eventually come around.

"You know he doesn't think you're a coward," I said.

Everyone else seconded the comment, and Miller gave a half grin to no one in particular.

"I know. Do you think he'll get over the Rambo insult?"

Kathy said, "Yes, but I'm going to edit the movie credits and put his name in there instead of Stallone's."

"I heard that."

We all froze because the Chief put just enough of an edge on the comment to keep us from being able to tell if he was still mad. Then one corner of his mouth went up.

"You came back sooner than anyone expected," said Jean.

"If you need more time to defend my point of view, I can leave for a bit."

"Chief, I think the Captain has a point," said Kathy. "What if Patriots Point attacks while we're gone? Whoever is still here could seal the shelter shut, but those people would occupy the surface. Not to mention the possible loss of life."

"I know he has a point. That's what I'm mad about. I just have to catch up with that lowlife who buried the kids. Sam had to feel alone before he ran out of air, and I need to make that guy pay."

Chief Barnes had a special bond with all of us, and we had been through a lot together, but his bond was undeniably the strongest with Kathy. Even though she had become Tom's girlfriend and Molly's new mother, the things they had done since the beginning of the infection made them closer than most blood relatives. That was why he slumped just like Miller had when Kathy walked over and hugged him.

Captain Miller opened his mouth to say something, but the Chief just held up a hand and said, "No, Jim. You don't need to say it again. You're right with one exception."

Miller wasn't sure what he had missed, but he was willing to wait for the Chief to finish.

"You need to do something about the birds on the surface. If Patriots Point does a preemptive strike, you'll have helicopters that don't fly. They weren't intended for combat, but whoever those people are, they don't know that."

"What do you suggest?"

The Chief turned to our group as he answered.

"We have an idea where this guy Stokes is going, and if we leave soon, we'll get there ahead of him. If Bus can convince his old friend on that oil rig to let us visit, we could land on the rig while his friend will be forced to use a boat. Before we go you could rotate the birds to the Air Force Base and retrofit some weapons."

"What about the Cormorant?" I asked. "I know those machine guns are deadly, but we've got to get something that packs a little more punch."

"The Cormorant might be why they haven't attacked us yet. They may be interested in taking her from us," said Tom. "I imagine they would take the helicopters if they could."

It was easy to see that the entire group was unnerved by the prospect of being attacked by this unknown enemy. Whoever they were, they had built a strong fortress from the top of the bridge all the way to the other side of Patriots Point. They had weapons, and they had small planes. The one thing they didn't have that we knew of was an ally.

"There's still the military," said Captain Miller. "I could let them know where we are."

Even though it wasn't being put up for a vote, it wasn't a secret how everyone felt.

"No way," said Kathy. "They might treat you like a deserter, and at the very least you know they would take over the shelter."

It sounded like we didn't trust the military anymore, but the simple fact was that we had survived for five years without them. As a matter of fact, other than the rare sighting of a ship in the distance, there had been no military presence that we were aware of. Wherever they were, we hoped they were making progress against the infected, but we had gotten used to being on our own.

The Chief and Captain Miller had a silent exchange that was a combination of eye contact, nods, and some hand motions that indicated they wanted to talk about something in private. I saw Miller hook a thumb toward the wing of rooms where he had set up an informal command center. The Chief took the invitation, and they both slipped out of the room.

There was more than one sigh of relief, and we left it to them to figure out the plan. In the end, they decided that Plan A was for the Mud Island survivors to go after Stokes, but we wouldn't leave until the Army felt like Fort Sumter was ready. If the people at Patriots Point saw one helicopter leave, they weren't likely to think much of it. They might wonder where we had been after being gone for more than a day, but they wouldn't think the Fort was vulnerable just because the executive chopper was gone.

Communications with the oil rig was the problem. We hadn't been able to get Maybank on the radio, but that was likely to improve once we were in closer range. If it didn't, we figured we could at least land on the rig and then convince him to let us in. That's where Bus came in. They had aged, but Bus could convince Maybank it was really him if they had a chance to speak. Bus said the oil rig has some serious armament. We just had to be sure Maybank didn't see us as a threat before using his defense system.

****

When we acquired our fleet of helicopters from the Air Force base, we found that North Charleston was saturated with the infected. Even over the years that had passed since that time, the city surrounding the Air Force Base had remained untouchable by survivors who weren't as well equipped as we were.

We had weapons, manpower, and flight capabilities, so we could get in and out in a hurry. We could approach by water when we wanted but only if we used the Ashley River. Whoever that was on the Yorktown, they controlled the Cooper and the Wando Rivers. Even the mouth of Charleston harbor was within their range, but so far no one was reacting when we sailed the Cormorant or our smaller boats out to sea.

We decided to fly into the Air Force Base in search of the munitions that could be most effective if Fort Sumter was attacked. Even though the base had been the home of the C-17 transports, there was an avionics maintenance squadron on the base that was used to repair and resupply fighter jets. If we were lucky, they would also have weapons that could be adapted for use on helicopters.

The Chief and Captain Miller agreed that we would only need one day to find what we needed and to bring it back to Fort Sumter. As soon as that was finished, we could head for the Florida panhandle to find Stokes. If we couldn't locate him, we would settle for meeting with Maybank at his shelter. If Stokes was really unlucky, he would pick the oil rig that was home to Maybank's shelter, and Maybank could settle the score for us.

We knew we were being watched by the people on the Yorktown, so only one of our helicopters was deployed to the Air Force Base with enough troops to search for weapons.

They hit the jackpot when they checked the cargo hold of a C-17 on the runway. It was apparently transporting munitions to a First Air Cavalry unit because it had a variety of door operated machine guns, rockets, and grenade launchers. They were all designed to be integrated into the navigation systems of specific helicopters, but they could be adapted to operate manually.

The biggest discovery was a guided missile system called GROM and GROM/B. It was all Greek to us, but Miller's men were really excited by the weapons. They did a lot of damage, but the best part was they were intended for surface to air defense, but they could be fired from helicopters. With the increased altitude, they could fire them a long distance from the target. One of the soldiers told us that they could almost hit the Yorktown from the Air Force Base. Captain Miller said he preferred that the unknown force across the harbor would never need to be hit by those weapons, but if they had to use them, the fight would be over in under an hour.

The C-17 was surrounded by the infected because the flight line was so exposed. Any movement or noise would attract more of them to the area, and as soon as they began their search, the infected began arriving. A large amount of precious ammunition had to be used to set up a perimeter around the C-17. Once the infected were eliminated to a safe distance, the helicopters could land and retrieve their cargo.

The Navy helicopters flew in relays between Fort Sumter and the Air Force Base until they had a sizable cache of missiles. We didn't want the missiles stored near the helicopters because one lucky shot could destroy all of them at once. We also needed to be able to load the missiles easily without taking fire, so an armory was set up in the escape tunnel near the Morris Island entrance. It was out of the line of sight from Patriots Point, and it couldn't be hit by anything that could penetrate the tunnel.

By the end of the day, Fort Sumter had become the closest thing to a super power that anyone was likely to become. If anyone tried to hit Fort Sumter, we could arm the helicopters in minutes and retaliate.

"There's only one thing left to do," said the Chief.

Captain Miller was nodding his head as if he knew exactly what the Chief was going to say. The rest of us waited to see if they were going to let us in on the secret.

The Chief gestured for Captain Miller to go ahead.

"The real power behind a weapon is in knowing that you have it and making sure that your enemy knows you have it."

"Deterrence," I said.

"Very good, Ed. If your enemy knows you can obliterate him, he might just decide not to attack you. As a matter of fact, sometimes it can lead to a truce or even peace."

Kathy had a frown on her forehead that caught the attention of everyone.

"Wait a minute guys, are you saying they showed us what they've got so now we show them what we've got?"

Jean and Colleen both giggled and said at the same time, "It's a man thing."

"Call it that if you like," said Tom, "but didn't they put someone in a boat with a rocket launcher?"

"What are we going to do," asked Jean, "put some of those missiles on the Cormorant?"

"No, I have something less subtle in mind," said Captain Miller.

Our mouths all dropped open, and I wasn't alone when I objected.

"We're going to attack them," I said. "That's really not who we are, is it?"

"No, we're going to tell them what we have," said Captain Miller. "There's bound to be some ex-military over there, so we're going to start by running up an American flag over Fort Sumter. That will establish who we are and what we stand for. Then we're going to hang a big sign on the wall of the fort that says GROM and GROM-B. If they don't know what that means, they'll find someone who does. In the meantime, it will give them something to think about."

"So, they won't attack because they probably can't defend themselves against that kind of weapon," said Kathy. "How soon will we know if they got the message?"

"Not long. While we've been talking it over, my men have been taking care of it. As soon as the signs are up, we should see some activity over there."

As if Captain Miller had timed it, one of his NCO's appeared at the door. They exchanged a few words, and when the NCO left, Captain Miller turned to us with two thumbs up.

"The boat in the marsh is gone. He pulled out less than five minutes after the signs were hung."

"I have a question," said Tom. "Why so subtle?"

"The message is only intended for them," said the Chief, "and it wasn't a threat, just information. Once we get done with our trip to the Gulf, we can start working on the peace part of deterrence."

******

Our son was growing like a weed, and leaving him was never easy for me or for Jean. Molly told us she didn't know what she had been thinking when she left the fort because leaving Joshua behind had been like leaving her little brother. Whitney stepped up and told Molly it wasn't all on her. If she hadn't forgotten how much Molly needed someone close to her age, she might not have turned to Sam as her only alternative. We weren't too hard on her because to hear her tell it, the last few hours of Sam's life had been nothing but fear.

Sarah Beth was still trying to come to terms with her part in it, but all of us had told her repeatedly that there wasn't anything she could have done differently. In an area that was infested with the infected dead, anyone would have taken a swing at a body dropping in from above. If they had really been infected, she would have been dead if she had hesitated.

The atmosphere around the shelter became different every time we got ready to go out on the road. There was the usual planning that was handled by the Chief. He shared the details with us, but he seldom needed input when it came to fuel and supplies. Kathy and Tom were working on weapons and ammunition while Jean and I prepared rations.

Because we had the unique ability to fly to the coast of the Gulf, we could carry less food. If we needed more, we could get to it easier than survivors on the ground. We also had enough fuel to fly out to the oil rig rather than to find a boat, so we didn't need to land before then. At least that had been the plan until the executive helicopter broke down.

To say the Chief was angry again was an understatement. Five years of routine maintenance on the Sikorsky hadn't made it impervious to engine failure, and the first reports weren't good. Even worse, getting parts for the repair wouldn't be as simple as cannibalizing another helicopter, especially at the Air Force Base. The last trip up to the base for weapons had gotten them a good look at the infected population, and it hadn't improved over the years. If anything, it had gotten worse.

Plan B made sense to all of us. The Chief and Kathy lobbied for one of their crazy missions, but the rest of us wouldn't hear of it. They wanted to take the de Havilland Beaver with maybe two other members of the group, and fly to New Orleans. There were reasons why it would make sense, but there wasn't one of us that wanted our group to get split up. Tom said he should go if Kathy did, but Molly almost went crazy when she heard about it.

It wasn't just the infected dead or other survivors they were up against. Molly spent a lot of time with Sarah Beth, and it was obvious that Stokes was one of those people who was just plain lucky. She said he should have died hundreds of times, but it was always the person standing next to him who died. He also had this way about him that made him always have someone else standing there. Sarah Beth had convinced Molly that Stokes would be expecting us to show up no matter how far away he got.

After so many years since that first day when I watched the police and paramedics getting bitten at the strip mall in Surfside, I knew that we had gotten a bit like Stokes when it came to luck. We had too many close calls, and we had seen too many people die. The Chief and Kathy couldn't come up with a good defense in favor of their argument to take the seaplane because we knew they could be shot down. On our very first trip away from the Mud Island Shelter we had taken a bullet that had forced us to abandon our first plane. It was shot down over Charleston harbor the second time, with the Chief and Tom's wife on board.

As much as we trusted the Chief, there was going to be a time when luck wouldn't be enough to get us all home, and after so many years since our trip to Columbus, Ohio, this was feeling more and more like a trip we shouldn't take.

That suggestion was put on the table, and this time the Chief and Tom were the ones who went crazy. The Chief wanted the madman who had buried Sam alive, and Tom wanted him for burying his daughter. There was no way we could convince them to just let Stokes meet his fate out on the road.

After debate that went on for hours, Captain Miller made a suggestion everyone could live with. He pointed out that their neighbors over at Patriots Point were used to seeing the helicopters leave for a few hours at a time. They had to assume we were foraging for supplies just like everyone else, because they couldn't possibly know we were sitting on enough food to last at least fifty years, even with the large number of people we had in the shelter. They also couldn't know we were sitting on a power plant that could recycle water forever. They couldn't have it as good on the Yorktown.

Captain Miller suggested that his men could fly us out about halfway and then we could travel the rest of the trip by ground. Traveling by water was also an option if we wanted to take the Cormorant around Florida to the Gulf.

The dining area was about as quiet as it could get with so many of us present for the discussion. We were all weighing the two options, and both had their good and bad points. No one wanted to cross the southeast by land. There wasn't a town or city that was safe from the infected, and the problem with traveling around Florida was the open exposure. We didn't know how many other ships were at sea, we didn't have accurate weather reports, but the worst part was we would be forced to refuel along the way. There were plenty of places where we could find fuel, but they were all going to be hot spots for the infected or for other survivors.

"I have one other issue I'd like to resolve before we make a decision," said Tom.

His voice broke the silence, and we were all glad to hear someone do it. We were surprised by his issue, though.

"We need to find out where we stand with Patriots Point before we go after Stokes. I think we should send someone over there under a white flag."

"We tried that," said the Chief. "I was convinced by their response that whoever was sitting under the flag was going to die. I don't think there'll be many volunteers."

"I wasn't planning to ask for volunteers. We have someone in a holding cell who could be given an offer he can't refuse."

Tom had a wry smile on his face that was anything but humorous. The Chief had a bigger smile.

"The dummy will think this is his chance to escape," he said.

"How do we know he won't just try to sell us out?" asked Colleen. "That's what I would do."

"We'll give him a specific message to pass along, but we'll tell him a few things that aren't true," said Captain Miller. "It's the same principal that's used to catch spies. Misinformation that the courier couldn't possibly know to be true or false."

The Chief picked up where Captain Miller left off.

"The written message will be sealed, but we'll tell Randal he's not the first courier we've sent over to Patriots Point. We'll tell him we have a deal with them that either side will kill a courier who shows up with an unsealed message."

"So, what will you tell him they would do if he loses the sealed message?" asked Hampton.

"Feed him to the infected," said the Chief.

Jean raised her hand even though it was a formality we all tended to ignore just for fun. This time she had an expression that said she wasn't kidding around, so we were all ears.

"We're putting a lot of faith on assumptions here. Like, what happens if they just kill him? We would never know unless they shoot him while he's on the water. Or he could make a deal with them and come back with some message that's just a setup. We would be assuming either way. If he doesn't come back it could mean they let him join them. If he comes back with a message, it could all be a lie by him or the people at Patriots Point. How do we know without assuming too much?"

Sometimes the Chief did joke too much, but Jean had known him before the apocalypse. When they served together on board the cruise ship, Atlantic Spirit, he was famous for making the ship run like a Swiss watch, but he was also famous for his sense of humor. This time he had a set to his jaw that said he wasn't kidding around. As a matter of fact, his facial expression was similar to the day they had been forced to start disposing of bodies when people died in sick bay.

"Have you met Randal?" he asked Jean.

"No, I got a look at him when he was brought in, but he was blindfolded and didn't speak. All I know is he's fat, so he hasn't been missing meals."

"He has been since we brought him in," said the Chief.

"We sent him some soup," said Colleen. "I understand you broke his jaw, Chief."

The Chief didn't react other than to give a slight shrug of his shoulders, as if to say it was no big deal.

Captain Miller said, "I think what the Chief means is that Randal is too stupid to pull off anything on his own, Jean. If we tell him what to do, he'll do it."

"So, it's decided then. We'll send Randal over to Patriot's Point and hope they respond to a message," said Kathy. "Next, we have to decide how we're going after Stokes."

Colleen asked, "How long would it take us to circle around the tip of Florida? I mean, wouldn't that be a lot faster than traveling on foot?"

Everyone turned toward the Chief because that was a logical question he could answer the best.

"If we could cruise straight there without any stops along the way, only a couple of days. It's about a thousand nautical miles, but I would prefer to go around the Keys, so add a hundred. That's two days at max speed, but the Cormorant only has a cruising distance of a little more than nine hundred miles. That means we have to risk stopping somewhere."

"Where?" asked several of us at the same time.

"That's not an easy answer," he said. "I'll have to spend some time with a few maps. Am I understanding everyone correctly? You'd rather go by sea than by land?"

A few of the group had been quiet. Olivia and Chase had always been better as support staff at home, but Sim would be a valuable navigator and Cassandra was undeniably a good shot from long range. Her military training wasn't as intense as the Chief's SEAL training, but she had proven herself to be a quick thinker and fast on her feet when the Mercy Mission ship had been overrun by the infected and then boarded by desperate survivors. Not many people could have survived one of those obstacles, but she had survived both.

"If this is a vote," said Cassandra, "I'll pick going to sea over mosquitos and humidity any day."

Sim said, "I'm with her and not just because she's pretty. I almost stayed up north when I had the chance just because of those same two things."

That earned him a smile from Cassandra and probably scored him a few points with every woman in the room.

"I guess that's settled," said the Chief. "Give me a day to study the maps, and in the meantime we can be getting the Cormorant ready to go home."

"Home?" asked Tom.

"She was built near New Orleans," answered the Chief.

"I'll take that as a good omen," said Sim. "I don't know if you people are superstitious, but I watch for the good signs whenever I can."

Hampton said, "You've been with us long enough to know this group believes in luck, but we also believe in each other. Right, Bus?"

Bus had been quieter than the rest of us and seemed to be a million miles away. He snapped out of it when he realized all eyes were on him.

"Don't mind me, guys. I was just thinking how good it would be to see Maybank again."

15 DEAD TIDE

Year One of the Decline

In those first days after the apocalypse, Maybank understood this had been what Titus Rush had been talking about. He watched news reports while they lasted and did his daily routines. Inspecting the shelter wasn't on the list for the rest of his life, but Titus had told everyone in the survivors club that they should look for things in those early days that they hadn't anticipated. Since they didn't know what kind of apocalypse they were going to face, they couldn't possibly anticipate everything.

By the end of the first month he knew that he had thought of everything that fit with this particular apocalypse. Or at least he felt like he had, although he had to admit he had never put much emphasis on getting ready for a zombie apocalypse.

"Or did I?" he asked himself.

Maybank noticed he was talking to himself more than before, and that was one thing that had come up in their survivor meetings. Everyone was planning to survive in shelters with important people. Some would be sharing their quarters with a lot of survivors, and some with a few. Titus was the only one who was planning on riding it out alone, and as far as Maybank knew, he not only wouldn't have any dignitaries staying with him, he also wouldn't have any family.

When Maybank and the other survivors all brought it up, he advised them to keep a journal. At first it was like keeping a log on a ship, then as technology improved, it became an audio and video record. He told them it would keep them from going crazy. After what he had seen so far, he didn't think keeping a record would stop him from going crazy. Maybe he already was.

The rains came so often that Maybank would have lost track of the seasons if not for calendars. He expected tropical storms and maybe even some hurricanes, but he didn't expect the heavy seas that were more like the North Atlantic than the Gulf of Mexico. They went on for so long that he was surprised when he finally woke up to weather he could enjoy.

It had done its job, though. The constant wind, storms, and high seas had washed the charred remains from the maze of catwalks, and the temperature was so comfortable that he decided to break the number one rule of survival. He was going topside.

Titus Rush had pounded it into all of them. Once you were inside, stay there. There was no reason to leave your shelter that was worth more than your life. Maybank wished Titus was around for him to talk to. He would tell him that he had found a reason to leave the shelter.

"Because I want to."

He didn't mean to say it out loud, but it was such a powerful feeling that it was almost a shout. Maybe it was because his reflection was looking back at him from the mirror, and for a moment his reflection was scolding him the way Titus would have.

"I've been by myself too long," he said, "and I've been inside too long. If I can go outside, then I should. I can tell when someone is coming from miles away, so I have plenty of time to get back inside."

Two hours later he was standing in front of the mirror again, and this time his reflection reminded him even more of Titus Rush. He didn't know why until he remembered his only visit to Mud Island. That was where Titus decided to put his shelter. It was on an island that was surrounded by water just like the oil rig. Titus was coasting a small boat up to the dock and jumped before he should have.

He learned a lot about Titus that day. For one thing, Maybank had always thought of him as larger than life, and larger than life people didn't get their feet tangled up in ropes and fall overboard. They also didn't laugh at themselves as hard as he did. It was something that made Maybank love and respect the man even more.

Titus had pulled his wet body up onto the dock and was laughing so hard he couldn't stand up. He laid there on his back with that long wet head of hair covering his face. His beard hid most of it, but the rest of his face was plastered with hair and seaweed. He laughed like that for so long that Maybank thought he had lost his mind.

He finally looked up at Maybank and said, "I think I may have forgotten how to have fun."

Maybank studied his own soaking wet and frustrated expression and agreed with what Titus had said. Long before the infected dead had seemingly appeared out of nowhere, he had stopped having fun, and along with that loss came the inability to laugh at himself.

His reflection said, "That's just what you needed. Now laugh about it and learn from it."

So Maybank laughed. He laughed until his side hurt, and he had to sit down. He couldn't believe that he had fallen off of his own oil rig. He knew the thing like the back of his hand, and he had done it just like Titus.

"Learn from it," he said.

He had gone topside through the main entrance, and the first thing he wanted to see for himself was the platform where the fires had been. What he didn't think about was how much damage the safety railings had taken. It was lucky for him that they were low areas closer to the water. When the railing broke loose from the platform, he instinctively grabbed for the nearest piece of pipe and held on. Too bad it was a piece that wasn't considered essential to the overall structure, so it snapped loose and went with him.

He dropped about forty feet, just enough distance for him to gain control of his body's position, and still low enough for the impact not to break bones. He went in feet first with his toes pointed downward. As he drifted toward the surface he told himself that even the Romanian judge would give him a ten for that dive.

The emergency hatches were everywhere if you knew where to look for them, and he didn't need to climb back up to the catwalks to get inside. He was just glad he didn't fall from too high or bounce on any catwalks below him. He got his bearings, took a deep breath, and swam to the nearest entrance.

All of the emergency entrances and exits were equipped with airlocks that could be pressurized, but this was one occasion when he didn't need it. He sealed the hatch behind him and climbed a steel ladder that took him back into the shelter.

After he dried off and changed clothes, he went topside again, but this time he went up with a little more respect for his predicament. He was a survivor, and if he was going to break one of the rules, he was going to be careful about it. He thought about Titus laughing on the dock, but a few minutes later he had been all business. Maybank had a good laugh at his own expense, but from now on he would watch where he put his feet and his hands.

Less than thirty minutes later he was climbing the steps up to the crew's quarters. The wind and rain had done a lot of housecleaning for him. The big red smears of blood had been washed enough to where it just appeared to be rust. The inside of the quarters was another matter. The guy who had been wounded had bled on a lot of things. Maybank checked the supplies and decided he would spend a little time cleaning up the blood. After a bit of scrubbing, he changed his mind and decided he would drop off a couple cases of food on his next trip topside. If anyone else made it this far, they could clean the place better if they wanted to.

The view from the landing pad was a welcome sight. As far as he could tell it had been almost six months since he had seen the horizon from this high.

There was something wrong with it, though. He steadied his arms on a railing and focused his binoculars. The line where the horizon met the sky was darker than he remembered. It was like someone had taken a black pen and colored it in from left to right.

Maybank wasn't sure, but he thought an oil spill would make the water darker in appearance, but there weren't any operating oil rigs between him and the coast of the US. He panned his view left and right to see if he could spot the end of the dark line. He wondered if there had been an oil spill drifting along the coast, and he was just now seeing it for the first time. That would make sense, and it would be an unexpected layer of protection for him. Whatever was happening on the mainland, it would have a harder time getting to him through an oil spill.

He eventually decided he would bring a camera up to get some pictures. He could run them through the computer and enhance the images.

An inspection of the rest of the rig showed what he had expected. The Army Corps of Engineers had built the thing to last, and other than a few scars from the fire, it would do exactly as they intended.

The last stop was the penthouse apartment that he had called home for so many years. It was still as well sealed as he had left it, and he let himself in by activating the hidden combination lock under one of the steps on the last catwalk. It was in a place where someone might look, but even if someone found it, they wouldn't know how to operate it.

Everything was where it should be, and he hadn't thought of it before, but there was a high resolution digital camera feed connected to his control room. He could save himself some time by checking that dark line from the penthouse instead of waiting until he got back to the shelter.

He powered up the computers and brought the image up on the largest monitor. It was a bright day with no clouds, but the dark line didn't reflect the light. He started scrolling the zoom bar as he panned lower to stay right on the horizon.

"What is that?"

It was expanding almost too slowly to see, but as he stared at it, he could see that it was moving in his direction. It was like a crooked black line that was getting wider and thicker at the same time. When he zoomed closer the details became pixelated, but he let the computer software take over, and gradually some of the details emerged.

Maybank was holding his breath. He didn't realize he was, but when the first details became too clear to deny, he finally let his breath out slowly. Arms, legs, heads…..bodies, and it was all moving. Not just moving on the surface, not just floating, but moving people as if they were all pushing at each other, trying to get enough room to break free.

He rubbed his eyes with the backs of his hands as if he needed to clear something out of them. It didn't do anything for his eyes, but it cleared his head. He remembered that he could take pictures and enhance them. Better yet, he could video everything. He hit all of the right switches and was recording it all to the drives in the underwater shelter. He could examine everything from safety if it turned out to be what he thought it was.

As the image became even clearer, individual bodies began to take shape. It was a massive tangle of bodies, and it was floating away from the mainland, held afloat by the gases building up in the decomposing dead.

Some of the bodies were floating on top of the bloated corpses under them, and Maybank was shocked to see some of them were actually crawling on top of the others. He knew there had to be hundreds of thousands of them, and as he watched the infected tide growing in size, he knew it was coming closer. He also knew why he had to be inside his shelter when the floating horde arrived. There was something else moving in between the bodies of the infected. At first it looked like body parts just bobbing in and out of view, but then he saw purpose in the movement. The floating graveyard was covered with rats that were feeding on the dead, and rats could manage to climb almost anything.

******

He stopped going topside days before the black tide of bodies reached his oil rig. It was one thing to see it through binoculars or digital photography, but it was another thing altogether to see it with the naked eye. Even without the binoculars, the height of the oil rig was enough for him to see how vast the stain was on the ocean. When he tried to make a journal entry to describe what he was seeing, he struggled with the words. Not how to describe it, but what to call it.

"Is it a floating island of bodies? Is it a killing field? A graveyard?"

He tried so many different things that he realized there was nothing in history that could compare. The floating island of plastic and other garbage in the oceans of the world were bad enough, but a floating, human debris field was beyond a one or two word title.

On his last day watching it approach from the landing pad on the top of the oil rig, he had let the binoculars hang on its strap and just leaned heavily on the railing. The gravity of the number of dead was beyond emotion.

He turned to the left and then the right and then tried to see beyond the bodies toward the coast. He couldn't see the end of it in any direction, but he was able to make out the details better. He was also starting to understand where they had all come from.

He turned on his audio recorder. He could have done video, but it was enough to know it was being recorded by the computer system in the shelter.

"The bodies will wash up against the rig for days. There are so many that I may even feel some movement inside the shelter. I don't know how many will get tangled up under the rig, because I just don't know how deep the bodies are. They're bound to catch on the moorings that hold the shelter to the frame of the oil rig. It's time for me to go below and watch from there. I caught a bit of the smell on the breeze a few minutes ago, and I imagine it's going to get a lot worse. I'll continue this entry when I get below."

The monitors were on when Maybank sealed his hatch, so he was able to see details he had seen from above. At that moment he doubted he would ever open the shelter door again.

"I can see details that confirm some things I already knew," he said after turning on the microphone by the computer.

"They are definitely what the news was calling them back at the beginning. They are all infected dead. Heaven help anyone in that mess who might be alive. They would have to think they're in Dante's Hell."

He switched off the microphone and just stared at the bobbing mass of bodies. Arms and legs aimed freely toward the sky and swayed with the motion of the water and the other bodies around them

"I'm sorry. I didn't mean to get all poetic. This is supposed to be a journal with observations. I guess I should say there isn't much chance that anyone is uninfected and alive in all of those bodies. I've also been searching for facts that would support the existence of this thing."

He searched again for the right thing to call it. He didn't feel like he could keep calling it the floating mass of dead people.

"The dead tide. I'll call it the dead tide. From what I could find on the Internet, millions of people were bitten in the first day alone, probably billions worldwide. People didn't all die at the same pace. Some went home to their loved ones, and some went to hospitals. When they died, they were able to bite other people, and from there the death rate became exponential. The question is obvious. How many of them went into the water?"

Maybank had a map of the Gulf coast spread across a large table, and he traced his finger along the line from Texas to the tip of Florida. An internet source said there were fourteen million people living on the Gulf coast in 2012. They didn't all go into the water, but the census only took into consideration the number of people who actually lived on the coast. It didn't consider how many tourists were visiting Tampa, New Orleans, Pensacola, Galveston, and all the other beaches along the Gulf. There were probably thirty million people on the coast when it started, and there was no such thing as an evacuation.

He pressed the microphone button again.

"Millions of people went into the water along the coast. They were either already dead when they went in or they died when they drowned or were bitten. The news wasn't clear about whether or not you had to be bitten before you died, but it didn't really matter. All dead bodies that sink eventually resurface due to expanding gases during decomposition."

He was trying to sound clinical, but the entire time his voice was shaking and beginning to break. He could see people of all ages in the tangle of bodies, and some of them moved like they were alive.

He decided to leave the recording running, but he couldn't watch anymore. There was only so much he could take.

The computer room reminded him of the control room in a submarine, so he went to the room he had designed for recreation. If he could ignore what was happening outside for a few minutes, maybe he could even get his appetite back.

It worked to some extent. Because the room was for recreation, the kitchen wasn't fully stocked with the ingredients he needed to make a home cooked meal, but it had plenty of frozen pizzas and beer. That was probably what he needed right now, and it wasn't long before the smells of dough baking and pepperoni crisping made his stomach growl. He was on his third beer by then.

He scrolled through the video library on his server and found a movie that he knew was loosely based on a book he had read. He had every movie in his collection that had anything to do with survival. He almost chose the movie about a guy who got stranded on an island for four years, but he wanted something that felt a little less real but also fit with what was happening outside. He settled on the movie about the sole survivor in New York who was trying to find a cure for an infection that turned people into zombies that could run. They only came out in the dark, and they hunted for survivors.

When he thought about it, the similarities between his apocalypse and the one in the movie ended with the infection. Yes, the infected would bite you in both situations, you became one of them if you were bitten, and there was no cure, but he was having problems with some of the details in the movie.

As far as he could tell, the infected in the movie would eat you if they caught you. They wouldn't feel pain because they were dead, and they could think to some extent. What he couldn't wrap his mind around was zombies that could run.

"Running zombies," he said. "That's against the rules."

There was also the day and night thing. The sunlight didn't seem to bother his zombies. The reports he had seen before losing the internet gave him the impression that the infected dead could find you in broad daylight or in a totally dark room.

A timer dinged, and his pizza was done. He would have called it denial if he thought about it, but he had pretty much put the dead tide out of his mind for the time being.

"Would Titus be proud of me for coping so well, or would he be worried that I was in denial?"

It wasn't difficult for him to answer his own question.

"He would be proud of me because I don't have an ounce of denial about what's happening out there."

He motioned with his head toward the ceiling.

"There just isn't a thing I can do about it, and I'm hungry."

There were crumbs left on the pizza pan, and he had washed it down with three more beers. Maybank felt relaxed and something else that he would have called satisfied under normal circumstances. But there was nothing normal about these circumstances. It didn't take much deep thinking for him to realize his satisfaction was simply the knowledge that they had been right. Titus and everyone in their survivors club had been right, and there were millions of people up there who had been wrong. A bunch of them were floating toward him now.

The swaying woke him up. His half awake half asleep mind told him he was at sea, and he was supposed to be swaying. When he was a little more than half awake, that part of his mind reminded him that the shelter wasn't supposed to sway. It was supposed to be steady. It was supposed to be as steady as it would be if was sitting on the floor of the Gulf of Mexico.

The lights were programmed to dim when he left a room, so they were still on.

"Maybe six beers were a few too many," he mumbled.

When he stood up he chose the wrong moment to do it. The whole room moved, and he heard a deep groan as the mooring cables that held the shelter in place were stretched as far as they could go.

Maybank knew every specification of the shelter right down to the sizes of the screws in the walls, and he knew the mooring cables were almost six inches thick. Whatever was pushing on the shelter had to have a lot of force behind it if the cables were going to stretch far enough to move the shelter. The groan meant something was going to give if they stretched much further, and there wasn't anything he could do about it.

With his arms stretched out to the sides and his legs spread for balance, he walked carefully to the door to the next compartment. From there he would be able to see what was happening outside.

The lights came up as soon as he stepped through the water tight door. Unlike the other shelters, all of his doors could be closed remotely and were replicas of the doors found on ships. He sealed the door and carefully worked his way into a chair that was fastened to the floor. He had questioned the need for such things when the engineers built his shelter, but one had patiently explained that he thought of the shelter as a ship, and ships didn't let things like chairs fly around a room full of computers.

The shelter stopped swaying just as he was situated in the chair with a seatbelt on. Now it was vibrating as if it was being pelted by something. He couldn't hear the shelter being hit, but he could feel it in his feet and as each jolt traveled up through the metal of the chair.

When the monitors came on, Maybank thought there was something wrong with the cameras. Every monitor displayed a dark screen even though they were definitely on. He tried turning them off and then back on again, but there was no change.

He had practiced disaster scenarios with the crew of a submarine, and he recalled they had told him sometimes you wouldn't know what was happening. Those were the disasters you worried about the most because you couldn't stop it or protect yourself from it until it revealed itself. If it was something you could control, the longer it took to reveal itself the more damage it could do.

Then there were the things you couldn't control, and you were possibly going to die without even knowing what was killing you.

Maybank swiveled his chair and furiously switched from one camera to the next. There was brightness on one monitor, and he transferred the feed of that camera over to the monitor directly in front of his chair. The view from the camera showed the surface just above the water, but the swells were traveling away from him.

He watched the swells doing the opposite of what he expected and was totally confused until the next unexpected thing happened. Something drifted across the camera and completely blocked his view.

He resisted the urge to reach up and tap on the monitor. It was a natural impulse, but he knew there wasn't anything wrong with it. He rotated the camera to try to see around whatever was blocking the view, and for just a moment he could see the swells again. This time there was something riding on the swells, and as he watched something else floated into view.

For a split second he saw the face, and he jumped back from the monitor. A quick glance at another monitor that had brightened a little, and he saw light between two faces. One was quickly replaced by another, and then the entire view was blocked again. He didn't know why he didn't recognize it sooner, and maybe it was the beer, but the dead tide had arrived. He just didn't want to believe that there could be so many bodies that it had moved the shelter, and his mistake had been to turn on the wrong cameras.

That much he could correct, and Maybank switched all of the cameras to an overhead view looking down from the top of the oil rig.

He had expected it to be bad, but even though he had watched the immense floating island of bodies approach for days, seeing it up close was unreal. There were so many bodies that the range of the cameras didn't show any water. He backed the view away on his highest camera until he could see water in the distance toward the Gulf coast. Rotating the camera to the west he could see that the dead tide was at least twenty miles long. He wasn't surprised to see the same when he turned it to the east. The dead tide was at least forty miles long and over twenty miles wide.

Bodies had drifted in between all four of his towers, and just as he had expected, they had become snagged on the top of the shelter where the mooring lines were connected. Bodies piled up on bodies until the weight of them had begun to put a strain on the massive cables. Fortunately, the current had continued to pull the tide of bodies around the sides of the oil rig, and most of the pressure was being pulled away from the rig. Some of the bodies from the middle even managed to be carried away with the rest.

Maybank saw he had also anticipated correctly what the rats would do. There were so many of them that they had begun to breed on the massive tide of bodies. Litters of baby rats left their nests in the clothing of the dead and scattered across an endless food supply, but when the bodies became lodged against the towers, some of the rats instinctively started to climb. Despite the fact there was no food supply for them to find on the oil rig, they climbed to get further from the water.

Some of them would eventually reach the crew quarters near the helicopter pad, but Maybank was certain they couldn't get inside. Even if they did, they would exhaust the food supply in a matter of days and be forced to go back down to the tangle of bodies that were stuck in the middle of the rig. He estimated that there were over a thousand bodies that would remain behind after the dead tide had passed, and that was far too many for him. It would take much longer for the rats to eat their way through that food supply, and there wasn't anything he could do about it.

"Or maybe there is."

The plans to the shelter and the oil rig were all on the computer, so Maybank opened an auto cad program and searched for the specs he needed. There they were.

The number one scenario they had planned for was a nuclear war. He opened the file to the scenario and didn't even need to use the search function to find the table he needed. It was a list of temperatures. The paint would start to crack and peel off as the temperature rose, but there wasn't anything he could do about that. If his plan worked, it was going to get pretty hot down there. Not as hot as a nuclear war, but hotter than normal.

What he needed to know was whether or not critical systems could handle the heat. His assumption was that anything that could withstand a nuclear explosion could easily withstand a regular fire.

"Maybe not a regular fire," he said. "It's going to be a big fire."

The mooring cables were probably not able to withstand the heat as well as the towers, but the narrow metal bars and grids of the catwalks were his biggest worries. The mooring cables at least had the water to keep them cool.

"Well, I won't be needing the catwalks if things are as bad on the mainland as they appear to be. Now I just need to figure out what kind of accelerant I could use to make waterlogged bodies burn."

He didn't need a degree in physics to know what the risks were. The fire had to be hot enough to keep burning, but a fire that hot could easily find a way to spread across the oil rig. It had occurred to him that the rats would climb higher to get away from the fire, and if the fire didn't fry all of his external electrical wiring, the rats would eat it in order to survive. Then they would turn on each other, but the damage would already be done.

He wasn't ready to give up on one of his defenses so quickly. The electrically charged catwalks had served him well, but he doubted it would be the last time he would use them if they were still working after he was done getting rid of the bodies.

In the end, he knew there was no way to set over a thousand bodies on fire and keep them burning long enough to break down the logjam. He had to find a way to get them to untangle from each other and drift away from the oil rig.

"What would Titus do?" he asked himself. "Titus would go out there and untangle them himself if that was the only way to get it done."

Maybank laughed at himself for having a conversation that included questions and answers, but he found himself actually visualizing what it would be like out there.

"Over a thousand snapping mouths, two thousand grasping hands."

He leaned back in his chair and noticed for the first time that the swaying had stopped. The monitors showing the east and the west gave him a good view of the bodies on the surface, and each side was a long, sweeping curve. The dead tide was tearing itself away from the oil rig on both sides. The view from the south showed more and more water as the gap between the tide and the rig increased. He switched to the camera view that showed the middle of the rig, and he figured he couldn't have snagged more infected dead if he had tried to with a net. He got an insane image in his head. He pictured himself wearing SCUBA gear, pulling at the squirming bodies as he yanked them free of the tangled mess one by one.

16 HOPKINS ON THE LAKE

Year Six of the Decline

The smell almost arrived before the sound of the horde as it pressed itself into the small gaps between trees. It came on the breeze almost a full day before the first group of them appeared. The dry underbrush was trampled flat with a great cracking and crunching, and trees that had weak spots or damage from lightning and wind were pushed over like they were nothing more than tall pretzels.

The children were too young to remember movies, but their parents remembered the silver screens and what it was like to see herds of elephants crashing through jungles. Some of them had forgotten about the dinosaur movies that had become so popular before the infected dead had arrived, but now they were being reminded of the scenes when the trees shook just before the monsters charged at their prey.

Even though the sun had only just begun to rise above the horizon, they could see the tops of the trees part and then come back together again. At any moment they expected to see the meat eating dinosaurs charging from the trees, not the slow moving, shifting shapes still too immersed in darkness to see. In a way, the people of the new town of Hopkins on The Lake would have preferred the monsters from thousands of years in the past because a horde large enough to move the big trees of the forest had to be beyond imagination.

From the time they had finished construction of the wooden town until now, they had been under siege. During the day they had seen the infected dead coming toward the dock and had to back away from the land defenses that were supposed to keep the infected from even reaching the lake. They doubled the guard and had every able bodied adult protecting their home. They worked frantically to build up the barricade at the single entrance that led out to their new town, and the guards fought off the infected that made it past the other obstacles. Sharpened trees were driven into the ground at random, and a crew worked full time to remove the bodies that had become impaled. It wasn't long before they were forced backward onto the dock to help the guards who were continually pushing the infected into the lake.

Pits between the rows of spikes were so full that the infected fell in and were only unable to get out because their legs were so entangled with the other infected. Some sank to the bottoms of the pits, disappearing among the squirming bodies, but eventually the new arrivals simply walked around them, and were joined by others that broke free of the melee in the manmade traps. They continued forward until they were pushed from behind onto the sharpened spikes. It was clear even before today that there was an increase in the number of infected, but scouts that had gone out to see what was happening didn't return to give their reports.

This was the day they had feared, but they had hoped it wouldn't be as bad as it was quickly becoming. They gave up their efforts at the end of the dock and raised the drawbridge they had built at the halfway point between land and the town.

When the sun came over the tops of the shaking trees, they could see that the infected had grown in numbers on the other side of the drawbridge, and even though they were walking off the end into the water, there were too many of them for the dock to support the weight. The wooden structure was swaying left and right, and rails were bulging outward. When they broke free, the entire dock seemed to fall over at the same time. Dozens of the infected fell with each other, but the path was cleared for hundreds more behind them. They walked into the water as if the dock was still there.

To the people watching the army of the infected trying to reach them, this was cause for celebration, and they cheered and shouted insults at the heads that bobbed in the water. The celebration was short lived, though. The dead couldn't reach them on their wooden town, but there was something about the growing numbers that was beyond comprehension. It was gradually dawning on the leaders and the planners in the community that they would never be safe if there were going to be hordes like this one passing through without warning. Yes, they smelled them coming. Yes, they could hear them. But why were there so many?

A hush fell over the people watching from the safety of their railings around the wooden town as the bobbing heads began passing under their homes. Hands reached up and slapped at the wooden walkways around the town and in the gaps between buildings. There were screams from inside the town as people were surprised by the infected that popped up in those gaps and held on for just long enough to reach for the legs of the frightened townspeople. Someone had been too close to the water, and the scream was from pain as teeth found bare skin.

The bumping started, and at first it felt like it should. Vibrations due to the collisions between the bodies of the infected and the pilings that supported the town. Vibrations they could accept, but the vibrations became strong enough for people to lose their balance as more and more of the infected managed to grab onto the pilings and the edges of the boards above them.

Everywhere the people could see fingers gripping the gaps between boards and the wider gaps between the buildings. It was a sturdy construction built by men and women who had done construction before the infected had arrived, and it was holding better than many places would, but this was no common horde. This was far more than they ever expected.

Someone finally got the nerve to begin fighting with the fingers reaching up from below. A woman with a hatchet chopped at a row of fingers, and the hand disappeared into the water. Feeling bolder, she singled out another hand and separated it from its owner.

The crowd of people who had been huddling away from the gaps, holding each other and crying came to life. At first it was one by one, and then it was large groups of people who began attacking the hands. There were fingers everywhere, and it became difficult to walk on the wooden planks without slipping on them until someone started going around the walkways pushing a broom in front of them, and slowly a gap appeared in the drifting bodies below Hopkins on The Lake.

They began to cheer again, but this time they were cheering each other on. Yelling and pointing where they saw new fingers appear instead of cowering away from them.

When someone pointed, someone near to the fingers would rush forward and neatly slice them off with knives and hatchets.

A hush fell over the people of the town for a second time. This time it wasn't because of the vibrations. This time it was because the town lurched under their feet. It was like a car suddenly stopping and its occupants continued forward. There was a scream from the back of the town as one of the occupants of that particular walkway was unable to stop their forward motion, and a man fell with his wife when he tried to keep her from going through the railing.

Then it was everyone's turn to scream as the vehicle that used to be their town began to lean too hard against the pilings that supported it, and the town began to slide across the tops of the poles. It was like they were launching a great ship, and the buildings of the town slid free onto the surface of the water and threw up a huge wave that rushed away in all directions. It had become a tremendous houseboat.

People who stayed on their feet began to climb the walls of the building to reach the rooftops. Hands that reached for them were the hands of their friends, but more than once when someone reached to help a friend it was not who they thought it would be. The people of Hopkins literally stuck their hands into the jaws of death, and only those people who didn't risk showing compassion reached safety.

The screams died away as people were dragged under and either eaten or drowned. What was left behind was the crying of mothers for their children or children who were unable to stay with their parents when they were pushed upward to safety.

The town of Hopkins on The Lake became quite literally on the lake as it floated away from its pilings. The few people who had managed to reach safety on the rooftops gauged the distance to the shore and hoped their momentum was strong enough for them to make it across that decreasing distance before they stopped moving. Their only hope was to coast to the far end of the lake and then to run when they reached shore.

One of the men yelled to the others that they weren't going to make it, and he dove into the water to swim ahead of the town. He dove in, but he didn't come back to the surface. He had forgotten that the infected had been falling into the lake for several hours before the town had slipped free of its pilings, and hundreds of the infected lined the bottom of the lake all the way to shore.

The people cried as they watched the bobbing heads in the water come and go. Some had been neighbors. Some had been family. All the while the horde continued to flow from the trees into the lake, and some of the more calm members of the remaining survivors realized that they were actually gaining speed. If the watertight integrity of the buildings held well enough, then they were really going to be pushed to the opposite shoreline. A quick assessment by those who were still not ready to die was enough for them to see that the buildings were closing the distance faster than they were sinking. Even as the momentum slowed when they reached shallow water, they saw that the buildings were going to beach without them having to get into the water to cover the remaining few feet.

Boards were stretched across the rooftops to allow everyone still alive to be able to jump to the beach, but it was almost a fatal flaw in the plan. The side of the drifting town settled deeper as more and more people crossed onto the rooftops to make the jump, and the town began to list and drag across the bottom. Ironically, the infected dead under the town were crushed into the shoreline at the edge of the lake, and the town literally slid across their bodies as if it had been lubricated to do so.

Some of the survivors waited until the town that had become a lifeboat stopped its forward motion, and then they crossed over the rooftops to join the others in their leap to safety. It was a miracle that so many had survived to make the jump, but to the remaining two dozen, they felt like the time to count their blessings would come later. For now, they had to run.

The sun was hardly an hour above the treetops, and the town of Hopkins was on the run for a second time. As they carried the handful of children who had survived, they ran for the trees on the opposite side of the lake. They didn't have a clue where they were going, but they knew the horde wouldn't need to stop and rest, so they couldn't either. One of the men had been a community leader, so when he said they should go west toward I-26, no one disagreed with him. He said that they needed to get to the interstate so they could move faster and out distance the horde that was crossing the lake in pursuit of them.

By the time the sun was past the middle of the sky they had found a road that led straight west. The sun sat above the middle of the road as if it was a street sign that had WEST printed on it. The road was also paved, so they were able to run much faster than they had before, and before the sun had reached the treetops to the west, they saw a red, white, and blue sign that said they were approaching I-26.

There was an overpass ahead that could only be crossing the interstate, so they knew they had made it, and as they approached it they saw there were several men along the right side of the overpass. They appeared to be heavily armed, but they were keeping their heads low beneath the concrete wall that ran the length of the overpass. One of them had binoculars to his eyes and was looking down the interstate in the direction of Columbia.

Caution made the Hopkins survivors hesitant about yelling to the men even though the guns would give them a measure of safety. Maybe it was the way the day had begun, but right now it seemed that the best way to stay alive was to be inconspicuous, and they could afford to be cautious.

They moved to the left side of the road into a ditch that ran along the shoulder. The men would probably be able to see them if they got much closer, so their newly elected mayor motioned for everyone to sit on the ground and get some rest. He climbed back up to the road and laid down in the grass where he could see the overpass. After a few moments, some of the other men crawled up and laid down next to him.

It was a good thing for the others not to see. The men on the overpass had company, and they didn't know it yet. On the far side of the overpass a group of about twenty infected dead had begun to cross the road. They were at the middle when they saw the living, breathing men hiding along the wall. They didn't need any further invitation, and they shambled in their direction.

Before the infected had even reached the overpass, they were joined by at least another twenty, and there was no way the men would be able to escape in that direction. One of the men spotted them. He alerted the others and started backing away at the same time.

From their hiding place the Hopkins survivors watched in horror as the men backed in their direction, but it wasn't the sight of the infected dead on the other side of the overpass that had them so startled. It was the large group of infected that emerged from the trees on the other side of the road directly in front of them.

They weren't exposed yet, but they would be in only a few minutes as the infected began to come up from the shoulder of the road only two lanes from where they were hiding. They couldn't even yell a warning to the men on the overpass without giving away their position.

A gunshot rang out from the overpass, and one of the infected across the interstate fell over. One of the men had panicked and opened fire. The infected were only one lane away from the Hopkins survivors when they turned in the direction of the gunshot. When the second shot was fired, it might as well have been a dinner bell. The infected in the road were joined by dozens more that were already in the ditch on the other side of the road, and they turned as one toward the men.

Down on the overpass the armed men hadn't seen the group in front of the Hopkins survivors. They had lined up across the road and were carefully taking aim at the infected that were coming from the other side. They were being efficient, but it soon became obvious to them that this wasn't just a little horde blocking the road, and they decided to retreat. That was when they saw what was behind them.

As the infected in front of them turned and walked toward the overpass, the men eased back into the ditch with their fellow survivors. No explanation was needed as they reversed their direction and followed the ditch back the way they had come. They made it to the first crest in the road, and when they looked up ahead, they knew they could run, but they also knew they wouldn't get very far. For miles down the road they had already traveled, the infected were crossing the centerline, and as the shots continued to ring out behind them, hundreds of them turned to face their way.

******

When the people of Hopkins jumped from their floating town onto dry land and ran for their lives, they assumed everyone came with them, but there were a few who believed they couldn't outrun a horde no matter how slow the infected were. Their best bet was to hide and wait for the infected to pass.

From the insides of their homes they watched through gaps in the boards as thousands of the infected walked by on the shoulders of the lake, and what seemed like just as many crowded into the water. Of course they couldn't swim, but they couldn't drown, either. They splashed, they pushed, they pulled, and they even walked on the backs of others, but they somehow managed to reach the shore and walk up onto dry land.

The infected that had been in the lake ranged from soaking wet all the way to full of water. The ones that were just wet were quick to resume the chase, and they followed the trail left behind by the horde. Those that were full of water were too heavy to chase anything. As a matter of fact, they were too heavy to walk. Some managed to crawl, and as they did, water of all different colors leaked from the openings in their bodies.

The survivors hiding in the former town of Hopkins on The Lake were forced to tie strips of cloth around their faces because of the smell. One cough would be a death sentence to all of them.

They heard gunshots later in the day, but then there was nothing but the sounds of the infected as the sun lowered toward the trees to the west. The constant groaning, splashing, and slapping of wet bodies against the water and the shore was deafening, but the gunshots seemed to almost invigorate the dead. They were determined to reach their prey before, and now they appeared to pick up speed. It was likely to be nothing more than wishful thinking on the part of the frightened people, but if the infected were moving faster, it meant they wouldn't have to wait much longer.

When the moon was high over the place where the town had once stood on pilings it gradually became quiet. A few of them dared to move quietly from room to room and whispered in voices hardly louder than breathing. They passed the word that there were still some infected in the water, but they weren't moving. When crickets and frogs began their nightly rituals, they knew it was safe to come out of hiding.

A woman who had been hiding in a place facing the forest behind them said she hadn't seen an infected come out of the woods for hours, and it had been at least that long since she had seen any movement in the water.

They passed around containers of fresh water they had been carefully protecting from contamination, as well as the few pieces of dried deer meat that had been cured and wrapped in preparation for this day. Someone produced a loaf of bread that was passed around with gratitude.

The main topic of discussion was why the others had jumped and ran from the town. The plan all along had been to stay on the rooftops unless you could get into a building and hide inside one of the many safe rooms they had made. Jumping and running wasn't part of the plan. Then again neither was breaking free of the supports that held the town in the middle of the lake and floating to the opposite shore.

Word was spread that they should stay in hiding for the whole night. It was uncomfortable, and it was hard to sleep curled up in a corner made of rough wood, but it was better than being chased through the woods at night. No one had any faith that the gunshots or the sounds made as their friends ran through the woods were signs of anything good. With a horde that size, nothing short of the sound of continuous automatic weapons fire would be reassuring.

Their decision to sit tight proved to be the right one on several occasions throughout the long night. The crickets would go silent, and everyone held their breath. The unmistakable slow march of an infected dead would drag on for the better part of an hour and then fade into the distance. The crickets and frogs would begin making noise again, and everyone relaxed…until the next time.

They thought they were discovered when a child whined to her mother that she didn't feel good. Her voice was followed by a moan somewhere outside, everyone stayed still for so long that it seemed like the infected would hear their muscles begin to creak. An infected approached the dark, primitive buildings that had been skillfully placed on top of the poles in the middle of the lake. It couldn't possibly know that people had lived inside, but if it had heard the child, it wouldn't leave until it found them.

With the moonlight behind it, they could see its monstrous features peering between broken boards. At least six people were within its field of vision if they moved, and the strain was taking its toll. The thing outside took a few more steps, and everyone realized it had managed to navigate the water and mud to somehow get onto the main platform that supported their homes. It was within inches of falling into the lake, but it was even closer to the door that would open easily if it was pushed.

When the town had slid off of the wooden supports that held it above the water, it had twisted and turned. Nails had popped loose. Boards had shattered. Even worse, doors had sprung free from their frames. There was nothing holding the door shut except for the gravity due to the slight down angle of the room.

The infected dead found a larger gap between some boards and reached through with an arm that was missing most of its skin. It didn't know the difference between a door and a hole in the wall, and that was a good thing because it was only a few feet from the door.

The hand groped in the dark only inches from the hair that hung from the back of the little girl who had whined. She was holding her breath, and her mother shuddered as she watched the hand come closer each time the infected dead pushed a little harder to get through the gap in the boards.

When the hand stopped groping, it just seemed as if the fingers were pointing at the child. It didn't move closer, it just pointed. Then it backed steadily away until it went out through the hole.

"Mommy?"

"Shhhh."

The sound telling her to be quiet didn't come from her mother. It came from the hole in the wall. A face that was framed by moonlight appeared at the hole, and a finger was pressed over its lips.

"How may people in this building?" asked the voice in a hushed tone.

The people inside could only go by what they knew before the sun went down, and one of them whispered back that there were six of them.

"Get some sleep," said the face outside the hole. "We'll move out at sunrise when we can see where we're going."

******

Iris and her companions had gained on the horde that was following I-26. They were amazed by the devastation left behind by so many of the infected. There was no way to imagine how many thousands of them were already on the interstate, but the noise they made was drawing more from the trees that bordered the interstate on both sides.

They discovered a fire tower in the middle of the forest, and despite their fear of becoming trapped, they wanted to see how big the horde really was. It was risky to go up when there were so many infected dead in the area because they would never go away if they saw a live person above them. The infected were mindless, and their singular purpose made them stay wherever they had last seen a living person. If you could last longer than them, you would see that they would rot before they would leave.

Iris and the others hurried up the tall flights of stairs to the top of the tower and surveyed the green trees that stretched away in all directions. Great swaths were cut through the forests where the infected had traveled in large groups, and smaller trails marred the landscape where the infected had followed each other in single file. Alone or together they all had the same goal, and that was to join the massive horde that moved like flowing lava down I-26 toward Charleston.

"Someone remind me why we have to follow the biggest zombie horde in the country," said George.

Iris didn't exactly give him a withering stare. It was more like an icy glance. She had explained it to all four of them, but it had been meant for George in particular. He had managed to hang onto his sense of humor despite the way life had turned out, but sometimes he didn't know when to quit. Iris told him not to test the Chief when it came to the topic of zombies.

"Okay, infected. Someone remind me why we're following them."

His wife gave him an elbow to get his attention. Her icy glance was a bit stronger than Iris', and he realized they were being serious.

"Sorry, Iris. It's just my way of coping with things. You're worried about the Chief, aren't you?"

Iris had been wondering which was crazier, following a horde or being in the path of a horde. At least someone in the path of a horde could honestly say they didn't know they were coming, but the last time she saw the Chief he had a plane. That meant he knew about the horde. As a matter of fact, more than once she had looked at the sky thinking she might see his plane.

"Anybody want to make a guess about that?"

Yuni had her binoculars at her eyes, holding them with one hand. She was using her other to point at a gap in the trees.

Iris aimed her binoculars in the same direction. She could see the gap, but she assumed it was nothing more than a lake. Then she saw what Yuni had to be talking about. At one end of the gap she could just make out a crude steeple on a building. It was at an angle that meant the building had collapsed under it.

"Post apocalyptic," she said. "Notice the gaps in the boards? None of the wood was milled. It looks like it was just shaped."

"So someone took the time to build a house in the middle of a forest where thousands of infected dead happen to be," said George.

"They could have done it back at the beginning," said Sora. " After the initial spread of the infected I seem to recall we saw more of them on roads than we did in the forests.

People stayed on the roads, so the infected did the same. This is a very remote stretch through here, so they could have pulled it off."

Sherry said, "I remember this place. It was some kind of recreational place owned by the Army. Their dependents could camp here, and I believe they had some decent cabins already. That could be part of a cabin."

"How come you know about this place?" asked George.

His wife was always surprising him with useful trivia, but it shouldn't have come as a surprise to him. She was a travel agent before the dead started rising.

Sherry locked eyes with George.

"Wait for it," said Yuni. "Wait for it."

When it dawned on George, he really did offer up a good defense.

"Forgive me for forgetting that there were actually careers over five or six years ago."

"We have company," said Sora.

He indicated a downward direction where at least six infected were navigating the steps at the bottom.

All four of the others spread out in the tower and checked the sides.

"Anything walking around the perimeter?" asked Iris.

They reported all clear which meant they needed to handle it as quietly as possible. If they could dispose of this group without drawing attention, it would give them time to get out of the area.

"Okay, everyone. Let's make this as fast as possible. They're already making noise, so we have to put them down quick and then keep going."

Iris was still their leader, and they liked the way she didn't hesitate. She didn't need to tell them it would be done without bullets. They all shouldered their rifles and pulled machetes from their belts.

"Which way when we get to the bottom?" asked Sherry.

"Towards your campground. We have to see what happened there, as if we don't already know. Could be survivors, though."

Iris gave Sora a nod since he was first in line at the top of the stairs. His wife followed, and Iris had to admit to herself that she was impressed with how quiet they were on the metal stairs. She knew that people used to think if you were Japanese then you knew martial arts, but she had never asked them. She just got to see for herself that they were light on their feet. George and Sherry were doing fine, too. She hoped she wasn't being the loudest one.

When they reached the group of infected they had only made it up two sets of stairs. That gave them a good advantage because others didn't have a chance to hear them. If they had gotten halfway or higher, they could have attracted others for miles around.

Sora cut the first one across the chest, missing his target, but it was enough to send them down like bowling pins. He followed them and slashed with more accuracy, but he was cursing at himself for giving them all the chance to groan one more time.

"Don't be so hard on yourself, husband. You made it easier on all of us."

Five of them against six infected was pretty good odds, but they took the last set of stairs in leaps and charged into the woods.

Sora was sure they would run into more infected any moment because it was hard to be quiet in the dense brush. He ran fast but watched for a trail and the infected at the same time. There was plenty of evidence that they had come through the area in large numbers, but if he was reading their damage right, he and the others were crossing their trail instead of following it.

He took a chance and glanced back to ask the others if they were thinking the same thing, so he wasn't watching when he reached the clearing around the old campsites. Without the dense brush to slow him down, he reminded the rest of his group of a baseball player sliding head first into second base. His momentum made him slide to a stop at the feet of several infected dead, and more began moving his way.

George had passed Yuni when they had cleared the area below the tower, and for all his jokes, Yuni would never have suspected the agility and speed he displayed to save her husband.

The first infected had practically fallen over onto Sora as he slid to a stop, and if he had been face down, he couldn't have protected himself. There was only a split second, but it was all he needed to get his blade across his chest and aimed at the face. The blade went through the rotten teeth and split the jaw on both sides. He shoved upward and was amazed to see the top of the creature's head disappear.

Iris pulled the body off of Sora, and he saw his friends had disposed of the other infected.

As he took her hand to get up she said, "You need to teach me that trick sometime."

Yuni hugged her husband for several minutes, but they knew they couldn't afford to waste much time. They knew they were seeing firsthand a futile attempt by someone to defend themselves against the infected, but whoever had built the walls and laid the spikes couldn't have known that a massive migration of infected was coming their way.

There was a main entrance to the barrier walls that surrounded what appeared to be the original campsite, and the pits filled with the infected were a mass of writhing arms and legs. The noise they were making would carry further at night and would draw more infected to the area, so they needed to move out quickly.

George had spotted a row of cars and RV's parked near the common building of the campground. A quick inspection near them produced several plastic jugs of gasoline and some propane tanks.

"What do you think?" he asked.

"I agree," said Iris, "but we have to time it right. After we set them on fire, they'll be like a beacon to plenty more."

Sora said, "So, let's check out the big houseboat and then set the pits on fire. We can clear out of the area while the fire draws in the infected. The best part is the way the stupid things will just walk right into the pits with their buddies."

"It's too close to dark," said Yuni. "We could run right into them. We have to wait until morning."

Iris nodded in agreement, "This changes everything, though. That horde is converging on the Interstate going southeast. When we light the fires there will be plenty that come back this way. When they do, we have to be moving east, straight for the coast."

"That's not where we want to go," said George.

This time Iris grinned, and that always meant she had a plan.

"I never thought it was a great idea to be following the biggest horde in the state. They're going to bottleneck when they reach the part of the Interstate that crosses swamps, and that's going to slow them down. Thousands will get stuck in the swamps or take forever to get through them. I think we should cut straight across to the coast after we light the fires.

We need to find a place the Chief told me about. It's called Mud Island."

17 VISITORS

Year Two of the Decline

It really wasn't a problem to have so many of the infected dead stuck in the bottom of his oil rig. The more he thought about it, the more Maybank realized it was another layer of protection. He imagined that other oil rigs had similar issues, and it would be worse for them. If there were survivors on other oil rigs, they wouldn't have the benefit of going inside an airtight shelter to get away from the smell.

Then there were the rats. He had been right that the rats would jump ship when they had the chance. There was something about their survival instinct that told them they shouldn't stay on the floating island of the infected, even though it was an unending supply of food. It didn't matter that their instincts were wrong, and they weren't going to have food forever on the oil rig. If an opportunity came along for them to jump ship again, he expected that they would. It wouldn't be a pretty sight if it was another pleasure craft like Hector's.

Maybank expected that it would be a good idea to throw the switch again, the one that would send current through the metal catwalks. He would need to do it several times because there would always be a few rats somewhere that the current didn't go, and one of those places was the tangle of bodies left behind by the dead tide. Then again, it was worth letting them clear out some of that food supply first.

After a couple of months watching the rats eat away at the bodies, Maybank could tell that they were making progress. At first, there didn't seem to be any change, but then it occurred to him that the pile was deeper than just what he could see. As the rats would eat an infected dead on the surface, another would pop to the surface and replace it. The entire time the pile moved in a bizarre waving motion as if they were fans at a rock concert swaying with the music, their hands reaching out toward the band.

Maybank took pictures of them from above and compared them with older shots. He couldn't figure out why the pile looked the same every day, but then he saw bodies being replaced, and he could only guess how many replacements there would be before the tangled mess got smaller.

When the change started to happen, it happened fast because the bodies under the pile were also the anchors. They were being pressed down from above all the way to the ceiling of the shelter. When they drifted upward, the bodies also began spreading apart. After three months of looking at the bodies, Maybank was excited when he saw water begin to appear between them. The island of infected dead started acting more like an ice flow as bodies broke away from the outside edges and drifted away on the current.

The rats were running out of places to nest in the remnants of the dead tide, so more and more were tearing scraps of clothing from the bodies and carrying them up to the catwalks. With so much metal above them, there weren't many places that made natural nests. The former quarters of the construction crew had proven to be well made because the rats hadn't found a way to get inside, although they certainly tried. They had ripped insulation from the bottom of the building to build one large nest, but they hadn't gotten to the food supply inside.

They finally got their chance to leave what was left of the bodies still tangled below almost six months after they arrived. It wasn't without worry for Maybank, though. He knew the oil rig would be tested over and over again. The drug lords and other unwanted guests weren't a big surprise. The dead tide was such a total surprise that he didn't think anyone in his survivor's club would have predicted it, but it was more of a long term nuisance than a real test of the oil rig. He also expected storms to pound the oil rig and test its ability to stay in one piece, but the real test was what he saw coming his way from the west.

He wanted the rats to leave, and a container ship was just what he needed to give them plenty of incentive, but he needed the ship to dock at the oil rig, not ram it. The derelict coming his way was drifting with no one at the helm. He could tell because it had the starboard side facing him, but it was still getting closer.

With good visibility, his worst fears were confirmed when he spotted infected dead on almost every level that had good safety rails. They weren't falling overboard, but he didn't expect to see any survivors trying to steer it away from a collision with his oil rig. This was the test he had feared the most, but with calm seas, it wasn't going to be as bad as it could be, especially since it was carrying a heavy cargo. He could tell the cargo was heavy because she sat low in the water.

The best case scenario was that the container ship would miss completely. The second best would be that it drifted close enough for him to attach the docking lines and get her to drop anchor. Those stacked containers might be full of TV sets and party favors, but they could also be full of MRE's.

Maybank mentally chastised himself for even thinking that was the second best outcome for this new arrival. He wouldn't need a single meal from the container ship for thirty years, and he didn't know why he was thinking it would be a good idea to cross over to take control of the ship. He wouldn't try that with the help of a SEAL team. For a moment, he questioned his own sanity again.

When he went back to considering the realistic possibilities, the most obvious hope was a miss, but the likely outcome was a collision. Charting its progress only confirmed that outcome.

He studied the ship for several minutes and estimated that its speed was slow enough for his rig to withstand the impact, but any damage was more than he wanted to give up. He also couldn't tell if it was going to be a glancing blow or a direct hit.

A spot appeared on the water at the bow of the big freight carrier, and it turned to race along the starboard side headed for the stern. It was a small boat, but it was fast, and Maybank couldn't tell how many people were on board. When it reached the stern, it turned the corner and disappeared. His best guess was that someone was trying to find a way to board the container ship. Other than the fact that it had infected dead on board, it wasn't the dumbest thing to do. That was a floating warehouse, and if even one container held useful supplies, it could spell salvation for someone for years.

A few minutes later it appeared at the bow again and made another fast turn, but this time it pulled away and throttled down its speed. Apparently, neither side was trailing a rope or a ladder that could be used to board the derelict. If they were going to board her, it needed to be from above, and Maybank considered what he would do if he was them.

It didn't take long for him to come to the conclusion that the people in the small boat would want the container ship to collide with the oil rig. All they had to do was be in the right place on the rig and drop down onto the ship. Of course they weren't aware of the problems that were waiting for them on the oil rig.

His conclusion was confirmed when the small boat pointed directly at the oil rig and throttled up again. Maybank had no doubt that whoever they were, they planned to board the oil rig and then cross to the container ship when it arrived. His dilemma was whether or not to help them.

Maybank had no intention of leaving the shelter. That much he knew for sure. Titus had made it perfectly clear to everyone that they would face situations when they were forced to play God. His number one rule was not to leave the shelter under any circumstances. Rule number two was not to open the door and let someone in. That wasn't going to be a problem for him, and if he had his preference, the people in the boat would never know he was even there.

He made his decision, and if he was lucky they wouldn't suspect it had been a living person who had helped. Maybe they would think it was divine intervention, but he felt like he had to take the chance.

To the man and woman in the small boat, the oil rig being in the path of the container ship had to be a good sign. If the ship hit the oil rig, maybe it would stop it from moving. Even though it wasn't moving on engine power, it was moving too much for them to get a line to the main deck. If it wasn't moving, they could climb aboard the oil rig and then lower themselves onto the containers. They would have some of the infected to deal with, but from what he had seen, the infected could be eliminated if they were careful.

Maybank threw the power switch that electrified the oil rig. He didn't have his audio turned on because he didn't really want to hear the sound of a few thousand rats being electrocuted. It was a good decision. As miserable as the rats were, the screams would have made him stop, and he was going to be forced to do this sooner or later. Besides, he didn't know how things were on other oil rigs, but his guess was that the dead tide had deposited rats everywhere it went, and the people approaching his oil rig had to know the rats were even more dangerous than the infected.

The catwalks, the pipes, the railings, the cables, and everything else made out of metal that could carry the current to the rats did its job. Thousands were eliminated in seconds, and all the people in the boat knew was that it was raining furry bodies up ahead. They made a sharp turn and cut power at the same time and put themselves broadside to the oil rig. Something had caused the rats to fall off of the oil rig, and judging by the fact that hundreds of them were on fire and trailing smoke as they fell, it had to be a power surge of some kind. There was only so much divine intervention they could accept, but they still didn't openly suspect that someone was watching from the oil rig and trying to help them. To them, that would have still been an act of God.

Besides the rats that were hit by the first wave of power and killed, hundreds more were jolted enough to make them fall from the oil rig, and hundreds jumped on their own. The remaining tangle of bodies above the submerged shelter was covered with them.

Despite the fact that rats are known to carry diseases and had become an even bigger threat to people in some places than the infected dead, they had been doing Maybank a big favor. Eliminating the floating tangle of bodies below the oil rig was something he couldn't have done without them, and they added another layer of security. It was too bad that they couldn't be dumped onto the container ship for a few weeks to clear out the infected, but if they found a container full of food and managed to get inside it, he would never get rid of them.

Maybank turned off the current and waited a full minute before turning it back on. In the sixty seconds with the current turned off, hundreds more rats had wandered onto dangerous places, and once again they rained onto the water below. He set a timer for five minutes and waited.

Out in the boat the couple began to slowly circle the oil rig. There were small fires burning on the island of bodies, but it was too soggy to be anything but the rats burning. Maybank could see them more closely on one of his monitors, and he could guess what they were trying to decide. They didn't know what was happening to the rats, but they could make an educated guess. The question was whether or not it was accidental. The last place they would want to be was on the oil rig when the next electric shock came along. Maybank knew that they would eventually decide that it was a chance they would have to take, but he had to be sure to remove enough rats for it to be safe.

At the ding from the five minute timer, Maybank threw the power switch again. More rats caught fire and dropped from the oil rig, but this time there were far fewer than the last time. He set the timer for ten minutes and felt a small bit of satisfaction when he saw them check their watches. If they were smart enough to start timing the electrical charges, they might reach a decision that the charges were becoming less frequent on their own.

They continued to circle the oil rig and were watching the time when five minutes went by. He saw the woman gesture toward her watch. At the ten minute mark Maybank did it again. This time there were distinctively fewer rats electrocuted, and he set the timer at a half hour. He also scanned the metal framework of the oil rig and knew he was accomplishing what he needed to with the rats. The only movement he saw was on the few bodies that were still floating above the shelter, and the really good news was that the bodies were finally drifting free of the place where they had been stuck when the dead tide passed through. He was finally going to be free of the ugly sight and the rats at the same time.

When the timer went off at thirty minutes and he threw the switch again, Maybank was glad that he had set the intervals to lengthen quickly. The container ship was drifting closer, and he wanted to give the couple the time they needed to get onto the rig. Only a few rats fell this time, and he set the timer for an hour. If they didn't climb one of the towers by then, he would burn off whatever rats were left, but he didn't believe they would wait. Of course he would also be watching them closely, and if they were in a safe place in one hour, he would throw the switch again.

Maybank extended the ladder rungs on every tower. He planned to do it when they weren't looking, but he could see by the woman's reaction that she saw the movement.

******

Janice Parker reacted the way anyone would in the same situation, and she scared her husband to death. He was steering the boat and was more concerned with the bodies in the water. Bodies from the death tide were scattered at random, but the furry bodies of rats were everywhere, and some were trying hard to get into their boat. It was amazing how they managed to get a grip on the boat even though he had increased speed.

David Parker swerved hard when his wife screamed because he thought she was warning him that they were about to hit something. The boat almost swamped in its own wake.

It seemed like they were finally in luck when they had spotted the container ship. Then there was no way to board it. The oil rig wasn't an unusual sight in the Gulf of Mexico, but so far they had steered clear of them because they were all occupied by people who didn't want company. They had been shot at every time they approached one. This was the first one that appeared to be abandoned, and it was even electrocuting the rats.

When the rats had started catching fire and falling from the big, ugly maze of pipes, they both agreed it was just a bit too coincidental, but if someone was behind it, they weren't shooting at their boat, and that was a first.

David got control of the boat and pulled it further away from the oil rig. Janice wasn't prone to panicking so he knew there had to be some reason she had screamed in his ear. She was still pointing at the big tower they had passed, but since he had already traveled so far away from it, he kept going to the next one.

"The ladder rungs came out of the side of that tower just as we were going by."

"You saw them come out?"

"Yes, they weren't there at first, then they all came out at the same time. Aren't you going back?"

"The current is moving toward that side of the oil rig. It's carrying rats and dead bodies that way. By the time we would be able to tie off the boat and start climbing, we would have the rats climbing with us. Let's check the other towers before we use that one."

They passed under the Power Module and saw that the ladder rungs were out, but David wanted to get as far from the current as possible, so he kept going toward the Wellbay Module. He was relieved to see that was a good decision because the rungs were out on that tower, too. David coasted up to it, and Janice used a boat hook to catch one of the rungs. There were bumpers at the waterline of the tower to keep them from ramming the boat against metal, so they tied against it.

David didn't have to say anything to Janice about climbing. She was on her way as soon as she was close enough to grab a rung. She wasn't sure if she was going to receive an electric shock, but they had to take the chance. Something told her there was someone inside the oil rig who was helping them, and she was so tired of trying to stay alive that she was ready to get help from someone.

She was halfway up the Wellbay tower when she finally remembered the container ship. She felt sick when she saw how close it was to the oil rig, and she wasn't sure David was going to make it. She knew for sure neither of them would make it if she didn't climb faster.

David saw her turn above him, and when she started climbing faster, he instinctively picked up his pace, too. He only took the time for a glance to his right, and all he could see were the sides of the stacked containers. They were a wall in front of his face, and it was coming closer so fast that it felt like the oil rig was speeding towards it instead of the other way around.

To David and Janice they were sure the container ship was moving at a speed high enough to crush the tower they were climbing. Janice flipped from the ladder rungs and threw herself flat on her back on a catwalk. David fell over her to shield her from the impact. The sound of metal bending and things being shattered was deafening, but they didn't really feel the bone jarring crash they expected. They shook and they swayed, but something was missing. They should have felt it deep in their bones.

There was a long drawn out sound as the rig and the boat settled back to their places in the water, and the two rubbed hard against each other. Waves washed across the entire area of the oil rig, and one really big wave led the charge. It hit the bodies that remained from the dead tide and the thousands of rats, dead and alive. They were all carried free of the rig, and for the first time in what seemed like forever to Maybank, there was clean water under the rig. He was elated, but the feeling was short lived. Now he wondered if he would be staring at the container ship for the rest of his life.

The people outside from the small boat had made it most of the way up the Wellbay tower before he took his eyes off of them. He wanted to see if they made it, but even more important to him was the test his oil rig was facing.

In the years that were spent designing and building the shelter, the engineers talked about making the shelter indestructible and the oil rig as indestructible as possible. He wasn't really worried about the shelter surviving a collision with a container ship, but he wasn't so sure about the oil rig. He wouldn't have been surprised if the ship ripped the rig apart, and he watched while holding his breath.

The engineers made a list of possible dangers to the rig. A nuclear bomb would melt it like ice, but the shelter would survive. They said it would be a rough ride, but if he was inside with the doors closed, he would be in one piece afterward. They had a long list of other disasters that were possible, and they were prioritized according to severity. Collisions were expected with all sizes and types of ships from pleasure craft to aircraft carriers, but container ships were far enough down the list to be considered survivable.

Maybank wanted to believe with his whole heart that the engineers were right, especially as he watched the ship grow in size as it approached. It filled the view completely of one monitor because the camera was on the Wellbay Tower. He braced himself when the impact smashed the camera. His hands were clamped onto the arms of his chair so hard that his fingers turned white.

He didn't feel a thing at first, but then he began to sway gently from side to side. The big crash and crunch he expected were missing, and his microphones out on the rig only relayed the sound of the ship's hull collapsing at the level of the deck. The ship bent inward along the starboard gunwales, and some of the containers continued on a collision course with the tower, but they were cracked open like eggshells when they hit.

Maybank heard the long sighing sound as metal rubbed against metal and the water rushed in again to fill the gap between the oil rig and the ship. He heard it all, and he swayed gently, but the engineers had been right. There was no hint of the dreaded breach in the tower.

The ship seemed to be bobbing on the surface next to the massive Wellbay Tower. Containers had been cracked open, and unknown contents had fallen like a landslide onto the deck, but other than the bent gunwales, the ship appeared to be ready to stay alongside the oil rig for a long time.

"Another houseboat," Maybank said out loud. "Complete with a crew of the infected."

He panned cameras around to the last place he had seen the people from the small pleasure craft. Panning upward he saw that they had gotten high enough that they had a front row seat to the collision, and they had to be wondering how a ship that size could hit an oil rig, and the total damage wasn't anything more than a bent gunwale and some spilled goods.

On the camera he could see they were approaching the edge of the catwalk that was now above the deck of the ship. From the way they were studying the damage, he could tell they were more than interested in the tower. Even the contents of the shattered containers didn't seem to be drawing their attention. It didn't take a rocket scientist to know that it wasn't right for a container ship to hit anything made of metal without leaving a scratch.

The man was running his hand along the tower where it continued up to the next level. It ended at that level, and the catwalks surrounding the fake Drilling Module were perched on top of it. What he was undoubtedly trying to understand was how the drilling module didn't fall over from the impact. It should have done the same thing as the stack of containers on the ship, but it had stayed perfectly upright as if it had been nothing more than a nudge by the ship. As a matter of fact, the man was going to realize sooner or later that he and the woman should have been launched through the air onto the deck of the ship.

While the man was inspecting the tower, the woman was turning in a slow circle taking in the metal and cables on the towers. Her eyes fixed on the building that resembled a large mobile home on the highest part of the rig. From her position on the Drilling Module, Maybank knew she couldn't tell that the platform above it was a helicopter landing pad. He also knew she would get around to finding that out for herself. They didn't appear to be injured, so they were going to be around for a while with plenty of time to explore.

Maybank had a sudden feeling that he had jumped to a conclusion when he assumed they would be around for a while. If he didn't know about the shelter in the oil rig but had escaped the carnage on the mainland, he would stay as long as he could, but he didn't know anything about them. For all he knew, they may have come from somewhere better than here. After all, they had to have been surviving somewhere since the spread of the infection.

He panned his camera downward toward the place where the people had grabbed the rungs to the ladder, and he searched for their boat. There was some big debris in the water from a container that had gone over the edge, but it wasn't hard to recognize the pieces of the broken hull. Their small boat had been caught between the metal of the hull and the tower and crushed to bits. They wouldn't be leaving anytime soon.

When he panned back up to the people, he saw they had just come to the same conclusion. The man was alternately pointing down at the spot where their boat used to be and gesturing with both hands at the oil rig. Just for good measure he broke up the routine by pacing back and forth a short distance from where the woman stood. If he was lamenting their predicament, Maybank wasn't sure what he was asking the woman to do about it.

******

Janice Parker leaned against a metal railing at the end of the catwalk and looked down onto the deck of the container ship.

"How can a ship that size hit an oil rig and just bounce off like that?" she asked her husband.

"At this moment, I don't really care," he answered. "I just want to know how we're supposed to get off of this oil rig now."

"Maybe there's a boat around here somewhere."

"Really? Do you really think we're going to be that lucky?"

It wasn't actually a question. It wasn't really like him, but so much sarcasm dripped from his tone of voice that she felt like pushing him over the side.

Janice pointed at the deck of the container ship and asked, "What do you think that is?"

David followed her finger with his eyes and saw a perfectly good boat hanging from a pair of davits, and it had a fair sized engine.

"I guess all we have to do is go down there and launch it."

"If you don't drop the sarcasm, you can go down there and launch it by yourself for all I care."

He was caught off guard because he wasn't used to her standing up for herself. When he counted the number of infected walking around out on the deck, he knew that he would never be able to do it without her help. The only area that was free of the infected was the part of the ship that had hit the oil rig. The containers had fallen over onto the infected that were in that area, and he saw that they would be able to climb down there, but they would never reach the boat hanging from the davits by themselves. One of them would have to distract the infected while the other one lowered the boat.

"We didn't chase this ship around all day just to try to steal a boat from its deck," said Janice. "I think we were trying to board the thing up until it hit the oil rig, but look at this place."

She made a long sweeping gesture with her hand.

"There's something up there that has to be some sort of crew's quarters. It looks like someone took a mobile home and fastened it to the top of this thing. And what about that place up there?"

Maybank could see that the woman was pointing at the sealed off area above where his apartment had been. He had no idea what she was saying to the man about it, but if he was them, he would feel pretty lucky to have been stranded on an oil rig. If they took the time to explore it, they would find out just how lucky they were.

"This place had people working on it. What happened to them after the infection broke out? If they lived out here, they must've had some supplies. They couldn't have just left and taken everything with them?"

She didn't give him the chance to answer. She brushed past him and went to the nearest ladder that went upward and climbed. Maybank knew what would happen next. She would take one look inside the crew's quarters, and he would have company on the rig for a long time.

Maybank sat back in his seat and watched her climb the ladder. It took a few moments to sink in, but it dawned on him he was watching her as a woman, not as a survivor who just happened to reach his shelter. He had been alone on the rig for months, maybe a year. For some reason he wasn't keeping track of how long, but when he considered events he had witnessed, it had to be somewhere right around a year. The infected showed up, the dead tide of bodies washed out to him, they stayed for about six months.

"Yeah, it's been about a year, I guess."

He said it out loud as if someone had asked him how long it had been since he had seen a living person, especially a woman.

Her hair was long, but she had it pulled back into a ponytail that swayed from side to side as she climbed the ladder. She reminded him of a teacher he had in high school. He had such a big crush on her that he almost didn't pass her class. He would have done anything to get a better grade, but he was too distracted to learn.

Maybank's trip down memory lane was interrupted by the man. He was climbing the ladder behind her and gaining. He was right behind her when she made it to the top, and he caught her by one arm. She tried to pull away, but he pointed at the door to the quarters and said something that made her pause long enough to listen. He was undoubtedly telling her she didn't know what was inside there.

There was something moving near their feet. After all of the electric shocks he had sent through the rig, rats had survived, probably by clinging to insulated wires. They were bigger than the others, and Maybank saw the rats weren't too happy about the intruders. The woman jumped away from one as her husband timed a perfectly aimed kick at a really big one that was closer to him. The rat sailed over the railing, and judging by the way all of the rats in the area ran for cover or jumped down to a lower level, the rat must have squealed when it was kicked.

One rat took advantage of the distraction and ran along the railing straight for his bare hand. When the man had delivered the kick he had reached for the railing to steady himself. To the rats, the only difference between these two people and the infected dead that had been a food source was that they walked upright and faster. These rats were accustomed to people who flailed their arms and legs but were unable to make a coordinated effort to prevent the rats from feeding on them.

It reached the bare hand quickly and took a big bite from the exposed flesh on the back. The rat was probably surprised by the hot blood that spurted from a vein. It was more accustomed to the cold, thick blood that didn't spurt at all when the rat had bitten the infected. Maybank didn't have to wonder what the rat thought of this discovery, because instead of running when the man screamed and then backhanded the furry creature from the railing, it attacked again.

Shock isn't the same for everyone at first. Some people get so angry that they keep carrying on as if nothing happened. That was this guy.

The cameras had a good view of the deck outside the crew's quarters, so Maybank saw the man's face and the woman's in one glance. Her eyes and mouth were wide, most likely because there was so much blood. His face was twisted and full of rage. The nerves in the back of the hand have very little protection, so it had to hurt badly, but the blood and pain made him mad before it made him smarter.

He should have run for the crew's quarters and tried to wrap something around his hand at the same time, but he wanted a piece of that rat.

She saw the rats coming, and her flight response kicked in. She ran for the door of the crew's quarters as he ran after the rat. With only one hand working right, he shouldn't have gone back to the ladder, but when several rats converged on his left ankle, that's where he was as the woman pulled the door shut.

It would have been better for him if the fall had killed him, or if he had missed the catwalk below and fallen all the way to the water, but he landed flat on his back on the catwalk. If Maybank had wired the entire rig with sound, he would have heard the man's back break. His head moved from side to side, but his arms and legs were spread heavily away from his body.

The rats jumped easily from the top level down to him, and as if they knew he would taste better than the cold bodies of the infected dead, they poured over him.

Maybank had seen plenty of death already, and he stayed detached from what he saw enough that he was able to ask himself one important question.

"If the rat had only bitten him, would he have been infected by the rat?"

18 EVOLUTION

Year Six of the Decline

It was really an amazing feeling to be on the Cormorant again and traveling over open water. We had been out on her plenty of times over the last five years, but traveling on the Ashley River or making a run up to Mud Island was different. Riding her decks on the Gulf Stream made me feel like the world was a better, safer place. Of course that was all an illusion because nothing had been done to change the world. There were still strongholds of people, pockets of civilization, but the world still belonged to the dead. As long as it wasn't safe to travel between those strongholds, the world didn't belong to the living.

I had picked up Molly's journal again when we decided to make the trip on the Cormorant. We knew more than a lot of people did about the world, but we didn't know enough. It occurred to me that the journal wasn't just for us and our children. It was for anyone who might read it. If something happened to us, someone still might find this journal and they would learn about the Mud Island survivors. It was important for them to know what we had done.

It was important for them, whoever they were, to know what had happened to the President. I made a detailed entry by interviewing Terrance Simmons about how his plane had been used to get the President out of Washington. I also made a long entry for Cassandra Gibbs, a security officer on a hospital ship who had survived a trip across the Atlantic with no one but the infected dead on board. She and Sim, as we liked to call Terrance, had been drawn to each other instantly.

It had become quite a project to bring the journal up to date. Tom and Molly's escape from Myrtle Beach and how they found Mud Island, Hampton and Colleen and their rescue from Lake Norman in North Carolina, and of course there was the best story of all. That was how the Chief, Kathy, and my own wife, Jean, escaped from Charleston Harbor on a cruise ship in the first days of the infection. What started as a journal was now a history of the survival of a large group of friends. If something happened to us, at least the world would know what we had done until our end had come.

******

Planning for the trip had been fast but thorough. Everyone did their part to get the Cormorant ready to go to sea. We loaded our supplies at night under the cover of darkness, not even using flashlights. We didn't want anyone to suspect that one of our most powerful weapon systems was going to be gone for a few days, and the amount of gear being loaded would have been a sure giveaway.

Three days before leaving the Chief and a squad of Captain Miller's men sailed her up the Ashley River to the Coast Guard Station for refueling. We wanted to start off with a full tank and we hoped to refuel when we were about eight hundred miles into our trip. We would refuel sooner if we saw the opportunity, but we didn't want to refuel too soon and be forced to find another fuel supply before getting to the oil rig. Maybank would be able to top us off for the trip home, but we were hoping to avoid making too many port calls. Bus told us the oil rig shelter held enough fuel for an aircraft carrier. We all took that with a grain of salt, but we didn't need that much fuel, anyway.

In the end, we decided to go with the simplest plan by stopping at the Key West Coast Guard Station. It was anybody's guess whether we would be right, but it was a logical choice.

First, the population was low before the infection. Second, there was a really good chance that the infected would have been reduced in numbers by falling into the water somewhere. The down side of that guess was that the isolation of Key West meant there was very little chance that anyone had survived.

The other advantage of stopping there was easy access. The Coast Guard Station was wide open and not as far from the mouth of the harbor as the station in Charleston. If they ran into any trouble, they would have a shorter run to open water.

Last but not least, the stockpile of digital satellite photographs in Fort Sumter had some good shots of the fuel storage tanks at Key West. One picture was marked with familiar symbols that indicated they could get fuel for the Cormorant or for aircraft.

"You should get out here and enjoy the fresh air and sunshine while you can."

I lifted my head up from the journal to see Jean standing in the door to the wheelhouse.

"Have you ever been to the Gulf of Mexico?" I asked. "That place is always sunny. We'll probably be sick of it by the time we get back."

The Chief was at the helm, and I could tell by his laugh that he was making fun of my theory about weather in the Gulf.

"The Gulf is just like anywhere else, Ed. Besides, it's likely that we're all going to get more sunshine than we planned to. Temperature gauges have been running higher than I like. I'm not happy about going into any big ports, but if we need to stop for repairs, we need to do it where we're most likely to find parts. We might not need any, but if we do, the Mayport Naval Base near Jacksonville is our best choice."

Hampton squeezed past Jean into the wheelhouse just as he said it, and his eyebrows jumped up to the middle of his forehead.

"You couldn't find a more populated area to make port? There were just under a million people living in Jacksonville when the infection started. Add in the tourists, and way over a million people were trying to get across three or four bridges at the same time."

"Mayport is surrounded by water. We should be able to at least get closer to a port that deep. There are smaller ports with less people, but I only want to stop once. If we hit a small port, we'll wind up stopping twice because we won't find what we need."

The wheelhouse was getting crowded, but Tom was next followed by Kathy. Both of them were covered with oil, and their hands were a black mess. Cassandra pushed from behind them, and when we saw how much oil was on her hands, we all pushed ourselves into the port corner of the wheelhouse to give them room.

"Good news," said Tom.

The Chief asked, "Did you find the problem?"

"With the help of these two ladies I found a blown valve seal. We don't need a shipyard. All we need is a place with a decent marina. This thing isn't like a destroyer or something bigger. We should be able to make a good replacement seal with parts from a marina that services deep sea fishing boats."

"Break out a map," said the Chief, "and give me a list of good candidates. Everyone else get yourselves armed with M4's. This is one time I don't want anything getting close to us. How much time do you need to replace that valve seal?"

Tom gave it some thought then reassured the Chief he could do it in a couple of hours, but he recommended that the sealant be allowed to set for a couple of hours before the engines are started.

"What if we need to get underway sooner?" he asked.

"It should hold. Letting it set is more of a precaution," said Tom.

Kathy had the charts of the coast spread out on the table and ran a finger along Florida.

"This is the only place after Jacksonville that has a marina with a full service repair capability, and we won't have to navigate along the Intracoastal Waterway to get there."

The Chief handed the helm to Jean, and leaned over the map. She had her finger on Camachee Cove marina. He let out a long, low whistle with a heavy sigh.

"What's wrong, it's the least populated area with easy access to open water?"

"Two things," he said. "That marina can handle a ship the size of the Cormorant, but there won't be any room for fast maneuvering. It's a tight fit."

Hampton said, "River traffic is like that. I grew up backing boats into docks and slips. We can do the same thing before we start the repairs. If things get bad, we can at least push away and be facing in the right direction."

"I agree," he said to both Tom and Hampton, "and do something about the second problem for me while you're at it."

"What's that?" asked Tom.

"Get your girlfriend to wash her hands before she handles the charts."

Kathy put her hands behind her back, but there wasn't anything she could do about the big black streak on the chart from our present position to Saint Augustine.

The Chief didn't push the engines up to full speed for fear of damaging the valves, so it took us a lot longer to reach Saint Augustine than we had planned. We stayed well off shore until we were close to the harbor entrance, but all of us were glued to our binoculars when we were within range.

We saw exactly what we expected. The beach wasn't crawling with infected, but no living person could be near the water without being attacked. After over five years, we had hoped to see wide open beaches with no infected dead, but we were realists. That's why we expected to see them. It was one thing to know how many people lived in America when the infection began, but it was another thing entirely to try to imagine most of them dead. They outnumbered the living even though thousands, perhaps millions of them had walked into the Atlantic, rivers, the Gulf of Mexico, and the Pacific.

The remaining living population had permanently destroyed some of them, but there would be no studies or census bureaus trying to capture the numbers. What saddened and amazed us the most was how many infected dead we saw that appeared to be in relatively good condition. Aside from being dead, that is. Some of them appeared to have died only within the last day or two, and that was disturbing. We had survived over five years, and so had they, only to eventually be assimilated by a stupid bite or a meal with crab meat in it. Maybe that was why the Chief took Sam's death so hard. He had made it so far.

Everyone was topside as we approached, and we were all on watch. Even though we were making note of the infected walking on the beaches, we were more concerned about the hazards that could reach us. Submerged boats were a major threat, but five years of storms and coastal drift of sand would make shoals pop up where they hadn't been before. We all knew the Chief would be staying toward the center of the entrance and hugging the line on the charts that showed the deepest water.

Fortunately, the location of the Camachee Cove was well away from the longshore drift, and there shouldn't be any new shoals, but the Chief had seen firsthand what Charleston Harbor had been like at the start of the epidemic. Charleston Harbor had been deep enough for fully loaded container ships back then, but sand builds up quickly on sunken ships, and hundreds sank in the harbor on that day. Saint Augustine was no different when it came to boats sinking in the chaos of the first day, but the harbor wasn't as deep.

We saw evidence of the way shallow areas seemed to reach out into the deeper water on our own Mud Island. It was actually mine, but I had come to think of it as belonging to my friends, as well. Without the jetties at the ends of the island, sand would fill in the northern and southern entrances to the waterway that surrounded the island. One huge boulder had been dislodged on the northern side, and it became shallow enough to walk across the waterway.

The evidence was raising its ugly head on the coast of Florida, too. We were entering the harbor outside Saint Augustine through an entrance that bore an eerie resemblance to Charleston but on a smaller scale.

Charleston sits in the confluence of the Ashley River and the Cooper River, and the inlet that led to the city was where we had set up our home at Fort Sumter. Unfortunately, the other side was occupied by unfriendly neighbors who had shunned our peaceful overtures.

Saint Augustine sits in the confluence of the Tolomato River and the Matanzas River. We were watching the sides of the Saint Augustine Inlet as we cruised into the harbor, hoping there were no unfriendly neighbors here.

Another uncanny resemblance was the bridge that crossed the northern side of the inlet. It wasn't as big as the one in Charleston, but it was high enough for us to pass under. Seeing it in the same place as the bridge in Charleston was a bit unnerving.

"The cove where we will make repairs is just north of the bridge on the mainland side," the Chief called out from the wheelhouse. "Everyone stay low on the forward deck in case I have to use the fifty calibers."

I don't think any of us had forgotten about the trio of deadly deck guns on the Cormorant. They didn't call it the Protector Class boat for nothing.

We rounded Vilano Point on the starboard side and turned diagonally upriver toward Camachee Cove, and as soon as we made the turn we knew Saint Augustine had experienced the same chaos as Charleston. Even after so many years had gone by, there were still hundreds of small boats piled up on Vilano beach and all of the shallows along the shores of the rivers. It was just like it would be if a large hurricane had made landfall in the harbor.

The Cormorant made very little noise as its bow sliced through the water, but the infected dead on Vilano Beach seemed to have no trouble seeing us. They flocked to the shoreline and walked into the water. It reminded me of when we entered the Folly River, and the dead followed us to the southern tip of Folly Beach. One by one they walked, waded, and then disappeared in the deeper water. Some may have washed ashore onto the new spit of land forming at Vilano Point, but most of them were washed out to sea in the swift current. Heads bobbed on the surface for a few yards making one last appearance before becoming part of the food chain.

The Chief let the Cormorant enter the marina at an angle and then began a slow turn to the right. He skillfully aimed the bow into the current and let the Tolomato River push the Cormorant back toward Camachee Cove. He gave a small burst of reverse from the engine, and the Cormorant drifted neatly up to the dock. Most people had trouble parallel parking a car, and the Chief had just parallel parked an eighty-seven foot long boat as if he did it every day.

It would have been nice to have a moment to tease him about bumping the curb with his tires, but we didn't get the chance. We already had company coming our way.

We had faced the infected on docks more times than we could count, and in the past we would shoot the ones in front to cause a logjam behind them. This time that tactic wouldn't work because the dock was concrete that was at least twenty feet wide, and the other side of it was occupied by a long building where repairs could be done. It was exactly where we needed to be, but we would have to find a way to close off the dock where it met the shoreline.

One quick glance in that direction was all I needed. There were dozens of infected coming to welcome our arrival. I was about to voice the question we were all thinking when Hampton yelled out the answer.

"They're coming out of the river."

There was a boat landing about fifty yards from the dock, and the asphalt surface disappeared at a gentle slope into the water. Waterlogged dead were walking heavily up the slope onto the main pier that was lined with slips and docks. They made a left turn and marched as a horde in our direction.

Camachee Cove was a curved opening into the Tolomato River that was acting like a net. The infected dead that walked into the water upriver were washed right into the cove. Worse, the infected that walked into the water inside the cove weren't being washed out into the river. That could mean only one thing. The bottom of the cove had to be full of them.

Even though the dock was too wide for us to cause a logjam, we had to start shooting. The horde coming down the dock had grown quickly, and they would be on us in a few minutes.

We all felt the vibration through the deck as the Chief started the engines again, but instead of pulling forward away from the dock, the Cormorant backed up toward the advancing horde. Because the bow was facing out toward the entrance of the cove, the fifty caliber machine guns were facing the wrong way, and the Chief had a plan, but he didn't have time to explain it to us.

The Cormorant's stern stayed close to the dock, but the Chief left about ten feet between the boat and the dock. Just enough to be out of reach. At the same time the bow rotated to the left, and the synchronized guns were facing straight at the boat ramp.

We all moved to the stern to get a better angle, and laid down a withering wall of fire. Whatever we didn't kill was shredded to the point where it couldn't even crawl in our direction, and the horde dwindled in size. The wheelhouse was blocking our view, but as we finished off the last of the slow moving, waterlogged infected, we saw that the fifty calibers had created the logjam we needed on the boat ramp.

The Chief maneuvered the Cormorant back into position and signaled for us to tie her off at the dock.

He called down to us, "I need two people on deck shooting anything that comes out of the water onto that boat ramp and two people shooting anything that approaches the dock from those restaurants over there. Everyone else will be making repairs. When we're done feel free to get a bite to eat at that place."

Needless to say we knew we weren't getting off the boat to sample the local cuisine, but when someone points you have to see what they're pointing at. The Chief was pointing at a restaurant named The Crab Shack, and there was a big wooden cutout of a blue crab above the front door.

Jean yelled up at the wheelhouse, "You know we could shoot you, right?"

The Chief had already closed the wheelhouse door and throttled up the engine so he couldn't hear her.

******

We were still sitting alongside the dock at sunset because the repairs had been more time consuming than expected. We decided that we would be better off staying where we were for the night rather than to navigate the cove and harbor without using our lights. Bright lights were not only an invitation to the infected, they were another way of painting a target on our backs. We didn't know if anyone was out there to see the lights, but we didn't want to give away the advantage if there was.

There were enough of us to have three people on watch at the same time. One watch was on the bow and stern, and one was in the wheelhouse. That person would be able to start the engine in a hurry if we needed to make a fast exit. Night vision goggles were passed out as we took our posts. I drew first watch on the stern, so I was facing down the length of the dock toward the pile of bodies.

If you stare long enough at something at night, it will eventually appear to move. If you stare at a tree, you'll swear there's someone standing next to it. If you stare at a window, someone will walk by on the other side of it. If you stare at a dark corner of your room, that coatrack or bookshelf will be someone just waiting for you to go to sleep.

From the stern of the boat, the largest thing in my field of vision was a pile of bodies. They were a bright green, but if I saw any movement in that pile, I wasn't going to be surprised. My problem was that I kept thinking there was something moving in my peripheral vision, but every time I faced straight at it, there was nothing there.

I finally got tired of thinking something had moved and radioed Cassandra on the bow and Sim in the wheelhouse.

"Stern to bow and wheelhouse. Please check my nine o'clock, over."

"Roger, stern."

I knew that both of them were staring into the darkness to my left while I faced straight ahead, and it seemed like I had only asked them to check the dock when Cassandra opened fire. She didn't come close to shooting me, but it sounded like the bullets went right by my head. I don't know if I dropped to the deck, or if my legs collapsed.

Something on the dock ran for cover, too.

"Stern, what was that, over?" Sim asked over his radio.

I didn't get a good enough look at it to answer Sim, but Cassandra did because she fired again. I lifted my head in time to see something change directions as bullets hit where it would have been. Another burst from the bow and whatever it was she was shooting at flipped over, but it didn't stop moving.

Cassandra came all the way to the stern and stood next to me, and Sim was right behind her. The door to the cabin below the wheelhouse was big and heavy, but it literally flew open as the Chief and the others all emerged onto the stern with their rifles ready.

"Everyone stay in the boat," said Cassandra.

She turned to the Chief and said, "We need to pull in the mooring lines and drift clear of the dock, and we can't drop the anchor."

The Chief always said there was a time to talk and a time to do things, and this was obviously not a time to talk. He would let Cassandra explain herself after we did what she said. We all scattered and brought in the heavy mooring lines. A shove on the dock from fore and aft was enough to get us away from the dock.

The stern of the Cormorant dropped down in the middle. The area was roped off because it was a boat ramp. The stern literally opened like a big door while the ship was at sea to allow a raft to enter at high speed. Cassandra peered over to check the bottom of the ramp and appeared satisfied that there wasn't anything down there to worry about.

"Is that thing still moving on the dock?" she asked me and Sim.

"Yes," I said, "but I still can't tell what it is."

I spoke to her, but I had stepped up on a piece of gear to get a better view. Whatever it was, it was moving a lot, but it wasn't going anywhere.

The Chief borrowed my goggles and stared in that direction for a minute.

"Now I know why you said we couldn't anchor," he said. "That thing could climb the anchor chain. How close was it?"

"Almost on top of Ed when he asked us to check his nine," she answered.

Kathy had taken the goggles next, and she practically gasped, which wasn't something she normally did. She was about as cool under fire as anybody could be, but whatever that was on the dock, it really scared her. She gave me a big hug, and that scared me.

"Somebody tell me what we're looking at up there," I said. "It's moving so much I can't make it out."

The rest of the group hadn't been able to see it yet because it was so dark, and they were waiting along with me for one of the others to say something.

The Chief said, "It's a crab. It must have flipped over on its back when Cassandra shot it."

"I had a dog smaller than that thing," said Hampton. His voice sounded almost reverent he was so awestruck.

"I was thinking the same thing," said Colleen. "If that thing had jumped Ed..."

There was no need for her to finish the sentence.

"That explains why I didn't see it every time I turned to face straight at it. It must've moved to its right every time my head turned. It's not only big, it's smart."

There was a flurry of movement and a clacking sound as more dark shapes moved out onto the dock. Some were bigger than the first one. They moved our way at first, found that the mooring lines were gone then moved to the flailing crab on its back. The sound of crab claws breaking another crab was enough to turn my stomach as it dawned on me what that would have felt like.

The Chief said, "Good work. If you hadn't asked for someone else to check your zone, that thing would have gotten you, and the others would have gotten on board."

We had drifted out about twenty feet, and we realized that the crabs had moved on. They were climbing over the pile of bodies at the end of the dock like it was a buffet.

"Big rats and now big crabs," said Sim. "What next?"

******

I never liked that question, "What next?" It didn't just imply that something else was going to happen. Not to me. To me it meant something was definitely going to happen.

At sunrise we had drifted about twenty yards from shore. We had only left a watch in the wheelhouse, and we all squeezed into the cabin below with the steel door dogged shut. We didn't know if those big crabs were also good climbers even without the anchor in the water, and we didn't want to find out the hard way.

The splashing and rocking of the Cormorant would have woken us up even if Tom hadn't raised the alarm from the wheelhouse. His warning wasn't what we expected, though. We scrambled out to see what was happening, but we stayed amidships and didn't go closer to the stern.

Alligators are better climbers than most people realize, and a big one had a firm grip on the stern door. We could see its claws hanging onto the stern railing and most of its head above its claws. Since he was slightly off center, the

Cormorant would rock every time it tried to raise a rear leg high enough to get a grip.

Since alligators did their fair share of eliminating the infected, we didn't want to shoot it. Call it our morning entertainment, but we gave short turns of the screw to get the boat in position at the end of the boat ramp. The crabs hadn't shown up the night before until after dark, so they had retreated to the water. It was no surprise that more infected were walking up the ramp, and the end of the dock had a large pile of bones where the infected had been. The crabs had feasted on them until there was nothing left. The cycle at the end of the dock would repeat itself every day if there was something to draw the infected out of the water. I didn't doubt that it happened all day long on the bottom of the river. No wonder the crabs were so big.

The infected didn't know an alligator from a grasshopper. All they knew was that it was moving. We couldn't see what was happening below the alligator, but we had a pretty good idea. The infected closed in, they tried to bite the leathery hide, and the alligator took it badly. It let go of the stern rail and dropped into the middle of the boat ramp.

Kathy nudged me and pointed to a spot out in the cove not far from where the ramp entered the water. Several sets of eyes moved in deadly silence straight for the infected. About ten feet behind the eyes there were tails moving from side to side, propelling the alligators toward breakfast, and the one that had tried to climb our stern had been a baby compared to these well fed monsters.

The Chief had taken over in the wheelhouse, and he decided it was time to go. A short burst of forward throttle made us pull away fast enough, and with a clear view of the boat ramp we saw why it would never be safe to stick our feet in the water again. The alligators ran right up the boat ramp and dragged down several of the infected.

"I feel like I'm in an episode of Animal Planet," said Jean. "Does anyone else feel like we're in a foreign country? Those were alligators that were bigger than crocodiles."

"It makes me wonder what else might have evolved by now," said Colleen.

Kathy said, "Not trying to be too scientific, but it must have something to do with the virus. Normally I would just say the crabs and alligators are being well fed, but that would just cause them to breed a larger population in the area. Why are they also growing bigger?"

The Chief couldn't hear everything from the wheelhouse, but we were near enough that he picked up some of it, and had the Cormorant cruising so slowly that we weren't leaving a wake. There were things to watch for in the water that we might have missed when we arrived.

"Which leads to another question," he called to us. "What else has evolved or changed just because there are so many rotting bodies walking around?"

Jean said, "I'll leave that one for all of you to figure out. I'm going to make breakfast while I still feel like eating it."

She ducked down through the cabin hatch just as Tom asked, "Is she pregnant again?"

"Don't ask Ed," said Kathy. "The last time everybody else figured it out before him."

"I'm more comfortable talking about the previous topic," I said.

Jean sounded far away, but we all heard her loud and clear when she yelled, "I heard that."

"Okay, let's see who can come up with the next evolution," said Hampton. "I think it's going to be insects.

They feed on the infected. Mosquitos feed on the infected and the living. What if they evolve to carry the virus?"

Colleen was shaking her red hair enough for all of us to notice.

"You don't think so?" asked Kathy.

"No, just the opposite. They already carry the virus, but something in their digestive system kills the virus or makes it dormant. By the time a mosquito that bit an infected dead gets around to biting a living person, the virus isn't capable of infecting them."

That wasn't the answer any of us had expected, and it was extremely disturbing. If Jean had been topside, maybe she could have given a medical opinion about it. Being a nurse, she had obviously taken her share of classes about infectious diseases and how they spread. Our group expertise was limited to the flu and hand washing.

Cassandra was frowning like she did every time I had talked with her about the doctors on the Mercy Mission hospital ship. They spent weeks bent over their microscopes staring at slides prepared from the blood of the infected, and when they realized people were getting sick after eating meals made from Ghost Crab meat, they wanted to know why the Ghost Crabs didn't get sick and die, too.

"We had it bad at sea," said Cassandra. "We had people on board who were bitten when we left port."

"So did we," said Kathy, "and their families didn't tell us until it was too late."

"We had medicines, research facilities, and doctors who knew research protocols," continued Cassandra, "but it didn't do us a lot of good because no one would ever tell the doctors when they were bitten. Then we had contaminated food and rats. I always wondered why the fleas on the rats didn't spread the infection."

"Bubonic Plague or the Black Death," said the Chief.

He stepped out onto the deck as Tom took over the helm.

"Sailors throughout history worried about rats on their ships because the fleas on the rats carried the plague. From what I understand it's a bacteria and not a virus."

"We've always gone with the assumption this infection is viral," said Kathy. "Any chance it's a bacteria?"

Cassandra shook her head this time.

"The doctors on my ship tried antibiotics, but they knew they wouldn't work. They said so. They only hoped to stumble across a cure while they studied the virus. They actually thought they were close to a cure, but we'll never know if it was just wishful thinking."

"So, putting two and two together," I said, "if it was a bacteria, we'd be in big trouble because fleas could carry it, and if fleas could carry it, there's at least some chance that mosquitos could too."

"I guess the same principle would apply to HIV. I never heard of any studies that said it could be transmitted by insects," said Kathy. "When I was a police officer, we always worried about direct contact with body fluids like blood, but beyond that I couldn't have explained why mosquitos or fleas couldn't carry the virus."

Jean appeared in the doorway of the cabin while Kathy was talking, and immediately guessed what everyone was concerned about.

"Without trying to deliver a college level lecture about the reasons we don't have to be afraid of mosquito bites, I'll just say the virus probably can't replicate inside mosquitos or fleas because an antigen found in humans is not present in insects. The body of an insect doesn't have the immune response that ultimately would kill it, such as the fever someone gets after being bitten by the infected dead."

Hampton said, "I don't believe it. My biology teacher in high school tried to get that across to our class all year, but we just didn't get it. Now I understand it completely."

"We all do," I said. "Now all she has to do is tell us what will evolve next."

"Better yet, find a cure," said the Chief.

19 FUGITIVE

Year Six of the Decline

Stokes ran into a small group of survivors in Claxton, Georgia. They were cautious around strangers, and Stokes probably would have tried to kill them all if they hadn't learned what to do when they ran into someone on the road. There were six people in the group, all around the age of thirty, but despite being young, they were experienced.

One thing they never did was let themselves get bunched up in a crowd. They always seemed to be too spread out for Stokes to be able to see them all without turning his head. They also made sure that there was always some distance between them.

Stokes was smart enough to know that he was more at risk than they were, so he decided to move on before they figured out that he wasn't safe. One man traveling alone meant the man was either good at staying alive or dangerous, and this group would detect which one he was in due time.

His next planned stop was Jesup. It was a town just big enough to possibly have transportation without the risk of going into a big city to find a car. The route he was planning to use was going to take him closer to Tallahassee than he wanted to be, but his only other alternative would be to spend a week or two going around big cities. He was already forced to go through Waycross and Valdosta, but he would stick to back roads as much as possible.

It was almost a confirmation of his belief that he was too lucky to die when he saw the big billboard advertising Honest Bob Horton's Jeep dealership on Hwy 84 near Jesup. He didn't really expect to find a Jeep at the dealership after over five years of rummaging by scavengers, but it meant there would be Jeeps in the area. All he needed to do was find a rural home where loyal customers of Honest Bob Horton lived. There had to be someone who grew up in the area and only bought from their good friend from high school. Small farms were his best bet.

Stokes was still on Hwy 301 when he saw the billboard, and that was perfect for him because he could cut across a few acres of farmland to the south and head straight for Jesup. He saw barns in the distance to the west and took it as a good sign that there would be others to the south. The second farm he spotted had several Jeeps parked between the barn and the main house, and there was a thin trail of smoke coming from a chimney.

"Now that is a good sign indeed," he muttered.

Stokes considered everything to be fair game, so he thought of those Jeeps as his, and they were parked at his house where someone was cooking over a wood fire. He could smell something like ham or pulled pork, and if that's what it was, it was his too.

The house sat back from the two lane highway that passed out front protected by a tall fence with a strong gate, and he was coming up from behind it. There were small hills that had something like wheat growing wild on their slopes, but for the most part the property was ringed by trees. A barbed wire fence seemed to connect the wooded places to each other, and a little investigating was all he needed to learn that the fence continued right through the trees. He sat at the edge of one of those wooded areas and watched the house for over an hour before anyone came out the back door.

It was the first time he didn't feel like things were going totally his way. The man who took the steps from the back porch two at a time was agile and muscular. That didn't bother Stokes because he was no slouch himself. What bothered him was the camouflaged outfit he was wearing. The man was a hunter, and good hunters could tell whether or not a man was a hunter or prey. One reason there were no ripe meat walking around this place was possibly because of who lived in that house.

The man cut across to the Jeeps and reached inside the passenger window of one. Stokes lifted his binoculars and sighted in on the man as he turned around and headed for a small wooden building. He had a roll of toilet paper in his hand.

Stokes thought about it for a moment. There were times when he talked his way into what he wanted, and there were times when he just went after it. The question was obviously how many more people would be in that house, and how much trouble would he be in if they weren't talkers.

Most people didn't live in the same place they did before the epidemic. He was proof of that because he had lived in someone else's house since it started. That guy who was dressed like a hunter probably took that house from its original owners.

The decision to take what he wanted was made without much deliberation about the consequences. The only thing he had to decide was which gun to use. He had kept the powerful elephant gun he had liberated back at the beginning of the apocalypse, but the weapon had unfortunately been lost when Randal decided to do a little sport shooting at the ripe meat outside the house. He had acquired a sawed off shotgun from Turk when he had died back in South Carolina. It was just right for close targets. From Franco he had liberated a .270 Winchester that was supposed to be right for bringing down the biggest bull elk at long distance.

Stokes lifted his hunting rifle and laid the barrel across a stump. He sighted in on the little outhouse door, and put the crosshairs of the scope in the center about four feet from the bottom. He pulled the trigger without emotion and saw a piece of wood fly off of the door, but instead of watching to see if he had gotten the results he wanted, he rotated and put the sights on the back door of the house as he chambered another round. He was right on time.

Stokes pulled the trigger just as the door flew open, and if he guessed right, there would be two of them coming out the door at the same time. The rifle sent its big bullet through the first man and into the chest of the second. Both flew back into the house in a heap.

He doubted there were only three men in the house, but he was feeling lucky again. No one came through the door of the outhouse, and if there was anyone inside the main house who was alive, they were trying to figure out where the bullet came from. One thing was certain. They knew someone outside wasn't taking prisoners.

Stokes had time on his side because he was inside the barbed wire fence. If any ripe meat heard the shots and tried to reach his hiding spot, the fence would cover him on that side. He also had the high ground, so he would be hard to spot. The vehicles were all parked far enough from the door for him to pick off anyone who tried to make a run for it, and he wasn't stuck inside a house with dead meat sprawled on the floor in the doorway.

One of the two men he had shot was already sitting up, and the second one behind him was trying to do the same.

"Here comes the good part," said Stokes. He had a toothpick hanging out between his lips, and he used his tongue to pass it from the right side to the left. To him this had always been the most entertaining part of the infection. When friends and relatives had to come to terms with seeing someone turn into ripe meat.

If the people inside the house weren't smart enough to go out the front door and try to flank him, he figured they weren't smart enough to live.

The two victims of his second shot were just making it to their feet when the outhouse door flew open, and the first guy fell flat on his face. It didn't faze him at all, and he awkwardly pushed himself up from the ground. He immediately fell a second time because his pants were still around his ankles. The two in the door were drawn toward him because of the noise, but something crashed inside the house and got their attention. They turned and walked inside while the man in the yard stumbled and stepped on his pants until he got one foot out of them, and he moved toward the steps of the porch. He stepped on the pants again on the stairs and fell face first onto the porch, but that last step managed to accomplish what the first steps hadn't. The other leg came free, and the pants were left behind.

There were screams before two women fell out the back door and ran straight into the dead meat on the steps. Both had blood running down their arms, and Stokes didn't need two guesses to know what caused the bleeding. They were moving so fast that the three of them landed in a heap on the ground.

It was possible that there really were only three men at the house, and it was all but confirmed when they made their second appearance in the door.

When they got back up, the women didn't run for the Jeeps. They just ran for the open yard like they thought they would get help from someone else, not really understanding how this could be happening to them.

Stokes shook his head and clicked his tongue in mock disgust.

"How did you people survive this long?"

He walked down the hill through the tall grass and wheat. It was far enough away that none of them would see him, and he only needed that pair of pants that was now left behind on the steps. His guess was that would be where he would find keys to the Jeep where the first guy stashed his toilet paper.

To Stokes it sounded like a bee flew straight into his right ear and stung him, but the warm wetness of blood hit the back of his hand at the same moment that he heard the distant crack of a small caliber rifle. When he grabbed at his ear he found that about a half inch was gone from the tip.

The grass was tall enough for him to disappear, but he couldn't see the person who shot him any better than they could see him. He didn't have any formal combat training, but he knew he wasn't supposed to stay where the shooter had last seen him, so he crawled across the field. There was just enough breeze for the grass to be swaying, but he was leaving a trail that would be easy for the shooter to spot, and he was amazed at how much an ear could bleed. He looked ahead for gaps and figured he could flank the shooter if he found a gap that went back up the hill. It never occurred to him that there might be more than one shooter behind him.

Down by the house the women heard the shot and saw Stokes go down. From where they were they could also see him crawling parallel to the men who had been patrolling the fence around the property. The women ran wildly up the hill, pointing and yelling. The resulting confusion was the kind of luck that always seemed to go Stokes' way.

He parted the grass to see why the women were screaming and getting closer and saw them running toward his new position.

"Stupid people," he said under his breath. "Just like football. Watch the quarterback's eyes to be able to tell where he was going to pass the ball."

Stokes turned in the grass and pointed his body roughly in the direction the woman was pointing, and even though his ear was full of blood, he listened to her voice. As soon as he heard what he was waiting for he pulled the trigger on his sawed off shotgun.

The woman was trying to give away the position of the man in the grass, but she saw she had done it to her own man, too.

She screamed, "No, wait. He's...."

The blast from the shotgun drowned out the rest, and she saw one of her friends fly backward from the impact. The second guy should have done what Stokes had done when he had clipped his ear with the small caliber rifle, but instead of dropping to the ground, he turned and ran back up the hill.

"Where you going?" yelled Stokes as he stood up and shot the man in the back.

He chambered another round and shot the woman who had run too far in his direction to get away. Stokes tried to see where the second woman had gone, but she was nowhere in sight. He knew she must have gotten away fast because the three men who had turned into dead meat were all walking up the hill. If she had been slow, they would be following her. The shotgun blasts were more than enough to get their interest.

Instead of walking toward the house, Stokes walked up the hill and found the guy who had shot him. The rifle he used was only a few feet away.

"You shot me with a lousy 22?"

He kicked the body just because he could and then got down to the business of finding the keys to the Jeep. He had his pick from four that were all parked out of sight from the road and figured he would take whichever one had a full tank of gas.

Gas had become more and more scarce over the years, and even when he found a big supply, a lot of it had been contaminated by ground water and corrosion. Sometimes it just sat in its container too long until it turned to varnish. He had learned that the hard way, but it only had to happen to him once.

Each of the men had keys in their pockets, so he would have to figure out which set went to each Jeep. At least he knew which one was owned by the ripe meat he had nicknamed pant-less.

It only took a few minutes to get rid of the ripe meat entourage that was following him all over the backyard. Normally he wouldn't waste his time with them, but he needed to check their pockets. While he was at it, he collected their guns, and one had a ring that he really liked. Despite the years making everything that had been precious turn into something useless, he still couldn't get enough of the old treasures like gold rings and necklaces.

Pant-less had the most gas in his Jeep, and Stokes liked the way he had gotten it professionally painted in hunters camouflage green. It started up easily and purred like a big cat, so he knew the dummy had taken care of the engine. He almost felt bad about killing the guy.

He checked out the house and found smoked meat, fresh baked bread, and some home brewed beer. That made him feel bad about killing all of them. After a few of the home brews he was a bit misty eyed and wished he would have recruited them. In his mind they would have welcomed the opportunity.

Less than an hour later he was heading south and making good time. He was still laughing because he had caught up with the woman who had escaped from the house. When she saw the familiar Jeep barreling down the road, she had run straight to him. She realized her mistake far too late.

******

At sunrise the handful of survivors from Hopkins on The Lake timidly whispered at the door to see if their rescuers were still there. They didn't know who was out there, but they were grateful.

Iris eased the door open and found a small group of women and children inside the house with one older man who didn't move as if he could see very well. They only took a few minutes to talk about what had happened to their community. It didn't take much imagination to know that the horde had moved through the area and overrun the town.

One of the women explained to them that they thought they were safe out on the lake. They told them about how they had built their settlement on land at first, but they were forced to relocate as more and more of the dead came into the area. If the lake had been deeper, and if they had been given more time, maybe the idea would have worked, but time and safe places were both luxuries that most people couldn't find.

When the citizens of Hopkins asked Iris where they had come from, she didn't have the heart to tell them they had left a perfectly safe shelter in North Carolina where the dead couldn't reach them, and where supplies were practically endless. It would be hard to explain to people who had lost so much.

George reminded Iris that they needed to get out of the area soon, and that presented another problem. As much as they wanted to help the defenseless people, they were going to cut across some very hostile terrain, and they weren't really equipped to protect them all the way to the coast.

The survivors surprised Iris and her group when they said they had plans of their own. All they knew was that some of their men had followed the horde, so they planned to do the same. Iris told them they planned to set fire to the infected that filled the original pits, and that the fire would attract the infected from all directions. She tried hard to convince them to head north because the horde was massed to the south, but they were convinced their people would be back at any time.

In the end, the survivors of Hopkins promised Iris that they would wait for one more day, and they would light the pits on fire themselves. Iris Mason had always been a practical person, and she didn't have much faith that the people of the lake settlement would see their friends again, but it wasn't up to her to convince them otherwise. She pulled her group off to the side for a chance to see if any of the others disagreed with leaving the people to set the fires.

Sora was willing to say what they were all afraid to put into words. They were leaving the people behind to die. Yuni sadly watched the children play and wanted to say they should stay to help them, but she knew they would need a lot more than the five of them to survive against the stray infected dead that were spread out through the woods. The main horde had gone by, but there would be stragglers for days.

George said, "You know the longer we hang around the more chance that we'll get hemmed in with them. I say if they don't want us to light the pits on fire, then we don't have to."

"I just have a hard time passing up on the opportunity to torch a hundred of them," said Iris, "but I get your point. These woods will be crawling with the infected for a long time. We need to go back to the next major highway and head east while we can."

Sherry was having as much trouble with leaving them as Yuni.

"You sure we can't get them to just follow us north? They won't last more than one week out here."

"They've already made up their minds," said Iris. "I have to be honest with them, though."

Iris took the woman who had assumed the role of leadership off to speak with her alone. It didn't take a lip reader to know that the woman thanked Iris for saving them the night before, but they were set on following the plans they had made.

When Iris came back, she said, "Well, that wasn't the answer I expected."

"What did she say," asked Sherry, "are they going with us?"

"No, she said when we saved them last night, we were just delaying the inevitable. She doesn't think any of their people are coming back for them, and she doesn't think it would be right for us to die trying to protect them. She said we should go while we can. They'll light the pits on fire at sunset to get the strays in the woods walking toward them instead of us."

"Let's go before she changes her mind," said George.

They said their goodbyes quickly and left at a trot along the gravel road that led to the lake. They were moving to the northwest to try to reach the interstate where the horde had already been, and they would turn back to the east as soon as they felt like they had enough distance between them and Hopkins. If they saw infected dead on the roads to the east, they decided to keep going and look for a road that was safer.

As it turned out, they went far enough to reach the Interstate that gave them the best visibility in the distance. I-20 was four lanes and went exactly where they wanted to go. When the Chief and Kathy had left them at Ambassadors Island, they had told Iris about Tom and Molly. How they had escaped from Myrtle Beach, and how they wouldn't have survived without the help of some very brave police officers and soldiers. A lot had changed since then, but Iris knew their best bet of reaching Mud Island was by retracing Tom's steps down the coast. She had asked to see where it was on a map, so she had a good idea of what they were up against.

Fortunately, Iris had four capable friends with her and some idea of where they were going. They were tired as they made the turn onto I-20, and they had a long way to go, but for some odd reason they felt like they were in the home stretch. Maybe it was because they weren't following the biggest horde in the southeast.

It took a week to travel from Columbia, South Carolina to the town of Conway. Iris remembered Conway was where Tom had been rescued by a police officer who got them into a convoy of small boats that escaped the chaos and death of the first night. She also remembered that the Chief's friend who owned the shelter was in Surfside when the infection broke out, and he had to race back to the safety of the shelter. She was glad the Chief had taken the time to tell her the stories of how all of his friends survived. If not, she would be traveling blind like the people in Hopkins.

Thinking of Hopkins made her realize it had been a week and what Sherry had said about how long they would last. They probably lit the pits on fire and then were overrun by the dead. Now they found themselves only a day or so away from Surfside and only a few hours more away from Mud Island.

Just like all of the other interstates, I-20 had been a vast wasteland of rusted cars and trucks. They moved fast while making very little noise, and they only stopped when they felt like they found a good place to spend the night that they couldn't pass up. A Greyhound bus had been a perfect place to sleep because someone had left the doors open. If the infected had been trapped inside until the heat had dried them into nothing but brittle skin and bones, the bus would have smelled like the inside of a coffin.

It was remarkable how few of the infected they saw along the interstate, but it was a true testament to how big the horde was that was using I-26 to reach Charleston. When they spotted lone infected or small groups, they detoured around them rather than try to eliminate them. They were tempted to do their part to help mankind take back the world, but their efforts would be a drop in a bucket, and it would take far longer for them to reach the coast.

The second night they made a unique discovery. An extension ladder under an overpass went up to the metal frame under the road. Someone had survived long enough to make a platform using scrap metal cannibalized from the vehicles.

George climbed up and tested it for stability so they wouldn't end their trip by falling to the median. He waved for them to come on up, and as they arrived he pointed out where crossbeams were located under the sheet metal. They were safe for the night, but they each had to admit they didn't sleep well trusting the engineering skills of a stranger. Sherry woke up twice with the sensation of falling.

Sora ran a rope around his waist and tied it around one of the support beams. The others teased him at first, but by the time they went to sleep, everyone had a lifeline.

When they climbed down the next morning, they were in general agreement that they would rather sleep on the ground than to be afraid of falling all night long. Yuni also admitted that she had been afraid the ladder would be gone in the morning, and they would be forced to use their ropes to get down.

There were farm houses within short walking distances of the interstate, and just as they expected, every house had already been searched for food and anything else that was useful. Thousands of cars and trucks lined both sides of the interstate, and those people had to have gone somewhere when the infection started.

They were checking a house as a potential place to spend the night, and no matter how many times they searched a house, they sensed the presence of the original owners, the people who stood in their windows and watched as the dying world forced its way in their front doors.

"They are called yurei by our people," said Sora. "Ghosts of the people who were denied a peaceful resting place when they died."

"The people who lived here?" asked Sherry.

Sora nodded at her.

"You are probably standing where one of them stood hundreds of times, and maybe even on the spot where they died."

Sherry glanced down at her feet out of reflex. She was a little pale, and when George asked her if she felt okay, she passed it off as just being tired from being on the move every day.

George and Sherry were only a bit older than the Tanakas, but they had gotten soft by being inside the shelter for over five years. It was going to take awhile for them to get as tough as they used to be. More time in the gym would have done them some good, and they both knew it.

Iris said, "Don't let Sora spook you. You don't really believe in ghosts, do you?"

"Do you believe in zombies?" asked Sora.

"Ouch," she answered. "I guess I deserved that."

George walked over and stood beside Sora at the window. From the window of the farmhouse, the interstate seemed to be out of place. Farmland and scenic forests dominated the view from the window, but the interstate was a gray and rust red scar in the distance.

"Sora's right," he said. "If I had lived here when the whole world fell apart, I would have been standing right here at this window watching it come to me. The cars and trucks were on fire with the exception of those that managed to pull out of line and then get stuck in the ditches and in the median. People were running everywhere. Some were infected, and they were chasing the living, and the living would have seen this house. Human nature would have made them think of this house as a refuge, but the people watching from their windows were really saying to stay away."

Sora had his eyes almost closed when he said, "I'm standing here watching them come toward me, but I have my gun, and I'll shoot the first person who sets foot on my property."

Yuni whispered to the others, "He is seeing it through the eyes of the yurei that live here now."

"Will the yurei mind if we spend the night?" asked Iris.

"They are not vengeful," said Yuni. "They simply did not get the peaceful passing they had hoped for during their golden years."

Now that they were less than a day from Surfside, there would be no need to stay in farmhouses with the yurei. If they didn't make it to Mud Island by nightfall, they could find plenty of commercial buildings that gave them access to the roof where they could sleep peacefully.

They left I-20 behind and were forced to use a road that was more narrow in some places. It made them nervous because they didn't want to get trapped between the river on one side and the woods on the other. By the time they reached the end of the road and it became wider with more commercial areas, they were exhausted, and they decided unanimously to find a place earlier than they had been doing. They could go the last few miles in the morning.

They were also unanimous about where they would stay when they saw a sign that pointed in the direction of a marina. One of the problems that had worried all of them was the famous moat around Mud Island. The Chief had told Iris about the man who had designed the shelter, and about how he had tried to think of everything to make Mud Island safe. His idea to put a moat around the island had been a stroke of genius, and they couldn't imagine how many of the infected had tried to cross the moat.

The good news was that the moat was effective at keeping people away from Mud Island, but that was also the bad news. There was no way for Iris and her group to cross the moat or take a boat across land to reach the moat. That left them with only one option, and that was to find a boat in Surfside and use it to reach Mud Island from sea.

They could see the marina ahead and they were hoping to find a boat before it got dark, but Kathy and the Chief had told them about the chaos and death at all marinas. There was only a slim chance that there would be a boat they could use that was tied to a dock.

Their best bet would be to find a sail boat that was at anchor far enough from shore to have been spared the damage of the first night, but anything that had been anchored that far out would have been forced to endure over five years of bad weather. Even if there had been no hurricanes or tropical storms, there were bound to have been storms bad enough to swamp a boat at anchor near the marina.

Even in daylight years after the infection began, it wouldn't take an expert investigator very long to describe the scene that must have unfolded at the marina. There were no more bodies, just piles of rags and bones spread around on the pier that led to all of the slips.

In its glory days the marina held over three hundred boats of all sizes. A seawall had been built across the entrance to protect it from the wakes of bigger ships as they passed by, and there was an entrance at one end and exit at the other. The area had been kept as pristine as possible, and it was unlikely that big ships ever came in too close, but the seawall was necessary. This marina was intended for important people, and accommodations must have been the best when the marina was alive.

On the day when money became worthless, so did the status of the people who could afford to dock their boats here. The marina had been swamped with desperate people who were trying to save their families, and they would do so even at the cost of someone else's life. The parking lot that was used to luxury cars was full of pickup trucks and minivans. Boats that managed to carry people to safety left the marina with bullet holes in their windshields and blood on their seats and decks.

The rest of the boats were upside down, resting on the bottom, or at least half full of water. Broken masts of sailboats lay across the wreckage like death shrouds, not a single one without a tear. The five survivors stood side by side and remembered their own first days of terror in Wilmington, and despite everything they had seen since leaving Charlotte, they realized they had blocked out in their minds just how bad that day had been. If they had remembered, maybe they would still be safe in their shelter on Ambassadors Island.

20 ROOM SERVICE

Year Six of the Decline

The marina featured a five star hotel for its rich clients, and it curved around the southern side of the slips. That way its guests could not only see their prestigious yachts, but they could see if someone famous was coming into the marina. Twenty stories tall, it had a grand view of the beach in both directions for miles.

George had his attention so focused on the hotel that he didn't hear Iris ask him if he could see something the rest of them might be interested to know about. Sherry poked her husband in the ribs and asked him what he was doing. The rest of them were feeling like they had come to the end of the road, but George was sightseeing.

"Do you think it's safe to go in there?" he asked.

"Safe?"

Sora was regarding his friend with an expression that said he might be going insane.

"Yeah, safe," said George. "The higher we get the further we can see. If there's a usable boat anywhere within a hundred miles we should be able to see it from up there, and check it out. It goes right down to the water's edge."

"I don't know if a hundred miles is accurate," said Iris, "but I get your point. I just don't know if I want to go into a building that was probably a death trap for a few thousand people."

"Maybe we don't have to go all the way to the top," said Yuni. "Maybe just high enough to see down the beach in both directions."

"Good point," said George. "Come on, Iris. It's worth a shot. If we can just get a look at the other side of that sea wall we might find something useful."

"I doubt it," said Iris, "but if we can see the other marinas from one place, it would save a lot of time on the ground going from one place to the next."

"You remember what the Chief said about buildings?" asked Sherry.

"Too clearly," said Iris. "Buildings are worse than finding one or two infected wandering around inside your shelter. Especially buildings that were meant to hold that many people."

"All we have to do is get into the stairwell on the end," said George. "We don't need to go near the areas that would've been crowded."

Sora asked, "You don't think the stairwell would have been crowded on that first day? I've got a news flash for you. Anyone with half a brain wouldn't have been waiting for an elevator."

"We're talking about rich people. They wouldn't have been on the stairs."

George was getting defensive, and they had all seen it before. If he got it in his head that it was a good idea, then it didn't matter how bad it was. They all knew he was going to go into that hotel.

"Let's play it by ear," said Iris. "If it looks safe from the fire entry at the end of the building we'll go in. We should find something down here to pry the door open. How about a lug wrench from one of those pickups out front?"

George couldn't have been happier and ran off to get a lug wrench. Sherry didn't seem to be too happy about it, and neither did the Tanakas.

"Why did you give in so easily?" asked Sherry. "You usually stand up to George until he backs down."

"This time he's right," said Iris. "We could save a full day or even two just by getting high enough to see down the beaches, but like I said, we'll play it by ear. If that place is full of the infected, we're getting out fast."

As soon as George got back they crossed a courtyard in the marina that led to the hotel. Golf carts lined one side of the brick sidewalks for people who preferred a slow ride over a little exercise. Everything was overgrown with weeds and tall grass, but it was easy to see that this had been an expensive place back when things like this mattered to people.

Getting to the end of the hotel proved to be more difficult than they had expected. The vegetation that was meant to make the courtyard feel like an island paradise had gotten so thick that it actually became dark walking through tunnels of tall vines. They followed the untended sidewalks much further than they would have gone if they had known it was so overgrown and found themselves at the back stairwell doors without even realizing they had gone far enough.

"That's one spooky garden," said Sherry. "George, this had better work because I don't want to have all of that be for nothing. We have to go back through that stuff again."

Iris wished she had listened to the others. The glass on the door was crusted with something on the inside, so they couldn't even see down the dark hallway. She hated to think what it was that had been smeared so thick on the glass that it blocked out the light. It was gloomy on their side of the glass, but it was midnight dark on the inside.

George stuck the lug wrench into the corner of the lock, and Iris held out her hand to stop him.

"This might not be the best idea. We can't even see in there?"

"I have a flashlight. Besides, we've come this far for nothing?"

It was getting late in the day, and it was either now or wait until the next day. They still had to go back through the courtyard and all that jungle, so Iris gave in again.

"At least listen at the door for any sound first. You can't just bust it open and hope nothing falls out on us."

George was getting impatient, but he knew he had to humor the rest of them, or they might change their minds about going inside.

He leaned his head toward the glass, and it felt cold against his ear. He wasn't sure, but he thought he heard rustling on the other side.

"I don't hear anything," he announced as he stood up straight and pushed the lug wrench into the lock for a second time.

The salt air had caused the gaps around the door to fill in with fine sand from the dunes. For over five years the door had remained shut, so it resisted at first. Then the strain on the frame caused the glass pane to shatter, and the entire thing came down in huge splinters. In the jungle enclosed area by the door the sound was deafening, and they found themselves being pushed back by something that was heavy and loose at the same time.

They fell into each other as they tried desperately to bring their weapons up in defense against the mass of junk that fell out on top of them. There were suitcases, handbags, shoe boxes, clothes, and a variety of room decorations. They were all tangled up with each other on the ground, and everything just seemed to keep coming out through the broken door.

As they untangled and scrambled to their feet, they realized they hadn't been able to see inside the door because it had been barricaded from the other side. It was still dark in the long hallway beyond, but someone had obviously been trying to keep something from getting in.

George shone his flashlight inside, and the light seemed to disappear into the darkness. It only lit up the area just inside the door enough for them to see the door on the left that was labeled with a little sign that said stairwell. He stepped into the darkness without hesitating and pulled on the stairwell door. It opened with a loud scraping sound that seemed to advertise their presence even more than the shattering glass.

If they had all told the truth at that moment, not one of them had ever been more afraid, and everyone was holding their breath. George disappeared into the dark stairwell as if he knew exactly what he was doing, and the others were forced to follow.

Everyone turned on their flashlights, and it got bright enough in the stairwell to see that nothing was moving, but people had died in there. They had to watch their steps as they avoided one pile of bones after the next.

Yuni asked in a voice so low she could hardly hear herself, "What happened to the rats that cleaned up all of the bodies?"

She still sounded to herself like she had been too loud.

"Hopefully they moved on looking for more food," said Sora. "They ran out of things to eat in this building years ago."

He hoped he sounded more convincing than he felt.

"How many floors should we go up?" George asked from the first landing above the others.

"If it feels right let's try for ten," said Iris.

"What do you mean, if it feels right?"

Iris had a moment when she seriously thought she might lose her grip on reality and shoot George. She was supposed to be the leader of the group, but right now she was as scared as she had ever been in her life. It was just so dark that every corner looked like it had someone standing in it.

"Stop at each door and listen. If you don't hear anything, go up to the next floor. If you hear something, we'll go back down one floor."

George stopped at the next door and then walked silently up the next flight of stairs. They reached the tenth floor without hearing anything on the other side of any of the doors, but while George was standing with his ear pressed against the cold metal, he heard something through his other ear. There was something in the stairwell above them. He held up one hand in their direction and whispered, "Freeze."

With the same hand he changed to one finger and pointed upward and then at his right ear. The moan that came from above had to be several stories above them, but it was loud enough for everyone to feel their legs go weak. Yuni was at the back of the group, and she lowered her feet down one step at a time. They all turned off their flashlights except George, and he put his hand over the lens of his.

"Do you think we can open the door at the ninth floor without making any noise?" Sora asked George.

There was a rustling sound above, and a piece of paper drifted down to their floor. They watched it as if they had never seen anything like it before.

"We had better get a grip on ourselves, or we won't be ready to go through the door," said Iris. "We all know what to do, and we all know how to defend ourselves, so get yourselves together."

Yuni motioned for Iris to come closer before she whispered to her.

"We've had it too easy. We haven't been running into the problems we expected so far, and George has gotten reckless. That's got you acting like you're not sure of yourself, and the rest of us are waiting for him to get us killed."

"Great time for a pep talk. Got any suggestions?"

Even in the darkness Yuni could see Iris was upset, but she knew her well enough to know she wasn't mad at her. She was upset because Yuni was right. If George didn't start acting like this was a dangerous place, he was going to cost someone their life.

Iris clicked her flashlight at George to get his attention, and he came down closer to the group. Iris put just enough anger in her voice to make him understand she was serious.

"You have the rest of us on edge. At any moment we could panic and run. If you don't start being careful, I'm taking the lead, and you can back me up."

George had never given even a hint that he couldn't follow Iris, and she didn't doubt it had something to do with the five years they had spent in the shelter. He was just being impatient, and she understood that he just wanted to keep making progress. They had already lost days by having to backtrack away from the I-26 horde.

A range of emotions flickered across George's face. He felt like he was being careful, but the way he had shattered the glass door had left them unnerved. There's something about the sound of breaking glass that stays in your memory and makes every sound after that seem amplified. The last emotion Iris saw in his features was the George she knew well. He understood, and he felt bad for making his friends feel so frightened.

He gave her a nod and held out a hand for the others to knuckle bump. He gave Sora a pat on the shoulder as he went back down the stairs one level.

They could tell George had gotten the point when he arrived at the door on the ninth floor because he approached it as if it was wired with explosives. He listened longer with one ear pressed against it and then motioned for Iris to do the same. Neither of them heard anything on the other side.

George got down on his knees and gently brushed away small bits of debris that would be in the way when the door opened. When he finished, he brought everyone in close and asked Iris if she had a plan in mind or anything to tell him.

"The doors will be spaced farther apart because these were expensive rooms. They also won't be easy to break into if the locks are manual, but if they're key cards, the batteries should have failed by now. We won't know until you try a door, but some locks fail to the locked position. You can always get out from the inside, but you might not be able to get in. If you have to pry a door, signal us first."

George gave her a thumbs up and turned back to the door. It didn't make nearly as much noise as the glass door had, but there was a noticeable change in air pressure in the stairwell.

"What was that?" asked Yuni.

Sora answered, "You don't smell that? This place must be airtight. Bodies decayed in their rooms, and if the HVAC system shut down, there were trapped gases."

"Nice. So we're breathing in dead people."

George held a finger to his lips, and the Tanakas stopped whispering. He slipped through the door and let it close, but Iris got her fingers around the edge before it could close all the way. She peeked through the gap and could see George's back as he moved along the wall. He had his flashlight pointed down at an angle, and she could see why.

The floor of the hallway was a mess. There were human remains, but there was no way to guess what had happened here. Some of the rooms were open, and furniture had been dragged into the hallway. She tried to imagine why there were minibars in the hallway with lamps and mattresses and could only guess that someone was trying to create barricades.

Sora leaned over her shoulder and said, "I think they blocked all the stairs and elevators, locked themselves in their rooms, and then called room service."

"How many do you figure were already bitten when they put up the barricades?"

"Too many. They put up the barricades and then couldn't tear them down fast enough. These people probably called 911 right up to the very end."

George's flashlight went out.

Iris stared into the darkness where the light had been and held her breath. Sora was practically on her shoulder, and she couldn't hear him breathing either.

Behind them Yuni was facing the stairs. She was trying to tell herself that she had imagined the sound of something being dragged. They had come up the stairs, so she reasoned the sound must have been somewhere above, but then she wondered if something had entered the stairwell on the eighth floor.

George's flashlight blinked on again, and he aimed it at his hand so they would see him motion to come forward. Iris opened the door just far enough to go through, and Sora squeezed through with her. The door clicked shut before Yuni knew they had even moved.

It was pitch black in the stairwell, and Yuni didn't even want to move her feet for fear that she would make a sound. It seemed as if her breath was stuck in her throat, refusing to go in or out. She was paralyzed with fear because she knew she hadn't imagined the last thing she had heard.

Without eyes to tell her what was there, her mind was filling in the blanks. The sound had come from the landing only eight steps up, and it was low to the floor. Whatever it was, it moved as if it was sweeping garbage ahead of it. When the blanks filled in, she pictured an infected dead dragging its useless body along the floor through the debris, and as if to confirm what her mind was seeing without her eyes, some debris went under the railing of the landing and dropped to the bottom of the stairwell. That made her breath move again as she gasped through her open mouth, and she could taste the old odor of decay.

Yuni wasn't able to stop the shaking that started with her knees and moved upward. She was afraid she would cry out loud or gasp again, and as the debris hit the bottom of the stairwell, the infected dead did what they always do. It moaned.

In the few moments it took for Yuni to be left alone on the landing, she was so focused on the source of the sound that she forgot how far she was from the top of the stairs and where the door was. She was so disoriented that she became sure she was closer to the door than she had been. She reached with her left hand for the door and only found empty air. She pressed hard with the toes of her right foot to see if she was standing on the top step or on the landing. All she felt was solid floor, and she no longer knew where she was.

Debris moved again, and this time she anticipated the next thing she would hear. Her mind saw an infected dead feeling its way along the floor and dropping one step at a time like a wet sack of flour. It couldn't see any better than she could, and as far as she knew, they couldn't smell a living person. That was one thing she didn't want to find out firsthand.

She was just starting to wonder how the others could have left her in the stairwell when she felt something touch the front of her shoe. At first it just bumped her, but then it came forward and put its weight on top of her foot. It was pressing down on her toes like someone had stepped on her foot with a round heel.

Her mind told her that the infected dead had been crawling, so it couldn't have stepped on her foot. If it had, that meant it had pulled itself upright at the railing, and now she was standing face to face with it.

She tried to smell the air in front of her to blindly see if she could sense a face in front of hers. There was a dusty smell with a wet taste, and her mind said it had to be there because she could feel it standing on her foot. She shut her eyes and pictured herself pushing out with both hands. She saw the vile creature fly away from her and bounce off the railing as it fell down to the next landing. She had to make herself do it, or she would die.

Even though she couldn't see, she had become sure of how the monster was standing. The weight on her foot made her sure she was facing the side of its head no more than an inch from her face, and it didn't know what she was about to do. It was time.

Yuni only bent slightly at the waist as her hands shot outward. The force made her exhale in a grunt as she expected resistance to meet with her palms. She still had her flashlight gripped in her right hand, and it was slippery with sweat, but she was counting on the weight of it to help knock the infected over. Instead, it flew out of her hand into the darkness.

The weight was still on her foot, but her arms were out in front of her like a basketball player who had just shot a free-throw. Her mind couldn't fill in those blanks.

The door opened and spilled light into the stairwell. The horror that crossed Sora's face was a stark contrast to the confusion and fear on Yuni's. There was no infected dead standing in front of her, and her arms were reaching out into the blackness.

It seemed like her head would only move with the greatest of efforts as she tried to look at her husband. The rest of her body was still paralyzed, and she felt weakness coming over her as the adrenaline faded. Then she saw the dirty mop of hair below her waist and what used to be a human face as it lifted upward to meet hers.

The thing she had feared most was really there, and it was leaning forward on one skeletal arm that was missing from the elbow down. The round end of the bone in the upper arm was pressed into the top of her shoe, and the face was bending toward her leg.

Yuni had resisted when her husband told her they would be working out at the gym every day, but he convinced her she would be doing it for him. He needed someone to practice his martial arts with. What she didn't realize was that he had been trying to teach her to react rather than to make a choice before moving. There was no time to make a choice now, and the time to react had passed. She tried to kick out with her left foot and swung at the head at the same time, but the teeth felt like hot metal as they tore open her leg above the knee.

She didn't know anything could be so painful, and she didn't think she could stop screaming. Sora's foot came up under the chin of the rotten skull and sent it flying down the stairs.

They picked Yuni up and carried her into a room they had checked before realizing she was missing, and Iris gave her a shot of morphine from their medical kit.

Sora eliminated the infected dead in the stairwell, but afterward he was a mixture of grief and rage. He blamed himself over and over for not staying with her. He was so sure the threat was inside the rooms, and he was doing his part to help them find a boat. It would have been better for him if the stairwell had been full of the infected so he could burn out the rage.

Iris checked the wound and saw that it was deep. They knew what the bite meant, and the most humane thing they could do for Yuni was to let her bleed. They tried to get Sora to go with George to search the rest of the ninth floor. That would give Iris time to give Yuni a merciful end, but he knew what they were doing and insisted that the honorable thing for him to do was to stay with her. He wouldn't let his wife become one of those things, and he wouldn't pass off his responsibility for ending it.

The others couldn't deny him his honor. He was already so damaged by leaving her in the stairwell that he would never forgive them for not allowing him the chance to do his duty to his wife. It was still difficult for Iris to believe he would be able to stop there. It was against her better judgment, but she took George and Sherry with her, and they left the Tanakas alone in the bedroom.

"What do you think he'll do?" Sherry asked Iris.

George took Sherry by the arm and whispered something to her. They left Iris sitting on the sofa in the living room. They were all worn out, and this had taken the last of her energy.

******

Iris woke up at sunrise. The balcony of the suite faced the northeast, so the sun wasn't right in her face, but close enough. There was an armchair pulled up to the big sliding glass door, and George was comfortably watching the sunrise. Sherry was stretched out on a mattress between him and the balcony. She didn't doubt that he was protecting her.

George lifted a cup toward his face, and she couldn't believe the smell that drifted from it.

"Is that coffee?"

He nodded but didn't say anything. He just got up and poured her a cup. She saw that he had found a box of sterno and kept the fire going long enough to heat up the water.

She accepted it gratefully.

"How long did I sleep?"

"You were passed out on the couch before we got back from searching this floor, so my guess is nine or ten hours."

"Don't look so guilty," he said. "You really needed it."

George was a little rough around the edges sometimes, but Iris could see why Sherry loved him. Besides being a little rough around the edges herself, Sherry had found herself a guy who was aware of other people's needs.

Iris was afraid to ask about Sora. She glanced toward the closed bedroom door and then back at George.

"Is he still in there?"

"As far as I know. We didn't go in when we got back."

"You've been awake all night?"

"No, my lovely wife let me get a few hours first. I guess it's time to move out, but you might want to see this first."

George walked over to the balcony and slid the door open. Iris followed him outside, and she saw what he wanted to show her almost immediately. He had been right about the view. The seawall that served as a breakwater along the front of the marina was in clear view, and there was a sailboat tied to it. The masts had been taken down and were lined up down the center of the boat, just waiting for someone to come along and sail her away.

"One problem," said Iris. "How are we supposed to reach it?"

"I can swim that far."

"Sure you can, but are you forgetting what's in the water? If you drained this marina it would be full of the infected and blue crabs."

"I wouldn't go out through the marina. It's deep water out there. I could go out on the beach, swim to deep water, and then swim back to the boat."

"You've been thinking about this, I can tell, but there has to be another way."

"Another way to do what?"

Sherry came out onto the balcony and leaned against George. She took his coffee from him and took a big swallow.

"He wants to swim out to that sailboat on the other side of that seawall."

"Of course he does," said Sherry. "Why not just jump from here?"

"That's one option," said Iris, "but I think we can get out there without having to get in the water first. Let's check on Sora and then decide what to do."

Opening the bedroom door was like going to a funeral. None of them wanted to face Sora and tell him it was time to leave his wife, but it was time. It was also time to admit that what they found was what they all expected.

They were side by side on the bed. Sora Tanaka must have known that he had to get it right, or he would have to recruit one of them to do it for him. He also must have known they wouldn't agree to do what he wanted.

They could tell he wasn't sleeping, but he was so well placed next to Yuni that they couldn't believe he had done it himself. It wasn't until they had gotten closer that they were able to see that Sora had placed a long knife under his own chin and shoved it upward. They could only imagine the grief that would give a man so much determination that he could kill himself that way.

George helped Sherry from the room. She could hardly keep her legs under control long enough to take a step. Iris found it difficult to move at first, but she broke free from her shock and moved to the bed. She lifted the covers and drew them over the faces of Sora and Yuni Tanaka.

She was wiping a tear from her cheek as she shut the bedroom door behind her. George was comforting Sherry, but he watched Iris closely. When she didn't say anything, he worked up the nerve to speak.

"It's my fault."

"It's nobody's fault," she said more forcefully than she intended.

"Yes, it is," he insisted. "Ever since we arrived here I've been trying to take control. You got us out of Wilmington despite the odds, and you helped us keep our heads together underground for over five years. I should've trusted you to tell me how to do this right. I got Yuni killed."

"Shut up, George. I don't want to hear another word. People are going to die, and sometimes we can't stop it. Yuni should have moved when we did. We've talked about this before. When the group moves, everyone moves just like we were trained to do."

Iris knew that George understood because they were both ex-military. Sora and Yuni weren't trained military, but Iris and George had taught them that a team moved as one.

"Besides, what's done is done. We need to focus on keeping ourselves alive, or we're next. How do we get to that sailboat?"

"I've been giving that some serious thought," said George.

"Serious thought that doesn't include you swimming out to it, I hope."

He nodded. "We only need to find something that can float that far. Something that might not be seaworthy but floats well enough to reach the seawall. I think that pontoon boat on the other side of the marina will work."

George walked to the balcony as he told her about it. Iris scanned the pile of wrecked and burned boats and saw the pontoon boat half buried in the mess.

"I guess we won't know if it will float until we get there," she said. "There's also the probability that we won't be able to get all the junk off of it."

They redistributed the supplies the Tanakas had been carrying and got ready to go without saying much. The sadness of losing their friends had put a dark cloud over them that was hard to ignore.

Iris checked the hallway and then moved to the stairwell. The infected that had bitten Yuni was a heap in the corner, and she resisted the urge to kick it as they went by. She didn't doubt that George wanted to do the same.

They stayed close to the walls as they circled downward, but as they came to each new landing, Iris checked to be sure the doors were still shut before they went by. They had briefly considered using ropes to leave the hotel by climbing down the balconies because it eliminated the need to be in the dark stairwell again, but it added other risks. George was sure he could shoot any infected that happened to be in the rooms below, but Iris wasn't convinced. For one thing, there may have been groups of people in the rooms, and they could be mobbed. Then there was the chance of falling. There was no way to eliminate that risk.

They reached the first floor quickly but not soon enough for any of them. They had entered the stairwell fast the day before, so they didn't know if they should expect company on the first floor. The stairwell door opened outward because it was a fire door, so it opened into a small alcove where it couldn't hit people who might have been escaping the building during a fire. Someone had decided it didn't need a little window, so all they could do was hope there wasn't anything waiting for them.

Iris opened it just far enough to be able to see, and she was glad the light from outside the building reached the alcove. Nothing was outside the door, but something fell in the distance. It came from the direction of the main entrance of the hotel and was far enough away for her to know they had to move now.

She whispered a warning to George and Sherry but let them know they were moving on three. George put himself behind Sherry to bring up the rear, and on three Iris went. The same thought probably went through all of their minds.

"This is how we should have done it last night."

21 STRANDED

Year Two of the Decline

Janice leaned against the door with her face and screamed until she couldn't scream anymore. All she could see when she shut her eyes was the rats, and in the darkness of the crew's quarters she was sure she would find herself surrounded by the brown creatures. They were worse than the dead people that tried to bite them. At least they were slow.

David had called the dead people biters, zombies, carriers, and everything he could think of when he was killing them, but the news had called them infected.

It suddenly dawned on her that she really didn't know if she was alone in this dark room. There really could be rats scurrying around her feet, and she wouldn't know it without lights.

She stopped screaming and listened, but all she could hear was the ringing in her ears from her own screams. She couldn't even hear her own breathing, and she hadn't been able to get that under control. If her life depended on her being totally quiet, she would be dead because her breathing was so loud.

She didn't dare to move. She just kept her face pressed against the door of the dark room. Her forehead was cooled by the metal, and there was only the faintest of smells. The place had been closed up for a long time was all she could guess. Still, nothing had bitten her exposed ankles, and she didn't feel any furry bodies by her feet. Nothing groaned or dragged itself toward her....and that smell. It wasn't the ammonia smell from rat urine or droppings.

Her breathing grew more shallow and less ragged. Eventually she began to believe she was in a safe place, and that made her think of David. It made her remember that he had just died outside. She kept her forehead on the door as the tears streamed down her cheeks, and for the very first time since it had all begun, she was alone.

Her thoughts drifted away, and it felt like she was going to sleep. She was so tired, but in her mind she saw bright sunshine and sandy beaches. David was trying to catch something in the water but kept falling down. She was laughing and making fun of him. She could remember wishing it wouldn't have to end. That their honeymoon was almost over, and they were going to be getting on a plane in less than twenty-four hours to fly back to their real lives.

"Why can't people just run away from all of their responsibilities and be happy doing nothing but sunning on beaches, swimming, and spending nights with the one they love? Why does it have to end?"

Somehow she took her left hand from where it was pressed to the smooth surface of the door and lowered it to where a doorknob should be, and to the left of doorknobs on that side there was supposed to be a light switch. Her rational mind told her that's where light switches were in the real world. She felt the sill around the door and moved her hand onto the wall and upward. She almost couldn't believe it when her hand hit the flat plastic plate that surrounded the switch.

In one motion Janice Parker pushed the switch upward and spun around to face the attackers that would be able to see her now that the lights were on. She screamed again.

Her own reflection was more than she could stand. It didn't look like her, but she was startled just because it was a living, breathing person. A full length mirror was hanging on a door across the room, and it had appeared to be rushing toward her because she had turned ready to fight. She was also a mess. Her tear streaked face would have been right at home on the head of a zombie.

As her back pressed against the door, she slid into a sitting position with her knees drawn up to her chest and cried for a second time. This time it wasn't despair, and she wouldn't have called it relief. It was more like the confusion of finding herself in a room that was nicer than their honeymoon suite had been.

The living room felt like it had been used as a recreation area for a group of people because it was so large. It reminded her of a fire station she had visited once. There was room for a lot of people to live together without getting on each other's nerves.

The door with the mirror on it was partially closed, so she couldn't see beyond it, and during the last year that had been as good as a death trap. There was usually something behind it. There was a big kitchen with nice appliances, and the dining room table confirmed her fire station theory. It finally came to her that oil rigs were operated by people, and people had to live somewhere.

"But where are the people?"

Her voice sounded like it belonged to someone else because her throat was raw from screaming, and it actually hurt to speak.

There was no answer from the other rooms, and the weakness she had felt was leaving with the certainty that she was going to die. David was dead. There was no way to change that, but this was the first time she had been truly alone since they had gotten married. Even when he had gone out to find supplies, she had tagged along and just followed him. He had always been the hunter, and she had just been there for him to take care of.

Janice didn't grow up in a home where the women needed to know how to kill for food or skin a rabbit. She was more of a Home Shopping Network type person, and she was more in tune with the famous people of the entertainment world than she was with people who could start a campfire without a match or lighter. She could make a gourmet meal with the proper ingredients, but she really couldn't explain what some of those ingredients were before they were put in seasoning and spice bottles.

She wasn't as helpless as she had been, though. She wasn't entirely sure, but it had been close to a year since she heard the screams and saw someone attacking a guest at the check-in counter. When she saw the blood spray across the white shirt on the hotel employee, she had passed out. Nothing made sense after she woke up.

From that day forward she had learned how to cope in a different world. The progress was slow, but it eventually got through her thick head that she would evolve or die. It was probably the day she tried to call her parents that was the turning point in her re-education. It was at least four months after the infected, as the news people called them, began biting people. She had simply snapped, and insisted that

David should take her home. She stupidly picked up a phone and dialed her parents. It wouldn't have mattered so much if she had snapped in private, but she did it as she was following David through a grocery store that smelled like rot. They had made it almost to the door without being detected when she simply turned back the clock a few months. She stood up and announced that she had run out of patience, and it was time to go home.

David had reacted with surprise at first, but then he saw her eyes. They were wet with tears and unfocused as if she was somewhere else. He was a survivor, and he did what needed to be done. A right hook to her glass jaw knocked her out cold. He lifted her over his shoulder and ran.

She didn't wake up for almost eight full hours, and he was worried that he had injured her, but then it occurred to him that she was getting the best sleep she had gotten in months. He took the chance that she might have a concussion and let her sleep.

When Janice opened her eyes, she was back to reality. Her jaw ached something fierce, and she had a bit of a headache, but she knew who he was and why they were hiding in an RV at a campground.

"Did you hit me?"

"I had to. You were back in high school, and you wanted to call your parents to tell them you were having a lousy time at the prom."

"Was I that bad?"

"Well, I embellished a little, but you were bad."

Her image of waking up that day was very similar to the way she woke up against the door inside the crew's quarters. She didn't remember sinking to the floor and going to sleep.

She didn't know she was so tired, and she didn't know how long she had been asleep, but her rear end felt sore. She must have been there for a long time. There were no windows, so she didn't know if it was still daylight outside, but reality flooded back over her the same way as it had when David had knocked her out, and she knew things had changed again. For a split second, she felt like picking up the phone and calling her mother.

When her rear end started to get numb, she somehow forced herself to get up. First, she just took her back off of the door. Then she put her feet under her legs and pushed. Her legs had gone to sleep, too. She was forced to stand there with one hand on the door while the circulation came back. There was a lock on the door, and she clicked it to the locked position without giving it much thought.

It was time to explore her new home, but as soon as she had that thought, she collapsed again. She went to the floor and was wracked with sobs that wouldn't stop. It was the realization again that she was without David. The man that had protected her so well was dead, and for all she knew, it was the day of their first wedding anniversary.

The carpet under her face was wet with tears when she sat up for a second time. This time she was emotionally numb, but her body was a bit more rested. She didn't know why she expected to find there was water at the kitchen sink, but she walked straight to it and washed her face. Maybe it was because there was electricity.

All she could think as she explored the quarters was how much David would have liked this new place. It was safe, comfortable, and all stocked with supplies. She had water and food, and they had come so close to having it with each other. After all their suffering during the last year, they would have had so much to share, and they were so close.

A long hallway had several bedrooms on each side, and they were nicely furnished with queen sized beds. The pillows on the bed in the first bedroom were inviting, and Janice laid her head down again. She told herself it would just be for a little while.

******

Maybank hadn't gotten around to finding out why the cameras didn't work in the crew's quarters. He wasn't so sure he would have spied on the woman if they did work, and the only reason he had known they had stopped broadcasting was because that monitor had been on and the picture was gone.

He had seen everything outside, but there wouldn't have been a way for him to change things. He would have electrocuted the rats before the people arrived if he had known in advance what it was going to take to get the job done. He should have been doing it a few times a day until no more fell from their hiding places. That's what he would have done if he had known what was going to happen, but that was in the past. It was too late now, but what he didn't do before, he could do now.

He didn't think the woman was going to take any chances by coming outside, but if she did, he didn't want to see her swarmed by the ugly creatures. He uncovered the red switch to the electrical circuits and sent voltage along the catwalks and rails. Judging by the amount of smoke that drifted up from burning fur, he was glad he couldn't smell or hear what was happening out there.

To his surprise, hundreds of rats began falling from the oil rig into the water. He thought he had eliminated them before, but there must have been more safe places for them than he realized.

He also saw one more reason why he should have done it before the container ship had drifted to a stop against the oil rig. All along the side that faced the ship, the rats were jumping to safety before they could be electrocuted. On the ship they would find a new supply of the infected to feed on, and Maybank would be faced with the problem of keeping them from coming back to the oil rig after they were done eating all of them.

He sat back in his chair and shut his eyes. It was something Titus Rush liked to do when he was faced with a problem. If he had the time to think it out, then there must be a solution.

As soon as it crossed his mind that he would think of a solution, he remembered that he had given up when he tried to find a way to get the dead tide to break up and move on. He had time, but he couldn't do it.

One thing the survivors club had preached was that people would have less problems if they solved them before they happened. The only way to do that was to think of the problems in advance.

"Okay, let's make a list of all the things I didn't think of in advance," he said out loud. "Why? Because that would be a longer list than things I did think of in advance."

"No one had really expected a zombie apocalypse, and even if they had, they wouldn't have guessed that millions of them would jump into the Gulf of Mexico. Then they would float until they got stuck on my oil rig. Oh, and let's not forget that they would carry a few thousand rats with them."

He made it that far and realized there was one thing he did predict in advance, and it was stuck against the side of his oil rig. He predicted that a ship would eventually run into him because ships were supposed to be in the Gulf. As a matter of fact, it was logical to assume another one might come along after this one.

Maybank opened his eyes and stared at the container ship.

"What did I plan to do when I predicted you?" he asked the image on his monitor.

He couldn't have moved out of the way, and he couldn't have controlled its course, so it was going to hit his rig no matter what he did.

"So, let's assume I thought of you in advance. What did I think I could do, sink you?"

Satisfaction made him lean back and shut his eyes again. He knew he couldn't blow it up because it would be too close to the rig. His shelter could withstand the explosion needed to sink a ship that size, but he couldn't think of anything he had that could produce an explosion like that. He could, however, scuttle the ship if he could put a hole in the right place.

"It would have to be on the port side," he said. "That would make her list away from the rig. The weight on her deck would make her roll and capsize without hitting the rig."

Now that he knew what he wanted to do, he realized he was either totally insane, or he was delusional. There was no way to put a hole in a ship that size without explosives. In the end, he came to the conclusion that the club had been right about thinking of things in advance, and if he had thought this all the way through, he would have armed the oil rig with cruise missiles. Since he didn't do that, the answer was to live with it parked there, but work on the rat problem.

That was when he remembered. When he told the military he wanted his shelter on an oil rig, he was asked what he would do if the rig was hit by a ship. It was decided that it was likely to happen, but the rig would survive. Someone had mentioned that ships carry rats. No one thought the rats would arrive on an island of dead bodies, but they did think they would arrive on a ship. That's why there was a large supply of rat poison in one of the supply rooms. It was in liquid form and could be delivered through a sprinkler system. The idea was to rinse every inch of the outside structure. He would start delivering it tomorrow, but before he did, he was going to fry his fair share of them with electricity.

In his many discussions with members of the survivors club, the topic of routine was one of the most popular. It was the closest they came to being philosophical because it was based totally on hypothetical situations. In other words, it was all guesswork. If they didn't know what type of apocalypse they were facing, they wouldn't have a clue about what would influence their routines.

Some of the disasters on their list were so bad that they would be forced to get their heads down and keep them down...forever. Others were short term events that would pass in time. He remembered when he was asked to give an example, he suggested conventional war. His theory was that they would simply remain undetected, and his routine would be influenced by how well he hid in plain sight. When the war was over, he would just continue to hide while the world sorted out the mess they had made.

He couldn't go up to the rig anymore and hang out in his old apartment, but that had always been too risky anyway. If he had known the rats were that aggressive, he would never have gone up there in the first place.

The woman in the crew's quarters had yet to show her face on the observation deck by the front door, and he didn't blame her. The rats had been dealt with for the time being, but she didn't know that. Even so, he did a review of the security videos to see if there had been any activity that hadn't been detected by the motion sensors.

The shelter had layers of security and layers of backup systems. The engineers had called them redundant support systems. He wished they had been as diligent when they installed the security cameras in the crew quarters, but it was his understanding that the people who had built his shelter didn't want anyone spying on them when they went to the quarters for the night. He wasn't really surprised when they quit working, and he wasn't able to switch to a backup camera.

The other support systems gave him more than enough to keep him busy. Despite the fact that the shelter had automation that made it futuristic, there were still things that could only bring peace of mind if there were visual inspections. So, the rules had been spelled out at every meeting, and one of them was to inspect your shelter.

Maybank started his morning tour as soon as he finished breakfast, and he could have done it wearing a blindfold. It only took two hours, but every compartment was visually inspected for water leaks and ventilation issues. If he was going to live underwater, he was forced to be sure the water stayed outside, and the air remained breathable.

When he arrived back at the central living quarters, he checked on the woman in the crew quarters. He knew he hadn't given her much chance to show herself, but there was no indication that she planned to do anything except keep her head down. It was almost as if she had been to the meetings, too.

It was during one of his inspection tours that Maybank thought of a way he could at least tell if she was alive. For all he knew, she could have locked herself in and then died from a rat bite.

He was checking data that monitored his activities, and he ironically laughed at the thought that he already knew what he had done, and all he was doing now was verifying that his systems were operating at peak efficiency. He was checking power usage and could tell from the data that he had used more electricity when he fried bacon for breakfast. He pictured the woman doing the same thing in the kitchen of the crew quarters.

Maybank opened his laptop and then the spreadsheet that showed power usage throughout the oil rig. He saw that the power usage fluctuated in the crew quarters just the way it would if there was someone living there. If she had died, the power usage would be constant. He ran a finger down the column that showed usage per hour, and he saw that there was a spike at about the time he had finished doing his morning inspection. It was only a small spike that meant some lights had been turned on, but it meant she was alive.

A motion sensor beeped, and he looked up just in time to see the woman in the doorway of the crew quarters. She had a very bloody towel around one arm, and she was throwing a rat with the other. He was amazed that a rat could tear someone up that bad, and his heart sank. She was alive for now, but he couldn't take the chance of making contact with her now that she was likely to be infected.

******

Half awake and half asleep, Janice didn't know what to do about going outside. She knew she would have to open the door sooner or later, but she was afraid she would find the rats waiting for her. She was also keenly aware of the fact that her husband's bones were out there somewhere, and she wouldn't be able to avoid seeing them when she was finally forced to go outside. The thought that they were bones was somehow more comforting than finding a corpse with flesh on it. Whatever was left, she didn't want it to resemble him.

With her eyes still closed, she thought about the last moment she had seen David. It was when a big rat had bitten his hand. She tried to remember the details of his face better, but it had happened so fast. She tried to recall if he had yelled for her to run. She thought he did, but what she knew for sure was that he had screamed in pain and then become too mad to run. He had attacked instead. He didn't come pounding on the door, yelling for her to let him in. She knew she had waited for those pleas, but they never came.

When she woke up in the strangely comfortable bed, she didn't know where she was and had called David's name before her mind gave her back the painful memories. She immediately scrambled backward away from the open bedroom door, dragging the blankets and pillows with her into a heap. She backed completely off of the bed into the corner, breathing heavily and trying to hear through the blood pounding in her ears.

Her long, dark hair was matted across her face and stuck to the dirty streaks on her cheeks. Her jeans and long sleeved pullover shirt were stiff against her body and felt uncomfortable from being out in the saltwater spray, but they still managed to show off her slender body. Over a year of survival hadn't made her tough and muscular because David had protected her too much. Now she felt even less equipped to face what the world had become.

Janice hid in the corner behind the covers and listened to the silence. There was no pattering of rodent feet on the roof and no scratching inside the walls. She also didn't hear any of the dreaded groans that would mean instant death, and her sense of smell wasn't finding the rot that would have made her stay in the corner forever.

She crawled out from under the safety of the blankets being careful not to make any noise, but she noticed the lamp on the nightstand was already on its side. She didn't think she had heard it fall when she backed into the corner. There was also something brown on the shade that reminded her of the hundreds of old, dried bloodstains she had seen in the last year. What was missing was the copper smell. David had always told her how long ago someone had died. His estimates were based on the color of blood fading from black to brown and whether or not he could still smell the copper odor that was nauseating when the blood was still red or black.

Her eyes instinctively went to the floor searching for footprints. David had also told her there would still be a body anywhere that the dead didn't get up and walk out of where it died. There wasn't a body in the bedroom, so it must have walked out of the room.

Janice didn't know that she was seeing what had been left behind by the security officers when one had been bitten. They had only been in the quarters long enough for the man to die and then attack his friend who had dragged him inside. It was long enough ago for the blood and smell to fade away.

The floor had dirty smudges on it where wet combat boots had tracked through blood, but they were as old as the smears on the lamp. Janice noticed the smudges only went one way in the hall outside. She stuck her head around the corner keeping low to the floor and strained her eyes against the dim light. She couldn't see any footprints going in that direction.

To the right the footprints went back toward the common areas and the kitchen. Her memories of the night before became a bit more clear, and she was also becoming more sure that she was alone in the crew quarters.

Without windows she was suddenly aware that she could still see well enough not to be staggering around in pitch black darkness. The lamp laying on its side was off, so her eyes scanned the room. There were several wall outlets, and low power nightlights were plugged into each of them. One more thing she had forgotten about the night before.

"There's power in here."

It came out as a low whisper, but the lump in her throat was all that prevented her from shouting it.

A rifle was leaning in the corner by the nightstand on the other side of the bed. The one thing David had made sure she would learn, besides survival cooking, was how to handle guns. They didn't have one of their own at the beginning, but they were easy enough to find in the months that followed. Janice quickly retrieved the heavy weapon as if it would disappear. She didn't know what type of gun it was, but it didn't appear to be terribly complicated.

With the barrel pointed ahead of her, Janice walked out of the bedroom into the hallway. Her eyes adjusted to the gloom, and she found the light switch. They weren't terribly bright, but the lights were a welcome addition. With them on, the quiet quarters weren't as foreboding as they had been, and Janice boldly went from one bedroom to the next.

There were ten bedrooms all together. None had anything special about them, and only the first one showed any signs of ever being inhabited. Whoever had stayed in the room where she had slept, they had been traveling light. Besides the rifle, nothing else had been left behind.

The last room at the end of the hallway was a large bathroom that had private showers and a row of sinks.

"Must be coed," she said.

There were medicine cabinets above each sink instead of fixed mirrors, and Janice was happy to see each was stocked with first aid supplies, as well as toiletries. She saw her reflection in a mirror when she smiled, and she was immediately flooded with guilt. Her husband was dead, but she smiled when she saw bandages.

The feeling washed over her the way she had felt on days when her blood sugar had dipped dangerously low, or how dizziness made her sway when she stood up too fast. Her mouth went dry, and she desperately wanted water. Through a wave of nausea she saw a glass sitting on the edge of a sink and clumsily grabbed at it, fumbled it, and tried to stop it from falling to the floor by pinning it against the sink.

She tried to stop herself, but the whole thing happened in one tick of the second hand on a clock. Her hand went through it as it broke into razor blades of glass. There was no pain at first, just lots of blood. Then came the pain.

Nausea, dizziness, vertigo, and blood meant only one thing to her. She would pass out. She knew what was happening and somehow managed to keep from hitting her head on the sink as she went by.

She woke up covered in her own blood, and there was a new pain traveling up her right arm toward her shoulder. When she twisted her arm around to see what hurt so much, she saw she had fallen on a shard of glass, and it was sticking out of the back of her arm about midway between her elbow and shoulder. She almost passed out again, especially when she impulsively grabbed it and yanked it from her arm.

Blood followed the glass in a gush, but she knew she had been lucky and missed the artery because it didn't shoot from her arm. Janice clamped her hand down hard on the cut and couldn't even feel the pain from the cut on her hand because the new cut hurt so much.

"Give yourself first aid, you idiot," she said through clenched teeth. She said a lot more, and it included a few words she had never been comfortable saying.

A towel rack behind her offered the first thing she needed, and she grabbed the towel with her good hand. It wasn't easy, but she managed to tie one end of the towel around her upper arm using her teeth to draw it tight. The other end of the towel reached her right hand where she struggled to tie a second knot around the cut that started all of this.

She didn't see another glass in the bathroom, and before she could even consider cleaning her wounds, she was going to need a drink of something. Instead of water she was hoping someone had the brains to put a bottle of bourbon in the place.

The rifle would be safe if she left it in the bathroom, but right now it was making a passable cane just to keep herself steady down the long hallway. She fell into the wall on the right side and let out a scream with a long smear of blood before she could push herself to the other side.

White dots floated across her eyes, and she didn't think she would make it, but something kept her going. She knew she would feel better if she just had a moment of rest with some water. One final surge of adrenaline, and she found herself reeling into the kitchen and throwing up into the sink.

Even through the heaving she had the presence of mind to reach up with her good arm and turn on the water full blast. She stuck her head under it and shuddered when the cold hit her. That was when she realized she had to be careful not to let herself go into shock, or she would die.

The cold water was enough to revive her, but she couldn't overdo it. Leaning on the sink using both elbows she surveyed the kitchen. She saw plenty of cabinets, a large refrigerator, and what had to be a pantry. Across the kitchen in the common area there was a bar with plenty of bottles lined up along a shelf.

"Just what the doctor ordered," she said.

She almost fell again because the rifle now rested on top of her foot. She picked it up and laid it across the counter then staggered toward the bar. The cuts on her right arm and hand had taken on a different kind of pain. It wasn't that pain where the skin had been cut. It was that deep ache down in the muscles that said she might have nerve damage.

"Right now, I'll medicate myself. If I have nerve damage, I'll medicate myself again."

She knew she was only trying to keep herself going by saying out loud how she felt, but she fully intended to take the biggest gulp of bourbon she could handle. As soon as her body was in range to lunge across the bar, she let herself fall forward. It knocked the wind out of her, but it got her where she wanted to go. She carefully gripped the neck of the bottle and held it against her body as she unscrewed the cap. The brown liquid rushed down her throat, and for the first time since reaching for the glass in the bathroom she felt like something went the way it was supposed to.

Janice eased herself onto a barstool and slowly lowered her head onto the cool bar. She stayed there for almost an hour, and every few minutes, she managed another sip of bourbon while she collected her strength.

"Okay, I'm a mess, but I can fix this," she croaked through a throat that had been numbed by the bourbon.

Before getting off of the barstool, she rotated it left and right, taking in everything. She couldn't wait to go through the cabinets, but that would have to wait until after she gave herself the medical attention she needed. She eased her feet to the floor and got herself steady before she let go of the bar.

If she hadn't been injured she probably wouldn't have been looking toward the floor, but something made her check every inch from the bar back to the hallway. In between was where she had come in through the front door, and light from the hallway washed over that spot. Something was on the floor that she hadn't seen when she had first come in the door, and she had gone right by it when she came in search of bourbon. If it was what she thought it was, she had to be sure it was dead.

Janice gingerly supported her right arm with her left, leaving the bourbon where it was. She sidestepped her way across to the kitchen and retrieved the rifle from the counter. She had to carry it in the cradle of her left elbow, and she wasn't sure she could even shoot it, but using her right arm was out of the question.

The rifle felt heavier by the time she got close to the big lump of brown fur, but from what she could tell the rat was dead. She poked it with the barrel, and it didn't react. She circled it to get a better angle from the light. She knew she would fall apart if it moved, but she also knew she would have to do something with the body. No matter what she could find to put it in, she didn't want to keep it inside.

She poked it again and then pushed hard enough to turn it over. That was when she saw how it had probably died. She had the vaguest memory of slamming the door shut, yanking it open just a little, and slamming it shut again. Now she knew why.

The rat had gotten inside with her, and when she closed the door the first time, she had closed it on the rat's head. When she yanked it open and then slammed it again, the rat had been freed just long enough to fall away from the door. It was probably dead as soon as its head was crushed, but its body was pushed aside by the door when she opened it. There was a streak of blood on the floor where it had slid. She was glad she didn't see it happen.

Janice was in no condition to make a big project out of rat disposal, but she was determined not to live a single day with the body inside. Moving as if she was on a mission, she forced herself across the room to the bar and took an even bigger swallow of bourbon than she had before. Before she could change her mind, she went back to the rat and lifted it from the floor by its tail.

It hurt like hell, but she used her bandaged hand to open the crew quarters door and put all of her weight into swinging the rat through the opening. It sailed through the air and landed at least twenty feet away, but Janice didn't see how far it went because she had already closed the door.

22 LOSING THE WAR

Year Six of the Decline

When someone close to you dies, the world seems
different the next day. Not just the fact that a loved one is
gone. The pain, the emptiness, the strangeness of a world
without them all add up to such a high total that the planet
appears wrong to the eyes. The sky is not a blue or a gray
you've ever seen before, the air smells different, and in this
world all noises are the sounds of danger. The senses are in
chaos.

The other side of that coin is a total shut down of what
can be felt, and in Iris' case the coin was being flipped from
one side to another. When the numb side came up, she was
ready to walk into a burning building, over the edge of a
high cliff, or into the path of the horde that was advancing
on the city of Charleston.

When the chaotic side flipped up, she was a one woman
army that could cut down that entire horde. She was afraid
of nothing, but she felt the purpose in living to avenge the
death of her friends, even if she had to destroy every
infected that was walking the earth.

When they retraced their steps from the previous day, they knew they had accomplished their goal of reaching a high enough place from which they could see the terrain, but the cost had been high. They all felt the loss, but George and Sherry weren't at all surprised when Iris took the lead. In a sad sort of way they were pleased that she did, but only because they knew it was a better thing for her to be responding to the death of her friends with anger than resignation.

Iris had been especially close with the Oriental couple. They had left Wilmington with almost three hundred people, but they were not prepared to support the logistics of a group that size. Just feeding them was impossible, but protecting them all was even harder.

In a group that big there would always be someone who thought they should be the leader. Their ideas were always better than anyone else's, and the alpha mentality would lead to violent challenges to authority. The first time a challenge rose up against Iris as leader, the Tanakas had taken up positions to protect her. Their loyalty had caused others to rally around her in a way that had permanence.

Over a hundred of the group broke away from the pack for various reasons. Some wanted to go in different directions thinking things would be better closer to the nearest military bases or even Washington DC. Some didn't want to follow her but were afraid to confront her or the Tanakas. Others died in different ways, and of course some were bitten by the infected but kept it a secret from the rest of the group.

By the time they reached the safety of the shelter on Ambassadors Island, they were down to less than ninety people. Some were relatively new to their group, but most were from the original survivors of the cruise ship in

Wilmington. Among them were the Tanakas, and Iris was feeling the empty space they had left behind.

Clouds were rolling across the sun filling in the gaps between the trees, and it would be raining within the hour, but rain had its advantages. It would cover the sounds they made as they worked their way through the thickly overgrown grounds of the hotel. If it was heavy rain, the sound of the drops hitting the wrecked boats and docks of the marina would be deafening, and they could move about even easier.

Iris set the pace, and as long as she was moving without being reckless, George and Sherry were content to let her decide when it was safe to move and when it was time to stop and listen. She did both, or the others would have been worried. Her right hand came up, and they immediately dropped to a knee. Both of them strained to hear or see what she had.

Two fingers stayed up on her hand while the others folded downward. That hand signal was obviously letting them know there were two infected between them and the marina. It was the next signal that made them get ready for combat. Her fingers came back up, and she placed her hand on the back of her neck. That signal meant the infected were coming straight at them.

They didn't expect Iris to make a move so soon. One moment her hand was on the back of her neck, and the next moment it was wrapped around the hilt of her machete. She sprang from her knee and used every muscle in her body to launch herself at the two infected that had barely come into view. As a matter of fact, George only saw them because Iris was moving their way. He doubted the infected had seen them before Iris attacked. It only took a split second for him to know which side of the coin had flipped up for Iris, and he hoped it was anger that kept her alive and not resignation that got her killed.

Iris was much faster than the infected, and even though one bite would be lethal, at the moment she was more deadly. Her first swing was a powerful forehand, and it neatly severed the head of one infected. What amazed George and Sherry was that the swing continued onward to the second infected until the blade sank deep into the side of the skull.

Iris was well aware that getting a blade stuck in the bone of an infected was a good way to lose your weapon when you needed it the most. In this case it had disposed of both infected, so she had time to plant her foot on the head of the corpse and pull her blade free...or so she thought.

The gardens surrounding them smelled wet and thick, and the humidity made it a happy place for insects of all kinds. Fetid pools of water were great breeding grounds for swarms of mosquitoes. Gnats were already biting at their exposed skin and burying themselves in their hair. Even worse than the other insects were the black flies that fed on the infected dead even as they walked on the bricks that were slippery with moss.

When Iris had suddenly sprung into the open with her blade high in the air, a group of infected between her and the entrance to the marina turned to face her. One of them turned too quickly on the moss and fell in front of the others. Iris watched the inevitable pile up, frozen at the sight of so many and knowing she had just made an amateur blunder. The first one was already getting up by the time she broke free from her mental paralysis, and she pulled frantically on the machete. George and Sherry hadn't reached her yet, but they could see by the expression on her face followed by the desperate energy she suddenly put into retrieving her blade, that there was something around the corner she hadn't seen.

The black swarms of flies were everywhere. There were so many that they were even landing on the blade of the machete still embedded in the skull of the infected. George made the mistake of opening his mouth to yell that they should retreat, and the flies that hit the back of his throat sent him into a spasm of coughing and gagging. Every time he involuntarily sucked in air through his blocked throat, he sucked in more flies. He was making a great whooping sound with each breath, and he had become the new target of the infected.

Sherry yanked a scarf free from around her neck and literally pounced on her husband. He was doubled over at the waist and was an easy take down. She had to fight him to get his hands away from his mouth and nose, but she eventually had the scarf in place and tied behind his head.

"Chew and swallow," she screamed in his ears. "Chew and swallow."

He heard the words, and to a man who was choking on flies, the words didn't sound like he was being asked to do something. It sounded like an order, and the changing world had made it necessary to follow orders. George chewed and swallowed.

When the bolus of dead and alive flies made it from his mouth to his throat, he threw up with so much force that Sherry had to hang on hard or he would break away before she could pull the scarf from his face. He almost wrestled her off of him, but she knew he would have to gasp in a huge gulp of air one more time. As he reared back onto his knees and threw back his head, she slapped the scarf across his mouth again.

They went down in a heap, but Sherry had accomplished what she had intended. George still had more than his fair share of flies stuck in his teeth and nose, but the majority had landed in a big mess on the bricks.

The taste in his mouth was unbelievable, and all he wanted was water. He didn't care if it was rain water filled with mosquito larvae. With the group of infected back on its feet and moving their way, George stuck his whole head into a pool of water and tried to suck it in past the scarf.

The second time he threw up, Sherry didn't have a chance to remove the scarf. Most of what came up went into his airway, and this time there was no whooping sound as he opened his mouth wide because air couldn't get by the blockage. George began to thrash around on the bricks like a fish pulled from the ocean. He didn't even hear the screams from his wife as the weight of an infected dead pushed her onto his squirming body just before its teeth found her right ear. He passed out when his lungs were too starved for air, so he didn't feel the muscles in his right leg being torn free from the bone.

The mind works in ways that can't be explained under normal circumstances, so it shouldn't be surprising when abnormal circumstances cause abnormal reactions. Iris had always been a warrior, and she had been referred to as the female version of Chief Joshua Barnes, but even she had her limits.

Iris watched in numb horror from the entrance of the marina. She didn't remember when she had pulled the blade free, and she didn't remember yelling for the others to run because there were too many infected. Something told her the infected were being distracted away from them, and that was fine with her, but she never realized it was George and

Sherry. Her survival instincts had won over her desire to protect the people who she cared for, and she felt beaten.

She backed away on legs that belonged to someone else and didn't snap out of it until she felt the sunlight on her skin and a breeze that smelled of salt. When she turned to see where she was, the wrecked marina lay before her, and she remembered that they had found a pontoon boat on the far side. The sun was in her eyes, but she could see the torn canopy above the boat gently waving in the breeze. She was crying, and someone was arguing with her that only she could see.

"We should get to the boat while we still can," said Sora.

Iris shook her head at him and said, "We can't. We have to wait for Sherry and George. George is sick, and Sherry is helping him. They'll be along at any minute."

"They're dead," said a new voice. Sora was gone, but Yuni was standing where he had been. She had her machete above her head as if getting ready to protect her from something.

"Here they come now," said Iris. She pointed toward the opening to the gardens where her good friends were emerging with a group of people she thought had stayed behind at the shelter.

She took several steps in their direction and waved at them. She wondered why they didn't wave back.

"What's wrong with them?" she asked Yuni, but Yuni was gone. The Chief was standing where Yuni and Sora Tanaka had been.

"Are they mad at me about something?"

Her subconscious was blaming her for all of their deaths, and maybe her subconscious was right. She couldn't have guessed that George would be overcome by the flies, but the flies had only been disturbed by her blind charge at the infected dead in the gardens. If she had waited, they almost certainly would have put their scarves over their faces before attacking the infected. It wasn't the first time they had encountered the infected under those conditions.

"It wasn't our first time, but it would be their last time," she said.

No one answered because no one was there. She fixed her eyes on the spot where they had all appeared and almost stayed too long. When the groans made her turn back to the group of friends coming her way, they weren't her friends anymore.

This time she understood that it was her own mind that yelled.

"Run."

******

Mud Island was only a few miles down the coast from the marina, but the world had passed the location by. It could have been developed into a resort getaway years ago, but real estate investors had never been able to buy the land or get the permits they needed in order to do environmental impact studies on the area. They never knew it was because the government had a closely guarded secret along that stretch of beachfront property.

Iris didn't know the exact location, but the Chief had told her she would know it when she saw it. He had only chuckled when she pressed him for more information.

The wooden docks that divided the slips of the marina were impassable in places, but that worked to her advantage. Where they were passable, they were intended to keep rich people from falling into the water, so they were coated with a non-slip surface. That helped her to move fast, showing less caution than she would have on a smooth dock. Iris was also able to climb over the debris and leave the infected behind. They gathered at the spot where she climbed into one badly damaged boat and then hopped into another. They tried to follow, but all they did was get themselves stuck or fall into worse places they couldn't get out of. When they fell into the water between the boats, they sank very quickly. She figured they didn't have any air in their lungs, so they weren't buoyant.

The marina had been a tangled mess, and it took over an hour to navigate the debris. When she finally reached her goal, she was seriously disappointed and beaten. The pontoon boat might as well have been nothing more than a mirage in a desert. From the hotel it had appeared to be in good shape, but even if it didn't have too much damage, it was wedged into its slip on top of another boat. There was no way to get them apart, and she doubted it would stay above water once it was free. Iris was going to have to find another way to reach the sailboat.

Iris sat on the stern of the wrecked pontoon boat and peered into the water. With the sun at just the right angle and no clouds in between, she could see the hull of another boat beneath her. A large blue crab propelled itself across the white hull on its way toward some food.

She shivered at the thought of what that food might be and instinctively pulled her feet back farther from the edge. The people in the settlement at Hopkins told her about the dead walking on the bottom of the lake to try to reach the floating town. Iris could imagine them floating to the surface when decay caused pockets of gases to build up in their bodies. It would be disturbing to have one pop up in front of her. She shaded her eyes to see through the spot in front of her and find out what the crab had been after.

A vague thought took shape when she saw her own reflection in the water superimposed over the hull of the boat. It reminded her of an aquarium, but it reminded her of something else. A trip to Sea World and another theme park nearby. A row of paddle boats lined up along a dock as eager tourists were helped into their seats.

Iris jumped to her feet and started turning in circles.

"Where would they be? Away from the slips but in walking distance."

The area would have a safety line across its boundary, and there would be a sign that says NO PADDLE BOATS BEYOND THIS POINT. The other side of the sign facing the marina would probably be a caution not to cause a wake because there were paddle boats in the area.

There probably had been a sign before the chaos of the first day when ownership of boats changed hands more than once inside the seawalls of the marina. Hundreds of small boats made it from their slips to open water, but judging by the wreckage, more of them weren't so lucky.

Boat owners shot people who were stealing their boats, but it happened just as often the other way around. Collisions caused more shots to be exchanged between boats that were already free of their slips, and fires broke out as bullets punched holes in motors and fuel cans. Explosions sent fireballs racing across the marina, catching people exposed on the docks. Burning boats that were either drifting or being driven by injured people had crossed into the paddle boat area and caused another tangled mess. From where she was, Iris could see plenty of the small two-seater boats bobbing on the water. If she could navigate one out of that area, she could definitely reach the sailboat if the tide was in her favor.

It took over an hour to get from the slips to the tourist attraction. Besides having to climb over boats and damaged docks, there was the constant threat of stumbling upon the infected that had been trapped or pinned under something. They had been like that for years and had been picked at by crabs and birds until there wasn't much left, but they could still bite.

There were also the ones that had strayed into the marina more recently and found the damp, overgrown gardens where she had last seen her friends alive. She wondered if the living would ever outnumber the infected again. The hulls of the boats that weren't too jammed against their neighbors caused a deep, rubbing sound when small swells reach the inside of the seawalls, and a perpetual moaning sound from every corner of the marina called the infected to come investigate.

Iris held her breath when she began pushing anything away that would separate from the rest of the wreckage. She found one small fishing boat that would have been perfect if it had been on the outside of the paddle boat area, but there was no way she would be able to get it into the clear. She climbed over one boat after the next until finally, there it was. One paddle boat sat inside a long curve of wrecked boats, almost like it was at anchor in its own private slip. She saw that she could climb out to it and drop straight down into a seat from above.

She showed less patience and caution than she should have, but she had no choice. Almost halfway to her goal she saw that it would become a race for her to get the paddle boat out in time.

In her mind's eye she saw herself pushing the paddles with her legs and driving the small boat straight at the gap between the last dock and the last upended boat. If she didn't get to that gap first, a group of the infected would be dropping from the dock right into the other passenger seat. She climbed faster.

Her arms and legs were aching, but somehow she managed to build up a slim lead in the race. If there wasn't anything keeping the paddle boat where it was, she would be able to start it moving as soon as she reached it.

The last boat was in front of her. A small sailboat, and its bow sat upward above the paddle boat. Its keel was exposed where it ran up and over a single engine powerboat. For a moment she considered jumping from the powerboat to the paddle boat, but she didn't like the idea of coming up short. At least it was a straight drop from the sailboat to the seat below.

Iris climbed over the side rail and up the sloping deck of the sailboat until she reached the bow. She didn't hesitate because the small horde had reached the beginning of the dock and were stumbling in her direction. They were already moaning with excitement.

She went over the bow, hung until she stopped swaying, and dropped before she could change her mind. It hurt worse than she expected, but that was because her small pack of gear managed to reach the seat first. She landed with the full weight of her rear end on top of it.

Despite the pain, she was so mad at herself for the painful bruise she was going to have that she pumped her feet immediately. It was pointed in the right direction, so the little paddle boat stroked the water and seemed to have enough speed for her to get to the gap first. It felt like it was gliding, and Iris realized this wasn't your average tourist attraction. This one was made for older, rich people who wanted everything to be easy. If she hadn't landed on her gear, she would have found out just how soft the seat cushion was.

She gauged her speed and the progress of the infected on the dock and saw she needed to give it just a little more effort. Out of reflex she looked down at her feet when she pushed them harder and was surprised to see the paddle boat had a glass bottom. She saw just how close she had come to making a critical error as the paddle boat passed over a wrecked boat that was only inches below her. If she had become stuck on something in that gap at the end of the dock, the infected would have been piling in the boat with her.

She was looking down at the hull of the sunken boat as she passed over it, sure that she would get snagged on it. When she lifted her head, she was surprised to find that she had passed the end of the dock, and only seconds later the infected arrived, too. They kept going as if they could walk on the water to reach her, and Iris heard the first one hit the solid hull beneath the surface.

The gap was only about six feet across, and as the infected fell from the dock, they made a pile that filled the opening. She was clear of the groaning infected as they reached for her, but it had been too close. Even though it didn't matter anymore, she paddled harder and steered toward the opening in the sea wall where the sailboat was anchored, hidden from view.

Iris couldn't believe it when she climbed easily into the boat and began to gather the lines. The anchor came up easily, which was a small miracle after so many years of sitting on the bottom, and the breeze was blowing across her starboard bow. As soon as she pulled up a sail and pushed away from the sea wall, the small sailboat began sliding away from the marina. If the Chief wasn't kidding, she would know Mud Island when she saw it.

******

Riding on small waves but at a brisk pace, Iris kept her eyes peeled to the coast, watching for something obvious. The Chief said it wasn't far by water, but there was time to think about the friends she had lost on the way. The four friends she had taken with her on the road would have enjoyed this last leg of the trip. It had the feeling of finality to it that said she was almost there. It also had the sadness that came with a certainty that they were losing the war with the infected. She asked herself how they were supposed to rebuild when they were still being torn down. The boat leaned slightly with the breeze, and she skillfully used it to gain even more speed.

Several times she thought she saw landmarks that fit the description of obvious, but something told her they didn't make her know without a doubt she was in the right place. The Chief said she would have no doubt. She admitted to herself that the Chief had only given her some of the details about Mud Island because she had never really committed to finding him. He had said she should look him up after the radioactivity dropped far enough for her to leave Ambassadors Island, and she had only said maybe she would. He had responded by giving her enough directions to get her this far. The rest seemed almost like he was joking.

The sun had passed into the west, and Iris didn't want to still be searching for Mud Island at night. She didn't think the Chief meant they would have a light on the dock. She was getting more and more concerned when she saw a jetty poking out into the surf.

"A jetty would be obvious."

She gave the rocks plenty of room as she steered a little further out to sea. She couldn't help being grateful that she made it this far in daylight. It wasn't likely that she would have been close enough to shore to hit the jetty, but if she had come within even a few feet of it in the dark, it would have scared her to death.

As she rounded the tip of the jetty, she understood what the Chief had meant. Several craft were parked along a wide dock that pointed toward the jetty, and one of them was a beautiful, yellow seaplane. Her heart was a big lump in her throat when she realized just how close they were when she lost her four friends. Somewhere under those trees was another safe haven like Ambassadors Island, and all she had to do was find it.

The Chief had given her just enough information for her to locate the shelter if she had to, but he told her the easiest way was for someone to bring her in from the dock. That's where she thought he was joking. She steered into a current that was moving toward the shore, and she had to be careful not to overshoot the dock. Having spent so many years on the water, she was an accomplished sailor, and she timed her jump perfectly.

She was impressed by every detail of the dock. Someone had built it to last. The cleat she had tied her line to had been so strong that it had allowed her to let the sail boat stretch the line tight as the current grabbed it.

"What did the Chief call the water on this side of Mud Island? Oh yeah, he called it the moat."

The houseboat wasn't what she had expected, but it fit with something else she had heard the Chief say. He had commented that the big homes on Ambassadors Island were like something he had protecting his shelter. It didn't make sense at the time, but it did now.

If she was supposed to do something to get herself noticed by the people inside Mud Island, it would most likely be something she could do in the houseboat. She had wondered about the playfully cryptic things he told her to do after she arrived, but she had let him have his fun. He had a good sense of humor, and he was always testing people to see how far they would go. In this case he had told her there was a rubber chicken on the dock, and she was supposed to swing it around in circles over her head. She didn't think so.

The door of the houseboat was unlocked when she tried the handle. It smelled a bit musty from being closed up for too long, but if she had nowhere else to go, she would have found it to be more than adequate as a place to live. Of course it was only intended to distract people into thinking there couldn't be anything better nearby.

She stepped through the door and stood just far enough inside to be able to get a sense for whether or not she was alone. She would have had security attached to the door, so she stood on one spot and just rotated to take it all in. It didn't take long to spot the hidden security camera above the door, but she recalled the Chief said they had added more of them throughout the houseboat because there had been too many blind spots.

"Hello. Can I help you?"

The voice came from behind her and off to one side, or she would have seen that someone was there when she turned far enough to see the camera.

Despite the fact that the voice had been anything but threatening, she dove inside the houseboat, rolled, and came up with her machete blade aimed toward a stocky, bald man who had to be in his sixties but looked like he could fight a bear bigger than him.

He held one hand out with his palm up to show it was empty and immediately tried to make up for scaring her to death.

"I'm so sorry, Ma'am. I should have called to you from a distance, but I've learned not to raise my voice outside."

He smiled and didn't draw a weapon, but Iris thought he didn't have to when he had a soldier behind him with an M4 aimed at her, and he wasn't smiling.

"Let me start over again. I'm Doctor Bus. I saw how you handled your sailboat when you brought her in. That was a pretty experienced move you did to tie her off. Normally I would have stayed hidden, and you would never have known I was here, but I'm in somewhat of a hurry. I need to take that plane on a trip."

The soldier hadn't so much as blinked, and her arm was getting tired anyway. She lowered the machete but tried to keep one eye on each of them. The short man was speaking so calmly that she didn't feel like he was just going to execute her.

"Are you a friend of Chief Barnes?" she asked.

The man looked positively happy about the question and his smile became even more broad.

"I'm beginning to think everyone knows Chief Barnes," said Bus. "Yes, as a matter of fact he's a good friend. That's where I'm going with the seaplane. I'm taking it to him in New Orleans."

23 NEW ORLEANS

Year Six of the Decline

Stokes felt right at home in New Orleans. It was as neglected as any city he had seen but worse than most. What had taken hundreds of years to be constructed by man had taken half a decade to be torn down and reclaimed by nature. Repairs and upgrades to the flood protection systems after hurricane Katrina had helped at first, but as the first year went by, there were more and more failures.

Without maintenance crews monitoring weak spots and breaches, the levees conceded to the forces of storms and allowed the Mississippi River to enter the streets. Silt collected in the twists and turns of crucial areas and the river became impassable in many places.

Stokes found the right boat for traveling the flooded streets and began collecting the supplies others wouldn't have tried to reach. It had a flat bottom, and he used a pole to push himself along the surface. Most streets were under ten or more feet of water, so the ripe meat walking on the bottom couldn't reach high enough to grab his boat as he passed over them, but they tried. There were thousands of them reaching as high as they could, and he laughed at them.

One thing about Stokes had never changed. Before the end of civilization he figured anyone who was dead must have been stupid. So what he was seeing under his boat were a lot of stupid people, and he didn't feel even an ounce of sympathy for the souls that had died horrible deaths. It was what made him feel even smarter.

He fancied himself to be a modern day version of the early explorers in this territory, and he proclaimed it all as belonging to him. If he found anyone living in this tropical hell, they were living on his property. What they owned was really his, and they would be his servants.

The downtown streets were so flooded that he could coast up to the second floor balconies of the storefronts, and he was searching for the things he would need to take an oil rig. Most of it was common survival gear, but there were still a few pleasures in life he didn't want to forget. A supply of cigarettes and liquor were just as essential to him as weapons.

A few of the windows were shattered, so he assumed other boaters had been through those stores. He was searching for the ones that had a high death rate and high numbers of ripe meat to protect the stores. They were the ones with faces pressed against the glass.

He came to an intersection and could see a disturbance on the surface where hundreds of hands were reaching from the water. Most were visible from the wrist up. They were swaying with the current in a grotesque dance that almost seemed choreographed. The sun was low in the east and shining on the hands from behind. Stokes didn't have an artistic bone in his body, but even he recognized the possibility that he was seeing something that may not have been seen by anyone who lived to tell about it. His appreciation for it was short lived because he knew he couldn't go over those hands.

The current was pulling him in that direction, so he steered up against a balcony and tied a line to the black iron railing. There were faces against the row of windows in front of him. Most people would have left, but the sight brought a smile to his face. He stepped easily over the railing for a closer look.

Stokes estimated five or six faces at each of the four windows, so there must have been around two dozen ripe meat inside.

"There must be something really good in there with ya'll," he said and tapped on a window with his knuckles. That caused a frenzy of pushing and shoving inside.

He stepped back over the railing and loosened his mooring line, allowing himself to drift away by about six or eight feet. Stokes hefted his long pole and punched one end at a pane of glass. He considered himself a bit of an expert at breaking glass windows, if there was such a thing, and he was a little irritated that the pane didn't crack with the first punch.

Stokes pulled his mooring line in a couple of feet to get a little bit closer and tied it off again. This time he could put more of his shoulders in the punch, and the glass made a popping sound as it fell away. The rest of the window gave in to the pressure from inside, and the ripe meat spilled over the sill onto the balcony. He adjusted his angle and popped the second window the same way. He let the other two stay because the ripe meat had packed the balcony so tight that no more would fall out until he got them into the water.

The railing burst from the iron posts that held it in place. It went down on one end as ripe meat fell off of the balcony into the water. The other end of the railing flew up in the air and landed neatly on his flat bottom boat, right over his mooring line. Ironically, the mooring line was tied to one of the posts that stayed anchored to the balcony. The current caught some of the infected at just the right moment, and they were dragged into the part of the railing that had gone into the water first. They either held on or got tangled in the melee of bodies, and the railing wound up making a nice little bridge from the balcony to the boat.

"Are you kidding me?"

The infected were barely capable of walking a straight line, so there was no chance of them using the railing to walk aboard the boat, but they certainly could fall onto it, and they could get their legs stuck between the railings. Stokes could see that he was going to have a devil of a time untangling them enough to get the railing off the boat. Normally, he would just back up, and the makeshift bridge would fall, but he couldn't reach his mooring line under the tangle of bodies.

What he considered stupid from other people was brilliant when he did it, so nothing he ever did was a mistake. Stokes got comfortable on a deck chair and took aim at the head of the first ripe meat on the railing. The sound of the rifle echoed loudly between the buildings. The intersection of waving infected became a solid mass of hands as others were drawn to the blast.

Stokes probably would have pushed someone overboard for shooting a gun in the narrow street, but since everything he did was brilliant, he figured it was a good idea to draw the infected into the area before he left.

The first ripe meat he had shot didn't fall from the bridge the way he hoped. Instead, it fell face down. A second infected was taking the opportunity to crawl across to the boat over the back of the first one.

"Oh, no you don't."

Stokes pulled the trigger again, and this one fell sideways into the water and disappeared. By the time he had repeated the process, Stokes was thinking it was what he had planned all along.

Large numbers of the infected had fallen out of the windows and then fallen directly into the water. Stokes watched one that had some kind of backpack on that made him float, and when he passed by on the surface of the water the current grabbed him and sent him straight toward the waving hands.

Stokes watched with fascination and considerable enjoyment as the ripe meat went straight through the waving hands like a bowling ball through the pins. He laughed out loud and wished he had something he could throw into the water that would float, but that gave him another idea. If he picked up enough speed, he could drive right through there.

The last of the ripe meat to fall through the windows had also fallen off the balcony. Stokes used a boathook to clear the bodies out of his way and walked across using the railing. He used the boathook again to dispose of a few more infected that were still trying to come out through the windows, and then he used it to pry open the door.

This was the store he had been trying to find. He knew it would be here somewhere, but the streets were hard to remember with all of them so flooded. The first floor was completely flooded, and there were two stairwells behind fire doors that would keep him from being disturbed while he picked out his supplies. The first floor had been the showroom of the sporting goods store, and the upper floors were the offices and inventory storerooms.

It took over an hour, but he eventually had everything he needed to survive a trip out as far as the oil rigs. Now all he had to do was navigate out of the city and find a boat that could get him there, and if he was lucky he would find a few people on the way who would want to have someone like him for a boss.

What happened in the intersection wasn't because he had underestimated the ripe meat. There were just more of them than there should have been. At least that was how he saw it.

When he pushed off from the balcony, he was a little heavier than before, so he drafted deeper. He gave the balcony a hard shove with his pole as soon as his mooring line was off, and he picked up speed. He was surprised that it wasn't faster. He quickly checked to see if there were any ripe meat clutching the boat and saw none, so he steered closer to the side of the street to be able to reach the buildings with his pole as he went by. He reached out as far as he could and gave himself another push. There was a surge of speed when he drifted back to the center, and he steered toward the side for one last push before reaching the intersection.

The speed increased again enough to make his body lean to the aft, but the jolt of hitting a traffic light at such a speed almost threw him over the bow. It also caused his boat to go into a tailspin, and he was sideways when he reached the intersection, but that wasn't the worst thing about to happen.

From the balcony where he had been docked he hadn't been able to see the debris that was in the water between all of the waving hands, and the other side of the intersection was completely blocked. His only choice was to attempt a right turn at the intersection.

If there was such a thing as dumb luck, Stokes got more than his fair share. The hundreds of hands caught the boat in the middle of a spin when it was completely sideways coming into the intersection. It was almost like hitting a cushion because the momentum slowed so smoothly. Then the hands came forward again as they tried to grab the side of the boat. The hands slipped from the hull, and they pushed forward at the same time, causing the boat to go down the street to the right. It quickly gained forward speed and left the intersection behind.

"Worked just like I thought it would."

Stokes gave a wave of appreciation to the hands that seemed to be waving at him and turned toward the bow. In the distance there was something new, and he wasn't totally sure what it was.

When he put the binoculars to his eyes he saw it wasn't something new, just new to him. He was already moving too fast to try another turn at the intersection he was crossing, and using all his strength with the pole he didn't think he could get turned at the end of the block. His only choice was to be ready for a turn at the street that ran across the front of one of the biggest cemeteries in New Orleans.

The wall of the cemetery had been restored, and was much taller than it used to be. In an attempt to gain control of the graffiti and vandalism problem and to restore the beautiful burial sites, the city had closed this cemetery to tourists and restored the wall first. The new gates leaked at first, but apparently survivors had retreated to the cemetery and sandbagged the gates from the inside. When the levees failed, the cemetery didn't flood along with the streets, and the top of the wall was above the water by a few feet.

Stokes wasn't the best sailor in the world, but he had enough experience to realize that things were not as bad as they appeared to be. The current that carried him forward would take him to the cemetery, but it wasn't strong enough to hurt his boat unless he hit it head on. He turned his rudder hard to starboard, and as soon as he was sideways, he brought the rudder amidships and created as much drag as he could.

He sent a wall of water ahead of him that crested the wall of the cemetery, but there was only a slight jolt as he bumped sideways into the front gates. He stared with satisfaction at the grass and weeds that filled every inch of dry ground between the graves and the vaults.

"If there's any ripe meat in there, I'll be able to see where they are just by following the tall grass they walk through."

He scanned the old cemetery for almost an hour using his binoculars. He only found four trails between the rows of burial sites, and they had to be recent because the tall grass was bent over and pushed to the ground.

At first he considered firing a couple of rounds into the cemetery to draw the ripe meat out into the open. He was just shouldering his rifle when he had another thought that maybe he would be able to use them for something down the road. He didn't know why, but it felt almost like he was at home, and there were ripe meat wandering around at the cemetery when he had buried those kids. It had a familiar, good feel about it.

Stokes tied off the boat against the cemetery gates and tossed a rope over the wall. Satisfied that he could climb back up to his boat he went over the wall and slid down into the cemetery. He had the handy boathook with him, and he went down the rows testing the locks and doors on the burial vaults above ground.

When he found an old lock he used his machete and the boathook to break the lock and pry open the door. A musty smell escaped, and he backed up away from the darkness inside. Then he used his machete to clear away tall grass and vines to create an open area around that vault.

He climbed on top of a tall memorial to get his bearings so he would remember where this vault was. His run of good luck continued as he saw the grass moving only a few rows past his open vault, and he hurried to the ground so he could greet the new arrival.

Stokes stood boldly in the open near the front of the vault and watched the ripe meat stagger into view. It groaned when it saw him but didn't stop moving forward with its arms outstretched toward him.

"Not so fast, Sparky."

Stokes held the boathook out and let the infected walk straight into it. Instead of pushing him away, Stokes redirected his movement toward the open vault. He easily got him to the doorstep and gave a mild shove that sent the creature falling backward.

"Sorry about the smell," said Stokes as he closed the door. He slid the broken lock back into place.

"I'm going to use the honor system with you and not lock the door, so you gotta promise me you won't try to escape."

He laughed at his own joke.

"I'm really funny. I'll bet I could've made a good living hosting one of those late night shows."

When he thought about it for a moment more he asked in a loud voice, "Do you think I'm funny?"

He was answered by a loud groan from inside the vault, and there was a chorus of groans from a few places around the cemetery.

406

"Uh, oh. Better find some more vaults."

Over the next hour he repeated his process and had the other three infected in vaults spread out in the cemetery. He had cleared four areas of grass so they were easy to spot when he climbed up to the top of a memorial, and for good measure he cleared one area to use as a campsite. He could use a place that he could come back to where he would feel safe. He surrounded it with steel traps that he had gotten from the sporting goods store. He had planned to use them on an oil rig, but they came in handy here.

Now all he had to do was find a boat that was capable of reaching the oil rigs out in the Gulf. His flat bottomed boat wouldn't work for that, but he would be able to get a lot of things done with it as a backup.

Stokes judged that there was enough time left in the day for him to start searching for a boat, and his best chance of finding one was with the binoculars. He climbed up onto the wall, and using his pole for balance, he walked along the top of the wall that surrounded the cemetery. He stopped walking when he thought he could see something worth checking in the distance, and he finally saw what he was sure he would find.

To the south of the cemetery he could see the Mississippi River, and there had to be a marina somewhere between him and the Gulf. Tomorrow he would go toward the river and then follow it until he found a boat that would meet his needs. For tonight, he would pitch a tent and even heat up some food over a camp stove. He went back to the clearing he made and settled in.

******

I had to admit that traveling on the Cormorant had been a welcome change from traveling by helicopter to Ohio. I imagine the weather had something to do with it. It was snowing in Ohio, and if that wasn't cold enough, we flew up to International Falls, Minnesota. This trip was nothing but sunshine, and the water was so calm that the Cormorant seemed to be gliding across it.

We started having engine problems again as we cruised up the western side of Florida, and this time we didn't like the idea of finding a port that had repair facilities. After we stopped the first time we saw too many coastal towns and marinas that were still heavily populated with the infected. We decided that it was a one in a million chance that we would find another repair facility, make the repairs, and not run into serious trouble.

We still had to pass some major cities, so we could change our minds if there was no other choice, but we saw too many situations happening in broad daylight for us to justify being in port at night. Passing the Everglades we saw alligators fighting over bodies of people. Whether the people had escaped to the Everglades to get away from the infected or the people had washed ashore after dying we would never know for sure. It was likely to be some of both.

Not long after the Everglades we were cruising by Naples when we saw more of the huge crabs. They were dragging an infected across the sand and into the water. Rather than to risk having to stop near one of the major cities like Fort Myers or Tampa, the Chief made the decision to cut our speed way down, and we all started to worry about how we would get back home if the Cormorant needed major repairs.

The Chief called us all together on the aft deck below the wheelhouse. It was comfortable outside, and Cassandra could relay what he was saying to Sim since he had the helm.

"I hope everyone doesn't mind, but I've already made the decision to cut our speed rather than to stop for repairs. I still think we can get to New Orleans around the same time as Stokes unless he found some really good transportation, but if we don't, I have an idea I should have considered to start with."

All of us chimed in that the Chief was the boss, and that we would support whatever decision he made. He knew that already, but he was fair about everything. If one of us had a problem with his plans, he really wanted us to say something.

"Finding Stokes was always going to be the hard part, but if he reaches the Gulf before us, it'll make it easier to find him if he's on the water."

"And we're in an airplane," Kathy finished for him.

He smiled at her and nodded.

"If we could have gotten on station off the coast of New Orleans before him, all we would have needed to do was turn on our radar and wait for him to come to us. Whatever he would be using to get to the oil rigs, it wouldn't be fast enough to get by the Cormorant and her machine guns. Now that she's having problems, we need to get Bus to fly the Beaver down to New Orleans. At our present speed, we should be able to get a message to him, have him hop a ride to Mud Island, and fly to New Orleans. We can meet him at one of the fuel depots marked on our maps."

The Chief turned to each of us one by one and waited for us to voice an opinion, but none of us disagreed with the idea. It was the most logical thing to do.

He continued, "Once we find Stokes and deal with him, we can find a way to repair the Cormorant, but if anyone wants to hop a ride back to Fort Sumter with Bus, he's got plenty of room."

"That's a noisy ride," said Kathy. "I think I'll stick around for the repairs. Besides, we're still going to see about visiting the oil rig shelter, right?"

"That's the plan."

"Count me in," I said. "I'd like to meet Maybank and see what else he might be able to tell us about the early days of the shelters. It would be fun to sit down with him and Bus and hear some of their tall tales about my uncle, too."

Tom had some different feelings about the plans. Because Stokes had almost killed Molly, Tom was going to stay angry until he caught up with Stokes. He was seeing the negative in everything and was looking ahead to other problems with a cynical eye.

"We need to get back to Fort Sumter to head off whatever it is that's happening over at Patriots Point. I don't know what they're doing over there, but it's pretty clear that they are hostile, and they're organized."

"You think they have something to do with the increased presence of the infected at Fort Johnson and James Island?" asked the Chief.

"I don't see how they could, but we might be facing a double threat."

It was a quiet crowd on the deck of the Cormorant. It was bad enough to watch our cities fall into ruin over the last six years, but now we had a double threat that would prevent us from saving what little bit that we could. If not for the people at Patriots Point, we would have already established a forward base in Charleston. The idea was to take it all back a little at a time. Now we also had to worry about why there were suddenly more infected dead in places where they should have run out of people by now.

The Chief climbed up into the wheelhouse with Sim and contacted Fort Sumter. Captain Miller said things had been quiet at Patriots Point ever since we had hung up our warning sign about having missiles, so he didn't have a problem with sending a helicopter up the coast to drop Bus off at Mud Island. He said he also liked the idea of having the seaplane with us in case we couldn't get the Cormorant repaired. It would be a shame if we lost the Coast Guard ship. She had proven to be worth her weight in gold. A few minutes later, Captain Miller reported that Bus was on his way.

Within the hour we had to make another change of plans. We were going to turn northeast at Naples and go straight for New Orleans, but we spotted smoke on the water. It appeared to be a ship on fire, and the black smoke meant its fuel was burning.

As we got closer, the Chief identified the burning ship as an American built destroyer, but it was flying a foreign flag. It took a few minutes, but we found the manual in the wheelhouse that showed all foreign navy flags, and this one was from Chile. We all automatically waited for the Chief to fill in the blanks.

"The US sells or leases ships to friendly countries all the time," said the Chief. "This one must have been on the wrong side of the Panama Canal when the infection started. Whatever it's doing here, the fact that it's on fire is a bad thing. It means someone with a better ship just sank her."

"What if she's just being scuttled by an infected crew?" asked Hampton.

"That's possible, but whatever the reason, we have to give it a wide berth."

He turned to Sim and told him to steer for the coast of Florida and to hug the coast as closely as possible without running aground. He explained that there was less chance of us catching a torpedo in shallow water.

We moved as close as we could to the coast and found that the water was so blue and clear that we could see the bottom in plenty of places. The big discovery was the numbers of infected we saw that were in various stages of their miserable existence.

Some were walking on the bottom, their buoyant arms often floating away from their sides. Some were suspended between the bottom and the surface, apparently building up enough body gases from decay to equal their weight. Eventually they would pop to the surface. Plenty of them were in pieces. Body parts were everywhere, and the jaws were usually snapping as if they had something in their field of vision they wanted to bite. That was usually us. They could see us going over them, so the snapping increased.

The most disgusting part of this human debris field was that it was like any garbage dump on the surface. At the garbage dumps there are always plenty of birds and rats crawling over the mountains of garbage searching for food, but out here they weren't having to search. It was all laid out like a buffet right in front of them. Crabs roamed over all of them, not particular about whether or not they were pieces or whole. Sharks swam through the middle of the floating bodies as if checking for the best selections and suddenly choosing one. With spectacular ferociousness they would charge one and wrap powerful jaws around them. They would speed away with their prize, often leaving a trail of loose pieces that would either fall to the bottom or float to the surface.

Gulls took care of the surface cleaning. The passing of the Cormorant hardly bothered their pursuit of another meal, and we were morbidly amazed when we would see a bird lifting an arm from the surface. Sometimes they were too heavy, and they fell back into the water, but the birds were not deterred. They had others they could manage when something proved to be too much for them to handle.

As morbid as it was, we watched quietly for the most part, but from time to time we reminded ourselves that these had been people in the past, and it could just as easily have been us. We were fortunate, and we needed to remember to have sympathy for the dead, not disgust of them, but disgust of what they had become.

By evening we could see New Orleans in the distance. It resembled Charleston with the darkened buildings under a dense canopy of vegetation. What was being reclaimed in Charleston was being reclaimed ten times faster in New Orleans. Both cities were accustomed to the heat and humidity when they were vibrant tourist centers, but without people they were being taken back by nature.

As we drew closer we saw that New Orleans had paid a high price for being below water level. The levees had been breached, and we could have sailed the Cormorant straight into previously dry, residential parts of the city. Water went into many places that weren't able to stand up against the undercutting of the currents, and buildings sagged over onto their sides.

The Chief checked the time and asked to no one in particular if anyone had heard Bus check in by radio. We all shook our heads, and we saw the attempt he made to hide his concern when he said it could be anything.

"Bus should already be here, so everyone listen for a hail from him, but whoever has radio duty, please give him a call once every fifteen minutes. We need to know where he landed so we don't have to search the whole coast for him."

We all acknowledged the Chief, but there was no escaping the nagging dread of understanding. Some of the reasons why we hadn't heard from him were bad. As a matter of fact, more of them were bad than good.

24 REALITY

Year Two of the Decline

Janice spent the rest of the day cleaning the wounds on her arm and hand. The cut on her hand wasn't as deep or as ragged as the place on her upper arm where she had stabbed herself, but the numbness worried her. She had seen too many ladders outside to have only one useful hand to climb with.

Her mind drifted back to David every time she was faced with doing something that he had always done. There was no avoiding those things now. She would have to do everything without his help.

When David had put a big gash across his own chest with a piece of sheet metal, she hadn't been strong enough to stitch it for him. He had asked her to, holding out a curved needle with a long piece of thread dangling from one end. She had looked at the ugly wound and cried, finally shaking her head and telling David she couldn't do it. She had felt like such a coward.

David had gone through enough that day, and she couldn't give him the first aid he needed. He had discovered a supply of food that was as good as finding King Solomon's

Mines, but when he tried to drop into the building through a skylight, the roof had collapsed, and the sheet metal ripped him open as he fell by.

Despite the searing pain and so much blood, he had filled several sacks and a backpack with food and come back out through the roof. In the supplies had been a medical kit that had been so complete there were antibiotics, morphine, antiseptics, and a stitching kit. He was worried about tetanus from the metal and hoped to find something he called tetanus immune globulin in the supplies, but that was hoping for too much. His best bet would be to clean and stitch the wound as soon as possible and start taking the antibiotics.

She had let him down. Sitting there in front of a mirror, he had cleaned the wound with hydrogen peroxide and started from the top. The cut ran from the top of his breastbone to only two inches above his navel. He had to keep stopping to wipe away the blood and then to squeeze the two sides of the cut together at a new spot. He wouldn't take a morphine shot because he said we might need it for something worse one day.

Janice couldn't imagine what he would have considered worse, but in her heart she knew he was saving it for her if she ever needed it. Even then, she couldn't make herself be brave enough to take the needle from him. She could only watch as each time he drew another stitch together, he winced and held his breath. He would let his breath out, rest a moment, and start another stitch. A couple of times he had taken a swallow from a precious bottle of bourbon, but as bad as it was for him, he always offered her some. She didn't know which was worse, her helplessness or his generosity in the midst of such suffering.

After David had used scissors to snip the thread, he covered it all with antiseptic and a bandage. The last thing he did was sort through the antibiotics until he found the one he was looking for. He took one and told her to give him another in four hours if he didn't wake up on his own. Janice helped him get comfortable, and he had gone to sleep.

Janice nursed him for more than three days before the fever broke, and the whole time all she could think of was how worthless she had been. She couldn't think of a single excuse for not even trying to do the stitching for him. She could have given him the morphine and let him sleep while she repaired the wound, but now she had to live with the memory of her husband holding out that needle and thread.

Now that memory changed a bit. David was handing her the needle and thread, not for him but for her to stitch herself. David was sitting across the bar from her. He was watching as she got ready to sew herself up. She wasn't very coordinated with her left hand, and she was having to watch herself do the stitches in a mirror.

"Payback is hell," she said as she took a long swallow from the bottle of bourbon. "I can't even use a pair of scissors looking in a mirror. Every time I want to go left, I go right. Every time I want to go right, I go left. This stinks."

She had just enough bourbon in her to think that was funny, and she giggled. She took aim at the cut on her upper arm with the needle and pushed it in for the first stitch.

It sounded like someone else had screamed, but when she did the tilt of the curved needle that would put the tip where the exit of the stitch should be, she did exactly what she had expected to do using a mirror. She went the wrong way.

Janice sat on the barstool and screamed obscenities at herself until she was crying. She focused on which direction would be correct, and she succeeded in piercing the other side of the cut. On a positive note, she was in so much pain that it couldn't get worse. She was actually surprised when she made the next entry with the needle because it wasn't so bad after she had screwed up the second one. This time she went the right way when she crossed back to the other side, and she drew the second stitch tight. As she closed the wound it felt better, and the only thing that made it still hurt was the memory that she couldn't do it for David.

She eventually reached for the scissors, missed the thread several times by reverting to her reverse mirror problems, and then blindly snipped it off. Bandaging wasn't so bad, and by the time she was ready to stitch up her hand, she was at least feeling like she was almost done.

Her hand proved to be worse than the upper arm because of the nerves. She wasn't sure, but it seemed to sting more, maybe because she would hit a numb spot and then surprised herself by crossing into a sensitive area. Since the cut on her hand was smaller, she was surprised for a second time when she realized she was done with the worst part. She swabbed it with antiseptics and placed a fresh bandage on it. It had a dull ache, but overall her arm felt like it wouldn't fall off.

The bar seemed like a good place to stay if she would have had a bartender who could pour drinks and order food from the kitchen. The thought of a big guy polishing glasses and taking her food order made her giggle again.

"Bartender, gimme another round, and let me have a look at your menu."

She went to sleep with her right arm curled across the bar and the left side of her head tucked into the curve of her elbow. It never occurred to her that was the best way to keep her arm positioned for a few hours, but it seemed to ease the pain a bit. When she woke up, the kink in her neck didn't agree, and being right handed, she instinctively reached for her neck with her right hand.

"Ouch."

Janice studied her arm and saw that she had earned herself some more time among the living, but it all still came back around to David. He was out there somewhere. Dead, she knew that, but this oil rig was her world now, and sooner or later she would have to go out there.

******

Maybank watched the door of the crew quarters while he ate his meals as if it was a television program on at a regularly scheduled time. The monitors were on in the background while he did his routine reviews of the shelter's systems and while he searched the horizon for new threats.

He watched the drama unfold on the derelict ship that had drifted up against his oil rig, as the rats at first went to the deepest and darkest parts of the ship to set up house. In a moment of cruel irony, he realized that they had done nothing more than the lady who had ducked inside the crew quarters. He knew that sooner or later the rats and the lady would come back out, but maybe for different reasons.

Inside the big container ship there was undoubtedly a large food supply wandering around in the compartments. After building their new, more secure nests, the rats would start eliminating the infected dead that were below decks. Given time, they would have a few more breeding cycles before they ran out of that food supply. Then they would arrive on the decks of the ship. Maybank decided that would be a good time to put the rat poison at the right locations.

The rats would have to cross the poison to get back on the oil rig.

In the meantime, Maybank had let himself become obsessed with the lady in the crew quarters. It was like he was holding an oyster and knew there was a pearl inside. He knew she had been bitten by a rat, and for all he knew, she was dead. If she was dead, she would be wandering around inside the crew quarters and bumping into the furniture. The lamps would all be broken on the floor, and she would be slowly decaying in one room at a time.

His obsession with her started when he pulled up a security video of the day she had arrived. When she appeared on the screen, he froze the image and enlarged it. She was much younger than him, but she was beautiful. Long brown hair spilled over her shoulders, and it was so full that it was almost like it had just been washed. Maybank was seeing her through the lenses of lonely eyes, but it would never occur to him that he had missed other people. If she had been homely, he would have still seen beauty.

It never crossed his mind that he had been alone on the oil rig for years before the apocalypse, and when it all ended, he had been alone for another year. He was much older than her, and even though she was probably dead, he couldn't stop the fantasy that had begun to build up around her.

The simple fact was that she wasn't beautiful, but she was pretty. She was younger than him, but that wouldn't matter because she was also certainly grateful to him for saving her. She would also be kind and understanding that he was lonely, so the age difference wouldn't be a problem. As for the man who had been with her, he must have been her brother, and if he wasn't, he was just someone she had run into as she tried to survive. She was unhappy that he died, but she would get over him.

As each day went by, Maybank built on his fantasy, reviewing security tapes he had already watched, trying to see if he had missed anything moving at that closed door.

He almost missed the arrival of the rats on the deck of the Titanic because he was so preoccupied with that single door. That's what he had started calling the ill fated derelict even though it was a container ship.

The infected dead that still roamed around on the upper decks were diminishing in numbers because the rats were taking them down at night. He just happened to glance at a monitor that showed a view of the ship when a large rat scurried across the deck dragging a snapping head with it. The teeth caught the rat's tail, and the rat attacked the head more viciously than he could believe. He had never seen one behave that way, and he understood why he had to keep them from coming onto the oil rig again. If they did, and if the lady was still alive, they would get her. He couldn't stand the thought of losing her even though he didn't know her name or if she was still alive.

The sun had been down for an hour when he went topside with the rat poison. It wasn't a difficult task. It was just time consuming because there were so many places he had to fill the sprinklers. Three hours later he skimmed the list of locations on a chart he had prepared in advance and saw that he had checked off each location.

Standing on a catwalk by the Wellbay Tower, Maybank saw the tattered clothing clinging to the bones of the man that had been attacked by the rats. Some of the remains had fallen over the edge to the waters of the Gulf, but he recognized there was still a pair of jeans attached to the bones. Out of reflex, his own right hand reached back to his rear pocket, and he felt the lump of his wallet there. Even though he had been on the oil rig since long before the end of the world, he still held to the habit of carrying a wallet. Something inside him was convinced that there would be a wallet in those jeans.

Maybank wasn't motivated by a desire to know who the man had been. He was motivated to know if there was a picture of the lady that he could see more clearly than the grainy images of the security cameras.

He crossed the short distance to the remains and didn't hesitate. He had no feeling that he was committing an act of desecration. He just had to know.

The wallet was right where he expected it to be, and he was smiling when he opened it. There were two pictures. One was a pose of the couple together. He saw that she obviously wasn't his sister. The affection in the picture was palpable. The second picture was her alone. He held it in a beam of light and saw on the back was written "Jan in Texas".

"Jan," he said out loud. "Janet."

Maybank glanced at the drivers license, but all he saw was the last name. His fantasy filled and lonely mind blocked out the rest. He tucked the picture inside his own wallet and made the long climb back down to the shelter, secure with the new knowledge that she was Janet Parker. He erased David Parker from his thoughts.

Once he was sealed inside the shelter, his habit of checking the security camera footage didn't change even though he had just been out there. He was horrified when the recording showed the darkness around the crew quarters interrupted by light from the straight line of the door.

Sharp at first, it flared as all of the light spilled out through the open door, and a silhouette stood in the light. The dark shape with the light behind it walked to the railing at the end of the deck outside the quarters and stood looking down at the catwalks below…right at the spot where he would have been standing over the remains of the man. One hand came up and balanced the silhouette as she leaned forward to see what was happening below, and then suddenly the shape ran for the open door and shut it quickly behind her.

He checked the timestamp on the video and looked at his watch. He knew instinctively that she had seen him going through her dead husband's wallet, but he had to know for sure. He switched to a different camera that showed him standing over the body and saw the timestamp. There was no doubt about it. They were the same.

"So, you survived the rat bites."

He was both excited and confused. He had seen it for himself, and she should have been dead by now. His thoughts were moving at a hundred miles an hour as he tried to sort out the facts from the theories.

"Maybe she's immune. Maybe not all rats are carriers. Maybe she found the antibiotics in the supplies and took them in time."

In his mind, which had already detached from reality, he rationalized that it didn't matter what had kept the woman alive. She was alive because of him, and the woman would come to the conclusion that he had saved her life, and it didn't matter what she had seen.

******

Janice didn't keep track of time, so she didn't have a clue how long she had been inside the strange place with everything she needed except windows and David. Hunger made her check the kitchen for food, and what she found only made her miss David more. Dry goods in a large pantry, frozen food in a large walk-in freezer, and a refrigerator that was filled with nonperishable items that could have come from a grocery store. A coffee pot and enough coffee to last a lifetime.

The kitchen was fully equipped, and there were dishes and all of the necessary utensils for cooking and baking. If that wasn't enough, there was cold beer and the bar, and another storeroom revealed a supply of MREs that would last for years. This was the motherlode they had searched for, and it was in a relatively safe place. All she needed was David to make it complete.

Janice took the antibiotics, and the wound would heal. Hunger more than appetite drove her to eventually push the guilt back far enough for her to eat. The smell of meat cooking in a pan made her dizzy. She thawed potatoes and green beans in a microwave and savored them with the forgotten flavor of steak. When she finished, she was surprised to find she had the strength to stay on her feet and clean up the dishes. She left the kitchen spotless and wandered to the bedrooms.

She hadn't noticed there was an entertainment system in each room, and the movie collection was as good as walking into a DVD store. Even better, when she turned on a TV set, the menu showed there was a central movie channel that was a lot like having cable. She scrolled the menu and felt like she would never be able to watch every movie that was listed. It was the same for music. There was an endless supply that would satisfy all tastes.

Besides the one where she had collapsed, there was only one room that appeared to have been slept in. The other rooms all had beds with covers stretched tightly across them, but this one even had a pillow that was still dented in the middle. Janice wondered who the previous occupant had been and what had happed to him or her.

Another rifle just like the first one leaned into the corner where a writing desk met the wall, and she realized there hadn't been any other weapons in the rooms besides the two she had found. It must have belonged to the person who had stayed here before. She instinctively hefted it with her good arm to check the weight.

David would have claimed the rifles if he had been there, but he had taught her a few things when they were lucky enough to have weapons. He had shown her the difference in weight of a full magazine from an empty one, and he had repeatedly drilled into her the importance of knowing the difference. She had gotten good enough to tell when one was half full.

She couldn't help but wonder why it had been left here in the room. The fact that it was abandoned here spoke volumes to her. Whoever had owned the rifle had gone out and not come back. Either that, or they were still on the rig somewhere, perhaps wandering around as an infected dead.

There was something else different in this one bedroom. There was a pad of paper on the desk, and someone had left a note. She turned the pad and tried to understand the poor handwriting.

"Someone is here. He talked with me on the phone a couple of times, but he wouldn't open the shelter. He said something once about Jones having the infection and that he wasn't sure about me. He also said something about us not being authorized to be here. Jones is getting worse, but I don't know when he could've been bitten, so I think it's something else. I'm going to try to reason with the guy and get him to let us in."

That was all there was to it, and it didn't make sense to her.

"Let them in where?" she asked herself.

She suddenly felt sleepy after the long day and the hot food. This time she chose the bedroom at the far end of the hall, and she took the rifle with her. She laid down on the bed and immediately started to settle down in the soft pillow, but something tugged at the back of her mind.

Janice switched on the light and took in every detail of the room. There wasn't a telephone anywhere that she could see. She tried to recall if she had seen one out in the main room or the kitchen, and she didn't think she had, but she had been so focused on the injury to her arm and everything else that happened after that. Alexander Graham Bell could have been out there, and she might not have noticed.

She giggled at her own joke and bitterly remembered it was the same giggle that David sometimes liked, but there had been times when he had told her it was immature. Part of her was angry at him for dying and leaving her alone like this, but the best part of her said he was only hard on her so she would survive. Maybe he was right, because she was alive, and he wasn't.

Sleep took over for her a few minutes later, and she stayed in one position for over four hours. She woke up with that nagging feeling first of not knowing where she was, then of someone watching. When she rolled over, she cried out at the pain in her right arm, and then there was the stiffness in her neck and left side of her body. Nonetheless, it was a clean and comfortable bed, something that they hadn't found in over a year, and whatever was left to be solved she could do the next day. She took more antibiotics and went back to sleep.

There was no alarm clock, but she wasn't counting the ache in the back of her right arm and the stiffness in her hand. Combined, they were as good as any alarm clock. It was strange to feel so much pain but be happy that her hand hurt more than it did the day before. The numbness was gone, which meant less nerve damage than she first thought.

"Given time, I'll play the piano again. Not that I could before."

Janice had some unfamiliar cramps in her stomach and made a right turn for the bathroom instead of the front of the quarters. She had forgotten what that much fiber and red meat could be like the next day.

She hadn't noticed she had her choice of showers and bathtubs, which was a great relief. The shower would have played hell with her bandaged arm, but the idea of soaking in a hot tub was beyond imagination.

There were already towels in the big bathroom where everything appeared to be stainless steel, and she decided between hunger and how much she craved a long, hot bath. She stripped standing next to a large tub with seats in it and climbed in before it was even half full. A row of switches confirmed it was a whirlpool, and she leaned back to let the jets of water pummel her body.

Time had no meaning as she floated neck deep in the hot water, but time healed wounds faster than she had known. There were a million thoughts going through her head, and most of them went from life with David to life without David. That had been before, and this was what her reality had become.

She knew that she had to grieve, but she had gone through a tremendous amount of grief already even before they had arrived at the oil rig. Even before David had died. She understood when you get used to grief, you almost lose perspective about how long you should grieve. So, she gradually came to the conclusion that grieving for David was only going to stop her from recovering, and perhaps stop her from completely relishing the comforts of her surroundings. She didn't want to ignore the good things happening to her out of guilt.

Despite sleeping well the night before, the hot water and the whirlpool jets put her into a slumber that lasted three more hours, and she felt so relaxed when she went back to her room. There was no way she was going to put those old clothes back on her clean body, and since there was no one else to see her, she enjoyed the freedom of walking down the hall with just her towel.

The closet and the dresser in her room had a surprising collection of unisex clothing. There was something like a navy blue jumpsuit that fit comfortably, and the cleanliness alone was a dream come true. Add to that the cotton socks and women's underwear in one of the drawers, and Janice felt like her good fortune was the reward for David's sacrifice. The grieving fell away with every new comfort and every remembrance of how he had kept her feeling helpless without him. She mentally closed the lid on his coffin when it crossed her mind that he would have taken credit for all of this if he had survived.

Revived by the sleep and the long bath, her appetite had returned, and she went to the kitchen on a mission. Powdered eggs tasted pretty good when you hadn't eaten eggs in a year, and a stack of pancakes smothered in real maple syrup gave her a sugar rush that would make her smile for a few hours.

When she finished eating, she explored every room again, examining the contents of every drawer and making a mental list of the supplies. Each room seemed to offer something she needed. There was a laundry room through a side door of the bathroom. She had missed it the first time, but that told her she could have clean clothes for the rest of her life.

That made her think for the second time about something that had no explanation.

"Power...where's the power coming from?"

Janice found a picture of the entire oil rig among the stacks of paperwork in a desk. Probably left there by someone who had built the oil rig, it gave her reason to hope that the power was no fluke. She saw that one of the structures was labeled as the Power Module, and it undoubtedly supplied the power to the drill, the oil processing tower, and everything else. As long as the power module kept working, she would be okay.

When she was done exploring, she went back to the common room that had served as a social gathering place and found herself wondering what to do next. She was rested, medically repaired, clean, and well fed. Now she had to think about what that meant to the rest of her life. She could see herself doing all of the same things tomorrow, minus the stitches, but she couldn't imagine doing them for the rest of her life. Especially since there were no windows.

The thought of going outside and being confronted by rats was enough to deter her from opening the door for the time being, but she wasn't sure how long she could go without seeing the outside. Sometimes seeing the sky meant she and David hadn't been able to find a safe place to spend the night, so sleeping under a roof in a room without windows wasn't going to be a problem. The daylight was what she would miss.

The big flatscreen television mounted in one corner where it could be seen from anywhere in the room was a good place to start, but when Janice found the remote and turned it on, she was disappointed to find it was only linked to the library of movies and TV shows. Not that she expected to find any live broadcasts, but she had hoped to at least see snow on the screen where the stations used to be.

The bonus, besides catching a few movies she had never seen, was the DVR setting. Someone had set the DVR to record news broadcasts at the end of the world. She saw by the menu that the storage drive was full, so someone had recorded everything. She had been there for some of it, but she knew she had to see the reports with her own eyes. It had been bad in her little corner of the world, but she imagined it had been ten times as bad in places like New York, Paris, and London.

She noticed there were smaller TV screens strategically placed around the large room and had assumed they were all linked to the main screen. That way everyone could see what was on without having to face in the same direction. She thought it was like any sports bar she had been to, and then she remembered the screens in sports bars weren't always on the same station.

There weren't remotes laying all around the room, so Janice assumed there was a control panel somewhere. If not, the bartender probably controlled them from his station. When she checked under the bar, she was rewarded for her thinking when she found a stack of labeled remotes in a box. She sat them on top of the bar and started figuring out which one went to which TV.

She was distracted by the bourbon she had left sitting on the bar and couldn't help herself.

"This could become a bad habit, but I think I deserve to indulge myself for a day or two."

She poured a glass and enjoyed the warm feeling of the drink as it reached her stomach.

The drink also cleared her head, and she realized all she had to do was press the power buttons on the remotes to identify which one went where. She pressed the first one and saw a screen light up. She laid the remote on the bar so that it was pointed at the screen. She kept going until they were all on except one that seemed to be situated at a private wall table. Under the bar there weren't any remotes she missed, so she walked over to inspect the screen more closely and found it wasn't a tv. It was a computer monitor.

Janice stuck her head below the table out of habit. That's where she expected to find the computer's CPU. There wasn't anything there that resembled a CPU, but on the way back up she spotted a thin cord that led her to a mouse.

She went low-tech and ran her fingers along the edge of the monitor until she found a power switch. When she pressed the button, she was surprised when the screen lit up and showed her a grid of small screens. They weren't big, but they were clear enough for her to see they were security cameras at various locations throughout the oil rig. One of them showed the bright blue, clear sky beyond a flat platform that she guessed was a landing pad for helicopters.

"This will do very nicely," she said, but a dark feeling passed over her, and she moved her eyes from one small screen to the next. Part of her was hoping that one of the cameras would show her David's body, and another part of her hoped it wouldn't. If his body was there, she didn't know if she would ever be able to turn this monitor on again.

She didn't see anything that resembled the place where she had last seen him, nor did she see an angle of the catwalks below. She experienced a small twinge of guilt at the relief she felt, but if this was to be her window to the outside world, she wanted to see it without being reminded of David by seeing his body.

Janice spent a few minutes studying each small screen but didn't see anything interesting except for the absence of rats. Either the cameras didn't cover where the rats were hiding, or they were gone.

There was one view of the ship that they had been following when it collided with the rig, and she leaned closer when she saw movement. A rat ran across the deck of the ship and literally leaped into the air at something out of her view. A moment later an infected dead staggered by with the rat clinging to its stomach. She was sickened by how the rat was digging its teeth into the rotten flesh. She turned away, knowing David had likely suffered as the rats fed on him.

When she turned back to the monitor, the view of the ship was empty, and she hoped it stayed that way. She played with the menu settings for a few minutes and finally stumbled across a list of the views. She found she could select any view to enlarge it, and she could also do it by double-clicking on that view. She enlarged the view that showed the most open sky and left it like that.

There were plenty of things to keep her busy for now, but she decided she needed to heal more than anything, and that meant rest. It would be a good time to watch the news reports on the DVR.

She poured herself another shot glass of bourbon and carried it to the couch, but before sitting down she went back to the bar and got the bottle.

25 DISCOVERY

Year Six of the Decline

Iris had never flown in a de Havilland Beaver, but she was no stranger to the fun of small planes. She watched as Bus expertly pointed the nose of the plane toward the open sea and picked up speed. He had told her it would be noisy and handed her protective gear, but she wanted the full experience and the headset rested on her lap. By the time the plane lifted from the water, the headset was where it was intended to be, and she didn't know if it was too late to avoid permanent damage to her ears.

Bus teased her by pretending to talk, and when she finally figured out he wasn't saying anything, her first thought was that this man had spent a lot of time around the Chief.

They reached cruising altitude a few minutes later, and Bus switched their headsets to interior communications. It made them able to speak easier without shouting, and he was curious about this attractive woman who was trying to find the Chief.

He kept glancing over at her startling silver hair and her sculpted features. She probably worried about the small wrinkles at the corners of her eyes, but Bus thought they gave her character. Being a smart man, he didn't say that out loud, though.

She had already given him enough information for him to know she was close to being the same age as the Chief, but she was so much like the Chief in the way she carried herself. He was also sure that by the time he got her to New Orleans, Kathy would never forgive him if he hadn't gotten every detail to pass along to her.

"I'm dying to know how you happen to know Chief Barnes."

Bus figured it was natural enough that he could be straight with her, and he was grinning from ear to ear when he said it. If he wasn't blessed with hair to charm the ladies, he did have an infectious smile.

"We were both cruise ship security directors."

Iris was more like the Chief than Bus knew, and she noticed the smile and how he didn't beat around the bush.

"I guess we have a couple of hours for me to tell you everything about me, but remember I've already met Kathy at Ambassadors Island. Are you going to tell me she didn't give you the details?"

Bus felt his smile become frozen on his face, and he saw her reaction. She saved him by laughing and telling him that she was teasing him.

"Listen Bus, women sometimes keep things to themselves for their own reasons, and I imagine Kathy picked up on my feelings for the Chief. She knew we would be forced to be apart for several years once we sealed Ambassadors Island against the radiation. She would have played her cards close to the vest about me because she didn't want to think about how long it would be. Now that the radiation is low enough, and I'm meeting up with the Chief, watch how excited she gets."

Bus understood, and as a matter of fact, he was likely to have handled it the same way if he had been in Kathy's shoes. The difference was that Kathy would still have choked him for withholding the information.

"Do we have the radio power to raise the Chief?"

"I don't think so, but I'll try anyway."

Bus turned on the radio and sent out his callsign on several frequencies, but he only got static when he listened.

"We lost contact between Mud Island and Fort Sumter a few days ago, but we haven't had contact with the shelter on the oil rig in a few years. We don't know if Maybank had some kind of emergency, or if his radio equipment had problems, but while we're in New Orleans, we're going to visit the oil rig and see if he needs a hand. That's why the Chief needs the plane. We have helicopters that would have been better, but we need to keep them at Fort Sumter for now."

"You have helicopters? You guys are light years ahead of the rest of civilization."

"We also have some Army personnel with us. That's why we're trying to get the shelters online. Has anyone told you we found the President's shelter in Ohio?"

Iris almost hurt her neck when her head snapped around so she could face Bus.

"Don't get your hopes up. It's a long story, but things went wrong there. He didn't make it. We can fill you in on all the details when we can tell you the whole story, but for now that shelter is sealed and offline."

Iris turned to her window, and Bus left her alone with her thoughts. It was obvious that she needed to be alone with her thoughts for a minute, but this was also her first time seeing what had happened to the countryside below.

There wasn't much to see because the landscape had turned so green. Towns and cities came into view, and as the plane passed over them, she saw that vegetation had covered everything in five years.

Entire suburban neighborhoods had burned to the ground. The lawns had grown tall with grass. When the grass died and turned to large patches of overgrown, brown straw, all it took was a lightning strike to get the fires started. In some places it was survivors who were careless with campfires or people who tried to use rusty propane gas grills for heat or cooking. Whatever the causes, there was no one to put out the fires, and people who tried to stop them learned the hard way that the infected were attracted to fire.

Iris was amazed by the devastation, and where cities weren't destroyed, they had been devoured by nature. That reminded her. She hadn't seen any infected dead yet.

"Where are all the infected?"

"Good question," said Bus. "We do reconnaissance when we can, but the last thing we saw was they all seem to be moving toward the coast. We can't explain why, but we were searching for this guy named Stokes, and we noticed the area had more infected dead wandering around than it used to."

"Tell me about Stokes. Why would the Chief be so mad at one guy that he would travel around Florida to New Orleans? Did he kill someone?"

"Yes, a young boy who's been with us for a long time, and he almost killed a girl who has been like my granddaughter. There was another boy that he killed with Sam, and you know the Chief. He took it pretty hard."

"If the Chief's protecting you, he would take failure personally," said Iris.

"We know from a survivor that Stokes was headed for New Orleans with the idea of reaching an oil rig and using it as a shelter."

"He knows about the shelters?"

"We don't know for sure that he knows about the oil rig shelter, but he thinks he can survive on an oil rig and plans to set out from New Orleans to find one. The shelter belonging to Maybank is in a direct line with New Orleans, so Stokes would be likely to find it."

"So the Chief wants to dispose of Stokes and check on Maybank at the same time?"

"That's the plan. I don't know if he would be so determined if it hadn't been one of our kids, but he's going to catch Stokes if he has to swim to the oil rig."

Iris knew Bus was right. Chief Joshua Barnes was a man of honor, but getting on his bad side by killing a child would unleash the part of him that would cause fear in anyone with half a brain. She silently hoped she would get to him before he caught up with Stokes. Six years of living with the infected dead must have hardened him, but she hoped it hadn't taken his soul.

She knew what he was about to do, and she understood why it had to be done, but a part of her worried that either one of two things could happen besides Stokes getting the justice he deserved. The Chief needed to be judge, jury, and executioner, but he needed to do it in a way he could live with afterward. The other thing was that Stokes was that special kind of maniac that somehow caught the Chief off guard and turned the tables. Good men have fallen before to evil men who seemed to have that kind of dumb luck that made them come out on top.

It suddenly occurred to Iris that she had gotten quiet. Bus kept glancing at her with a worried expression.

"I forgot to tell you, I think you're right that something is drawing the infected toward the coast, but they aren't taking the shortest routes, and they aren't taking shortcuts."

Bus had been worried. Now he was confused.

"What does that mean? I mean, I understand the part about them all going toward the coast, but the rest of it didn't make sense."

"They could use roads and highways that go straight to the coast, but they're gathering together into a massive horde and going toward Charleston. They could go toward Myrtle Beach or Georgetown, but they're not. Hell, they could use I-95 all the way to Florida, but they're even coming from that direction to join up with the big horde headed for Charleston."

"If I remember my South Carolina maps well enough, they're going to bottleneck on I-26 where the swamps close in on the interstate on both sides," said Bus.

"Exactly, so that gives us some time to get ready for them. I lost four close friends on this trip from Charlotte to here, but we all agreed the horde was well over a hundred thousand. After that many you can't even estimate them anymore."

"We can do some reconnaissance after we get back, but a horde that size could even reach Fort Sumter if enough of them come around the harbor onto James Island."

Iris laughed a little, but was still a bit grim when she answered the last comment by Bus.

"You need to brush up on your maps just a bit. They will bottleneck, but once they get strung out, imagine a half million or more of them on I-26 reaching all the way from Orangeburg to the Cooper River Bridge. They won't be able to cross to James Island and come up behind you at Fort Sumter, but I wouldn't want to be anywhere near the Cooper River and the Ravenel Bridge when that parade arrives."

******

Year Two of the Decline

Janice was stunned to find that there were enough recorded broadcasts on the DVR for her to put together a timeline. A calendar in one of the rooms was over a year old from what she could figure, and if she was right, she had just passed what would have been her first wedding anniversary. David had celebrated it out there while she celebrated it inside the safety of the crew quarters. Part of her knew he would have wanted this for her, and that eased the pain a little.

She wasn't sure if it was the bourbon that just made her think that last thought about David, but it didn't really matter. She held a glass of the amber liquid to catch the light from the TV.

"Here's to you, David. Happy anniversary. You kept me alive for a year. I'm sorry I couldn't do the same for you."

She might not have been sure about what the bourbon was doing to her thoughts about David, but she was sure it had helped her watch the news reports. She would have most likely turned them off if not for the numbing effects of the bourbon.

Of course the DVR started at the beginning, and even though she remembered it like it was yesterday, she felt like she owed it to someone to watch the history of the end of the world as it unfolded. She pressed play on the remote and recognized the familiar faces of TV anchors she had watched for years before this recording. They were American faces, but they had adopted the name of the worldwide crisis used by their European counterparts. They were calling it The Decline of Man.

A banner was running across the bottom of the screen that was trying to keep up with the new reports of attacks worldwide. The anchorwoman was talking to four reporters who were in different cities across the country, and their broadcasts were in four separate squares on the screen. Each of them tried to describe the same thing while taking their eyes off their nervous camera crews to point at attacks that were happening far too close for comfort. Screams permeated the sound from each of the squares as the anchor desk switched between them, and the anchorwoman began pleading with all four to seek shelter. She could see that the attackers weren't going to spare anybody just because they were reporters.

In one square a man walked into the field of vision behind the young girl holding the microphone. Reporters doing remote broadcasts had always endured the antics of people who realized they were on camera. Whether it was rabbit ears behind a reporter's head or someone dropping their pants, reporters have always had to do retakes. There would be no retake on this one.

The man kept coming, and the cameraman moved to get between the man and the reporter. She was slow to realize what the man was doing, but the cameraman wasn't. He turned his camera into a weapon, and before the picture was lost, the viewers got a dizzy ride as seen through the lens of a camera being swung like a club.

The camera hit the stumbling, reaching man across the face and sent him flying, but there was only a glimpse of the action before the square went totally blank.

Janice wondered why reporters had been so slow to understand they were in danger, she imagined each of them was thinking they had to get this story.

The first bottle of bourbon was long gone by the time she used the fast forward button on the remote. There was nothing new for a long time, and the anchor people were being replaced by office staff who had never been on camera before. Eventually, the cameraman in the studio was sitting on a stool in front of the camera.

He was explaining that no one else had come into the studio that day, and that the only reason he was there was because he couldn't leave. He did the best he could to get a camera view of the street outside, but he had been forced to move to a higher floor because those infected people had made it onto the floor below. He said he would stay on the air as long as he could, but he thought he might have to move to the roof soon. He even made a halfhearted joke and said it might be the decline of man, but at least he was on the rise.

There was a brief burst of snow on the screen, then the DVR recording resumed on another channel. Apparently whoever had recorded this broadcast had lost the last channel, searched for another while still recording, then stopped on this new one.

The news anchors were dressed in casual clothes and reading various articles they had gotten from the Internet. Apparently, it had stayed in operation longer than the TV stations could, and as long as there was a server connected somewhere, they could still get information.

According to the female anchor, most places that could still connect to the Internet could only get access to shopping websites because their servers were automated.

Janice was a little too far past drunk because this news made her cry, even though she hadn't cried through the tragic events. For some reason she found it incredibly sad that she could have logged onto her favorite sites and shopped to her heart's content longer than she had known. As a matter of fact, she thought it would be wild if she could find a computer and do some shopping now.

"Oh, darn. I don't know the address here."

She let out a giggle and a hiccup at the same time and then couldn't stop more of them from coming. She turned off the DVR and laid down on the bench seat where she had stretched out earlier.

Sometime during the night she woke up with a bad headache and remembered she had forgotten to eat before she started drinking and watching the news. She knew she was going to pay for it, but at least she had gotten the rest she knew she needed. She managed to make it to her bed and she figured she could finish watching the recordings while she ate breakfast in the morning. She wolfed down a pack of crackers before she shut off the lights, and she got her second night of deep sleep in a row.

The next morning was a repeat of the previous morning, but she had more black coffee than food. She stared at the bar across the room with the thought of putting an off limits sign on it.

"Just because I can drink any time I want to doesn't mean I should."

Her voice sounded raw to her own ears, and she wondered exactly how much crying she had done the day before. She reassured herself that it had been the bourbon, and this time she carried a cup of coffee over to the table and sat it down next to the evil, empty bottle from the night before.

She picked up where the news had ended and found she was watching something that wasn't being broadcast from a studio. It was an old man who said he was broadcasting from some kind of bunker out west. He said it used to be a Minuteman Missile silo, and that the government had turned it into a shelter for him.

"How nice of them," she said.

Janice didn't believe a word of it, but it was entertaining. The man claimed there were other shelters like his around the country, and that some people would survive the apocalypse because they had planned for it.

The man would have been right at home pushing a shopping cart full of aluminum cans. Wool cap, 1970s' style CPO coat, and gray beard, talking crazy, but entertaining.

The man said he had an internet connection that was letting him get some news out of England. There had been some skirmishes between the Royal Navy and the Russians. Apparently the Russians had tried to grab a little extra territory during the apocalypse, and enough ships had left port without the infected on board for England to put up a good defense of their homeland.

The man would have been doing himself a favor if he had proven he had the Internet by putting his computer in front of the camera, but he explained something about not being able to synchronize the computer screen with the TV camera.

"Yeah, right. Give me some more excuses."

Eventually the man said he was losing his Internet connections, but he wanted to share the last bit of news that he had, and ironically it made a believer out of her.

"Yesterday, I was able to log into the website where I do all of my shopping, so I ordered a few things. Before the connections started dropping this morning, the website said that my order had shipped."

The man started laughing, and once he got going, he couldn't stop. His last few seconds of broadcasting was an attempt to say he hoped he could get back on the air and let everyone know if his order was delivered, but he was pretty sure that he would get a message that his order was still on the way, but it was delayed.

Janice laughed with him. He might be bug-eyed and crazy, but he was entertaining. After he went off the air, the DVR continued to run. From time to time a bulletin would appear on the screen. She didn't know who was sending them, but she assumed they were from different government entities because they were generally tips about how to avoid getting infected. Eventually the messages stopped, and the recording on the DVR came to an end.

"Well, I guess I need to get a hobby."

Janice didn't think she could watch movies to pass the time, but she didn't rule it out. She sat and watched the snow on the TV screen for a few minutes before she remembered the security cameras. As if she had just realized her favorite show had already started, she jumped up and practically ran to the table where she had found the monitor.

The screen lit up with the same grid of views she had seen before, but the light was brighter outside, and she could make out more details. She leaned closer and tried her best to find something new. It was like going to the mailbox and finding nothing. Not even junk mail. She remembered many times that she had swept her hands around inside her mailbox even though she could see it was empty.

She mentally swept across the screens a second time, and she pictured herself doing nothing for the rest of her life except watching movies, cooking, cleaning, and checking the security screens. Of course there was sleeping and grooming, but this was getting more and more like prison.

Janice found herself getting emotionally upset about the prospect of living for years in a place where she had everything except something to alleviate the boredom, and that made her wonder about her new home. The more she thought about it, the more she felt like there was something odd about it.

"Why didn't someone come here after the apocalypse began? If we had known about this place, we would have."

She said it out loud, and hearing her own voice again made her understand what was really bothering her. This was like finding the winning lottery ticket when you had never played the lottery in your life. The odds of winning were already astronomical, but winning by finding the ticket would be somewhere around impossible.

The answer came to her as a list. Someone tried to come here and didn't make it. Someone came here already and died afterward. She thought about the rifles and the odd streaks that were most likely blood. Someone came here and left. Someone came here and is still here.

That last item on the list made her get goosebumps, and she turned to see if someone was behind her. All she could imagine was that there were cameras just like the ones she had been using every time she checked the computer monitor. She faced it again, this time searching the views for signs of life. There were thirty little TV screens arranged in neat rows, but nothing was moving on any of them.

"That's a lot of cameras," she said. "What am I missing?"

Her eyes wandered around the room, and she saw the one thing she had come to ignore wherever she saw it. There was a telephone in the kitchen on the wall, but there weren't any in the rooms, and there wasn't another one in the big commons area. That meant it was for internal communications only.

"Communications to where?"

She felt dense when it came to her, and she couldn't help wondering if David would have figured it out first.

"This place must have a control room somewhere, but it isn't one of the views on that screen."

Janice was on her feet without even thinking about it, and she didn't know what to expect when she put the phone to her ear. The dial tone hummed just like any she had heard in her life before cell phones came along. It was amazing how an entire generation had never used telephones with a dial on it, but everyone still used the same terminology.

"Dial the number still meant to call someone even when the dial was gone, so what's the first thing I hear on this phone? A dial tone."

The phone didn't have any buttons, and it certainly didn't have a dial, so she did what people used to do when wall phones were high-tech. She tapped the little thing in the middle of the phone cradle that went up and down as she tapped.

The dial tone disappeared, and on the other end of the line, there was a ring tone. Janice listened to it like she had never heard ringing before, and she held her breath as she waited for someone to answer.

Disappointment wasn't the right word to describe how she felt when she finally let out her breath. It was worse than all those times right after the infection started. She would see a phone, snatch it from its cradle and listen to the silence on the other end. If she got a dial tone she would frantically dial her parents' number and listen to the fast paced beeping sound that came through the phone. At first she would get those automated messages that said, "I'm sorry, but your call cannot be completed at this time. Please try again later." She had broken a lot of phones.

Cell phones were almost as bad because she left voicemail messages for almost a month, until she finally got a message that said the voicemail box was full. Of course it was. She had filled it.

She knew while she was waiting for someone to answer the phone that she was actually thinking she would finally be able to dial her parents again, and this time they would answer.

Janice became acutely aware that she was regressing. David had talked with her about how she had a habit of going back to something that had happened and start going through all of the "what if" scenarios.

"What if we had flown home a day earlier?"

"What if we had waited to go on our honeymoon?"

"What if we had brought my parents along?"

"What if they were safe in some Army base, and they were worried about us?"

In a moment of total frustration, David had screamed, "What if they're dead?"

He felt bad about it, but she knew it was the truth.

"I'm going to go crazy in here," she said as she slammed the phone down in its cradle.

Somehow she found herself back over at the bar again. She was just about to pour another glass of bourbon when it occurred to her that she should ration everything because she couldn't exactly rely on the resupply ship.

The brown liquor was in her glass without much conscious thought because she had a flash of inspiration. She carried her glass back over to the computer monitor and leaned in toward the little TV screens. She found the one she was searching for and used the mouse to enlarge that one screen.

The ship that was resting against the side of the oil rig was a container ship, and the reason David had steered their boat on a course to intercept it was because there could be food in the containers. He had shouted to her over the roar of their engines that there could be as many as ten thousand containers stacked on the ship, and one of them had to have food.

On her screen she could see the place where the rat had attacked the infected dead that had been a member of the crew. Despite the voracious way the rat had attacked the infected, and even despite the fact they had killed David, Janice felt like there had to be a way to get onto the ship and avoid the rats or at least defend herself against them.

"The rats would go to the deepest, darkest parts of the ship. If I could stay on the main deck and open the containers, I could find supplies without attracting their attention."

She knew from what she had seen that it was going to be risky, but it was what David would have done. She also knew that she had plenty of time to sort out the details because she had so many supplies already. She could take her time and figure out how David would have done it. In the meantime, she could let her wounds heal, and she could watch the outside views to see if there was anything else to worry about.

Janice picked up a remote and aimed it at the TV. She thumbed through the menu of movies and settled on one that had been a favorite of hers before it came true. The main character woke up in a hospital in London to find an infection had wiped out most of the population. He hooked up with more survivors and managed to stay one step ahead of the infected until they ran into some soldiers that had gone rogue.

Janice hit the stop button and found a sitcom that included the entire series. She pressed the play button for the first episode and went to the kitchen to make some lunch.

"I hate reality TV," she mumbled.

******

There was something to be said for binge watching a TV series, even if she had seen them before. The familiarity of the actors was comforting. They were friendly faces of people who had been there for her when times were good, and now they were here for her when times were bad. For hours on end she could pretend that everything was fine outside her windowless world. It was something David would have criticized, but Janice told herself she had to heal, and what did it matter if she chose to mentally escape while she healed. At least it was a way of passing the time until she was better.

And she did get better. As the days passed, she went about her routines anticipating the hours she would get to spend in front of the TV.

She cut her stitches out when the skin around the thread began to turn a healthy color, and the scab covering the wound became dry and fell off. She didn't even notice that she didn't have to concentrate on left and right movements as she watched the threads pull free in a mirror. She would cut with the scissors and then switch to tweezers to tug on the loose ends. Before she knew it, she was examining a ragged but healed scar. She moved from the wound on her arm to her hand without hesitating.

Now that she was free to move without further damage to her arm, she began exercising. She would have loved some gym equipment, but the men who had stayed here probably got enough exercise out on the rig. She settled for jogging to build up stamina, and it wasn't hard to find makeshift weights. Once she was sure that she wouldn't reopen the healed wounds, she started doing pushups. The way she figured it, she had better build up her upper body strength for when she would tackle the container ship.

Adding exercise to her daily routine made the days go by faster, and during the entire time she never once saw movement on any of the outside cameras. She watched during the day because there was more light, and she had learned by studying the views at different times of day where the sun was. Once she had that figured out, she was able to put together a puzzle in her mind that resembled the oil rig. She felt like she could visualize where she was in relation to the camera views.

She only watched them at night to try to detect whether or not the rats had returned. She felt like sooner or later she would have to go outside to get a closer look at the ship so she could put together her plan to open the cargo containers.

Janice watched the camera views at places where rats might run past a light, and was relieved after so many nights without seeing a single furry body. Some of the views were darker than others, and she learned not to stare at any of them. If she stared long enough at any given spot, it would start to move. She also learned not to do it when she was tired or had too much to drink for the same reason.

That was why she knew it wasn't her imagination when she saw the movement. It wasn't out of the corner of her eyes, and it was deliberate. It stopped for a few moments and then moved out of range, only to reappear in the frame of another camera. It was also too big to be a rat.

Janice held her breath and watched the movement reflect light and then block it out. When it left the view of the camera, she checked the mental map she had created of the oil rig and turned her eyes to the exact camera view where the movement should appear next. It did.

She blinked her eyes and then shut them for just a moment. It was moving closer to her position in the crew quarters. She could tell by the length of the shadows she had seen in each camera view. She sucked in an involuntary gulp of air when she realized that the movement should be very near the last place she had seen David, and she didn't think before she moved.

She didn't remember crossing from the table to the door that had been sealed shut for so long that she couldn't say if it had been weeks or months. It was someone else who was unlocking the door without any thought about taking the rifle with her. It was someone else who went from the brightly lit safety of the crew quarters into the darkness outside.

There was a slight stumble on the steps that led down to the deck, but her legs were strong, and she only needed to hold out one hand to the railing to steady herself before she leaned down toward the next level below. She saw that she was in time to know she had been right. That she had seen the movement outside.

An old man was standing up from a crouched position and doing something with his hands. He had long hair and was slightly slumped at the shoulders, but it was too dark to see him clearly.

He was holding something and turning from side to side at the waist, and she couldn't understand it at first, but she finally figured out that he was trying to get more light onto whatever it was he was holding.

He eventually mumbled something in frustration and the bright beam of a flashlight lit up the area. At his feet was a scattered corpse wearing jeans and a shirt she recognized too well. The center of the light played across the man's hands, and she was close enough to see the thumb and forefinger of his left hand as it slid a drivers license from the wallet. David's wallet. David's drivers license.

She felt like she had been dreaming when she had run from the crew quarters to the railing of the deck. As she ran back for the safety of the bright light pouring from the door, she knew she wasn't dreaming. The infected dead don't go through wallets.

26 STOKES

Year Six of the Decline

The Cormorant limped into what used to be called New Orleans barely making way against the current, and the worst part was that they felt like they were blind and deaf. They couldn't make contact with Bus to see if he had made it to New Orleans ahead of them, they couldn't make contact with Maybank on the oil rig, and all they got was static when they tried to reach Fort Sumter. That would be inconvenient when it was time to go home, but the Chief had already decided they would send Bus back to get Captain Miller to send the helicopters.

The city was in worse condition than Charleston. The buildings were collapsing under the weight of the water that was soaking into walls and the green plants that covered everything. In most places the vines seemed to grow out of the water and straight to the rooftops.

We were all on deck watching in silence as we coasted into a port that would have been more at home somewhere on the Amazon River. All that was missing was the rain forest, but none of us would have been surprised to see natives watching us from the jungle.

We were being watched, but it wasn't by natives with face paint and spears. There were infected dead that had long ago given up their efforts to free themselves from the tangled foliage where docks used to be. As we approached, their arms extended toward us, and their groaning sounded more like swamp frogs than the dead. They wouldn't be a threat to us as long as we gave them room.

We were also being watched by a combination of predators. Eyes coasted through the water just above the surface as alligators positioned themselves at a safe distance from us, but not out of range if they decided we were more defenseless than we appeared to be. A few of them turned away from the new arrivals and returned to their previous attempts to reach the infected that were now reaching for us. Alligators were good climbers when they put their minds to it, and if they were hungry enough, they would eventually snack on the infected dead that were like low hanging fruit.

There were competitors for that food supply, though. Cassandra called out and pointed to a thick patch of jungle above several entangled infected, and we saw the way the vines drooped under the weight of something just passing through. The heavy vines sprung back up to where they had been as something big moved from a rooftop down to the docks.

"What is it?"

Jean was on the bow and could see the movement but not what was causing it.

Hampton said, "It's a big snake of some kind. Probably a boa constrictor, but if this was South America I'd guess anaconda."

No one was surprised when Colleen pointed out a second snake and then a third. She also pointed to the oversized crabs that were shuffling more easily toward their prey.

"I don't understand," said Sim. "Those infected should have been eaten a long time ago. I mean, there seems to be no shortage of things trying to eat them."

"There's a fresh supply," said Kathy. "Something caused more infected to come this way recently. It's possible that Bus landed somewhere near here, and the noise from that plane would have been like a dinner bell."

The Chief decided there were no safe places to dock, so he dropped the anchor and idled the engine. The air was so still that we could all hear him without the need for him to even raise his voice.

"We have some problems, people. We don't know where Bus landed, or even if he made it to New Orleans. We can't dock and search the area, that's obvious. So I need ideas, because I only have one."

For once the Chief wasn't telling us what the plan was, and it was unsettling. He saw that we were all at a loss for ideas, and I didn't doubt for a second that everyone was waiting to hear his one idea.

"You might as well tell us," I said.

"Everyone keep your eyes on the water and the surrounding area, but come in closer."

We gathered around the Chief in a loose circle between the machine guns mounted on the bow. Everyone kept rotating between him and the shore. I had to admit, if someone was watching us, we had to appear to be a formidable group.

We were surprised when the Chief said in a low voice that he wanted everyone to stay as natural as possible, because we were being watched by someone hiding in a building that wasn't completely buried by the jungle.

"Who would be crazy enough to get within a mile of this place on land?" asked Kathy.

The Chief did his best not to lose his temper when he said the name.

"Stokes."

"What makes you think it's him?" said Tom. We could see the anger rising in him, and the Chief had to stare him down.

"You aren't going to stop me from killing him," said Tom.

The Chief said cooly, "The only thing that will stop you is if I get to him first, but I'll try to wait for you. I spotted the Beaver before I dropped anchor."

It was impossible not to react, but if Stokes was watching from somewhere, he would expect us to be on guard and a bit jumpy.

The Chief kept talking as if he wasn't restraining the urge to aim all three 50 caliber machine guns at the window where he saw what had to be Stokes. It would have been satisfying to watch the big bullets chew up the bricks around the window, but something familiar was tugging at the Chief's mind.

"The Beaver is camouflaged in the back corner of the docks to our starboard. Bus wouldn't have hidden the plane after he landed. He must have cruised in to see if we were here ahead of him, and Stokes got the drop on him."

Tom was seething with anger.

"That jerk should have been strangled by one of those snakes by now."

I added, "Or bitten by a crab, an infected, or an alligator."

"Some people are just too mean to die," said the Chief. "Good people are dying because they stepped on a rusty nail. This guy will have to be put down by one of us, someone who knows how evil he is."

I stole a glance at the place where the Chief said the seaplane was hidden, and if he hadn't said it was there, I would never have spotted it. I could just make out the bright yellow of one wing.

"He has Bus," said Jean. Her voice shook as the words came out with a sob.

"Better that than dead."

The Chief said it so calmly that all of us felt like he knew Bus was alive. It was reassuring and nerve wracking at the same time.

"So, what's our next move?" asked Kathy.

"I hate to say it, but we have to wait for his next move. We can't rush him or blow him to pieces without risking Bus' life. By the time we got here, Stokes knew we were coming. He had time to hide the plane and make a plan, so all we can do is pretend like we're waiting for Bus to arrive."

Tom was furiously shaking his head at the Chief.

"Let's go back out where he can't see us. We can make our landing somewhere safe and then come back in behind him."

"Stokes would kill Bus as soon as we sailed out of sight. This guy has a plan, and if it doesn't work, he's got a backup plan. If we leave, he can kill Bus and leave."

Tom opened his mouth to argue, but Kathy put a hand on his chest and stopped him.

"Stokes is playing chess with the Chief. Which one would you put your money on?"

The Chief explained to all of us, if Stokes was watching, he was seeing exactly what he expected to see. A group of people who didn't know what to do next. That wasn't enough reason to kill Bus. The Chief was sure he was keeping Bus alive for a reason that suited his own needs. He said he wasn't sure why, but it felt familiar.

In the end, Tom reluctantly agreed that we had to let it play out. There were no guarantees, but they had to let Stokes feel like he was in control until they knew if Bus was safe. All we could do was settle in and wait for him to make his next move. We just hoped it was a move the Chief could live with.

******

Stokes was thrilled to see the Cormorant as it came into view. He couldn't tell that they were having engine trouble, and that was one piece of information Bus had managed to keep to himself, but he didn't hesitate to tell Stokes they were coming. Bus knew that was the only thing that would keep him and Iris alive. If Stokes knew his friends were coming, he at least would see the value in having them as hostages. He had been half right, and he hoped with his entire soul that Iris was still alive. He just didn't know.

When the Beaver had landed, Bus coasted into the port and began searching for the Cormorant. If the Chief had been able to maintain half speed, he would have been there already, and Bus wasn't even worried when he didn't see the familiar Coast Guard vessel because the port was so big and so overgrown. He also didn't see the small boat easing up behind him until the Beaver dipped slightly to the left. He turned his head and realized it had dipped under the weight of Stokes as he stepped onto the float.

"Permission to come aboard."

Stokes had a big, ugly grin, and the barrel of his Glock was only an inch from the window. The only thing Bus could do was show Stokes his hands, and Iris knew Bus would die if she tried to take her gun from its holster.

Iris didn't have to be told this man was Stokes. Even though the population was a small fraction of what it had been, Stokes had an air about him that made her know from instinct that this was the man that could kill children by burying them in the ground. He was everything the Chief hated in a man.

Stokes motioned with one hand toward a slip that had been cleared of the vines and debris that covered everything else in the harbor. The remains of a huge snake was being eaten by dozens of crabs. Bus didn't need it spelled out for him, but like any floatplane pilot, he hated to navigate into a slip. It almost always ended with a bent wing because there wasn't the same kind of control as with a boat.

The light seemed to diminish as the plane coasted into the narrow channel. Hidden under the thick vines were the hulls of the unfortunate that hadn't been able to escape at the beginning of the infection, and Bus expected to hear the grinding of metal as the floats glided within inches of the wreckage.

Stokes almost casually turned toward the tail of the plane and shot an alligator between the eyes. The sudden report of the gun in the stillness caused the jungle to come alive with movement. More alligators slid from the banks into the water but only to put distance between themselves and this newcomer. They could smell blood in the water and moved in a wide circle to investigate.

Bus was holding his breath as he let the plane begin to slew to port. Its momentum was carrying it to the back of the marina, but the same momentum was going to risk damage to his left wing. There were no breaks on a coasting vessel. He could only try to diminish forward speed as he made the turn.

Stokes grinned the entire time. He knew Bus wouldn't risk his only transportation out of this green and humid hell, and he knew he could shoot both hostages before Bus could try anything that stood a chance of working.

The tip of the right wing grazed the vines and caused the Beaver to rotate just when Bus thought they were going to bury the left wing and do serious damage. He saw a power pole in the middle of the green that would have ripped the wing from the plane.

The pivot to the right was perfectly timed, and the float on that side brushed gently against the dock. Cushioned by long abandoned bumper guards and fresh growth of plants, they came to a stop.

For a man of advancing years, the work of hacking down the jungle and covering the plane took its toll on Bus. Iris was younger, but she was old enough for it to leave her completely drained. Stokes told them they would get water only after they were done, and the humidity was so high that they were drenched in sweat almost as soon as they started working.

Stokes stood nearby and watched for the predators along the docks. Iris was worried about the crabs more than anything, but she had seen how quickly an alligator could take its prey when they came from the water. Fortunately, Stokes wasn't ready for them to die, and he shot another alligator before they were done hiding the plane.

The most frightening part was when he tied their hands behind their backs and then pulled moldy smelling burlap bags over their heads. He added short ropes as leashes around their necks and dragged them behind him for almost an hour. They could tell he was taking them through the heart of the overgrown jungle and then along a city street to a building with stairs. They were both sure they would feel at any moment the agonizing crush of teeth from an infected dead, and so much energy went into bracing themselves against the attack that they were exhausted when he finally pushed them to a floor.

Iris heard the familiar sound of blunt force and waited to hear if it was an infected dead or if it had been Bus. She had hit the skulls of enough infected to know the sound.

Stokes leaned in close to her head. She could feel his sweaty arm against hers.

"You and I are going somewhere. Your friend can stay here."

Iris was frantic.

"You can't leave him here alone. What if something finds him? He won't even be able to defend himself."

"Now isn't that sweet the way you're worried about him, but he won't come to for at least an hour. If something finds him, he won't feel a thing."

It was disgusting the way Stokes laughed. Even blinded by the burlap bag she could tell he was overjoyed. He pulled her to her feet by grabbing the rope that was looped around her neck and she gasped for air.

"Please don't do this. You don't have to do this."

"Shut up."

It was only two words, but the menace in his voice was unlike any she had ever heard in her life, and it was more than enough to make her bite back another sound. She couldn't remember the last time she had cried for any reason, but she didn't think she had ever cried from fear. She could feel the salty tears roll down her cheeks and into her mouth.

Stokes dragged her from wherever it was he had left Bus, and all she could think of was Bus blindly waking up to find himself being eaten by the infected. She fell on the stairs, and every part of her hurt as Stokes just picked her up and forced her to move.

She was much taller than him, but he was stronger. Iris only knew what Bus had told her about him, but it was enough to know he was dangerous, and if he didn't get his way, he would strike quickly and without warning.

They were outside again, and Stokes made her move faster than before. Whatever it was he had in mind, she didn't think his first choice was to kill her, or she would already be dead. The same thing applied to Bus, but if he was willing to leave him somewhere unprotected, his plan didn't require Bus to be alive, just being held hostage.

The rope around her neck was jerked from side to side, and at one point Stokes let go of the rope. His gravelly voice was over her left ear. She felt dirty every time he touched her even if it was just on her arm.

"Go ahead and run if you want to, but if you could see what I see right now, you would stand right where you are."

The truth was she was afraid to run, and she drew her elbows into her sides as if she could protect herself more. If she could see what was happening around them, she would have known how little it would help. The sounds of infected groans were everywhere, and Stokes was laughing as his machete whistled when he swung it.

Stokes was having more fun than even he could believe. They had almost reached his goal when he saw they were surrounded by infected, and although he was protecting his hostage from being bitten, he enjoyed the way they got close to her before he stopped them. He pushed her up against a wall and kept circling from side to side.

When it was finally quiet, Stokes pulled on her leash again and dragged her over a slippery pile of bodies.

"Watch your step," was all he said to help her.

Iris was terrified that she would fall on them and make contact with their mouths, and even her denim jeans made her legs feel unprotected. She stumbled behind him and heard as he opened a gate with rusty hinges. He pushed her roughly forward, and the gates were closed behind her. She imagined herself inside a cage even though she was still outside, and she wondered if she was in the cage alone. She tried to remember if New Orleans had a zoo.

"Where are we? Why are you putting me in a cage?"

For some reason Stokes thought that was funny, and he laughed as he pushed her forward again.

"Walk."

Iris walked straight ahead, but for some reason Stokes would correct her direction by a foot or so every few seconds. She was scared, but she was also smart enough to realize she was walking between things, and he was keeping her on a gravel path.

She was about to ask him where they were going again when he stepped up closer to her. She could feel his body getting close even though this time he wasn't touching her, and she could hear the crunch of the gravel under his feet. Light seemed to flare brightly behind her eyes. Then it was dark.

Iris woke up once, but the shooting pain on the back of her head made her roll onto her side and throw up. The smell made her heave a half dozen times until her stomach cramped. She tried, but she couldn't pull her knees up to her stomach to ease the cramps.

It was still totally dark, but she didn't feel the texture of the rough burlap bag against her face. She reached with one hand to the back of her head, and it came back damp. Iris instinctively looked at her fingers expecting to see blood, but she couldn't see her fingers at all. As the realization flooded over her, she threw up again and then passed out.

******

"I blew it," said the Chief. "I got it wrong."

After an hour of total silence on the Cormorant, the sound of his voice made everyone jump.

We had just been sitting and watching the jungle, thinking the whole time that Stokes would be doing the same. The Chief had instructed everyone to use binoculars to make Stokes think we were doing what we could to locate Bus. He said it would be natural for us to zero in on the window where he had seen Stokes, but it was probable that he had relocated after being spotted.

"Stokes meant for us to see him," yelled the Chief. He raised his voice as he climbed into the wheelhouse and raised the anchor. He was cursing the lack of power from the engines, but the last thing we needed was for him to ram the end of the dock.

We moved forward as several of us got ready with the bowlines, and the Chief cut the engine power to let us coast. We could all hear Tom yelling questions to the Chief. The Chief's only answer was that time was important. We needed to get there fast.

When we were close enough to make the jump from the deck, we saw that Stokes had left us a clear dock. All of the vines were chopped away from the area, and there was enough room for us near the Beaver. From where we had dropped anchor in the harbor the area was hidden from view. Stokes may have meant for us to see him, but he didn't want to make it too obvious.

"Handguns and machetes," yelled the Chief.

Tom was in the lead, and the Chief didn't even try to slow him down. It was easy to spot the path that had been cleared through the jungle straight toward the building where the Chief had seen Stokes. Kathy was right on his heels to give him as much cover as she could. Cassandra was almost on Kathy's back covering anything Kathy might miss.

The vines growing over the narrow streets had become so thick that it was almost a tunnel that led us to an iron gate that served as the entrance to a courtyard. The building had probably been one of the first permanent homes built in New Orleans, and it felt as old as it looked. Moss grew everywhere, and the path was slippery. Tom slid with all of his weight right into some kind of moving mess on the path and went down hard, but Kathy and Cassandra had time to throw on the brakes. They caught him by his arms and pulled him away from a snake that was making a meal out of an infected dead. Half of its body had already been swallowed feet first.

I had seen the infected eaten by sharks and alligators, and each time there had been that look of indifference on their faces. Even as they were being eaten, they wore detached expressions that said there was nothing left in their minds that told them what was happening. Tom's first instinct was to use his machete to end the miserable existence of the infected, but Kathy caught his arm in time.

"It will keep the snake busy."

Cassandra had passed them and found the door into the building. She took the stairs to the right three at a time and began yelling that Bus was there almost as soon as she reached the top.

We all had to know that Bus was alive and unhurt, so no one bothered to stay downstairs. We quickly filled the room where Cassandra was helping Bus to a sitting position by the window. He had a big red mat of dried blood on the right side of his head, and Jean examined it first. Bus was trying to say something, but she stopped him.

"Don't talk until I've had a chance to see how bad you're hurt."

She was using a small flashlight to see if his pupils were responding.

"You don't understand," he said. His throat was dry, and his voice was barely loud enough to hear.

Jean didn't want to hear it and tried to scold him, but Bus became determined to be heard. He put all of his will into three words.

"He has Iris."

We moved aside for the Chief. He had just reached the top of the stairs in time to hear Bus give us the bad news, and all of our eyes turned to him.

I could see the pain in Kathy and Jean's faces, but the cold anger on the Chief's face was something I would never forget.

Bus said in a weak voice, "He said to tell you something. He said find her if you can."

Even though it was obvious to all of us, the Chief added, "So he will have time to get away."

"Did he tell you anything that would help us find her?" asked Kathy.

Jean gave Bus a sip of water, and we could understand him better when he answered.

"He only said we would figure it out."

"What does that mean?" asked Tom.

He turned toward the Chief, and he could tell by the way the color drained from his face that the Chief knew where to find Iris.

"Is Bus okay to defend himself here?"

Jean immediately protested and said she should stay with him, but the Chief was already moving. He stopped on the stairs and told Jean that Iris may need her more than Bus.

We were all talking at once, but no one was listening to each other. Most of us were asking the Chief where we were going, and he was arguing with Jean about Bus. I could tell that the Chief didn't want to put his wildest fear into words, so I broke the stalemate for him.

"He buried her, didn't he?"

Everyone went silent at the same time.

"Where's the nearest cemetery? Who knows New Orleans well enough to lead the way?" I asked.

"Follow me," said the Chief.

Jean didn't have to ask Bus if he would be okay by himself. She knew what he would say. Not only did they need her for her medical skills, they needed every pair of eyes they had if it was going to be anything like finding the kids in the cemetery on James Island. Considering the differences between that cemetery and what they would find in New Orleans, it was going to be a nightmare.

There was plenty of daylight left, but they had no idea how long Iris had been buried. They also didn't know if Stokes had given her a way to breathe, or if she was injured before she was buried. If he hadn't at least given her an air tube, she was already dead.

Bus took a couple of guns from us along with extra ammunition and reassured us that he could take care of himself. We added water and some ration packs, and he waved impatiently for us to get going. I heard him whisper something to Jean, and she said something back.

When Jean caught up with me, I didn't ask, but she read my expression and knew that I was curious.

"He told me that Iris had traveled to Mud Island to find the Chief. She wanted to tell him she was tired of acting like she wasn't in love with him."

Both of us knew the Chief felt the same way about Iris, but it wasn't something he would have talked about. He was quick to tease me about such things, but the Chief was private about his own feelings. It was a double standard, but the Chief wasn't perfect, and if that was his biggest fault I was willing to let him have a free pass.

We caught up with the rest of the group before they reached the end of the street, and we were relieved to see how close we were to a cemetery. It was possible that he had chosen a different one, but we didn't have the luxury to start guessing which one to search when time was so critical. Besides, it was a good chance that someone living had been here recently, because there was a crowd of infected dead around the front gate, and the gate was standing open.

Several of the infected saw us at the same time that we saw them, and they filed out into the street. Everyone rushed toward them with their machetes held out in front, and it was only a matter of seconds before we were all inside the cemetery. We closed the gates behind us, but judging by the way the tall grass had been trampled inside, there would be plenty more of the infected wandering around where we couldn't see them.

Judging by the way we all faced the jungle that had overgrown thousands of gravesites, we were all thinking the same thing. We didn't know where to start.

In front of us were paths that stretched away in all directions. Some were completely covered in vines and green plants of every kind, but it was hard to tell which were actually paths, and which were only places where the infected had stumbled through, chasing something that had run from them.

The grass was over six feet high where it hadn't been trampled, and it was hard to walk more than a few feet without tripping on gravestones or vaults. The cemetery had been poorly maintained before the infection, and the neglect had turned it back over to nature quickly.

"This is worse than the swamps around Mud Island," I said. "Stokes let as many infected inside as he could so we wouldn't be able to search for Iris."

Cassandra was the one who seemed to attack the problem with the most focus. She went down on one knee and stared hard at the different paths through the grass. We spread out, instinctively thinking we needed to split up so we could cover more ground.

"Everyone freeze," she yelled.

Even the Chief stopped in his tracks. He was a born leader with good tracking skills, but right now he wasn't the most objective person in our group.

Cassandra swept her hand from left to right.

"Count the number of trails and judge how wide they are. Have they been used more than once over a period of time? Were they trails cut by someone who took steps or dragged their feet? Figure out which ones were used by Stokes by finding me a normal footprint."

The ground was soft, and even the gravel paths gave up their histories where gravel was pushed deeper into the ground because someone wearing boots had stepped on them with his weight instead of shuffling his feet.

We could see she was right as soon as we knew what to look for. There were twelve clear paths that led away from the gate. Six were gravel and had obviously been intended to be walked by visitors to the cemetery. Six were random, and the muddy spots gave a picture of the infected traveling together in groups.

Cassandra pointed at one path.

"He would have used the clearest path first because he wanted to lose himself in the middle of the cemetery as fast as possible. He may also have been carrying her, so his footprints would be deeper."

She turned to the Chief.

"I heard you say she was tall. Would you guess one hundred and twenty-five pounds?"

The Chief nodded, and Cassandra said, "Anyone see a footprint that could have been made by an aggressive male weighing over three hundred pounds?"

It was like telling us to find the path with the signs and arrows saying, "He went this way."

Our eyes scanned the ground, and it was only seconds before Sim called out, "I've got a winner."

"Everyone stand perfectly still," said Cassandra. "Watch for infected while I check it. We don't want to be thrown off because someone stepped on his footprints."

She circled Sim and focused on the spot where he pointed at a footprint. She noted which way the toe of the boot was facing and which part of the print was deeper. Then she lifted her head to see further down the path.

"Jean and Colleen, you have the smallest feet, so you follow me and give me cover. The guys should follow the other paths and eliminate the infected that are still inside the cemetery, and one last thing. He planned this. That means he was here before and picked a place to bury her. It might be something symbolic or just something that caught his eye, but don't rule out unique gravestones or vaults."

I had to admit, Cassandra had galvanized the group. We were a mob when we entered the cemetery. Now I felt like we were part of a rescue squad.

We split up into the groups as she dictated and disappeared into the rows of gravestones, vaults, and jungle. It wasn't long before I heard my friends making contact. The familiar sounds of machetes hitting their targets and warnings being called out seemed to go on for a long time, but they became more distant from each other as we continued away from our starting point.

I ran into Tom and the Chief as our paths converged into one, and we followed it, realizing that it had to be a group of infected that was being drawn to the sounds made by Cassandra, Jean, and Colleen. We came up behind them just as the ladies had turned to face them.

"This is going to take forever," said Tom.

He tried to keep the anger out of his voice but it sounded almost as if he was accusing Cassandra of having a bad plan. She was unfazed.

He continued, "I've already opened four vaults that had broken locks on them, and he had planted infected dead inside them. How will we know if she's in a vault or a grave?"

"Here's where he doubled back and went that way."

She pointed toward the coast, and we could see a path that took a shortcut to the wall of the cemetery. The Chief didn't hesitate. He charged down the path and jumped high enough to grip the top and pull himself up onto the wall. He got his balance and faced back our way.

He cupped his hands to his face and yelled, "There was a boat tied up over here, and there's a clearing behind you."

He pointed past us, and we followed his hand. There was another path that crossed ours, and the white gravel of a visitor path had muddy footprints on top of the places that had been dragged by the infected.

"It's worth a shot," said Cassandra.

We could see that someone had camped in the clearing, and our first impression was that Stokes wouldn't have been that obvious, but Kathy pointed out Stokes had already shown us he liked to be obvious when he let the Chief spot him in the window. He had also existed under our noses for years by never leaving Fort Johnson.

Our whole group had reached the clearing, and everyone was reading the names on gravestones and vaults. Knowing that Stokes would be drawn to irony, we were sure we would see something familiar, but nothing was ringing a bell. We shouted out the names as we read them to see if anyone had a reaction.

When Jean yelled that she had one named "Stokes" we converged on the spot and started digging, but the ground hadn't been recently disturbed on the grave.

"I was sure that would be it," said Jean.

Our adrenaline had shot through the roof at first, but now we were drained as it wore off. The Chief leaned on the Stokes gravestone from behind and tilted his head to one side.

I turned in the direction he was facing. About twenty yards away was a worn marble statue of a tall, slender, angel. She had her left arm extended with the palm facing upward and the fingers pointed straight at the Chief... or straight at the headstone he was leaning on. The right arm was draped gracefully along her right side with her hand pointing downward. She wasn't exactly pointing, but that's how Stokes would have seen it.

The Chief took the shortest path to get there, and it didn't escape my attention that he left deep footprints right down the middle of the grave in front of him.

27 BRIDGE

Year Three of the Decline

Janice began keeping track of time on the morning after she had learned she wasn't alone on the oil rig. Each day she would go to the security cameras before doing anything else. She studied each frame, each detail, and even made precise notes of the position of everything in the picture. If anything moved, she wanted to know it had.

She also wanted to make her supplies last as long as she could, and one year later she was finally able to see the back wall of the supply room. She estimated that she would have to go out in search of food in another month.

There had been endless nights of doubt. Times when she played out every possibility in her own mind. She wondered if she was being watched the way she was watching the security monitor. She wondered why she wasn't seeing the old man again. Most of all, she was wondering why the rats hadn't come back.

Janice imagined herself going over to the ship and finding supplies in the top row of containers, but she also imagined opening a container door only to find the contents infested by an entire year of rat breeding cycles. But if that was possible, she couldn't imagine why they weren't also climbing onto the oil rig.

She remembered the way electricity had arced across the metal framework, and rats had fallen to the water with their fur sending up smoke and steam as the bodies disappeared below the surface. She thought about how they had been electrocuted and not the old man. She always came back to the question of why the rats were on the ship but not on the oil rig, and where the old man had gone.

That part had been easy to explain away. She decided that he had searched the oil rig for food, and finding none he had gone onto the ship where the rats had gotten him. Imagining the rats killing him didn't help, because it still didn't explain why the rats hadn't come back, and if he had searched the entire oil rig, he would have come knocking on the door of the crew quarters. Too many questions…no answers. The only thing she knew for sure was that she was running out of supplies.

She came to the conclusion that she at least needed to venture outside. After a year of wind and storms, she was sure that there would be nothing left to show David had died on the catwalk below. She would find it difficult to walk past the spot, but it would be worse if he was still there. She decided that she would accomplish two things when she went out the first time.

Before she could cross over to the ship, she had to find the best location. It had to be a place that allowed her to go both ways, and she had to be able to carry back supplies. So, it wouldn't help to climb out above the ship and drop down to the tops of the containers.

The second thing she had to do was locate the cameras that had been her eyes to the outside world. She wanted to find at least one and try to reorient it so that it was aimed toward the place where she would cross to the ship. If she could watch the spot for a couple of days, she would know if it was safe. If she could find two cameras, she would feel even better.

Once the decision was made, she knew there was no reason to put it off. There were no other options. After checking the security cameras, she got dressed to go outside.

The blue jumpsuit was her best choice. The denim was tough enough for her to be comfortable and safer from the bites of the infected or rats. She hadn't seen a single infected on the rig, but she knew there was always a chance that someone from the ship had been infected and found their way onto the oil rig. They were just stuck in an area where she didn't have a camera view.

There were thick gloves in a dresser drawer, and she used duct tape from a repair locker to cover the gap between the gloves and the sleeves. If there were rats, she was going to make it hard for them to bite her.

Janice tucked a long knife from the kitchen into her belt and held the rifle in front of her as she slowly opened the door and breathed in the outside air for the first time in a year. She was almost stunned by how clear and fresh it smelled. She had forgotten it could be like that, and it made her remember standing on the beach on her honeymoon. A wave of sadness rushed over her, and if she had seen the old man or anyone else out on the deck, she probably would have shot them.

After a few tentative steps, she remembered that she couldn't leave the door open. She didn't have a key, so she couldn't lock it, but she could picture herself hunting down rats if she left it open while she was gone.

Her legs seemed to have a will of their own, and she walked with no more hesitation over to the railing where she could look down at the spot where David had died. She had been right. The weather had scrubbed away any evidence of his death, and it was easier for her to walk by the spot than she had expected. It was like David had never been there. Like he had never happened. Now she had to find the best place to cross over to the ship and change the cameras.

The ship was exactly where she had last seen it. She guessed as much given the lack of change in the camera views. The containers on the top row had slid and rolled like the cars of a railroad train when it jumped the tracks. Some had turned to point directly at the oil rig before beginning to slide, and she was shocked to see several rested with one end on the oil rig catwalks and the other ends on top of the stacks of containers.

"It's practically a damned bridge," she said out loud.

It was too good to be true in some ways because it meant the old man had been able to search for supplies through the upper containers. She could see that the twisting and turning when the ship had collided with the oil rig made some of the doors literally pop open, and anything inside would have been exposed to the elements for a year. She hoped those were the containers full of TV sets.

She considered the possibility that other survivors might have also pillaged the containers by now, but even though she had seen no sign of anyone else on the security cameras, she doubted anyone else had reached the rig. From where she was standing, she could see no sign of the mysterious handholds that had been on the towers.

Satisfied with the first results of her sightseeing trip, Janice moved on to the second task. Finding cameras only meant finding the spots she had studied for a year. She climbed from one catwalk to the next, always keeping her eyes at a down angle. She reasoned that the best approach was to go up and around until she saw a spot she recognized below her.

Her stomach did a flip when she saw something that matched her security monitor frame perfectly. Since there were thirty frames, she had called this one number twenty-four. A fire extinguisher was on a beam above a catwalk where it turned, and she was standing at exactly the right angle to it. She could hardly believe her luck when she turned at the waist and found the camera just above her head.

It was mounted on an adjustable ball that was tightened inside a socket. It was difficult to turn, but she was eventually able to loosen it and aim it in its new direction. It was a guess, but she tightened it down when she was fairly sure it was aimed at the containers forming her bridge.

Now that she had number twenty-four, she felt like she had a frame of reference for the others, and she found twenty-three less than five minutes later. As a bonus, she found twenty-two. If she was off a little with her aim, she could always come back and realign them, but she only really needed one to be exact.

She celebrated that night with a movie about a man who was stranded on a desert island who finally figured out how to get a boat past the reefs. She wasn't trying to escape. She only wanted to stay alive long enough for someone to fix things on the mainland. She would know when they had done that when people showed up or if the news came on the TV one day. Until then, she at least felt like she was doing something about it.

******

Maybank stopped shaving three months after the lady in the crew quarters had come outside and seen him. He was talking to himself nonstop by six months when he quit showering.

He was having a daily debate with himself about the woman. She shouldn't be alive. He had seen the blood, and he knew she had been bitten by the rats. That had been a death sentence before, and if she was alive it could only mean one thing. She was a carrier.

Still, he had her picture, and knowing that the woman in that picture was so close but yet so far from his reach made him willing to accept that anything was possible. He didn't know that had been a year ago, because he lost touch with reality as easily as he lost track of time.

He was making rounds to check on the systems that operated his shelter, but he had stopped recording the data from the instruments. They would last the rest of his life, and as far as he was concerned that would be long enough.

Maybank had turned the radio off after he received an SOS from someone. He didn't tell them where he was even though the man had pleaded for help. He wouldn't stay safe in his shelter if he told everyone where it was. Still, he fantasized about the woman in the crew quarters and would have taken her into his confidence if she would just show herself.

He debated just walking up to the door of the crew quarters and knocking. He could explain everything, she would be happy to know the truth, and she would welcome him into her arms as her hero.

That was how he saw it half of the time. The rest of the times he knocked on the door, she answered with the rifle in her hands, and she shot him as soon as he told her the truth.

Both scenarios played out in his mind so many times that he didn't know which one was more likely.

He dismantled the radio after the next SOS. It made him angry that the people on the radio didn't understand why he wouldn't help them, but he also felt compelled to answer. Without the radio he didn't have to listen to their pleas. They would just have to understand that he wasn't going to make Janet share with them.

It had been a long time since he had sat for hours on end watching the security cameras. The last of the motion sensors to go was the one facing the container ship. There had been no motion on it for so long that he had assumed it wasn't working, but when it finally sounded an alarm, it startled him so much that he had overreacted. He broke the camera and the alarm with a fire ax.

Maybank missed Janice's excursion out on the oil rig until the last camera moved. He was passing through the operation center and saw the view changing as the camera was aimed at the containers laying across the gap between the oil rig and the ship. Then he saw that two others had also been moved.

At first it didn't occur to him that she had anything to do with the cameras moving. It couldn't be a coincidence that they were all pointing at the same thing, but they were nowhere near the crew quarters.

He leaned in close to the monitor as if he would be able to see what was causing this phenomenon when a face filled the screen. Maybank fell over backward across a rolling chair that did exactly what it was meant to do. He wasn't able to get back in front of the screen until the face was gone. Even then he didn't understand that Janice had moved in front of each camera when she had tightened them into place.

Maybank had always known where each camera was located, and he knew what could be seen by watching them. He could have turned off the feed that went to the crew quarters a long time ago, but he simply chose to avoid those catwalks. He didn't have a reason for leaving them on except that it felt like it would be mean to turn them off.

Maybank got up in the middle of the night after trying unsuccessfully to sleep. He finally figured out what he had to do. He didn't feel like he was being mean as he flipped the switch that disconnected the feed to the crew quarters. On the contrary, he felt like he was doing her a favor. The only reason he could think of that she was aiming cameras at that particular spot was because she was planning to do something stupid.

"She's going to go over to the ship, and I need to stop her. I need to tell her about the shelter so she can stay here and be safe."

If Maybank had been standing in front of a mirror when he decided to tell her, he might have realized how she would take that information.

******

Janice was satisfied with her first foray into the maze of metal and cables. She had to give herself some credit for finding the cameras and adjusting them. She had made a plan and followed it. Even a year after David's death, she was thinking of how proud he would be to know she had succeeded.

She grabbed a celebration drink over at the bar and went to the monitor. The three cameras were all almost exactly where she wanted them. From what she could tell, she didn't leave any blind spots. She could leave the crew quarters and approach the container bridge without worrying that there would be something or someone waiting for her. The only thing left to do was decide when to go, and just like making the decision to go locate the cameras, there was no reason to delay. She originally planned to watch the security cameras for a few days, but that was just an excuse to put it off. It would be nice to have the cameras so she could check the bridge every day before going, but she had seen all she needed to see. The weather was showing signs of making it an unpleasant trip, but the rain wouldn't kill her unless the container became slippery.

Just for this one night, she doubled her rations in her evening meal, and she indulged in one more cocktail than she had allowed herself for some time. The extra food was for the energy she needed. The extra cocktail was because she had an excuse to drink it. She was excited and nervous at the same time, but kept to her evening routine by watching a movie before going to bed.

Janice didn't think she would be able to sleep, but she did. When her alarm went off, she didn't hit the snooze button. She stayed with her morning routine just like the night before, and before she knew it she was at the door with her hand on the knob. The morning coffee had tasted better than ever, and breakfast had been a way of congratulating herself for taking matters into her own hands. She knew she might not even find supplies on her first trip over, but at least she was getting it done.

As Janice opened the door, she had that nagging feeling that she was forgetting something. She thought it was like when she would leave home and remember the keys were in the kitchen. One glance back around the room was all it took for her to remember she forgot to check the cameras, but to do it now would mean sitting everything down and lifting it all again. She decided she could live without it just this once.

Now that she knew exactly where to go, it didn't take long to reach the bridge. The only thing that slowed her down was the heavy bag of kitchen utensils and items in the repair locker that she thought she might need to open a container. She already decided she would only have to carry back the items that had proven themselves to be useless as tools.

The container was a dirty yellow color with plenty of stains running down the sides. It had slid from the top row of containers and turned toward the web of catwalks, wedging itself neatly between two steel beams. The end on the catwalks would remain in place forever as long as the ship stayed where it was.

At the moment, the other end, the end that still rested on top of the stacked containers, was gently moving up and down as waves rolled past the ship. Each time it changed directions there was an eerie sound of metal rubbing against metal, and she saw that one corner of the container had a post connecting it to the container below it. The posts at the other corners had all snapped from the force of the ship hitting the oil rig. The storm had arrived, but it was just an inconvenience. The rain was drumming on the metal container and running off onto the catwalk as the water followed a seam like it was a gutter.

The heavy container had crushed the handrails on one side of the catwalk, and there was just enough room at her end to open its doors. Janice stood before the door and had to laugh at the possibility that the first container would have anything useful inside. She had a better chance of winning the lottery twice.

There was no reason at all to believe there were any infected dead inside the container, so she went to work on the lock. When it broke under the pressure she applied with the handle of a large pipe wrench, she silently hoped they were all that easy, and she was looking forward to the ones that had already popped open. She swung the door open wide and tried not to be disappointed by the contents. Her best guess was that the container was being delivered to a manufacturer of clothing. She didn't know if the ship was going to or from the US, and she didn't care as long as it had something on it she needed.

"Well, if I ever take up sewing my own clothes, I won't have far to go."

Janice closed the doors and stepped back to get a good look at the top of the container. She didn't know what she was looking for, but if she was honest with herself, she would admit that she was stalling. Deep down she knew it and shook her head as if it would help to clear it.

She spotted hand and footholds and easily climbed the door. Getting to the top wasn't a problem, but when she stood up straight, the forty foot container might as well have been as long as a football field because of the way the other end was going up and down. What translated to a small amount of motion on her end appeared to be violent chaos at the other end, and the eight foot wide container looked like the four inch wide balance beam at the Olympics.

Janice didn't know yet that it would get worse as she got closer to the other end. That was when she would start to feel the strain in her legs as the container rose to push against her muscles as she put weight on them, and then suddenly she would feel like gravity was gone as the container dropped below her.

She started walking with her arms out to her sides for balance, but she finished the trip by crawling on her hands and knees, stopping every time the container changed direction. She tried not to think about what it would be like when she found something that had to be carried back to the crew quarters, but when she finally admitted it would be too hard, she decided it wasn't a total loss. She would carry back what she could and wait for calm weather to carry the heavy stuff.

Her feet dangled over the edge of the container, and she felt like she would never stop learning about the laws of physics as she watched the container below hers.

"No wonder people get seasick. One moment it looks like I'm going up and down, and the next moment it looks like the other container is doing all the moving."

Instead of dropping over the edge, she climbed down as if she was descending from Mount Everest. She reached with her foot for the roof of the next container like she had just learned to walk, and she let go of her handholds so fast that she wound up on her butt.

"I don't know if that's an Olympic sport, but I don't think I made the team."

She was relieved to find there was less movement now that she was on top of the containers, but it wasn't until she got her bearings that she discovered she was standing at an angle. She was on top of the stack that had leaned toward the oil rig on the day the ship had rammed into it.

"Relax, dimwit. It's been leaning for a year, and this isn't the worst weather we've had."

She regretted saying it when she saw the gap between the stack that was leaning and the stack next to it. It was too far to jump. The only way across was by climbing the two containers that had tried to follow the first one. They weren't going up and down like an elevator, but there was going to be a lot of climbing in her future.

Janice had enough time on her hands to be methodical in her search, so she decided to search each container from the top down. That meant hanging over the front of the containers as she worked her way down, and she would prefer to do that with a safety line. Fortunately, she had one in her handy bag of tricks she had lugged with her.

She didn't know if there was a special way that container ships were loaded, but if she had to do it, she would take weight into consideration. The heaviest would be on the bottom. That wasn't much help when it came to guessing what was in each one. If she could logically guess which ones contained food, she would have been a valuable person at any port in the world.

"Stop playing mind games and start searching," she said out loud.

Even though she had made progress, she was still stalling, and it wasn't because she was going to be playing on a steel wall all day. It was because she was afraid she wouldn't find anything. If she went home at the end of the day empty handed, she could tell herself there were still thousands of containers to check, but the question would be whether or not she had to check thousands before she found food.

She took a deep breath, gave herself a mental kick in the rear end, and went to work on the lock of container number two. Her theory about lighter containers being on top was supported by the contents. She doubted she would need wicker furniture in the crew quarters, but she told herself she might feel differently in ten years.

After closing the door, Janice quickly moved to the next container that had tried to follow the first one across to the rig. She moved even faster to close the door after she saw more boring contents. Janice climbed the door of container number three faster than the first one and hurried to the other end. She hooked her safety line to the frame and dropped over in front of the door of the first container that was at the top of the stack.

It wasn't really hard to get enough leverage to break the lock. It just took time, and when she opened that door, all she could think was that it was going to be a long day.

******

Maybank didn't see Janice climb the container and cross to the ship. If he had, he doubted he could have stopped himself from going after her. Even though he hadn't seen rats in a long time, he didn't doubt that they were still the dominant species on the ship.

It took almost an hour for him to figure out what was different about the container that rested on the catwalk. Even though it had been there for over a year, he never had the slightest bit of curiosity about its contents. The cameras had only been aimed at it for one day, and he hadn't studied the image closely. When he realized the lock was only hanging in place, he knew that someone had opened the container.

His heart skipped a beat when her head appeared above the other end of the container, and she climbed into full view. The storm had passed, so there was far less motion than before. She had also become more at ease and confident as she climbed up and down the mountain of containers. She made it look easier now as she hurried across the bridge and smoothly descended the door onto the catwalk.

He hadn't really thought about what he would do if he saw her, but he felt almost frozen in his chair as she disappeared from the view of the camera. He switched to another view and saw how quickly she had reached the door of the crew quarters. He was especially impressed that she could move so quickly with a backpack that was bulging at the seams.

******

The day had felt like she was breaking even, or as David used to say when a sporting event ended in a tie, it was like kissing your sister. It wasn't a total loss because she was searching the containers instead of just thinking about doing it. She was happy with herself for working up the nerve to dangle almost a hundred feet above the deck while she forced open the locks, but she felt like she needed a win, not a tie.

The one container that held food was going to take a long time to unload, but there was no reason to bring all of it to the crew quarters before she found a better shipment. When she dangled in front of the open door she thought she had hit the jackpot.

The cardboard boxes were definitely canned food, but she wondered how many cans of corn she could eat before it started to kill her. She made a mental note that the answer was likely to be when she felt like shooting herself because all she had to eat was canned corn. She brought back a backpack full, and when she added it to her existing supplies it felt like a small win. At least she wouldn't starve….yet, and she could bring some back on days when she didn't have anything else to carry. She went to bed feeling like she had gotten some much needed exercise, but she also had a reason to get out of bed in the morning.

The next day started the same, but her muscles ached. She checked the security cameras as she was about to leave, and she was stunned by the snow that filled every little screen. All thirty were the same, and since she had not seen her adjustments the day before, she thought it was possible that she had broken them.

Janice didn't know what it meant, and she wondered if she would be safe crossing to the ship again. She wondered if someone didn't want her to see what was waiting for her where the cargo containers formed her bridge. She unslung her rifle and made sure a round was in the chamber. She flipped the safety off and decided she would meet this development head on. If she had to shoot someone, she would.

Without the stormy weather of the previous day, she made the trip across much easier and felt almost cheerful by the time she started climbing down the wall of canisters. There had been no surprises waiting for her at the bridge, and she decided to just keep her eyes and ears open.

The containers were stacked twelve high, and where they hadn't slid apart on top, she saw there were poles, or corner posts, that held them in place. She was happy to learn they wouldn't fall from where they were.

After finishing an entire column of containers she had found her TV sets, computers, and household appliances. She used a Sharpie to write a note on the door and doubted she would ever need to open them again.

She moved to the next container in line and started the process over again. It only took a minute to open it because she had better leverage standing on the main deck. That was when it dawned on her where she was. She stopped what she was doing and listened. It was quiet with the exception of the waves lapping against the sides of the ship and the occasional groan of stressed metal.

Janice decided it was a good time to take a break and find out what was happening around her. She followed the deck across the bow to the starboard side and peered around the corner. That was where the cameras had shown large rats and a few crew members that had become infected dead.

The deck was totally clear without any debris. She thought that this was probably one of the few places where nature kept it neat and clean instead of crumbling into crowded streets, and she had a wave of emotion she hadn't experienced in a long time.

Home…what had happened to it? Her parents, family, friends were all dead. She didn't have the slightest amount of hope that any had survived. If they had, they would be competing with other survivors for dwindling resources and defending themselves from the infected at the same time. She had lived in the lap of luxury compared to them.

A hundred feet above the deck was her bridge crossing to the oil rig, and for the first time since arriving over a year ago, she was getting a close look at the massive towers that supported the rig. She could see the indentations where the handholds had formed a ladder. They were gone now, and she doubted she would ever be able to explain them.

The need to explore outweighed her search for supplies long enough for her to make the long walk along the rows of containers, and as she got a closer look, questions about how the containers were stacked and kept in place were answered. She saw that she would be able to reach the doors of almost every container, but she more importantly learned that the ships were most likely loaded based upon where they were going next. Food could be on the top or the bottom.

Janice found herself at the bottom of the ship's superstructure, facing an open doorway. It towered above her, and she wondered if any of the crew had escaped to the living spaces. She couldn't see anything except blackness inside the door a few feet in front of her, and when she leaned inside the opening to let her eyes adjust to the dark, she could see it was a steep set of stairs that went up and down. If it was dark at the door, it was pitch black above and below.

She knew they had battled rats and the infected, but if she had lived so well in a glorified mobile home, she considered it at least possible that there were people surviving in the safest parts of the ship. If they were watertight in some sections, maybe they had been able to seal themselves inside.

She reached into her backpack and pulled out a flashlight, and before she could change her mind, she stepped through the door. It felt like an empty tomb, but as far as she knew, tombs were silent. The hollow metal chambers above and below echoed the slightest sounds, and somewhere in the distance was the clang of metal against metal.

Janice didn't have the slightest idea of where anything would be located on the ship, but she guessed that the bridge was at the highest level. She had more reasons to choose up than down, so she climbed the stairs.

Maybank was horrified to see her go through the door. He had been easily able to follow her and remain undetected. He didn't have a plan for what he would do when he revealed himself to her, and when he saw the rifle slung across her back, he realized he'd better think of something that would keep him from getting shot as soon as she saw him.

He was watching from above on the top row of the containers closest to the superstructure, and when she disappeared into the ship, he panicked.

Like most people his age, he still believed himself to be far more athletic than he was. That included his ability to do things quickly. In his youth he was strong enough to free climb, so repelling had never been a challenge. He took pride in being a healthy nerd, and being a member of a group with people like Titus Rush made him act like he could do anything.

He was wrong. He lost control of his ropes and slammed into the deck. The only thing that saved his life was the fact that he had kept his legs under him, but that was bad news for his legs. Both hurt bad enough to be broken, but there were no bones protruding through the skin, so he silently begged that they were only bruised.

Maybank didn't know how much time had passed when he finally pulled himself to a standing position. The fact that he could put his weight on his legs was good news, but walking was incredibly painful. He took a few tentative steps and felt like something moved in the wrong direction in his left leg. His right leg did better, but the knee was already beginning to swell.

He pushed himself away from the face of the container where he had landed and let his momentum carry him across to the open door of the superstructure. The bright light outside made him feel blind, but he could hear well enough, and there were footsteps on the metal stairs above him. It sounded like she was coming down.

He couldn't let her see him the first time like this. If she saw him limping as much as he was, she would think he was infected and shoot him even though he would be speaking. Maybank did the only thing he could do to hide. He forced himself to enter the darkness and go down the stairs. It was like walking into black ink.

Janice had come to a watertight door that she couldn't open. It frustrated her to make it this far and be stopped by a door, so she decided to come back with anything she could find that would help her gain enough leverage to turn the big wheel in the middle of the door. There was a sound below her that was partially muffled by the echo of her own footsteps.

She stopped and listened. A dragging sound that was all too familiar. The infected all shuffled their feet or dragged their mangled legs. She had always considered that a good thing because she would be able to outrun most of them, but in this case it had given away its position somewhere below her.

The sound of her getting her rifle ready to fire would be too loud, and she didn't relish the idea of blowing out her own eardrums, so she hefted her pipe wrench and got ready. She needed to see the steps and knew the infected would see her flashlight, but she couldn't bring herself to turn it off. She would just have to face the infected from the advantage of a higher step, and if she was lucky, the creature would be at a lower level than the door she had entered.

Luck was definitely on her side when she made the turn from the landing above and saw the light from the open door. The shuffling sounds were coming from below the first level, and she could feel the vibrations in the metal stairs as the infected climbed below her.

Her only question was whether it was climbing up or down. If it was coming up, she had to hurry. She tried to stay as quiet as possible, but she noisily banged into the railings with her pipe wrench as she took the steps faster. The metal banging startled her, and she screamed just as if she had come face to face with an infected.

Maybank screamed too, but his old man's voice didn't rise to the level of the woman's scream, and to her it was no more than a loud moan.

"Nooooooo...," was all she heard.

When she slammed the heavy door shut, she slid the handle of the pipe wrench into the locking wheel to wedge it shut and ran for the bow. Her frightened mind didn't even see the ropes left by Maybank when he fell from the containers.

Adrenaline carried her back to the bridge above, and she crossed quickly to the safety of the oil rig. Once she hit the catwalks, she didn't think she was safe yet. She felt like danger was still behind her so she ran in the direction of the Wellbay Tower and climbed ladders toward the crew quarters. She didn't know she had taken a wrong turn until she found herself climbing onto a large flat area that had to be a helicopter landing pad. She was confused and lost, but a slight turn to her left brought the crew quarters into full view below. She had never gone upward, always preoccupied with the ship and the catwalks below her, but she had seen the top of the ladder ended at a higher level.

"So, this is what's up here."

Aside from the view, she didn't see where it would ever be of any use to her. The observation hut was probably so someone could watch a helicopter landing without getting blown over, but it was the strange hatch next to the hut that caught her eye. It was similar to something she would expect to find on a ship, and when she thought about it, it wasn't so strange to see it on an oil rig. There were probably hundreds of hatches and doors just like it that she had never found.

Curiosity was what had given her the nerve to walk through the open door on the ship, and curiosity was what made her tug on the hatch and lift it open. A ladder descended into a well lit chamber, and it was far less threatening than the dark stairwell of the ship, so she climbed down.

As soon as she reached the bottom and turned from the ladder, there was a faint hiss of air, and the door above her closed on its own. It frightened her at first, and she almost retreated up the ladder, but she felt safer with the door shut. Then she saw the panel on the wall with labeled buttons. One said Escape Hatch Lock, so she pressed it.

******

In the blackness of the ship, Maybank could only hear the blood pounding in his ears. He had broken the one rule that Titus Rush said would get survivors killed. He had left his shelter. Now he couldn't see his nose, and he couldn't hear because he was having a heart attack. It felt like an elephant had stepped onto his chest, and he fought to breathe.

He pressed his face against the cold steel of the door, and his arms were so numb from trying to turn the locking wheel that he could hardly feel them. His left knee was swollen until it stretched the leg of his pants tight, but that was his good leg.

When he finally moved, he tried to remember where he was when he had put his hand on a metal rail. He wanted to go up, but his chest and his legs wouldn't let him. His only hope would be to go down and find a room that was safe.

He found the railing and shuffled down one flight. There was no one who would hear his screams, and the heart attack spared him from wondering why it didn't hurt as something used its teeth to remove the calf from his left leg.

28 ENDGAME

Year Six of the Decline

Pleasant Oaks had been terrible, but it had been a tiny cemetery compared to this tropical burial ground. People were being buried in the cemeteries of old New Orleans for hundreds of years, but the last six had turned the cemetery into a botanical nightmare. If the Chief was wrong, he would begin all over again. Stokes could have left clues everywhere, and the Chief would see clues where there weren't any, but this was a good place to start. He couldn't ignore the obvious.

The Chief tore away the vines at the base of the statue and almost missed the thin piece of pipe, but he was sure he had found a breathing tube. His only thought was how afraid Iris had to be at the other end of that tube. He didn't know if she could hear him, but he whispered across the top of the tube and then put his ear above it.

"Hang on a bit longer, Iris. We're getting you out of there."

He didn't hear words through the tube, but he heard the sobbing. He was so afraid that it had been a groan.

Everyone worked methodically, digging with our machetes first at the end farthest from the air tube so we wouldn't disturb it. Tom carried a small camping shovel in his belt and was able to remove large scoops of soft dirt. Stokes didn't have the luxury of digging with a backhoe this time, so the casket was only a few feet below the surface. He had tried to put it back into its original hole, but the sides had collapsed and filled it to half of its existing depth. It didn't matter that much to him because he never expected us to find her in time, but it was a stroke of luck for us. His only reason for putting an

497

air tube in was to make sure we spent time digging her up instead of coming after him. He knew we wouldn't let her die of suffocation in the coffin if there was the slightest chance she was alive, and we all hoped it wasn't a fake air tube like the one in Pleasant Oaks.

We were interrupted by an infected that fell over a headstone nearby, and Tom hardly skipped a beat digging by hitting it with the blade side of his camping shovel and then immediately shoving it back into the dirt.

The shovel made a hollow sound as it hit the casket, and we all moved to that spot. It was rapidly uncovered from that end up until we got to the tube, and we saw that it had been driven through the casket. At least it was real, and we heard the scraping of fingernails against the inside.

Each of us had our own private thoughts about what we would find. Stokes was so cruel that he could have selected any grave at random and simply put an air tube in it. There were plenty of caskets that were buried in shallow graves, and not all of them were enclosed with concrete vaults, but we didn't have time to worry about what else he had done. If we did, she would die while we worried.

As if our deepest fears were put into words, Hampton yelled a warning to us all not to open it yet. The Chief had his hands in position and was two seconds away from ripping it open. He only stopped out of reflex, and Hampton pointed at the next grave over. It had an air tube extended above the surface.

The Chief nodded his understanding and braced himself to be able to jump back if he had to move in a hurry. His big shoulders flexed, and the lid flew free of the casket.

The burst of stale air that rushed into our faces was old and musty with the odors of the corpse that had decayed inside it. She was wild-eyed and gasping for air, but Iris was alive. She reached above her with bloody fingernails and flailed at the air as if she could grab it and pull herself from the casket. Forced to breathe the foul smell of rot inside the casket had pushed her to a limit she had never experienced, but when the Chief got his arms around her and lifted her to freedom, they both sobbed with relief mixed with joy. Iris actually laughed between sobs.

Jean tried to get the Chief to hear her.

"Chief, let me check her for injuries. She's been bleeding."

Colleen and Tom unfolded a small camping tarp, and we got the Chief to lay her on it. Iris didn't want to let go of him, but gave Jean enough room to get a look at her scalp.

Cassandra got a water bottle in between all of the faces and had to wrestle with Iris to be sure she only sipped.

There was overwhelming happiness in the moment, but when I looked at the Chief I could see the anger boiling up inside. If he found Stokes, he would rip out his arms and beat him to death with them.

We also had to at least dig up the grave with the other air tube. There was no way we could be certain that there wasn't another victim. Just like Pleasant Oaks, we only expected to find Molly and Sam.

While Jean took the time to be sure Iris could be moved back to the Cormorant, we split up into groups to see if we could pick up Stokes' trail. We had to be sure the place the Chief had already found where a boat had been wasn't left by Stokes as a decoy. Colleen stayed behind to give them cover if they needed it.

The rest of us spread out, and about an hour into the search we found that the water had encroached all the way to the back wall of the cemetery. One more big storm would flood the entire area, and the walls would be breached one last time.

There was evidence in the mud at the base of the back wall that someone had very recently launched a boat from the spot, and it didn't take a genius to know it had been him. We knew his goal had been to reach an oil rig, and if he wasn't on one yet, he would be soon. We may have lost an hour, but his decoy would have cost us more if we had fallen for it.

Hampton had spent his life around small boats, and he examined the drag marks closely.

"V-shaped hull judging by the shape of the keel marks. Most likely twenty-three to twenty-six feet long. He would have tried for twin engines for the speed. Fuel wouldn't be a problem for him if he was satisfied with one of the rigs close in."

"How are we going to find which one he went to?" I asked.

We could see the Chief already had something on his mind by the way he was rubbing his chin. It was one of his habits I had noticed when we played poker. It was something he did when he had a good hand, so he did it when he bluffed. He wasn't bluffing this time.

"It depends on how fast we can get the Beaver in the air and how long ago he left. I'm only guessing, but since Iris is still alive, he's still on the water."

It was about as fast as I had ever run just to keep up with the Chief, and Hampton had to climb the wall first. He still passed me and caught up with the Chief.

The Chief took a couple of minutes to be with Iris, and I overheard him say to her that he would give her his undivided attention as soon as he got back. She knew him well enough to know what he had to do. It wasn't revenge. It was a guarantee that Stokes wouldn't do the same things to someone else. The last thing I heard made me move out of earshot because I didn't think they wanted anyone to hear something that private.

Kathy caught me before I could avoid her.

"Well?"

I tried to play dumb.

"Well, what?"

"What are they saying to each other? I can tell you were close enough to hear."

I pointed at some bushes and said, "Infected."

When she turned to see the threat I hurried away.

The Chief carried Iris back over to the others and sat her on the tarp. She insisted that she was okay to walk, but he said Jean would have to discharge her from treatment first.

It was an incredible feeling seeing Iris smile with her eyes on the Chief, but she had strong feelings for all of us. She could tell we were family.

"We're going to have to move fast," said the Chief, "that's why we're splitting up. Tom, Ed, and Cassandra, you're with me. Kathy, I need you back here to make sure everybody gets back to the Cormorant after you pick up Bus."

Kathy only halfheartedly objected to being left behind. As much as she wanted to be there when the Chief and Tom caught Stokes, she knew she was the best one to leave in charge of the safety of the rest of the group. What I couldn't understand was why I was picked to go along. Cassandra had combat training, so she was a logical choice, and she had maritime experience on the Mercy Mission ship.

Before I could ask the obvious question, the Chief told me my role.

"We don't know which oil rig we're going to visit, and we can't get radio contact to find the one from your uncle's survivors club, but if by some chance we find it, it won't hurt to have Titus Rush's nephew with us."

The reason was just as obvious as the question. It hadn't really sunk in that I might meet someone who was in on the shelter construction from the beginning, and I had to admit it was a bit like being told I was about to meet a rock star.

"Time to go, everyone."

It didn't take a second invitation from the Chief. We were ready to get out of the sweltering jungle, and there weren't many hours left in the day. We didn't want to try to find Stokes on the Gulf of Mexico at night.

We went back to the building where Bus was holed up, and we ran into several small hordes on the way. The noise in the area hadn't been as loud as it could have been, but the infected seemed to have good hearing, and they were being drawn to the area. After making several detours, we finally got back to the stairs.

"We've lost too much time," said the Chief.

"You go on from here," said Kathy. "You'll have the Beaver in the air by the time we get there because Jean's going to want to examine Bus first."

The Chief surprised everyone by pulling Iris into his arms and giving her a long kiss. She didn't resist, and the eye contact they shared in the brief moment before the kiss said all that needed to be said.

When they pulled themselves apart it was only because time was important, but it was going to be a big moment for all of us to see them reunited when we got back, and there wasn't the slightest bit of doubt in our minds that we would be back.

Those of us going on the plane ran ahead, leaving the others to make sure Iris and Bus were able to travel on foot. It wasn't far, but they had been through a lot.

We hadn't bothered to leave anyone on the Cormorant when we scrambled from her deck earlier in the day, but we weren't worried about it being stolen. It was still docked by the Beaver, and the Chief shouted instructions to us. It was in the right place for us to use its deck to steer the Beaver out of the slip faster.

Cassandra comically hopped into the cockpit to steer while the Chief and I guided the plane out of the slip by pushing on the struts on each side. She quickly hopped back out and helped push it away from the dock. She flashed a frown at me that said to keep it to myself.

Tom caught the wing as it got close to the Cormorant and held it far enough away to keep it from hitting the ship, and we all made the jump onto the floats. I was practically tossed into the passenger door when the Chief landed on the float on the port side. The doors shut all around and the Chief started the engine without bothering with a preflight check.

The roar of the Beaver was deafening, and we all searched for the headsets. Cassandra put them over the Chief's ears for him because he was too busy getting the plane up to speed for the take off, and he was building speed even in the turns to the mouth of the harbor. The plane lifted into the air, and we were on our way, hoping to find Stokes before he lost himself among the thousands of oil rigs in the Gulf of Mexico.

******

Year Three of the Decline

Janice felt like she had fallen down the rabbit hole years ago, and she thought she had lost the capacity to be surprised by anything, but the labels on the walls of the chamber below the strange hatch weren't handwritten or pasted on the wall. They were engraved signs, professionally made instructions for someone to follow.

She had already reacted out of instinct when she read the first one that said it was the button that would lock the hatch. It seemed like the right thing to do. So she did it. She didn't know that a nuclear blast could tear off the entire chamber, but the lock would probably stay in place. The next sign said to enter the chute feet first, keep your feet together, and your arms crossed at the chest.

"What chute?"

There was another hatch next to the sign, and when Janice turned in a circle, she saw there was nothing else besides the ladder, the recessed lighting, the instructions, and the hatch. She shrugged her shoulders and opened the hatch. Soft lights illuminated the descent chute, but Janice was not inclined to stick her body in a smooth tunnel that went down at a steep angle just to find out where it went. She closed the door and climbed the ladder to the hatch.

The locking wheel had a small sign on it that read, NO EXIT. Janice climbed back down and pressed the button that she had used to lock the door. Nothing happened.

This reminded her of one of her dates with David. She hated it, but he really had a good time. They were locked in a room with three other couples that they didn't know, and they were told they could only leave when they solved the clues that would unlock the door. One of the other women made it worse when she said we had to hurry because she forgot to go to the bathroom.

David was mad because one of the other couples worked on clues together and solved the lock. Despite her protests, he wanted to do it again in a different room.

Now Janice had to solve the clues alone, but down meant water to her. She really didn't want to survive all this time only to launch herself into the Gulf, and she didn't think she could get back on the rig once she got off.

She tried the hatch several times, pressed the button several times, and read the chute instructions several times, and it all came back to one thing. The chute was the only way out of the chamber, whether that meant out of the chamber and out of the oil rig, she didn't know.

Janice opened the door to the chute again and was so angry that she was tempted to go head first, but common sense told her the sign was instructions for safe use of the chute. She grabbed a handle that was on the ceiling of the chute and did a pull up to get her feet inside. It wasn't too narrow, but it reminded her of what she had felt like when she was inside an MRI machine. It was just narrow enough to make her put her arms where the sign instructed, and there was just enough room for her to pull the door shut before the slope became steep. For some reason, she felt like it was the thing to do, so she shut it behind her.

As soon as she was in position, she felt her ears pop and felt a slight change in air pressure. Now she knew what it felt like to be inside the pneumatic air tube at the bank drive-through.

Her whole body seemed to slip at once, and she felt the urge to spread her feet to use them as brakes, but her memory of a waterslide reminded her that was a bad idea. When she tried to use her feet as brakes she wound up reaching the bottom airborne and unceremoniously landing face first in the pool at the bottom.

Instead, she followed the instructions and thought about another Olympic event, but she was the bobsled.

It was over before she knew it, and before she could even scream she was slowing to a stop onto an open platform. Next to the platform was a tremendous door that would have been at home on any bank vault, and for some reason, it was open.

It didn't take her long to accept the fact that she should go inside, but this time she didn't shut the door. The platform had several other

503

doors around it, and there were two more of the smooth "laundry" chutes that appeared to arrive from other places on the rig. She figured one had to be an exit, but it wouldn't help much if she locked herself inside of the bank vault.

She stepped across the threshold into the shelter. The lights were on a low level but brightened as she walked in. She jumped because she thought someone had turned them on when she entered, but she didn't run.

All around her was technology she didn't understand, and she felt like she was in a science fiction movie. The setting was an alien spacecraft, and she was in the control room. But then she did understand what she was seeing. She suddenly understood, not where she was, but what she was in...or at least she thought she understood. Every oil rig had a control room, and she had found it.

"But why the bank vault door, and where is everybody?"

Her next guess was closer to the mark than she knew.

"A secret government oil rig, but what's the big secret?"

That made some sense, and it stood to reason that it was military, but she didn't see anything that resembled military. As far as she knew the military put signs on everything saying who they were, but this was more like NASA. Then she knew she had figured it out. It was NOAA. They studied the oceans, and that's what all this stuff was for. That made the most sense, but she would be happier if she saw NOAA printed on something.

"Hello?"

Her voice didn't echo, and there was total quiet.

"Well, I'm here, so I might as well have a look around."

The door to the next room was also open, and Janice found herself in a kitchen that was similar to the one in the crew quarters. There wasn't anything remarkable about it, but when she opened the refrigerator, there were leftovers and food that had obviously been made recently. She helped herself to a cold beer and something that tasted like fresh salad. It wasn't that she didn't think anybody would mind if she ate their food. It was because she didn't care if they minded. It had been so long since she had eaten fresh greens that she was sure her digestive system would be wrecked, but she craved a salad the way most people had craved drugs.

The beer was domestic, but after a year of nothing but hard liquor, it was refreshing. Just in case she had missed them, she checked the refrigerator for fresh eggs, but there weren't any.

"I guess they don't have any chickens around here."

Janice took another beer off the shelf and checked the cabinets. Judging by the variety of seasonings and spices, there was a good cook around somewhere.

The next compartment was a recreation center, and it was no surprise that it had the same TV setup. To be sure, she turned it on and saw the same menu of movies. Figuring there would be nothing of interest, she took a few steps toward the next door and then remembered the computer monitor. Since she had found hers, she had no trouble sorting it out from the TV monitors, plus this recreation room was geared more toward one person than several.

She turned the monitor on and saw that it had exactly the same camera views, including the three she had recently moved. That meant someone knew she had moved them, assuming someone was still watching. The fresh food, the open door, and anything else she was about to find all told her someone was there recently. She wondered if this discovery had anything to do with her camera views turning to snow.

There was one thing different about the next room. It appeared to be someone's personal living quarters. What bothered her was the smell. The bed was unmade, but the unmistakeable odor of bad hygiene permeated everything. When she thought about it a second, there was something she had missed in the kitchen. The sink was overflowing with dishes. She had been so caught up in the food that she had missed that detail.

Janice backtracked to the kitchen and checked everything from the oven to the top of the dining room table. They all needed to be cleaned. She went back to the bedroom figuring the bathroom should be nearby. She was right, and the bathtub was covered in mildew, as were the showers. Whoever lived here didn't believe in cleaning up after themselves until it was necessary, like maybe in a year or two.

Her mother always said, "Clean body, clean mind."

She wondered how clean the mind was of the person who lived here.

Janice picked up her pace and was astonished at the level of sophistication she found in the rooms. There was a medical center that had everything she would have needed to repair her injuries when she had first arrived. She had never used a medical stapler before, but she recognized it when she saw it.

"That would have beat the hell out of stitches," she thought.

There was an armory that included a shooting range, and she could pick from any kind of weapon she wanted. That was the first time she became aware of the fact that she had lost her rifle somewhere.

"Well, I can remedy that little oversight right now."

She tested the weight of several different handguns, and selected two. She filled her pockets with magazines and then found another rifle just like the one she had lost. Once again, she wasn't asking for anything. She was taking it. Whoever lived here had let her live on the edge of starvation and mental stability for over a year, and she wasn't going to give them her undying gratitude if she ran into them.

When she gave it some thought, she knew it wasn't if, but when, and the unsanitary living quarters were not a sign that she would be dealing with a sane person.

"So what if I wasn't making my bed? I was changing the sheets and showering, and I was washing my dishes."

The lower level of the shelter was down a set of stairs. As far as she could tell by the shape of the rooms, she was inside a circular structure, and she had circumnavigated the upper level. When she went down one flight she found the laundry room, which was much needed but ignored, and a hydroponics lab. Whoever the slob was, he knew how to grow plants because they were doing quite well.

Janice spent almost two hours exploring the rest of the shelter. The food storage areas were beyond description. She had been searching containers for something to replenish her supplies, while someone had been sitting on a grocery store.

"No, more like a food factory," she said.

She went back to the kitchen and made another big salad. She added canned chicken and ham to it, grabbed another beer, and went back to the room inside the big bank vault door. She got comfortable and waited for someone to come home so she could set a few things straight.

******

Year Six of the Decline

Janice had sat inside the door with her rifle across her lap for hours, but no one had come home. She finally decided to lock the door, but she was pretty sure whoever lived there would know how to unlock it. It was primitive, but she stacked bottles and cans in front of the big door and tied strings to them. If someone opened the door, she would hear them coming. Three years later, the stack was still standing undisturbed.

She had given in and eventually cleaned the bedroom and bathroom. She couldn't find any air fresheners, so she had washed the walls with the cleansers from the laundry room. It took almost a day to clean the kitchen.

Janice swore that if the owner of the place came home after she had done all the work, they could go live in the crew quarters.

She checked the cameras every day, and nothing ever changed, just as nothing changed when she was watching from the crew quarters. She wondered if the old man she had seen standing over David's body had anything to do with this place, and she wondered where he had gone. He had probably been someone from the ship, or he had found his way onto the oil rig. Regardless, she never saw him again.

Settling into a routine inside the shelter was far easier than it had been in the crew quarters because there was enough food to last a lifetime. She had tried to do an inventory, but eventually she knew it was more than enough for one person. She decided her time could be put to better use, and she went to the hydroponics garden.

Life was good. Almost four years later she was raising something in her garden that was a lot like potatoes, and she had figured out how to grow grains. It was something that grew like rice, but she was able to grind it into flour and make something she called rice bread. Getting it to rise was difficult until she found there was yeast in her dry storage.

There was an exercise room that had been neglected before her, and it stayed neglected for the first year after she had moved in, but along with the rice bread and the other regular meals came a few unwanted pounds and some slack muscles. It was like starting all over again on a new project when she decided to get back in shape. She had to strip down and service some of the equipment, but that would make it even more worth it when she started using the equipment.

Once she had finished that project, there was no excuse to get started on the physical part, but that didn't mean she didn't try to find excuses. When she ran out of things that she could say were more important, she started her exercise program, and as most people would admit, it became her passion. The rice bread was her reward for working hard, and besides being happy with her physical appearance, she realized that she was mentally content.

There had been a time when all she could think of was survival. She knew she couldn't get back to the mainland even if she wanted to go, but if things were as bad as she suspected they were, there was no reason to go back. She didn't want to leave her glorified mobile home at the top of the oil rig, but all she had up there was a kitchen, a TV set, and the necessities for staying clean. She just didn't have a food supply that would last. Now she had everything she needed, and she wasn't even lonely. She couldn't explain it, but she felt fine by herself.

******

Year Six of the Decline

Now

Janice saw the twin engine boat coming straight for the oil rig long before it arrived. She had learned the control systems well, and she would decide when the time came if she needed to rid herself of the problem, or if it was going to be a problem at all. One of her options was the switch that sent electricity through the catwalks.

This was likely to be the only oil rig that had a container ship parked next to it, but there were plenty of oil rigs that were being resupplied when the infection began. People escaping to the Gulf would be attracted to the ones that had the most food and water.

Over the last few years she had seen several small boats racing into the Gulf. Some circled a few times but eventually gave up because they couldn't find a way to board the ship or oil rig. She thought of them as being unprepared, but then again she and David didn't have some grand plan in mind when they started circling. Because there was so much interest in the ship, Janice had gone outside just once. She realigned cameras to cover more of the deck and the containers, and the remaining cameras were aimed at strategic points on the oil rig.

There was one group of survivors that climbed the port side of the container ship where she couldn't see with a camera. They were a wild bunch, judging by the way they acted. It didn't matter to her how they climbed on board, but apparently they thought the real prize was the ship. They never got around to crossing the container bridge onto the oil rig. Instead, they tore open containers and threw the contents out onto the deck as if there might be something hiding behind the worthless stuff. Some of it was thrown overboard, not that she cared, but she thought it was senseless behavior.

It did bear a resemblance to bad reality TV, though. Six fools living together only because they had to. She found it entertaining and was waiting for one of them to do something really stupid like fall from the containers or throw something without warning and having it land on someone in their group.

It finally happened when one of them slid a shiny casket from a container into the sunlight and let it drop to the deck. It wasn't a direct hit, but pieces broke off and flew into the faces of two men below. The next time he appeared at the entrance, they shot the man. After he hit the deck, they picked him up and put him into the broken coffin.

"Well, I guess I don't need that container."

Janice waited patiently for the real fun to start when the lid would open, but they decided to move on before then. They went into the superstructure door that she had gone through years ago. From her angle it was still ink black inside. Nothing came out when they opened the door, but she didn't expect there was still an infected hanging around in the stairwell. Whether anything had been there or not, she never saw the reality TV stars come out again.

She wasn't surprised when she saw another boat getting closer to the container ship.

Maybe the new arrival would find out what was going on inside. As she was reminiscing about other visitors, the boat disappeared around the bow of the ship. When it didn't reappear at the stern, she guessed the occupants of the boat had a way to climb the ship. She saw that she had guessed right when a head came over the far side of the boat. She expected another, but this one was a loner. He walked over to the coffin that still sat in the spot where it had landed a year or so ago. He knocked on the coffin lid with his knuckles and then leaned back and laughed.

"This might be one to avoid. Better yet, he might be one to electrocute."

Janice doubted she would ever use the electric shock system unless she had a good reason, but she also couldn't define what a good reason would be. Maybe it would be obvious when the time came, but something about this guy screamed dangerous. It could have been because he thought a coffin with an infected inside was funny.

The man was leaning backward to see the bridge from the ship to the oil rig. He was taking in everything before deciding where to start, and his options were wide open if he could go back and forth from the ship to the oil rig. As far as she knew, he couldn't get inside, so she didn't really care what he did, but she didn't think she would ever be comfortable with him around.

He walked from the coffin to the open containers and grabbed the rope that still hung from top to bottom. He was strong and made it look easy as he climbed all the way up. She thought he was going to cross over to the oil rig, but something made him stop and turn his head toward the sky. He held a hand to his forehead to shade his eyes from the sun and stared intently in the same direction for several minutes. Even on a camera monitor she could tell his body had become rigid, and his free hand had balled into a fist.

"This guy isn't just escaping from the mainland. He's escaping from somebody else."

There were cameras located on the other side of the oil rig facing toward the middle of the Gulf and toward the mainland. She checked the one toward the mainland but couldn't see what the man had been watching. Her eyes played back and forth across the surface of the water, but there was no telltale white wake from a boat. She glanced at the view that showed the man again, and didn't understand why she wasn't seeing anything, because he certainly was.

Something reflected light, but it wasn't where she had expected. It was above the water, and it was coming down from a higher altitude at a steep angle. As it got closer she could see it was a bright yellow plane with floats on it. She turned back toward the man and saw that he had changed directions. He was on his way back down the rope, and he was being quick about it.

The plane made a sweeping turn and passed the port side of the ship level with the deck. The man pulled a handgun from his belt and went into a shooter stance, but she didn't see the plane waver from its course. It disappeared quickly, and the man ran for the open door of the superstructure.

Janice had been listening to a lot of music lately, especially while she was working in the hydroponics garden or baking bread. Maybe because it was fresh in her mind, or maybe because it fit the occasion, but she started singing, "Welcome to the Hotel California."

The plane came back into view on the opposite side of the oil rig. She saw it was circling back and getting lower to the water. It appeared obvious that it was going to land on the other side of the ship where the strange man had left his boat, but it surprised her when it reappeared at the bow and circled toward the Wellbay Tower.

Running on the surface with a black cable stretched behind it, the plane stayed clear of the massive support pole, but whoever was in the plane wanted to be where the man couldn't see them. She got another surprise when she saw that the cable was pulling the man's boat behind the plane. They didn't plan to let him leave the ship on his own.

Janice wondered which drama she was watching.

"Is this a bad guy escaping justice, or is it the other way around? Should I stay out of it, or should I get involved?"

She knew what she would do if there was a hostage involved, but for the time being she couldn't assume the man in the boat was the bad guy just because he had a poor sense of humor.

The coffin was still where it had been for a long time, but it had gotten the attention of the man as soon as he climbed onto the deck.

"Aha," she said out loud. "Let's see what the new guys do when they see it."

Someone threw an anchor out of the seaplane, and she had expected that the water would be too deep for an anchor, but she saw an African American woman step out onto the float and draw the anchor line tight. When she gave it another moment of thought, she leaned back and looked up at the ceiling.

She had always wondered about the chute she had used to reach the shelter, and the best she could figure was that it crossed from the landing platform over to the Wellbay tower and then down to the shelter.

"Did you guys just anchor to the top of my home?"

29 THE DECLINE

Year Six of the Decline

Now

A huge man climbed out of the pilot seat and stood on the float. Janice didn't have great magnification, but it was clear enough to see he was giving instructions to someone else inside the plane, so that meant at least three people. The plane was turning against a current that passes under the oil rig, so she could see if from the front. They were pulling the boat toward them.

The woman held the boat steady while two men climbed from the plane onto the float, then she joined them. They started the engines and drove around to the other side of the plane, and the big guy jumped into the boat.

Over the last couple of years, Janice had not only cleaned the shelter and made it livable, she had learned everything she could about how to operate it. There were still some things that she couldn't figure out, but she was pleased with her progress. Making her own bread from crops she grew herself had given her a confidence she had never felt before.

David would be proud of her, but more importantly, she was proud of herself.

Somewhere along the line she had remembered the day they had arrived. The handholds on the tower had appeared out of nowhere. Either they did something out on the water, or someone had made the decision to help them. That decision had saved her life.

The people in the plane didn't seem like they were in a life and death situation, but the strange man in the ship had shot at them as they flew by. If they intended to go in after him, it was not a stretch to think he would be waiting to ambush them.

She watched as they used something that resembled a rifle to shoot something the size of a baseball over the railing of the ship. A line trailed behind it, and the woman expertly tugged the line at just the right moment to make the weight on the end loop over the railing and wrap itself tight.

The smallest man went up first with another, heavier rope trailing behind him. When he got to the top, he tied it off, and the others began to climb. She was so impressed by the way they went about their jobs that she wasn't keeping an eye on the door to the superstructure.

The strange man had moved quickly from the door and for a second time he climbed to the top of the containers. By the time the people from the plane had climbed onto the ship, he was crossing the container bridge onto the oil rig. Only seconds later he was on a catwalk level with the deck of the ship and very close to where the new arrivals would be soon.

The four people moved in single file from the bow toward the superstructure without a clue that they were about to pass within a few yards of the man. He was in a shooter stance again hidden behind a large support beam, and before Janice could react, he fired.

She saw the woman go down, and the three men were totally exposed. He fired a second shot, and she saw the next man in line spin into the side of a container from the force of the bullet's impact. Her hand was on the switch before she could complete the thought, but she had already decided she was right.

The electric current that hit Stokes was enough to kill him, but he didn't make the same mistake most people had. He didn't grab the railing in front of him. He jumped, kicked off the railing, and did a back flip from the catwalk. He hit the water feet first, but the last thing he expected was to land on something solid only a few feet under the surface.

The big guy had been last to climb onto the ship, so he was the last one in line. Janice couldn't believe how gracefully he dove over the railing to the water below. She only hoped he didn't hit the top of the shelter.

He must have felt like he had jumped through a manhole cover. He had entered the water straight down almost as if he suspected something was under the oil rig. He passed between the hull of the ship and the outer wall of the shelter. When he came up to the surface, the first man was floating not far away, and he was screaming for help. He still didn't realize he was in shallow water.

Janice expected the big man to drown the guy who had ambushed his friends, but he half carried, half dragged the injured man back toward the plane. Janice knew he needed to get him out of the water so he could get back to his injured friends, and she made the decision someone else had a long time ago. She hit the switch that extended the hidden handholds.

The Chief saw and heard the handholds come out of the side of the tower, and he threw Stokes over his shoulder to make the climb. Stokes tried to wrestle himself free, but the Chief ended that with a quick punch to the side of his head.

Over on the ship, Tom had a bullet in his left shoulder that was bleeding bad, but he was able to apply pressure on the wound and still make his way to where Cassandra was sprawled on the deck. I was climbing over him to get to her, too. The bullet had hit her in the neck. I had to push Tom away to get pressure on the wound and slow the bleeding. There was so much blood that I was afraid she wouldn't make it, and I couldn't tell if it was the carotid artery.

The Chief reached the catwalk that was level with us and dumped Stokes unceremoniously on the metal plates. When he turned to us, all I could do was shake my head at him.

"It's bad. She won't make it back for Bus to help her."

The woman seemed to come out of nowhere. She was standing on a catwalk a few feet away from the Chief, and she was scared to death that she was making the wrong decision.

"I can help her, but not over there. I need for you to go get her and then follow me."

The Chief didn't have a choice. Part of him wanted to just go ahead and kill Stokes, but he didn't have a second to spare. The woman pointed at the place where the catwalk held the container steady, and he raced for the ladder that would get him there the fastest. The woman followed as best she could.

"I'll show you a way back that will get us to the hospital faster."

The Chief knew he had heard her right, but he would figure it all out after he reached Cassandra. Despite his size he outdistanced the woman quickly. When he reached us, I had tied a shirt across the wound, but it would be hard for him to climb and keep pressure on it. I did my best to tie it in place without choking her, and after he took her from me, I turned to Tom.

He was in a lot of pain, and I didn't know if I should try to get him to the plane or over to the oil rig. He showed me just how tough he was when he reached for the rope and climbed up the same way as the Chief. I grabbed a line and went up with more difficulty than him, but I could hear him yelling something about breaking Stokes' neck.

When we crossed the container bridge there was a woman leading the Chief to a higher level where a hatch stood open. I wouldn't learn until later that she had used a remote switch to unlock it before exposing herself to the Chief.

The Chief handed Cassandra down through the hatch, and when I arrived I saw the Chief help to lift them both into a chute on the wall.

"I'll see you there," she said.

As soon as they disappeared, the Chief helped Tom into the chute and then followed close behind him. As I went downward, I could only think about all of the blood in the tube.

It was a familiar sight to us when we reached the bottom. The woman had left the shelter door open so we wouldn't be locked out, but then again, she didn't know that we could have opened it.

The Chief picked up the unconscious body of Cassandra and carried her inside right on the heels of the woman. When we got to the medical bay, she told the Chief to let her take over. Janice didn't know if she could save her, but she knew how to close a wound.

We had also gotten some experience over the years, and we knew Cassandra would need blood, so the Chief was already rolling up his sleeve to get ready for the transfusion. Tom brushed us off and said he could take care of himself for the time being.

The woman worked fast, and she lifted her head once and told us her name was Janice. That was all she had time for. After what seemed like hours, she stepped back from Cassandra and went over to unhook the line from the Chief's arm.

"The bleeding has stopped, and I'm going to put some morphine in her IV. That's all we can do for now. The bullet missed the artery and the spinal cord, so with one more miracle she could make it. I'm sorry I can't do more."

To us her apology was the most ridiculous thing we had ever heard. We could tell from the lack of blood coming through the clean bandage that Cassandra had a very good chance of making it. Bus was going to want to meet this woman.

She saw that Tom was about three seconds from passing out, so she got the Chief off the other bed and Tom onto it. I think he passed out as soon as his head was down.

"Where's Stokes?" asked the Chief.

"There wasn't time to worry about him," I said.

"Janice, how can I get back to that catwalk fast?"

She told him where to go, and the Chief took off.

"Ed, stay here and help Janice with Tom. That bullet is still in his shoulder, and she's going to need help getting it out."

I didn't want to stay behind, but I also thought the Chief might prefer to do this alone.

******

The Chief arrived to find the catwalk empty, but the trail of blood went to the ladder that would get him closest to the container bridge. He wanted Stokes so bad that he didn't feel an ounce of the exhaustion that would come later.

He crossed over to the ship and had to figure out which blood trail was Stokes', and it led back to the black door in the superstructure. It was a big ship, but if he had to guess, Stokes had never been on one like it, but the Chief felt right at home.

It was pitch black in the stairwell, so the Chief stopped to let his eyes adjust. His night vision was so good that the people who served in the Navy with him laughed when he put on night vision goggles. They said he didn't need them. While he often felt like that was true, he wished he had some on at the moment.

What he couldn't see, he would try to hear, so he stood perfectly still and listened. He could hear his heartbeat, so he forced himself to breathe slowly and brought his heart rate down. Stokes had a big head start, so he might already have found a place where he could just crawl in and stay quiet. Of course, that depended on what else was in here with them.

The Chief was able to make out the bulkhead in front of him, and he decided it would be easier for Stokes to go down than up, so he followed the wall to the stairs and knelt at the top. He ran his fingers lightly across the first step down and felt the warm, slippery fluid. It smelled like copper.

The Chief walked down the stairs so softly that he could have walked on toilet paper without tearing it. As he descended he listened for something that would give Stokes away. He remembered that rats were as common as people on ships and thought about what Sim had told them before. The rats had probably turned on each other when their food supply ran low. There could still be some, but the strong smell of ammonia left behind in their urine probably meant there had been thousands at one time.

A slight movement caused just enough sound for him to stop. There was a slight echo, so the Chief knew he was in a large chamber. There was a small squeak to his right that he recognized as a rat, but the groan that made the hair stand up on the back of his neck was an infected. It was below and to his left. The Chief visualized the room and thought about the layout above. This would be a hub with hallways leading off in different directions. Down the stairs would be the way to the hold. Further in would be the crew quarters.

The Chief thought about how Stokes would try to navigate this darkness. Instead of using his ears to judge how far he was from a wall, he would stretch out an arm. Since the center of the hub was to the right, Stokes would have put one hand on the wall to his left and followed it. That meant Stokes went down the first corridor on the left.

The Chief judged the distance to the corridor by remembering how wide the deck had been above, and he made the turn without touching the walls. He heard Stokes try to stifle a sound when something brushed past him, but he was loud enough to give away his position.

At the same time, the Chief felt rather than saw a presence only inches away on his right, and he had no choice. His hand shot out chest high, and he buried it fist deep into the torso of an infected. He closed his hand on something that had to be the ribcage, and he swung his arm forward.

The infected didn't have a chance to bite him as the entire ribcage ripped loose and flew forward, hitting Stokes in the face. He screamed and began to cry like a child who had just fallen on a playground. When the pasty decayed tissue got into his open mouth he got sick and was doubled over with nausea.

The Chief had no sympathy as he pushed the infected further away and grabbed Stokes by the hair. If there were more infected on this level, they wouldn't have any trouble finding them, so the Chief moved much faster getting to the stairwell and going up.

Stokes screamed and cried the entire time, but all it did was make the Chief think about how Sam must have screamed until he ran out of air, and how Iris' fingernails looked when they opened the casket. That gave him an idea.

When they reached the open door onto the deck, Stokes became bold and tried to hit the Chief. The Chief wanted him awake for what he was about to do, so he didn't hit him back. He just twisted his hair even harder as he dragged him across the deck to the coffin.

With one hand he pulled open the lid, and with the other hand he shoved Stokes down on top of the infected that was trying to get out. He stuffed them both in far enough before he slammed the lid shut, then he sat down on top of it and listened.

The lid shook and he could still hear the screams that were almost loud enough to drown out the hungry groans inside. When it finally stopped, the Chief picked up the coffin, carried it to the railing, and threw it overboard. He waited for it to sink, and then after it sank he waited almost ten minutes before he walked away.

When the Chief walked into the medical bay we knew from his expression that it had been brutal, but Tom had to know for sure. He had to know the man who buried his daughter was dead.

"You caught him?"

"Yes, and he won't be around to bite anyone, either."

******

The Chief flew from the oil rig straight to Fort Sumter where the Army medics could take Cassandra and Tom right into the surgical suite. There wasn't even time to stop in New Orleans to tell the others what had happened, so I took Stokes' boat back to the Cormorant. I had my hands full with Kathy and Sim when I broke the news to them about Tom and Cassandra being shot. Kathy was quick to pull herself together because Sim was taking it the hardest. I needed her help because Jean was a wreck even though I came back without a scratch.

Bus was sad because no one could explain what had happened to his old friend, Maybank. As far as we knew from Janice, he had survived in the shelter but disappeared sometime in the last six years. She told us she had seen an old man, but it could have been anybody.

The Chief had asked Janice to fly with him so she could take care of the injured pair, and he promised he would fly her back to her shelter as soon as possible.

"Are you kidding?" said Janice. "I never want to see this place again. Can I stay with you guys?"

The Chief had given her one of his patented laughs before giving her a bone crushing hug.

"Consider yourself a member of the family."

Captain Miller put helicopters in the air within minutes of their arrival, and even though the Cormorant had been our savior more than once, it was time to leave her behind. Maybe we would be able to go back for her someday.

******

Year Six of the Decline

Three Weeks Later

The Chief and Iris were sitting on a blanket on Morris Island, watching the stars climb above the horizon. The stretch of beach by the back entrance to the Fort Sumter shelter was one of the safest places where you could go to be alone, but the Chief was always listening and watching.

Iris leaned into him and asked, "Do you know how many times I wished for this?"

"It was a long time for you to be stuck in Ambassadors Island."

"I'm talking about before then, too."

"You wanted this before the infection happened? Why didn't you tell me?"

"You were supposed to want it first."

She gave him a playful poke in the ribs.

"Besides," she continued, "if we had gotten together before, then you wouldn't have been on that cruise ship in Charleston, you wouldn't have met Ed and learned about the shelters, and we wouldn't have run into each other in Charlotte."

"That makes my head hurt," he said.

They both laughed, and it was nice to be able to smile after what they had been through with Stokes. They kissed and then held each other in silence for a long time.

"How long will it stay like this, Josh?"

"You don't mean tonight, do you? You mean the whole world…the infection?"

She nodded.

He didn't answer, and she thought she knew why. She was just about to say it when he stopped her.

"We both know that we've already lost. This is the big extinction event everyone talked about before. Whoever it was who called it the decline of man, I think they were right. There are less people on the planet now than there were in the last ice age. I think we're done, but you and I have no choice. We have to last as long as we can."

"I'll settle for that," she said.

ABOUT THE AUTHOR

Bob Howard (1951-) was born in New Jersey to an Army Sergeant from Ohio and a mother from Romania. He was moved from one Army base to the next, and before he began high school in Huntsville, Alabama he had lived most of his life overseas in Germany and Okinawa with brief stays in Maryland and North Carolina. He credits his imagination to his exposure to different cultures and environments at an early age. He began reading science fiction and fell in love with post apocalyptic novels. He still has an original copy of the first one he read in 1966, The Furies by Keith Edwards. He joined the Navy after high school and continued to move from one base to another, including a submarine base at Holy Loch, Scotland. He eventually stayed in one place when he got stationed in Charleston, South Carolina. He graduated with a BS in Psychology from the College of Charleston. He married his wife in 1984 and together they raised a son and a daughter.

I would love to hear from you, and I value your opinions and comments. The best way to help an author become better at his craft is to write a review, so please feel free to write one. If you would like to know more about me or get in touch with me, please visit my website at *realbobhoward.com*. You can also sign up for my newsletter and be notified when the next book is released.

With gratitude,

Bob Howard

www.ingramcontent.com/pod-product-compliance
Lightning Source LLC
Chambersburg PA
CBHW020625020726
47494CB00001B/49